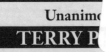

Terry Pratchett

WYRD SISTERS

A Novel of Discworld®

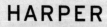

HARPER

An Imprint of HarperCollinsPublishers

This book was originally published in Great Britain by Victor Gollancz Ltd.

HARPER

An Imprint of HarperCollins *Publishers*
10 East 53rd Street
New York, New York 10022-5299

Copyright © 1980 by Terry and Lyn Pratchett 1988
Terry Pratchett® and Discworld® are registered trademarks.
ISBN 978-0-06-222573-3

First Harper premium printing: May 2013
First HarperTorch mass market printing: February 2001

HarperCollins ® and Harper ® are registered trademarks of Harper-Collins Publishers.

Printed in the United States of America

Visit Harper paperbacks on the World Wide Web at
www.harpercollins.com

13

WYRD SISTERS

Visit HarperCollins Publishers on the World Wide Web at
www.harpercollins.com

The wind howled. Lightning stabbed at the earth erratically, like an inefficient assassin. Thunder rolled back and forth across the dark, rain-lashed hills.

The night was as black as the inside of a cat. It was the kind of night, you could believe, on which gods moved men as though they were pawns on the chessboard of fate. In the middle of this elemental storm a fire gleamed among the dripping furze bushes like the madness in a weasel's eye. It illuminated three hunched figures. As the cauldron bubbled an eldritch voice shrieked: "When shall we three meet again?"

There was a pause.

Finally another voice said, in far more ordinary tones: "Well, I can do next Tuesday."

Through the fathomless deeps of space swims the star turtle Great A'Tuin, bearing on its back the four giant elephants who carry on their shoulders the mass of the Discworld. A tiny sun and moon spin around them, on a complicated orbit to induce seasons, so probably nowhere else in the multiverse is

1

it sometimes necessary for an elephant to cock a leg to allow the sun to go past.

Exactly why this should be may never be known. Possibly the Creator of the universe got bored with all the usual business of axial inclination, albedos and rotational velocities, and decided to have a bit of fun for once.

It would be a pretty good bet that the gods of a world like this probably do not play chess and indeed this is the case. In fact no gods anywhere play chess. They haven't got the imagination. Gods prefer simple, vicious games, where you Do Not Achieve Transcendence but Go Straight To Oblivion; a key to the understanding of all religion is that a god's idea of amusement is Snakes and Ladders with greased rungs.

Magic glues the Discworld together—magic generated by the turning of the world itself, magic wound like silk out of the underlying structure of existence to suture the wounds of reality.

A lot of it ends up in the Ramtop Mountains, which stretch from the frozen lands near the Hub all the way, via a lengthy archipelago, to the warm seas which flow endlessly into space over the Rim.

Raw magic crackles invisibly from peak to peak and earths itself in the mountains. It is the Ramtops that supply the world with most of its witches and wizards. In the Ramtops the leaves on the trees move even when there is no breeze. Rocks go for a stroll of an evening.

Even the land, at times, seems alive . . .

* * *

At times, so does the sky.

The storm was really giving it everything it had. This was its big chance. It had spent years hanging around the provinces, putting in some useful work as a squall, building up experience, making contacts, occasionally leaping out on unsuspecting shepherds or blasting quite small oak trees. Now an opening in the weather had given it an opportunity to strut its hour, and it was building up its role in the hope of being spotted by one of the big climates.

It was a *good* storm. There was quite effective projection and passion there, and critics agreed that if it would only learn to control its thunder it would be, in years to come, a storm to watch.

The woods roared their applause and were full of mists and flying leaves.

On nights such as these the gods, as has already been pointed out, play games other than chess with the fates of mortals and the thrones of kings. It is important to remember that they always cheat, right up to the end . . .

And a coach came hurtling along the rough forest track, jerking violently as the wheels bounced off tree roots. The driver lashed at the team, the desperate crack of his whip providing a rather neat counterpoint to the crash of the tempest overhead.

Behind—only a little way behind, and getting closer—were three hooded riders.

On nights such as this, evil deeds are done. And good deeds, of course. But mostly evil, on the whole.

* * *

On nights such as this, witches are abroad.

Well, not actually *abroad*. They don't like the food and you can't trust the water and the shamans always hog the deckchairs. But there was a full moon breasting the ragged clouds and the rushing air was full of whispers and the very broad hint of magic.

In their clearing above the forest the witches spoke thus:

"I'm babysitting on Tuesday," said the one with no hat but a thatch of white curls so thick she might have been wearing a helmet. "For our Jason's youngest. I can manage Friday. Hurry up with the tea, luv. I'm that parched."

The junior member of the trio gave a sigh, and ladled some boiling water out of the cauldron into the teapot.

The third witch patted her hand in a kindly fashion.

"You said it quite well," she said. "Just a bit more work on the screeching. Ain't that right, Nanny Ogg?"

"Very useful screeching, I thought," said Nanny Ogg hurriedly. "And I can see Goodie Whemper, maysherestinpeace, gave you a lot of help with the squint."

"It's a good squint," said Granny Weatherwax.

The junior witch, whose name was Magrat Garlick, relaxed considerably. She held Granny Weatherwax in awe. It was known throughout the Ramtop Mountains that Miss Weatherwax did not approve of anything very much. If she said it was a good squint, then Magrat's eyes were probably staring up her own nostrils.

Unlike wizards, who like nothing better than a complicated hierarchy, witches don't go in much for the structured approach to career progression. It's up to each individual witch to take on a girl to hand the area over to when she dies. Witches are not by nature gregarious, at least with other witches, and they certainly don't have leaders.

Granny Weatherwax was the most highly-regarded of the leaders they didn't have.

Magrat's hands shook slightly as they made the tea. Of course, it was all very gratifying, but it was a bit nerve-racking to start one's working life as village witch between Granny and, on the other side of the forest, Nanny Ogg. It'd been her idea to form a local coven. She felt it was more, well, occult. To her amazement the other two had agreed or, at least, hadn't disagreed much.

"An oven?" Nanny Ogg had said. "What'd we want to join an oven for?"

"She means a coven, Gytha," Granny Weatherwax had explained. "You know, like in the old days. A meeting."

"A knees up?" said Nanny Ogg hopefully.

"No dancing," Granny had warned. "I don't hold with dancing. Or singing or getting over-excited or all that messing about with ointments and similar."

"Does you good to get out," said Nanny happily.

Magrat had been disappointed about the dancing, and was relieved that she hadn't ventured one or two other ideas that had been on her mind. She fumbled in the packet she had brought with her. It was her first sabbat, and she was determined to do it right.

"Would anyone care for a scone?" she said.

Granny looked hard at hers before she bit. Magrat had baked bat designs on it. They had little eyes made of currants.

The coach crashed through the trees at the forest edge, ran on two wheels for a few seconds as it hit a stone, righted itself against all the laws of balance, and rumbled on. But it was going slower now. The slope was dragging at it.

The coachman, standing upright in the manner of a charioteer, pushed his hair out of his eyes and peered through the murk. No one lived up here, in the lap of the Ramtops themselves, but there was a light ahead. By all that was merciful, there was a light there.

An arrow buried itself in the coach roof behind him.

Meanwhile King Verence, monarch of Lancre, was making a discovery.

Like most people—most people, at any rate, below the age of sixty or so—Verence hadn't exercised his mind much about what happened to you when you died. Like most people since the dawn of time, he assumed it all somehow worked out all right in the end.

And, like most people since the dawn of time, he was now dead.

He was in fact lying at the bottom of one of his

own stairways in Lancre Castle, with a dagger in his back.

He sat up, and was surprised to find that while someone he was certainly inclined to think of as himself was sitting up, something very much like his body remained lying on the floor.

It was a pretty good body, incidentally, now he came to see it from outside for the first time. He had always been quite attached to it although, he had to admit, this did not now seem to be the case.

It was big and well-muscled. He'd looked after it. He'd allowed it a mustache and long-flowing locks. He'd seen it got plenty of healthy outdoor exercise and lots of red meat. Now, just when a body would have been useful, it had let him down. Or out.

On top of that, he had to come to terms with the tall, thin figure standing beside him. Most of it was hidden in a hooded black robe, but the one arm which extended from the folds to grip a large scythe was made of bone.

When one is dead, there are things one instinctively recognizes.

HALLO.

Verence drew himself up to his full height, or what would have been his full height if that part of him of which the word "height" could have been applied was not lying stiff on the floor and facing a future in which only the word "depth" could be appropriate.

"I *am* a king, mark you," he said.

WAS, YOUR MAJESTY.

"What?" Verence barked.

I SAID WAS. IT'S CALLED THE PAST TENSE. YOU'LL
SOON GET USED TO IT.

The tall figure tapped its calcareous fingers on
the scythe's handle. It was obviously upset about
something.

If it came to that, Verence thought, so am I. But
the various broad hints available in his present circumstances were breaking through even the mad
brain stupidity that made up most of his character,
and it was dawning on him that whatever kingdom
he might currently be in, he wasn't king of it.

"Are you Death, fellow?" he ventured.

I HAVE MANY NAMES.

"Which one are you using at present?" said Verence, with a shade more deference. There were people
milling around them; in fact, quite a few people were
milling *through* them, like ghosts.

"Oh, so it was Felmet," the king added vaguely,
looking at, the figure lurking with obscene delight
at the top of the stairs. "My father said I should
never let him get behind me. Why don't I feel angry?"

GLANDS, said Death shortly. ADRENALIN AND SO
FORTH. AND EMOTIONS. YOU DON'T HAVE THEM. ALL
YOU HAVE NOW IS THOUGHT.

The tall figure appeared to reach a decision.

THIS IS VERY IRREGULAR, he went on, apparently
to himself. HOWEVER, WHO AM I TO ARGUE?

"Who indeed."

WHAT?

"I said, who indeed."

SHUT UP.

Death stood with his skull on one side, as though listening to some inner voice. As his hood fell away the late king noticed that Death resembled a polished skeleton in every way but one. His eye sockets glowed sky blue. Verence wasn't frightened, however; not simply because it is difficult to be in fear of anything when the bits you need to be frightened *with* are curdling several yards away, but because he had never really been frightened of anything in his life, and wasn't going to start now. This was partly because he didn't have the imagination, but he was also one of those rare individuals who are totally focused in time.

Most people aren't. They live their lives as a sort of temporal blur around the point where their body actually is—anticipating the future, or holding onto the past. They're usually so busy thinking about what happens next that the only time they ever find out what is happening now is when they come to look back on it. Most people are like this. They learn how to fear because they can actually tell, down at the subconscious level, what is going to happen next. It's already happening to them.

But Verence had always lived only for the present. Until now, anyway.

Death sighed.

I SUPPOSE NO ONE MENTIONED ANYTHING TO YOU? he hazarded.

"Say again?"

NO PREMONITIONS? STRANGE DREAMS? MAD OLD SOOTHSAYERS SHOUTING THINGS AT YOU IN THE STREET?

"About what? Dying?"

No, I suppose not. It would be too much to expect, said Death sourly. They leave it all to me.

"Who do?" said Verence, mystified.

Fate. Destiny. All the rest of them. Death laid a hand on the king's shoulder. The fact is, I'm afraid, you're due to become a ghost.

"Oh." He looked down at his . . . body, which seemed solid enough. Then someone walked through him.

Don't let it upset you.

Verence watched his own stiff corpse being carried reverentially from the hall.

"I'll try," he said.

Good man.

"I don't think I will be up to all that business with the white sheets and the chains, though," he said. "Do I have to walk around moaning and screaming?"

Death shrugged. Do you want to? he said.

"No."

Then I shouldn't bother, if I were you. Death pulled an hour-glass from the recesses of his dark robe and inspected it closely.

And now I really must be going, he said. He turned on his heel, put his scythe over his shoulder and started to walk out of the hall through the wall.

"I say? Just hold on there!" shouted Verence, running after him.

Death didn't look back. Verence followed him through the wall; it was like walking through fog.

"Is that all?" he demanded. "I mean, how long will I be a ghost? *Why* am I a ghost? You can't just leave me like this." He halted and raised an imperious, slightly transparent finger. "Stop! I command you!"

Death shook his head gloomily, and stepped through the next wall. The king hurried after him with as much dignity as he could still muster, and found Death fiddling with the girths of a large white horse standing on the battlements. It was wearing a nosebag.

"You can't leave me like this!" he repeated, in the face of the evidence.

Death turned to him.

I CAN, he said. YOU'RE UNDEAD, YOU SEE. GHOSTS INHABIT A WORLD BETWEEN THE LIVING AND THE DEAD. IT'S NOT MY RESPONSIBILITY. He patted the king on the shoulder. DON'T WORRY, he said, IT WON'T BE FOREVER.

"Good."

IT MAY SEEM LIKE FOREVER.

"How long will it really be?"

UNTIL YOU HAVE FULFILLED YOUR DESTINY, I ASSUME.

"And how will I know what my destiny is?" said the king, desperately.

CAN'T HELP THERE. I'M SORRY.

"Well, how can I find out?"

THESE THINGS GENERALLY BECOME APPARENT, I UNDERSTAND, said Death, and swung himself into the saddle.

"And until then I have to haunt this place." King Verence stared around at the drafty battlements. "All alone, I suppose. Won't anyone be able to see me?"

Oh, the psychically inclined. Close relatives. And cats, of course.

"I hate cats."

Death's face became a little stiffer, if that were possible. The blue glow in his eye sockets flickered red for an instant.

I see, he said. The tone suggested that death was too good for cat-haters. You like great big dogs, I imagine.

"As a matter of fact, I do." The king stared gloomily at the dawn. His dogs. He'd really miss his dogs. And it looked like such a good hunting day.

He wondered if ghosts hunted. Almost certainly not, he imagined. Or ate, or drank either for that matter, and that was really depressing. He liked a big noisy banquet and had quaffed* many a pint of good ale. And bad ale, come to that. He'd never been able to tell the difference till the following morning, usually.

He kicked despondently at a stone, and noted gloomily that his foot went right through it. No hunting, drinking, carousing, no wassailing, no hawking . . . It was dawning on him that the pleasures of the flesh were pretty sparse without the flesh. Suddenly life wasn't worth living. The fact that he wasn't living it didn't cheer him up at all.

Some people *like* to be ghosts, said Death.

---

* Quaffing is like drinking, but you spill more.

"Hmm?" said Verence, gloomily.

IT'S NOT SUCH A WRENCH, I ASSUME. THEY CAN SEE HOW THEIR DESCENDANTS GET ON. SORRY? IS SOMETHING THE MATTER?

But Verence had vanished into the wall.

DON'T MIND ME, WILL YOU, said Death, peevishly. He looked around him with a gaze that could see through time and space and the souls of men, and noted a landslide in distant Klatch, a hurricane in Howandaland, a plague in Hergen.

BUSY, BUSY, he muttered, and spurred his horse into the sky.

Verence ran through the walls of his own castle. His feet barely touched the ground—in fact, the unevenness of the floor meant that at times they didn't touch the ground at all.

As a king he was used to treating servants as if they were not there, and running through them as a ghost was almost the same. The only difference was that they didn't stand aside.

Verence reached the nursery, saw the broken door, the trailed sheets . . .

Heard the hoofbeats. He reached the window, saw his own horse go full tilt through the open gateway in the shafts of the coach. A few seconds later three horsemen followed it. The sound of hooves echoed for a moment on the cobbles and died away.

The king thumped the sill, his fist going several inches into the stone.

Then he pushed his way out into the air, disdaining to notice the drop, and half flew, half ran down across the courtyard and into the stables.

It took him a mere twenty seconds to learn that, to the great many things a ghost cannot do, should be added the mounting of a horse. He did succeed in getting into the saddle, or at least in straddling the air just above it, but when the horse finally bolted, terrified beyond belief by the mysterious things happening behind its ears, Verence was left sitting astride five feet of fresh air.

He tried to run, and got about as far as the gateway before the air around him thickened to the consistency of tar.

"You can't," said a sad, old voice behind him. "You have to stay where you were killed. That's what haunting means. Take it from me. I know."

Granny Weatherwax paused with a second scone halfway to her mouth.

"Something comes," she said.

"Can you tell by the pricking of your thumbs?" said Magrat earnestly. Magrat had learned a lot about witchcraft from books.

"The pricking of my ears," said Granny. She raised her eyebrows at Nanny Ogg. Old Goodie Whemper had been an excellent witch in her way, but far too *fanciful*. Too many flowers and romantic notions and such.

The occasional flash of lightning showed the moorland stretching down to the forest, but the rain on the warm summer earth had filled the air with mist wraiths.

"Hoofbeats?" said Nanny Ogg. "No one would come up here this time of night."

Magrat peered around timidly. Here and there on the moor were huge standing stones, their origins lost in time, which were said to lead mobile and private lives of their own. She shivered.

"What's to be afraid of?" she managed.

"Us," said Granny Weatherwax, smugly.

The hoofbeats neared, slowed. And then the coach rattled between the furze bushes, its horses hanging in their harnesses. The driver leapt down, ran around to the door, pulled a large bundle from inside and dashed toward the trio.

He was halfway across the damp peat when he stopped and stared at Granny Weatherwax with a look of horror.

"It's all right," she whispered, and the whisper cut through the grumbling of the storm as clearly as a bell.

She took a few steps forward and a convenient lightning flash allowed her to look directly into the man's eyes. They had the peculiarity of focus that told those who had the Know that he was no longer looking at anything in this world.

With a final jerking movement he thrust the bundle into Granny's arms and toppled forward, the feathers of a crossbow bolt sticking out of his back.

Three figures moved into the firelight. Granny looked up into another pair of eyes, which were as chilly as the slopes of Hell.

Their owner threw his crossbow aside. There was a glimpse of chain mail under his sodden cloak as he drew his sword.

He didn't flourish it. The eyes that didn't leave

Granny's face weren't the eyes of one who bothers about flourishing things. They were the eyes of one who knows exactly what swords are for. He reached out his hand.

"You will give it to me," he said.

Granny twitched aside the blanket in her arms and looked down at a small face, wrapped in sleep.

She looked up.

"No," she said, on general principles.

The soldier glanced from her to Magrat and Nanny Ogg, who were as still as the standing stones of the moor.

"You are witches?" he said.

Granny nodded. Lightning skewered down from the sky and a bush a hundred yards away blossomed into fire. The two soldiers behind the man muttered something, but he smiled and raised a mailed hand.

"Does the skin of witches turn aside steel?" he said.

"Not that I'm aware," said Granny, levelly. "You could give it a try."

One of the soldiers stepped forward and touched the man's arm gingerly.

"Sir, with respect, sir, it's not a good idea—"

"Be silent."

"But it's terrible bad luck to—"

"Must I ask you again?"

"Sir," said the man. His eyes caught Granny's for a moment, and reflected hopeless terror.

The leader grinned at Granny, who hadn't moved a muscle.

"Your peasant magic is for fools, mother of the night. I can strike you down where you stand."

"Then strike, man," said Granny, looking over his shoulder. "If your heart tells you, strike as hard as you dare."

The man raised his sword. Lightning speared down again and split a stone a few yards away, filling the air with smoke and the stink of burnt silicon.

"Missed," he said smugly, and Granny saw his muscles tense as he prepared to bring the sword down.

A look of extreme puzzlement crossed his face. He tilted his head sideways and opened his mouth, as if trying to come to terms with a new idea. His sword dropped out of his hand and landed point downward in the peat. Then he gave a sigh and folded up, very gently, collapsing in a heap at Granny's feet.

She gave him a gentle prod with her toe. "Perhaps you weren't aware of what I was aiming at," she whispered. "Mother of the night, indeed!"

The soldier who had tried to restrain the man stared in horror at the bloody dagger in his hand, and backed away.

"I-I-I couldn't let. He shouldn't of. It's—it's not right to," he stuttered.

"Are you from around these parts, young man?" said Granny.

He dropped to his knees. "Mad Wolf, ma'am," he said. He stared back at the fallen captain. "They'll kill me now!" he wailed.

"But you did what you thought was right," said Granny.

"I didn't become a soldier for this. Not to go around killing people."

"Exactly right. If I was you, I'd become a sailor," said Granny thoughtfully. "Yes, a nautical career. I should start as soon as possible. Now, in fact. Run off, man. Run off to sea where there are no tracks. You will have a long and successful life, I promise." She looked thoughtful for a moment, and added, "At least, longer than it's likely to be if you hang around here."

He pulled himself upward, gave her a look compounded of gratitude and awe, and ran off into the mist.

"And now perhaps someone will tell us what this is all about?" said Granny, turning to the third man.

To where the third man had been.

There was the distant drumming of hooves on the turf, and then silence.

Nanny Ogg hobbled forward.

"I could catch him," she said. "What do you think?"

Granny shook her head. She sat down on a rock and looked at the child in her arms. It was a boy, no more than two years old, and quite naked under the blanket. She rocked him vaguely and stared at nothing.

Nanny Ogg examined the two corpses with the air of one for whom laying-out holds no fears.

"Perhaps they were bandits," said Magrat tremulously.

Nanny shook her head.

"A strange thing," she said. "They both wear this

same badge. Two bears on a black and gold shield. Anyone know what that means?"

"It's the badge of King Verence," said Magrat.

"Who's he?" said Granny Weatherwax.

"He rules this country," said Magrat.

"Oh. That king," said Granny, as if the matter was hardly worth noting.

"Soldiers fighting one another. Doesn't make sense," said Nanny Ogg. "Magrat, you have a look in the coach."

The youngest witch poked around inside the bodywork and came back with a sack. She upended it, and something thudded onto the turf.

The storm had rumbled off to the other side of the mountain now, and the watery moon shed a thin gruel of light over the damp moorland. It also gleamed off what was, without any doubt, an extremely important crown.

"It's a crown," said Magrat. "It's got all spiky bits on it."

"Oh, dear," said Granny.

The child gurgled in its sleep. Granny Weatherwax didn't hold with looking at the future, but now she could feel the future looking at her.

She didn't like its expression at all.

King Verence was looking at the past, and had formed pretty much the same view.

"You can see me?" he said.

"Oh, yes. Quite clearly, in fact," said the newcomer.

Verence's brows knotted. Being a ghost seemed to

require considerably more mental effort than being alive; he'd managed quite well for forty years without having to think more than once or twice a day, and now he was doing it all the time.

"Ah," he said. "You're a ghost, too."

"Well spotted."

"It was the head under your arm," said Verence, pleased with himself. "That gave me a clue."

"Does it bother you? I can put it back on if it bothers you," said the old ghost helpfully. He extended his free hand. "Pleased to meet you. I'm Champot, King of Lancre."

"Verence. Likewise." He peered down at the old king's features and added, "Don't seem to recall seeing your picture in the Long Gallery . . ."

"Oh, all that was after my time," said Champot dismissively.

"How long have you been here, then?"

Champot reached down and rubbed his nose. "About a thousand years," he said, his voice tinged with pride. "Man and ghost."

"A thousand years!"

"I built this place, in fact. Just got it nicely decorated when my nephew cut my head off while I was asleep. I can't tell you how much that upset me."

"But . . . a thousand years . . ." Verence repeated, weakly.

Champot took his arm. "It's not that bad," he confided, as he led the unresisting king across the courtyard. "Better than being alive, in many ways."

"They must be bloody strange ways, then!" snapped Verence. "I *liked* being alive!"

Champot grinned reassuringly. "You'll soon get used to it," he said.

"I don't want to get used to it!"

"You've got a strong morphogenic field," said Champot. "I can tell. I look for these things. Yes. Very strong, I should say."

"What's that?"

"I was never very good with words, you know," said Champot. "I always found it easier to hit people with something. But I gather it all boils down to how alive you were. When you were alive, I mean. Something called—" he paused—"animal vitality. Yes, that was it. Animal vitality. The more you had, the more you stay yourself, as it were, if you're a ghost. I expect you were one hundred percent alive, when you were alive," he added.

Despite himself, Verence felt flattered. "I tried to keep myself busy," he said. They had strolled through the wall into the Great Hall, which was now empty. The sight of the trestle tables triggered an automatic reaction in the king.

"How do we go about getting breakfast?" he said.

Champot's head looked surprised.

"We don't," he said. "We're ghosts."

"But I'm hungry!"

"You're not, you know. It's just your imagination."

There was a clattering from the kitchens. The cooks were already up and, in the absence of any other instructions, were preparing the castle's normal breakfast menu. Familiar smells were wafting up from the dark archway that led to the kitchens.

Verence sniffed.

"Sausages," he said dreamily. "Bacon. Eggs. Smoked fish." He stared at Champot. "Black pudding," he whispered.

"You haven't actually got a stomach," the old ghost pointed out. "It's all in the mind. Just force of habit. You just *think* you're hungry."

"I *think* I'm ravenous."

"Yes, but you can't actually touch anything, you see," Champot explained gently. "Nothing at all."

Verence lowered himself gently onto a bench, so that he did not drift through it, and sank his head in his hands. He'd heard that death could be bad. He just hadn't realized how bad.

He wanted revenge. He wanted to get out of this suddenly horrible castle, to find his son. But he was even more terrified to find that what he really wanted, right now, was a plate of kidneys.

A damp dawn flooded across the landscape, scaled the battlements of Lancre Castle, stormed the keep and finally made it through the casement of the solar.

Duke Felmet stared out gloomily at the dripping forest. There was such a lot of it. It wasn't, he decided, that he had anything against trees as such, it was just that the sight of so much of them was terribly depressing. He kept wanting to count them.

"Indeed, my love," he said.

The duke put those who met him in mind of some sort of lizard, possibly the type that lives on volcanic islands, moves once a day, has a vestigial third eye and blinks on a monthly basis. He considered himself to be a civilized man more suited to the dry air and bright sun of a properly-organized climate.

On the other hand, he mused, it might be nice to be a tree. Trees didn't have ears, he was pretty sure of this. And they seemed to manage without the blessed state of matrimony. A male oak tree—he'd have to look this up—a male oak tree just shed its pollen on the breeze and all the business with the acorns, unless it was oak apples, no, he was pretty sure it was acorns, took place somewhere else . . .

"Yes, my precious," he said.

Yes, trees had got it all worked out. Duke Felmet glared at the forest roof. Selfish bastards.

"Certainly, my dear," he said.

"What?" said the duchess.

The duke hesitated, desperately trying to replay the monologue of the last five minutes. There had been something about him being half a man, and . . . infirm on purpose? And he was sure there had been a complaint about the coldness of the castle. Yes, that was probably it. Well, those wretched trees could do a decent day's work for once.

"I'll have some cut down and brought in directly, my cherished," he said.

Lady Felmet was momentarily speechless. This was by way of being a calendar event. She was a large and impressive woman, who gave people confronting her for the first time the impression that they were seeing a galleon under full sail; the effect was heightened by her unfortunate belief that red velvet rather suited her. However, it didn't set off her complexion. It matched it.

The duke often mused on his good luck in marrying her. If it wasn't for the engine of her ambition he'd be just another local lord, with nothing much to do but hunt, drink and exercise his droit de seigneur.* Instead, he was now just a step away from the throne, and might soon be monarch of all he surveyed.

Provided that all he surveyed was trees.

He sighed.

"Cut *what* down?" said Lady Felmet, icily.

"Oh, the trees," said the duke.

"What have trees got to do with it?"

"Well . . . there are such a *lot* of them," said the duke, with feeling.

"Don't change the subject!"

"Sorry, my sweet."

"What I *said* was, how could you have been so stupid as to let them get away? I told you that servant was far too loyal. You can't trust someone like that."

"No, my love."

"You didn't by any chance consider sending someone after them, I suppose?"

"Bentzen, my dear. And a couple of guards."

"Oh." The duchess paused. Bentzen, as captain of the duke's personal bodyguard, was as efficient a killer as a psychotic mongoose. He would have been

---

* Whatever that was. He'd never found anyone prepared to explain it to him. But it was definitely something a feudal lord ought to have and, he was pretty sure, it needed regular exercise. He imagined it was some kind of large hairy dog. He was definitely going to get one, and damn well exercise it.

her choice. It annoyed her to be temporarily deprived of a chance to fault her husband, but she rallied quite well.

"He wouldn't have needed to go out at all, if only you'd listened to me. But you never do."

"Do what, my passion?"

The duke yawned. It had been a long night. There had been a thunderstorm of quite unnecessarily dramatic proportions, and then there had been all that messy business with the knives.

It has already been mentioned that Duke Felmet was one step away from the throne. The step in question was at the top of the flight leading to the Great Hall, down which King Verence had tumbled in the dark only to land, against all the laws of probability, on his own dagger.

It had, however, been declared by his own physician to be a case of natural causes. Bentzen had gone to see the man and explained that falling down a flight of steps with a dagger in your back was a disease caused by unwise opening of the mouth.

In fact it had already been caught by several members of the king's own bodyguard who had been a little bit hard of hearing. There had been a minor epidemic.

The duke shuddered. There were details about last night that were both hazy and horrible.

He tried to reassure himself that all the unpleasantness was over now, and he had a kingdom. It wasn't much of one, apparently being mainly trees, but it was a kingdom and it had a crown.

If only they could find it.

Lancre Castle was built on an outcrop of rock by an architect who had heard about Gormenghast but hadn't got the budget. He'd done his best, though, with a tiny confection of cut-price turrets, bargain basements, buttresses, crenellations, gargoyles, towers, courtyards, keeps and dungeons; in fact, just about everything a castle needs except maybe reasonable foundations and the kind of mortar that doesn't wash away in a light shower.

The castle leaned vertiginously over the racing white water of the Lancre river, which boomed darkly a thousand feet below. Every now and again a few bits fell in.

Small as it was, though, the castle contained a thousand places to hide a crown.

The duchess swept out to find someone else to berate, and left Lord Felmet looking gloomily at the landscape. It started to rain.

It was on this cue that there came a thunderous knocking at the castle door. It seriously disturbed the castle porter, who was playing Cripple Mister Onion with the castle cook and the castle's Fool in the warmth of the kitchen.

He growled and stood up. "There is a knocking without," he said.

"Without what?" said the Fool.

"Without the door, idiot."

The Fool gave him a worried look. "A knocking without a door?" he said suspiciously. "This isn't some kind of Zen, is it?"

When the porter had grumbled off in the direction of the gatehouse the cook pushed another farthing into the kitty and looked sharply over his cards at the Fool.

"What's a Zen?" he said.

The Fool's bells tinkled as he sorted through his cards. Without thinking, he said: "Oh, a sub-sect of the Turnwise Klatch philosophical system of Sumtin, noted for its simple austerity and the offer of personal tranquillity and wholeness achieved through meditation and breathing techniques; an interesting aspect is the asking of apparently non-sensical questions in order to widen the doors of perception."

"How's that again?" said the cook suspiciously. He was on edge. When he'd taken the breakfast up to the Great Hall he'd kept getting the feeling that something was trying to take the tray out of his hands. And as if that wasn't bad enough, this new duke had sent him back for . . . He shuddered. Oatmeal! And a runny boiled egg! The cook was too old for this sort of thing. He was set in his ways. He was a cook in the real feudal tradition. If it didn't have an apple in its mouth and you couldn't roast it, he didn't want to serve it.

The Fool hesitated with a card in his hand, suppressed his panic and thought quickly.

"I'faith, nuncle," he squeaked, "thou't more full of questions than a martlebury is of mizzensails."

The cook relaxed.

"Well, OK," he said, not entirely satisfied. The Fool lost the next three hands, just to be on the safe side.

The porter, meanwhile, unfastened the hatch in the wicket gate and peered out.

"Who dost knock without?" he growled.

The soldier, drenched and terrified though he was, hesitated.

"Without? Without what?" he said.

"If you're going to bugger about, you can bloody well stay without all day," said the porter calmly.

"No! I must see the duke upon the instant!" shouted the guard. "Witches are abroad!"

The porter was about to come back with, "Good time of year for it," or "Wish I was, too," but stopped when he saw the man's face. It wasn't the face of a man who would enter into the spirit of the thing. It was the look of someone who had seen things a decent man shouldn't wot of . . .

"Witches?" said Lord Felmet.

"Witches!" said the duchess.

In the drafty corridors, a voice as faint as the wind in distant keyholes said, with a note of hope, "Witches!"

The psychically inclined . . .

"It's meddling, that's what it is," said Granny Weatherwax. "And no good will come of it."

"It's very *romantic*," said Magrat breathily, and heaved a sigh.

"Goochy goo," said Nanny Ogg.

"Anyway," said Magrat, "you killed that horrid man!"

"I never did. I just encouraged . . . things to take their course." Granny Weatherwax frowned. "He didn't have no respect. Once people lose their respect, it means trouble."

"Izzy wizzy wazzy, den."

"That other man brought him out here to save him!" shouted Magrat. "He wanted us to keep him safe! It's obvious! It's destiny!"

"Oh, *obvious*," said Granny. "I'll grant you it's *obvious*. Trouble is, just because things are obvious doesn't mean they're true."

She weighed the crown in her hands. It felt very heavy, in a way that went beyond mere pounds and ounces.

"Yes, but the point is—" Magrat began.

"The point is," said Granny, "that people are going to come looking. Serious people. Serious looking. Pull-down-the-walls and burn-off-the-thatch looking. And—"

"Howsa boy, den?"

"—*And*, Gytha, I'm sure we'll all be a *lot* happier if you'd stop gurgling like that!" Granny snapped. She could feel her nerves coming on. Her nerves always played up when she was unsure about things. Besides, they had retired to Magrat's cottage, and the decor was getting to her, because Magrat believed in Nature's wisdom and elves and the healing power of colors and the cycle of the seasons and a lot of other things Granny Weatherwax didn't have any truck with.

"You're not after telling me how to look after a child," snapped Nanny Ogg mildly. "And me with fifteen of my own?"

"I'm just saying that we ought to think about it," said Granny.

The other two watched her for some time.

"Well?" said Magrat.

Granny's fingers drummed on the edge of the crown. She frowned.

"First, we've got to take him away from here," she said, and held up a hand. "No, Gytha, I'm sure your cottage is ideal and everything, but it's not safe. He's got to be somewhere away from here, a long way away, where no one knows who he is. And then there's this." She tossed the crown from hand to hand.

"Oh, that's easy," said Magrat. "I mean, you just hide it under a stone or something. That's easy. Much easier than babies."

"It ain't," said Granny. "The reason being, the country's full of babies and they all look the same, but I don't reckon there's many crowns. They have this way of being found, anyway. They kind of call out to people's minds. If you bunged it under a stone up here, in a week's time it'd get itself discovered by accident. You mark my words."

"It's true, is that," said Nanny Ogg, earnestly. "How many times have you thrown a magic ring into the deepest depths of the ocean and then, when you get home and have a nice bit of turbot for your tea, there it is?"

They considered this in silence.

"Never," said Granny irritably. "And nor have you. Anyway, he might want it back. If it's rightfully his, that is. Kings set a lot of store by crowns. Really, Gytha, sometimes you say the most—"

"I'll just make some tea, shall I?" said Magrat brightly, and disappeared into the scullery.

The two elderly witches sat on either side of the table in polite and prickly silence. Finally Nanny Ogg said, "She done it up nice, hasn't she? Flowers and everything. What are them things on the walls?"

"Sigils," said Granny sourly. "Or some such."

"Fancy," said Nanny Ogg, politely. "And all them robes and wands and things too."

"*Modern*," said Granny Weatherwax, with a sniff. "When I was a gel, we had a lump of wax and a couple of pins and had to be content. We had to make our *own* enchantment in them days."

"Ah, well, we've all passed a lot of water since then," said Nanny Ogg sagely. She gave the baby a comforting jiggle.

Granny Weatherwax sniffed. Nanny Ogg had been married three times and ruled a tribe of children and grandchildren all over the kingdom. Certainly, it was not actually *forbidden* for witches to get married. Granny had to concede that, but reluctantly. Very reluctantly. She sniffed again, disapprovingly; this was a mistake.

"What's that smell?" she snapped.

"Ah," said Nanny Ogg, carefully repositioning the baby. "I expect I'll just go and see if Magrat has any clean rags, shall I?"

And now Granny was left alone. She felt embarrassed, as one always does when left alone in someone else's room, and fought the urge to get up and inspect the books on the shelf over the sideboard or examine the mantelpiece for dust. She turned the crown around and around in her hands. Again, it gave the impression of being bigger and heavier than it actually was.

She caught sight of the mirror over the mantelpiece and looked down at the crown. It was tempting. It was practically begging her to try it for size. Well, and why not? She made sure that the others weren't around and then, in one movement, whipped off her hat and placed the crown on her head.

It seemed to fit. Granny drew herself up proudly, and waved a hand imperiously in the general direction of the hearth.

"Jolly well do this," she said. She beckoned arrogantly at the grandfather clock. "Chop his head off, what ho," she commanded. She smiled grimly.

And froze as she heard the screams, and the thunder of horses, and the deadly whisper of arrows and the damp, solid sound of spears in flesh. Charge after charge echoed across her skull. Sword met shield, or sword, or bone—relentlessly. Years streamed across her mind in the space of a second. There were times when she lay among the dead, or hanging from the branch of a tree; but always there were hands that would pick her up again, and place her on a velvet cushion . . .

Granny very carefully lifted the crown off her head—it was an effort, it didn't like it much—and laid it on the table.

"So that's being a king for you, is it?" she said softly. "I wonder why they all want the job?"

"Do you take sugar?" said Magrat, behind her.

"You'd have to be a born fool to be a king," said Granny.

"Sorry?"

Granny turned. "Didn't see you come in," she said. "What was it you said?"

"Sugar in your tea?"

"Three spoons," said Granny promptly. It was one of the few sorrows of Granny Weatherwax's life that, despite all her efforts, she'd arrived at the peak of her career with a complexion like a rosy apple and all her teeth. No amount of charms could persuade a wart to take root on her handsome if slightly equine features, and vast intakes of sugar only served to give her boundless energy. A wizard she'd consulted had explained it was on account of her having a metabolism, which at least allowed her to feel vaguely superior to Nanny Ogg, who she suspected had never even seen one.

Magrat dutifully dug out three heaped ones. It would be nice, she thought wistfully, if someone could say "thank you" occasionally.

She became aware that the crown was staring at her.

"You can feel it, can you?" said Granny. "It said, didn't I? Crowns call out!"

"It's horrible."

"No, no. It's just being what it is. It can't help it."

"But it's magic!"

"It's just being what it is," Granny repeated.

"It's trying to get me to try it on," said Magrat, her hand hovering.

"It does that, yes."

"But I shall be strong," said Magrat.

"So I should think," said Granny, her expression suddenly curiously wooden. "What's Gytha doing?"

"She's giving the baby a wash in the sink," said Magrat vaguely. "How can we hide something like this? What'd happen if we buried it really deeply somewhere?"

"A badger'd dig it up," said Granny wearily. "Or someone'd go prospecting for gold or something. Or a tree'd tangle its roots around it and then be blown over in a storm, and then someone'd pick it up and put it on—"

"Unless they were as strong-minded as us," Magrat pointed out.

"Unless that, of course," said Granny, staring at her fingernails. "Though the thing with crowns is, it isn't the putting them on that's the problem, it's the taking them off."

Magrat picked it up and turned it over in her hands.

"It's not as though it even looks much like a crown," she said.

"You've seen a lot, I expect," said Granny. "You'd be an expert on them, naturally."

"Seen a fair few. They've got a lot more jewels on them, and cloth bits in the middle," said Magrat defiantly. "This is just a thin little thing—"

"Magrat Garlick!"

"I have. When I was being trained up by Goodie Whemper—"

"—maysherestinpeace—"

"—maysherestinpeace, she used to take me over

to Razorback or into Lancre whenever the strolling players were in town. She was very keen on the theater. They've got more crowns than you can shake a stick at although, mind—" she paused—"Goodie did say they're made of tin and paper and stuff. And just glass for the jewels. But they look more realler than this one. Do you think that's strange?"

"Things that try to look like things often do look more like things than things. Well-known fact," said Granny. "But I don't hold with encouraging it. What do they stroll about playing, then, in these crowns?"

"You don't know about the theater?" said Magrat.

Granny Weatherwax, who never declared her ignorance of anything, didn't hesitate. "Oh, yes," she said. "It's one of *them* style of things, then, is it?"

"Goodie Whemper said it held a mirror up to life," said Magrat. "She said it always cheered her up."

"I expect it would," said Granny, striking out. "Played properly, at any rate. Good people, are they, these theater players?"

"I think so."

"And they stroll around the country, you say?" said Granny thoughtfully, looking toward the scullery door.

"All over the place. There's a troupe in Lancre now, I heard. I haven't been because, you know." Magrat looked down. "'Tis not right, a woman going into such places by herself."

Granny nodded. She thoroughly approved of such sentiments so long as there was, of course, no suggestion that they applied to her.

She drummed her fingers on Magrat's tablecloth.

"Right," she said. "And why not? Go and tell Gytha to wrap the baby up well. It's a long time since I heard a theater played properly."

Magrat was entranced, as usual. The theater was no more than some lengths of painted sacking, a plank stage laid over a few barrels, and half a dozen benches set out in the village square. But at the same time it had also managed to become The Castle, Another Part of the Castle, The Same Part A Little Later, The Battlefield and now it was A Road Outside the City. The afternoon would have been perfect if it wasn't for Granny Weatherwax.

After several piercing glares at the three-man orchestra to see if she could work out which instrument the theater was, the old witch had finally paid attention to the stage, and it was beginning to become apparent to Magrat that there were certain fundamental aspects of the theater that Granny had not yet grasped.

She was currently bouncing up and down on her stool with rage.

"He's killed him," she hissed. "Why isn't anyone doing anything about it? He's killed him! And right up there in front of everyone!"

Magrat held on desperately to her colleague's arm as she struggled to get to her feet.

"It's all right," she whispered. "He's not dead!"

"Are you calling me a liar, my girl?" snapped Granny. "I saw it all!"

"Look, Granny, it's not really real, d'you see?"

Granny Weatherwax subsided a little, but still grumbled under her breath. She was beginning to feel that things were trying to make a fool of her.

Up on the stage a man in a sheet was giving a spirited monologue. Granny listened intently for some minutes, and then nudged Magrat in the ribs.

"What's he on about now?" she demanded.

"He's saying how sorry he was that the other man's dead," said Magrat, and in an attempt to change the subject added hurriedly, "There's a lot of crowns, isn't there?"

Granny was not to be distracted. "What'd he go and kill him for, then?" she said.

"Well, it's a bit complicated—" said Magrat, weakly.

"It's shameful!" snapped Granny. "And the poor dead thing still lying there!"

Magrat gave an imploring look to Nanny Ogg, who was masticating an apple and studying the stage with the glare of a research scientist.

"I *reckon*," she said slowly, "I reckon it's all just pretendin'. Look, he's still breathing."

The rest of the audience, who by now had already decided that this commentary was all part of the play, stared as one man at the corpse. It blushed.

"And look at his boots, too," said Nanny critically. "A real king'd be ashamed of boots like that."

The corpse tried to shuffle its feet behind a cardboard bush.

Granny, feeling in some obscure way that they had scored a minor triumph over the purveyors of untruth and artifice, helped herself to an apple from the bag and began to take a fresh interest. Magrat's nerves started to unknot, and she began to settle down to enjoy the play. But not, as it turned out, for very long. Her willing suspension of disbelief was interrupted by a voice saying:

"What's this bit?"

Magrat sighed. "Well," she hazarded, "*he* thinks that *he* is the prince, but *he's* really the other king's daughter, dressed up as a man."

Granny subjected the actor to a long analytical stare.

"He *is* a man," she said. "In a straw wig. Making his voice squeaky."

Magrat shuddered. She knew a little about the conventions of the theater. She had been dreading this bit. Granny Weatherwax had Views.

"Yes, but," she said wretchedly, "it's the Theater, see. All the women are played by men."

"Why?"

"They don't allow no women on the stage," said Magrat in a small voice. She shut her eyes.

In fact, there was no outburst from the seat on her left. She risked a quick glance.

Granny was quietly chewing the same bit of apple over and over again, her eyes never leaving the action.

"Don't make a fuss, Esme," said Nanny, who also knew about Granny's Views. "This is a good bit. I reckon I'm getting the hang of it."

Someone tapped Granny on the shoulder and a voice said, "Madam, will you kindly remove your hat?"

Granny turned around very slowly on her stool,

as though propelled by hidden motors, and subjected the interrupter to a hundred kilowatt diamond-blue stare. The man wilted under it and sagged back onto his stool, her face following him all the way down.

"No," she said.

He considered the options. "All right," he said.

Granny turned back and nodded to the actors, who had paused to watch her.

"I don't know what you're staring at," she growled. "Get on with it."

Nanny Ogg passed her another bag.

"Have a humbug," she said.

Silence again filled the makeshift theater except for the hesitant voices of the actors, who kept glancing at the bristling figure of Granny Weatherwax, and the sucking sounds of a couple of boiled humbugs being relentlessly churned from cheek to cheek.

Then Granny said, in a piercing voice that made one actor drop his wooden sword, "There's a man over on the side there whispering to them!"

"He's a prompter," said Magrat. "He tells them what to say."

"Don't they know?"

"I think they're forgetting," said Magrat sourly. "For some reason."

Granny nudged Nanny Ogg.

"What's going on now?" she said. "Why're all them kings and people up there?"

"It's a banquet, see," said Nanny Ogg authoritatively. "Because of the dead king, him in the boots, as was, only now if you look, you'll see he's pretending to be a soldier, and everyone's making speeches about how good he was and wondering who killed him."

"Are they?" said Granny, grimly. She cast her eyes along the cast, looking for the murderer.

She was making up her mind.

Then she stood up.

Her black shawl billowed around her like the wings of an avenging angel, come to rid the world of all that was foolishness and pretense and artifice and sham. She seemed somehow a lot bigger than normal. She pointed an angry finger at the guilty party.

"He done it!" she shouted triumphantly. "We all *seed* 'im! He done it with a dagger!"

The audience filed out, contented. It had been a good play on the whole, they decided, although not very easy to follow. But it had been a jolly good laugh when all the kings had run off, and the woman in black had jumped up and did all the shouting. That alone had been well worth the ha'penny admission.

The three witches sat alone on the edge of the stage.

"I wonder how they get all them kings and lords to come here and do this?" said Granny, totally unabashed. "I'd have thought they'd been too busy. Ruling and similar."

"No," said Magrat, wearily. "I still don't think you quite understand."

"Well, I'm going to get to the bottom of it,"

snapped Granny. She got back onto the stage and pulled aside the sacking curtains.

"You!" she shouted. "You're dead!"

The luckless former corpse, who was eating a ham sandwich to calm his nerves, fell backward off his stool.

Granny kicked a bush. Her boot went right through it.

"See?" she said to the world in general in a strangely satisfied voice. "Nothing's real! It's all just paint, and sticks and paper at the back."

"May I assist you, good ladies?"

It was a rich and wonderful voice, with every diphthong gliding beautifully into place. It was a golden brown voice. If the Creator of the multiverse had a voice, it was a voice such as this. If it had a drawback, it was that it wasn't a voice you could use, for example, for ordering coal. Coal ordered by this voice would become diamonds.

It apparently belonged to a large fat man who had been badly savaged by a mustache. Pink veins made a map of quite a large city on his cheeks; his nose could have hidden successfully in a bowl of strawberries. He wore a ragged jerkin and holey tights with an aplomb that nearly convinced you that his velvet-and-vermine robes were in the wash just at the moment. In one hand he held a towel, with which he had clearly been removing the make-up that still greased his features.

"I know you," said Granny. "You done the murder." She looked sideways at Magrat, and admitted, grudgingly, "Leastways, it looked like it."

"*So* glad. It is always a pleasure to meet a true connoisseur. Olwyn Vitoller, *at* your service. Manager of this band of vagabonds," said the man and, removing his moth-eaten hat, he treated her to a low bow. It was less an obeisance than an exercise in advanced topology.

The hat swerved and jerked through a series of complex arcs, ending up at the end of an arm which was now pointing in the direction of the sky. One of his legs, meanwhile, had wandered off behind him. The rest of his body sagged politely until his head was level with Granny's knees.

"Yes, well," said Granny. She felt that her clothes had grown a bit larger and much hotter.

"I thought you was very good, too," said Nanny Ogg. "The way you shouted all them words so graciously. I could tell you was a king."

"I hope we didn't upset things," said Magrat.

"My dear lady," said Vitoller. "Could I begin to tell you how gratifying it is for a mere mummer to learn that his audience has seen behind the mere shell of greasepaint to the spirit beneath?"

"I expect you could," said Granny. "I expect you could say anything, Mr. Vitoller."

He replaced his hat and their eyes met in the long and calculating stare of one professional weighing up another. Vitoller broke first, and tried to pretend he hadn't been competing.

"And now," he said, "to what do I owe this visit from three such charming ladies?"

In fact he'd won. Granny's mouth fell open. She would not have described herself as anything much above "handsome, considering." Nanny, on the other hand, was as gummy as a baby and had a face like a small dried raisin. The best you could say for Magrat was that she was decently plain and well-scrubbed and as flat-chested as an ironing board with a couple of peas on it, even if her head was too well stuffed with fancies. Granny could feel something, some sort of magic at work. But not the kind she was used to.

It was Vitoller's voice. By the mere process of articulation it transformed everything it talked about.

Look at the two of them, she told herself, primping away like a couple of ninnies. Granny stopped her hand in the process of patting her own iron-hard bun, and cleared her throat meaningfully.

"We'd like to talk to you, Mr. Vitoller." She indicated the actors, who were dismantling the set and staying well out of her way, and added in a conspiratorial whisper, "Somewhere private."

"Dear lady, but of a certain," he said. "Currently I have lodgings in yonder esteemed watering hole."

The witches looked around. Eventually Magrat risked, "You mean in the pub?"

It was cold and drafty in the Great Hall of Lancre Castle, and the new chamberlain's bladder wasn't getting any younger. He stood and squirmed under the gaze of Lady Felmet.

"Oh, yes," he said. "We've got them all right. Lots."

"And people don't *do* anything about them?" said the duchess.

The chamberlain blinked. "I'm sorry?" he said.

"People tolerate them?"

"Oh, indeed," said the chamberlain happily. "It's considered good luck to have a witch living in your village. My word, yes."

"Why?"

The chamberlain hesitated. The last time he had resorted to a witch it had been because certain rectal problems had turned the privy into a daily torture chamber, and the jar of ointment she had prepared had turned the world into a nicer place.

"They smooth out life's little humps and bumps," he said.

"Where I come from, we don't allow witches," said the duchess sternly. "And we don't propose to allow them here. You will furnish us with their addresses."

"Addresses, ladyship?"

"Where they live. I trust your tax gatherers know where to find them?"

"Ah," said the chamberlain, miserably.

The duke leaned forward on his throne.

"I trust," he said, "that they do pay taxes?"

"Not, exactly *pay* taxes, my lord," said the chamberlain.

There was silence. Finally the duke prompted, "Go on, man."

"Well, it's more that they *don't* pay, you see. We never felt, that is, the old king didn't think . . . Well, they just don't."

The duke laid a hand on his wife's arm.

"I see," he said coldly. "Very well. You may go."

The chamberlain gave him a brief nod of relief and scuttled crabwise from the hall.

"Well!" said the duchess.

"Indeed."

"That was how your family used to run a kingdom, was it? You had a positive *duty* to kill your cousin. It was clearly in the interests of the species," said the duchess. "The weak don't deserve to survive."

The duke shivered. She would keep on reminding him. He didn't, on the whole, object to killing people, or at least ordering them to be killed and then watching it happen. But killing a kinsman rather stuck in the throat or—he recalled—the liver.

"Quite so," he managed. "Of course, there would appear to be many witches, and it might be difficult to find the three that were on the moor."

"That doesn't matter."

"Of course not."

"Put matters in hand."

"Yes, my love."

Matters in hand. He'd put matters in hand all right. If he closed his eyes he could see the body tumbling down the steps. Had there been a hiss of shocked breath, down in the darkness of the hall? He'd been certain they were alone. Matters in hand! He'd tried to wash the blood off his hand. If he could wash the blood off, he told himself, it wouldn't have happened. He'd scrubbed and scrubbed. Scrubbed till he screamed.

* * *

Granny wasn't at home in public houses. She sat stiffly to attention behind her port-and-lemon, as if it were a shield against the lures of the world.

Nanny Ogg, on the other hand, was enthusiastically downing her third drink and, Granny thought sourly, was well along that path which would probably end up with her usual dancing on the table, showing her petticoats and singing "The Hedgehog Can Never be Buggered at All."

The table was covered with copper coins. Vitoller and his wife sat at either end, counting. It was something of a race.

Granny considered Mrs. Vitoller as she snatched farthings from under her husband's fingers. She was an intelligent-looking woman, who appeared to treat her husband much as a sheepdog treats a favorite lamb. The complexities of the marital relationship were known to Granny only from a distance, in the same way that an astronomer can view the surface of a remote and alien world, but it had already occurred to her that a wife to Vitoller would have to be a very special woman with bottomless reserves of patience and organizational ability and nimble fingers.

"Mrs. Vitoller," she said eventually, "may I make so bold as to ask if your union has been blessed with fruit?"

The couple looked blank.

"She means—" Nanny Ogg began.

"No, I see," said Mrs. Vitoller, quietly. "No. We had a little girl once."

A small cloud hung over the table. For a second or two Vitoller looked merely human-sized, and much older. He stared at the small pile of cash in front of him.

"Only, you see, there is this child," said Granny, indicating the baby in Nanny Ogg's arms. "And he needs a home."

The Vitollers stared. Then the man sighed.

"It is no life for a child," he said. "Always moving. Always a new town. And no room for schooling. They say that's very important these days." But his eyes didn't look away.

Mrs. Vitoller said, "Why does he need a home?"

"He hasn't got one," said Granny. "At least, not one where he would be welcome."

The silence continued. Then Mrs. Vitoller said, "And you, who ask this, you are by way of being his—?"

"Godmothers," said Nanny Ogg promptly. Granny was slightly taken aback. It never would have occurred to her.

Vitoller played abstractly with the coins in front of him. His wife reached out across the table and touched his hand, and there was a moment of unspoken communion. Granny looked away. She had grown expert at reading faces, but there were times when she preferred not to.

"Money is, alas, tight—" Vitoller began.

"But it will stretch," said his wife firmly.

"Yes. I think it will. We should be happy to take care of him."

Granny nodded, and fished in the deepest recesses of her cloak. At last she produced a small leather bag, which she tipped out onto the table. There was a lot of silver, and even a few tiny gold coins.

"This should take care of—" she groped—"nappies and suchlike. Clothes and things. Whatever."

"A hundred times over, I should think," said Vitoller weakly. "Why didn't you mention this before?"

"If I'd had to buy you, you wouldn't be worth the price."

"But you don't know anything about us!" said Mrs. Vitoller.

"We don't, do we?" said Granny, calmly. "Naturally we'd like to hear how he gets along. You could send us letters and suchlike. But it would not be a good idea to talk about all this after you've left, do you see? For the sake of the child."

Mrs. Vitoller looked at the two old women.

"There's something else here, isn't there?" she said. "Something big behind all this?"

Granny hesitated, and then nodded.

"But it would do us no good at all to know it?"

Another nod.

Granny stood up as several actors came in, breaking the spell. Actors had a habit of filling all the space around them.

"I have other things to see to," she said. "Please excuse me."

"What's his name?" said Vitoller.

"Tom," said Granny, hardly hesitating.

"John," said Nanny. The two witches exchanged glances. Granny won.

"Tom John," she said firmly, and swept out.

She met a breathless Magrat outside the door.

"I found a box," she said. "It had all the crowns and things in. So I put it in, like you said, right underneath everything."

"Good," said Granny.

"Our crown looked really tatty compared to the others!"

"It just goes to show, doesn't it," said Granny. "Did anyone see you?"

"No, everyone was too busy, but—" Magrat hesitated, and blushed.

"Out with it, girl."

"Just after that a man came up and pinched my bottom." Magrat went a deep crimson and slapped her hand over her mouth.

"Did he?" said Granny. "And then what?"

"And then, and then—"

"Yes?"

"He said, he said—"

"What did he say?"

"He said, 'Hallo, my lovely, what are you doing tonight?'"

Granny ruminated on this for a while and then she said, "Old Goodie Whemper, she didn't get out and about much, did she?"

"It was her leg, you know," said Magrat.

"But she taught you all the midwifery and everything?"

"Oh, yes, *that*," said Magrat. "I done lots."

"But—" Granny hesitated, groping her way across unfamiliar territory—"she never talked about what you might call the *previous*."

"Sorry?"

"You know," said Granny, with an edge of desperation in her voice. "Men and such."

Magrat looked as if she was about to panic. "What about them?"

Granny Weatherwax had done many unusual things in her time, and it took a lot to make her refuse a challenge. But this time she gave in.

"I think," she said helplessly, "that it might be a good idea if you have a quiet word with Nanny Ogg one of these days. Fairly soon."

There was a cackle of laughter from the window behind them, a chink of glasses, and a thin voice raised in song:

"—with a giraffe, if you stand on a stool. But the hedgehog—"

Granny stopped listening. "Only not just now," she added.

The troupe got under way a few hours before sunset, their four carts lurching off down the road that led toward the Sto plains and the big cities. Lancre had a town rule that all mummers, mountebanks and other potential criminals were outside the gates by sundown; it didn't offend anyone really because the town had no walls to speak of, and no one much minded if people nipped back in again after dark. It was the look of the thing that counted.

The witches watched from Magrat's cottage, using Nanny Ogg's ancient green crystal ball.

"It's about time you learned how to get sound on this thing," Granny muttered. She gave it a nudge, filling the image with ripples.

"It was very strange," said Magrat. "In those carts. The things they had! Paper trees, and all kinds of costumes, and—" she waved her hands—"there was this great big picture of forn parts, with all temples and things all rolled up. It was beautiful."

Granny grunted.

"I thought it was amazing the way all those people became kings and things, didn't you? It was like magic."

"Magrat Garlick, what are you saying? It was just paint and paper. Anyone could see that."

Magrat opened her mouth to speak, ran the ensuing argument through her head, and shut it again.

"Where's Nanny?" she said.

"She's lying out on the lawn," said Granny. "She felt a bit poorly." And from outside came the sound of Nanny Ogg being poorly at the top of her voice.

Magrat sighed.

"You know," she said, "if we *are* his godmothers, we ought to have given him three gifts. It's traditional."

"What are you talking about, girl?"

"Three good witches are supposed to give the baby three gifts. You know, like good looks, wisdom and happiness." Magrat pressed on defiantly. "That's how it used to be done in the old days."

"Oh, you mean gingerbread cottages and all that,"

said Granny dismissively. "Spinning wheels and pumpkins and pricking your finger on rose thorns and similar. I could never be having with all that."

She polished the ball reflectively.

"Yes, but—" Magrat said. Granny glanced up at her. That was Magrat for you. Head full of pumpkins. Everyone's fairy godmother, for two pins. But a good soul, underneath it all. Kind to small furry animals. The sort of person who worried about baby birds falling out of nests.

"Look, if it makes you any happier," she muttered, surprised at herself. She waved her hands vaguely over the image of the departing carts. "What's it to be—wealth, beauty?"

"Well, money isn't everything, and if he takes after his father he'll be handsome enough," Magrat said, suddenly serious. "Wisdom, do you think?"

"That's something he'll have to learn for himself," said Granny.

"Perfect eyesight? A good singing voice?" From the lawn outside came Nanny Ogg's cracked but enthusiastic voice telling the night sky that A Wizard's Staff Has A Knob On The End.

"Not important," said Granny loudly. "You've got to think headology, see? Not muck about with all this beauty and wealth business. That's not important."

She turned back to the ball and gestured half-heartedly. "You'd better go and get Nanny, then, seeing as there should be three of us."

Nanny was helped in, eventually, and had to have things explained to her.

"Three gifts, eh?" she said. "Haven't done one of them things since I was a gel, it takes me back—what're you doing?"

Magrat was bustling around the room, lighting candles.

"Oh, we've got to create the right magical ambience," she explained. Granny shrugged, but said nothing, even in the face of the extreme provocation. All witches did their magic in their own way, and this was Magrat's house.

"What're we going to give him, then?" said Nanny.

"We was just discussing it," said Granny.

"I know what he'll want," said Nanny. She made a suggestion, which was received in frozen silence.

"I don't see what use *that* would be," said Magrat, eventually. "Wouldn't it be rather uncomfortable?"

"He'll thank us when he grows up, you mark my words," said Nanny. "My first husband, he always said—"

"Something a bit less physical is generally the style of things," interrupted Granny, glaring at Nanny Ogg. "There's no need to go and spoil everything, Gytha. Why do you always have to—"

"Well, at least I can say that I—" Nanny began.

Both voices faded to a mutter. There was a long edgy silence.

"I think," said Magrat, with brittle brightness, "that perhaps it would be a good idea if we all go back to our little cottages and do it in our own way. You know. Separately. It's been a long day and we're all rather tired."

"Good idea," said Granny firmly, and stood up. "Come, Nanny Ogg," she snapped. "It's been a long day and we're all rather tired."

Magrat heard them bickering as they wandered down the path.

She sat rather sadly amidst the colored candles, holding a small bottle of extremely thaumaturgical incense that she had ordered from a magical supplies emporium in faraway Ankh-Morpork. She had been rather looking forward to trying it. Sometimes, she thought, it would be nice if people could be a bit kinder . . .

She stared at the ball.

Well, she could make a start.

"He will make friends easily," she whispered. It wasn't much, she knew, but it was something she'd never been able to get the hang of.

Nanny Ogg, sitting alone in her kitchen with her huge tomcat curled up on her lap, poured herself a nightcap and through the haze tried to remember the words of verse seventeen of the Hedgehog song. There was something about goats, she recalled, but the details eluded her. Time abraded memory.

She toasted the invisible presence.

"A bloody good memory is what he ought to have," she said. "He'll always remember the words."

And Granny Weatherwax, striding home alone through the midnight forest, wrapped her shawl around her and considered. It had been a long day, and a trying one. The theater had been the worst part. All people pretending to be other people, things happening that weren't real, bits of countryside you could put your foot through . . . Granny liked to know where she stood, and she wasn't certain she stood for that sort of thing. The world seemed to be changing all the time.

It didn't use to change so much. It was bewildering.

She walked quickly through the darkness with the frank stride of someone who was at least certain that the forest, on this damp and windy night, contained strange and terrible things and she was it.

"Let him be whoever he thinks he is," she said. "That's all anybody could hope for in this world."

Like most people, witches *are* unfocused in time. The difference is that they dimly realize it, and make use of it. They cherish the past because part of them is still living there, and they can see the shadows the future casts before it.

Granny could feel the shape of the future, and it had knives in it.

It began at five the next morning. Four men rode through the woods near Granny's cottage, tethered the horses out of earshot, and crept very cautiously through the mists.

The sergeant in charge was not happy in his work. He was a Ramtops man, and wasn't at all certain about how you went about arresting a witch. He was pretty certain, though, that the witch wouldn't like the idea. He didn't like the idea of a witch not liking the idea.

The men were Ramtoppers as well. They were following him very closely, ready to duck behind him at the first sign of anything more unexpected than a tree.

Granny's cottage was a fungoid shape in the mist. Her unruly herb garden seemed to move, even in the still air. It contained plants seen nowhere else in the mountains, their roots and seeds traded across five thousand miles of the Discworld, and the sergeant could swear that one or two blooms turned toward him. He shuddered.

"What now, Sarge?"

"We—we spread out," he said. "Yes. We spread out. That's what we do."

They moved carefully through the bracken. The sergeant crouched behind a handy log, and said, "Right. Very good. You've got the general idea. Now let's spread out again, and this time we spread out separately."

The men grumbled a bit, but disappeared into the mist. The sergeant gave them a few minutes to take up positions, then said, "Right. Now we—"

He paused.

He wondered whether he dared shout, and decided against it.

He stood up. He removed his helmet, to show respect, and sidled through the damp grass to the back door. He knocked, very gently.

After a wait of several seconds he clamped his helmet back on his head, said, "No one in. Blast," and started to stride away.

The door opened. It opened very slowly, and with the maximum amount of creak. Simple neglect wouldn't have caused that depth of groan; you'd need careful work with hot water over a period of weeks. The sergeant stopped, and then turned around very slowly while contriving to move as few muscles as possible.

He had mixed feelings about the fact that there was nothing in the doorway. In his experience, doors didn't just open themselves.

He cleared his throat nervously.

Granny Weatherwax, right by his ear, said, "That's a nasty cough you've got there. You did right in coming to me."

The sergeant looked up at her with an expression of mad gratitude. He said, "Argle."

"She did *what*?" said the duke.

The sergeant stared fixedly at an area a few inches to the right of the duke's chair.

"She give me a cup of tea, sir," he said.

"And what about your men?"

"She give them one too, sir."

The duke rose from his chair and put his arms around the sergeant's rusting chain mail shoulders. He was in a bad mood. He had spent half the night washing his hands. He kept thinking that something was whispering in his ear. His breakfast oatmeal had been served up too salty and roasted with an apple in it, and the crook had hysterics in the kitchen. You could tell the duke was extremely annoyed. He was polite. The duke was the kind of man who becomes more and more agreeable as his temper drains away, until the point is reached where the words "Thank you so much" have the cutting edge of a guillotine.

"Sergeant," he said, walking the man slowly across the floor.

"Sir?"

"I'm not sure I made your orders clear, sergeant," said the duke, in snake tones.

"Sir?"

"I mean, it is possible I may have confused you. I meant to say 'Bring me a witch, in chains if necessary,' but perhaps what I *really* said was 'Go and have a cup of tea.' Was this in fact the case?"

The sergeant wrinkled his forehead. Sarcasm had not hitherto entered his life. His experience of people being annoyed with him generally involved shouting and occasional bits of wood.

"No, sir," he said.

"I wonder why, then, you did not in fact do this thing that I asked?"

"Sir?"

"I expect she said some magic words, did she? I've heard about witches," said the duke, who had spent the night before reading, until his bandaged hands shook too much, some of the more excitable works on the subject.* "I imagine she offered you visions of unearthly delight? Did she show you—" the duke shuddered—"dark fascinations and forbidden rap-

---

* Written by wizards, who are celibate and get some pretty funny ideas around four o'clock in the morning.

tures, the like of which mortal men should not even think of, and demonic secrets that took you to the depths of man's desires?"

The duke sat down and fanned himself with his handkerchief.

"Are you all right, sir?" said the sergeant.

"What? Oh, perfectly, perfectly."

"Only you've gone all red."

"Don't change the subject, man," snapped the duke, pulling himself together a bit. "Admit it—she offered you hedonistic and licentious pleasures known only to those who dabble in the carnal arts, didn't she?"

The sergeant stood to attention and stared straight ahead.

"No, sir," he said, in the manner of one speaking the truth come what may. "She offered me a bun."

"A bun?"

"Yes, sir. It had currants in it."

Felmet sat absolutely still while he fought for internal peace. Finally, all he could manage was, "And what did your men do about this?"

"They had a bun too, sir. All except young Roger, who isn't allowed fruit, sir, on account of his trouble."

The duke sagged back on the window seat and put his hand over his eyes. I was born to rule down on the plains, he thought, where it's all flat and there isn't all this weather and everything and there are people who don't appear to be made of dough. He's going to tell me what this Roger had.

"He had a biscuit, sir."

The duke stared out at the trees. He was angry.

He was extremely angry. But twenty years of marriage to Lady Felmet had taught him not simply to control his emotions but to control his instincts as well, and not so much as the twitching of a muscle indicated the workings of his mind. Besides, arising out of the black depths of his head was an emotion that, hitherto, he had a little time for. Curiosity was flashing a fin.

The duke had managed quite well for fifty years without finding a use for curiosity. It was not a trait much encouraged in aristocrats. He had found certainty was a much better bet. However, it occurred to him that for once curiosity might have its uses.

The sergeant was standing in the middle of the floor with the stolid air of one who is awaiting a word of command, and who is quite prepared so to wait until continental drift budges him from his post. He had been in the undemanding service of the kings of Lancre for many years, and it showed. His body was standing to attention. Despite all his efforts his stomach stood at ease.

The duke's gaze fell on the Fool, who was sitting on his stool by the throne. The hunched figure looked up, embarrassed, and gave his bells a half-hearted shake.

The duke reached a decision. The way to progress, he'd found, was to find weak spots. He tried to shut away the thought that these included such things as a king's kidneys at the top of a dark stairway, and concentrated on the matter in hand.

. . . hand. He'd scrubbed and scrubbed, but it seemed to have no effect. Eventually he'd gone down to the dungeons and borrowed one of the torturer's wire brushes, and scrubbed and scrubbed with that, too. That had no effect, either. It made it worse. The harder he scrubbed, the more blood there was. He was afraid he might go mad . . .

He wrestled the thought to the back of his mind. Weak spots. That was it. The Fool looked all weak spot.

"You may go, sergeant."

"Sir," said the sergeant, and marched out stiffly.

"Fool?"

"Marry, sir—" said the Fool nervously, and gave his hated mandolin a quick strum.

The duke sat down on the throne.

"I am already extremely married," he said. "Advise me, my Fool."

"I'faith, nuncle—" said the Fool.

"Nor am I thy nuncle. I feel sure I would have remembered," said Lord Felmet, leaning down until the prow of his nose was a few inches from the Fool's stricken face. "If you preface your next remark with nuncle, i'faith or marry, it will go hard with you."

The Fool moved his lips silently, and then said, "How do you feel about Prithee?"

The duke knew when to allow some slack. "Prithee I can live with," he said. "So can you. But no capering." He grinned encouragingly. "How long have you been a Fool, boy?"

"Prithee, sirrah—"

"The sirrah," said the duke, holding up a hand, "on the whole, I think not."

"Prithee, sirra—sir," said the Fool, and swallowed nervously. "All my life, sir. Seventeen years under the bladder, man and boy. And my father before me. And my nuncle at the same time as him. And my grandad before them. And his—"

"Your whole family have been Fools?"

"Family tradition, sir," said the Fool. "Prithee, I mean."

The duke smiled again, and the Fool was too worried to notice how many teeth it contained.

"You come from these parts, don't you?" said the duke.

"Ma—Yes, sir."

"So you would know all about the native beliefs and so on?"

"I suppose so, sir. Prithee."

"Good. Where do you sleep, my Fool?"

"In the stables, sir."

"From now on you may sleep in the corridor outside my room," said the duke beneficently.

"Gosh!"

"And now," said the duke, his voice dripping across the Fool like treacle over a pudding, "tell me about witches . . ."

That night the Fool slept on good royal flagstones in the whistling corridor above the Great Hall instead of the warm stuffy straw of the stables.

"This is foolish," he told himself. "Marry, but is it foolish *enough*?"

He dozed off fitfully, into some sort of dream where a vague figure kept trying to attract his attention, and was only dimly aware of the voices of Lord and Lady Felmet on the other side of the door.

"It's certainly a lot less drafty," said the duchess grudgingly.

The duke sat back in the armchair and smiled at his wife.

"Well?" she demanded. "Where are the witches?"

"The chamberlain would appear to be right, beloved. The witches seem to have the local people in thrall. The sergeant of the guard came back empty-handed." Handed . . . he came down heavily on the importunate thought.

"You must have him executed," she said promptly. "To make an example to the others."

"A course of action, my dear, which ultimately results in us ordering the last soldier to cut his own throat as an example to himself. By the way," he added mildly, "there would appear to be somewhat fewer servants around the place. You know I would not normally interfere—"

"Then don't," she snapped. "Housekeeping is under my control. I cannot abide *slackness*."

"I'm sure you know best, but—"

"What of these witches? Will you stand idly by and let trouble seed for the future? Will you let these witches defy you? What of the crown?"

The duke shrugged. "No doubt it ended in the river," he said.

"And the child? He was *given* to the witches? Do they do human sacrifice?"

"It would appear not," said the duke. The duchess looked vaguely disappointed.

"These witches," said the duke. "Apparently, they seem to cast a spell on people."

"Well, obviously—"

"Not like a magic spell. They seem to be respected. They do medicine and so on. It's rather strange. The mountain people seem to be afraid of them and proud of them at the same time. It might be a little difficult to move against them."

"I could come to believe," said the duchess darkly, "that they have cast a glamor over you as well."

In fact the duke *was* intrigued. Power was always darkly fascinating, which was why he had married the duchess in the first place. He stared fixedly at the fire.

"In fact," said the duchess, who recognized the malign smile, "you like it, don't you? The thought of the danger. I remember when we were married; all that business with the knotted rope—"

She snapped her fingers in front of the duke's glazed, eyes. He sat up.

"Not at all!" he shouted.

"Then what will you do?"

"Wait."

"*Wait?*"

"Wait, and consider. Patience is a virtue."

The duke sat back. The smile he smiled could have spent a million years sitting on a rock. And then, just below one eye, he started to twitch.

Blood was oozing between the bandages on his hand.

Once again the full moon rode the clouds.

Granny Weatherwax milked and fed the goats,

banked the fire, put a cloth over the mirror and pulled her broomstick out from behind the door. She went out, locked the back door behind her, and hung the key on its nail in the privy.

This was quite sufficient. Only once, in the entire history of witchery in the Ramtops, had a thief broken into a witch's cottage. The witch concerned visited the most terrible punishment on him.*

Granny sat on the broom and muttered a few words, but without much conviction. After a further couple of tries she got off, fiddled with the binding, and had another go. There was a suspicion of glitter from one end of the stick, which quickly died away.

"Drat," she said, under her breath.

She looked around carefully, in case anyone was watching. In fact it was only a hunting badger who, hearing the thumping of running feet, poked its head out from the bushes and saw Granny hurtling down the path with the broomstick held stiff-armed beside her. At last the magic caught, and she managed to vault clumsily onto it before it trundled into the night sky as gracefully as a duck with one wing missing.

From above the trees came a muffled curse against all dwarfish mechanics.

Most witches preferred to live in isolated cottages

---

* She did nothing, although sometimes when she saw him in the village she'd smile in a faint, puzzled way. After three weeks of this the suspense was too much for him and he took his own life; in fact he took it all the way across the continent, where he became a reformed character and never went home again.

with the traditional curly chimneys and weed-grown thatch. Granny Weatherwax approved of this; it was no good being a witch unless you let people *know*.

Nanny Ogg didn't care much about what people knew and even less for what they thought, and lived in a new, knick-knack crammed cottage in the middle of Lancre town itself and at the heart of her own private empire. Various daughters and daughters-in-law came in to cook and clean on a sort of rota. Every flat surface was stuffed with ornaments brought back by far-traveling members of the family. Sons and grandsons kept the logpile stacked, the roof shingled, the chimney swept; the drinks cupboard was always full, the pouch by her rocking chair always stuffed with tobacco. Above the hearth was a huge pokerwork sign saying "Mother." No tyrant in the whole history of the world had ever achieved a domination so complete.

Nanny Ogg also kept a cat, a huge one-eyed gray torn called Greebo who divided his time between sleeping, eating and fathering the most enormous incestuous feline tribe. He opened his eye like a yellow window into Hell when he heard Granny's broomstick land awkwardly on the back lawn. With the instinct of his kind he recognized Granny as an inveterate cat-hater and oozed gently under a chair.

Magrat was already seated primly by the fire.

It is one of the few unbendable rules of magic that its practitioners cannot change their own appearance for any length of time. Their bodies develop a kind of morphic inertia and gradually return to their original shape. But Magrat tried. Every morning her hair was long, thick and blond, but by the evening it had always returned to its normal worried frizz. To ameliorate the effect she had tried to plait violets and cowslips in it. The result was not all she had hoped. It gave the impression that a window box had fallen on her head.

"Good evening," said Granny.

"Well met by moonlight," said Magrat politely. "Merry meet. A star shines on—"

"Wotcha," said Nanny Ogg. Magrat winced.

Granny sat down and started removing the pins that nailed her tall hat to her bun. Finally the sight of Magrat dawned on her.

"Magrat!"

The young witch jumped, and clamped her knuckly hands to the virtuous frontage of her gown.

"Yes?" she quavered.

"What have you got on your lap?"

"It's my familiar," she said defensively.

"What happened to that toad you had?"

"It wandered off," muttered Magrat. "Anyway, it wasn't very good."

Granny sighed. Magrat's desperate search for a reliable familiar had been going on for some time, and despite the love and attention she lavished on them they all seemed to have some terrible flaw, such as a tendency to bite, get trodden on or, in extreme cases, metamorphose.

"That makes fifteen this year," said Granny. "Not counting the horse. What's this one?"

"It's a rock," chuckled Nanny Ogg.

"Well, at least it should last," said Granny.

The rock extended a head and gave her a look of mild amusement.

"It's a tortoise," said Magrat. "I bought it down in Sheepridge market. It's incredibly old and knows many secrets, the man said."

"I know that man," said Granny. "He's the one who sells goldfish that tarnish after a day or two."

"Anyway, I shall call him Lightfoot," said Magrat, her voice warm with defiance. "I can if I want."

"Yes, yes, all right, I'm sure," said Granny. "Anyway, how goes it, sisters? It is two months since last we met."

"It should be every new moon," said Magrat sternly. "Regular."

"It was our Grame's youngest's wedding," said Nanny Ogg. "Couldn't miss it."

"And I was up all night with a sick goat," said Granny Weatherwax promptly.

"Yes, well," said Magrat doubtfully. She rummaged in her bag. "Anyway, if we're going to start, we'd better light the candles."

The senior witches exchanged a resigned glance.

"But we got this lovely new lamp our Tracie sent me," said Nanny Ogg innocently. "And I was going to poke up the fire a bit."

"I have *ex*cellent night vision, Magrat," said Granny sternly. "And you've been reading them funny books. Grimmers."

"Grimoires—"

"You ain't going to draw on the floor again, neither," warned Nanny Ogg. "It took our Dreen days to clean up all those wossnames last time—"

"Runes," said Magrat. There was a look of pleading in her eyes. "Look, just one candle?"

"All right," said Nanny Ogg, relenting a bit. "If it makes you feel any better. Just the one, mind. And a decent white one. Nothing fancy."

Magrat sighed. It probably wasn't a good idea to bring out the rest of the contents of her bag.

"We ought to get a few more here," she said sadly. "It's not right, a coven of three."

"I didn't know we was still a coven. No one told me we was still a coven," sniffed Granny Weatherwax. "Anyway, there's no one else this side of the mountain, excepting old Gammer Dismass, and she doesn't get out these days."

"But a lot of young girls in my village . . ." said Magrat. "You know. They could be keen."

"That's not how we do it, as well you know," said Granny disapprovingly. "People don't go and find witchcraft, it comes and finds them."

"Yes, yes," said Magrat. "Sorry."

"Right," said Granny, slightly mollified. She'd never mastered the talent for apologizing, but she appreciated it in other people.

"What about this new duke, then," said Nanny, to lighten the atmosphere.

Granny sat back. "He had some houses burned down in Bad Ass," she said. "Because of taxes."

"How horrible," said Magrat.

"Old King Verence used to do that," said Nanny. "Terrible temper he had."

"*He* used to let people get out first, though," said Granny.

"Oh yes," said Nanny, who was a staunch royalist. "He could be very gracious like that. He'd pay for them to be rebuilt, as often as not. If he remembered."

"And every Hogswatchnight, a side of venison. Regular," said Granny wistfully.

"Oh, yes. Very respectful to witches, he was," added Nanny Ogg. "When he was out hunting people, if he met me in the woods, it was always off with his helmet and 'I hope I finds you well, Mistress Ogg' and next day he'd send his butler down with a couple of bottles of something. He was a proper king."

"Hunting people isn't really right, though," said Magrat.

"Well, no," Granny Weatherwax conceded. "But it was only if they'd done something bad. He said they enjoyed it really. And he used to let them go if they gave him a good run."

"And then there was that great hairy thing of his," said Nanny Ogg.

There was a perceptible change in the atmosphere. It became warmer, darker, filled at the corners with the shadows of unspoken conspiracy.

"Ah," said Granny Weatherwax distantly. "His droit de seigneur."

"Needed a lot of exercise," said Nanny Ogg, staring at the fire.

"But next day he'd send his housekeeper around with a bag of silver and a hamper of stuff for the wedding," said Granny. "Many a couple got a proper start in life thanks to that."

"Ah," agreed Nanny. "One or two individuals, too."

"Every inch a king," said Granny.

"What are you talking about?" said Magrat suspiciously. "Did he keep pets?"

The two witches surfaced from whatever deeper current they had been swimming in. Granny Weatherwax shrugged.

"I must say," Magrat went on, in severe tones, "if you think so much of the old king, you don't seem very worried about him being killed. I mean, it was a pretty suspicious accident."

"That's kings for you," said Granny. "They come and go, good and bad. His father poisoned the king we had before."

"That was old Thargum," said Nanny Ogg. "Had a big red beard, I recall. He was very gracious too, you know."

"Only now no one must say Felmet killed the king," said Magrat.

"What?" said Granny.

"He had some people executed in Lancre, the other day for saying it," Magrat went on. "Spreading malicious lies, he said. He said anyone saying different will see the inside of his dungeons, only not for long. He said Verence died of natural causes."

"Well, being assassinated *is* natural causes for a king," said Granny. "I don't see why he's so sheepish about it. When old Thargum was killed they stuck his head on a pole, had a big bonfire and everyone in the palace got drunk for a week."

"I remember," said Nanny. "They carried his head all around the villages to show he was dead. Very convincing, I thought. Specially for him. He was grinning. I think it was the way he would have liked to go."

"I think we might have to keep an eye on this one, though," said Granny. "I think he might be a bit clever. That's not a good thing, in a king. And I don't think he knows how to show respect."

"A man came to see me last week to ask if I wanted to pay any taxes," said Magrat. "I told him no."

"He came to see me, too," said Nanny Ogg. "But our Jason and our Wane went out and tole him we didn't want to join."

"Small man, bald, black cloak?" said Granny thoughtfully.

"Yes," said the other two.

"He was hanging about in my raspberry bushes," said Granny. "Only, when I went out to see what he wanted, he ran away."

"Actually, I gave him tuppence," said Magrat. "He said he was going to be tortured, you see, if he didn't get witches to pay their taxes . . ."

Lord Felmet looked carefully at the two coins in his lap.

Then he looked at his tax gatherer.

"Well?" he said.

The tax gatherer cleared his throat. "Well, sir, you see. I explained about the need to employ a standing army, ekcetra, and they said why, and I said because of bandits, ekcetra, and they said bandits never bothered them."

"And civil works?"

"Ah. Yes. Well, I pointed out the need to build and maintain bridges, ekcetra."

"And?"

"They said they didn't use them."

"Ah," said the duke knowledgeably. "They can't cross running water."

"Not sure about that, sir. I think witches cross anything they like."

"Did they say anything else?" said the duke.

The tax gatherer twisted the hem of his robe distractedly.

"Well, sir. I mentioned how taxes help to maintain the King's Peace, sir . . ."

"And?"

"They said the king should maintain his own peace, sir. And then they gave me a look."

"What sort of look?"

The duke sat with his thin face cupped in one hand. He was fascinated.

"It's sort of hard to describe," said the taxman. He tried to avoid Lord Felmet's gaze, which was giving him the distinct impression that the tiled floor was fleeing away in all directions and had already covered several acres. Lord Felmet's fascination was to him what a pin is to a Purple Emperor.

"Try," the duke invited.

The taxman blushed.

"Well," he said. "It . . . wasn't nice."

Which demonstrates that the tax gatherer was much better at figures than words. What he would have said, if embarrassment, fear, poor memory and a complete lack of any kind of imagination hadn't conspired against it, was:

"When I was a little boy, and staying with my aunt, and she had told me not to touch the cream, ekcetra, and she had put it on a high shelf in the pantry, and I got a stool and went after it when she was out anyway, and she'd come back and I didn't know, and I couldn't reach the bowl properly and it smashed on the floor, and she opened the door and glared at me: it was that look. But the worst thing was, they *knew* it."

"Not nice," said the duke.

"No, sir."

The duke drummed the fingers of his left hand on the arm of his throne. The tax gatherer coughed again.

"You're—you're not going to force me to go back, are you?" he said.

"Um?" said the duke. He waved a hand irritably. "No, no," he said. "Not at all. Just call in at the torturer on your way out. See when he can fit you in."

The taxman gave him a look of gratitude, and bobbed a bow.

"Yes, sir. At once, sir. Thank you, sir. You're very—"

"Yes, yes," said Lord Felmet, absently. "You may go."

The duke was left alone in the vastness of the hall. It was raining again. Every once in a while a piece of plaster smashed down on the tiles, and there was a crunching from the walls as they settled still further. The air smelled of old cellars.

Gods, he hated this kingdom.

It was so small, only forty miles long and maybe ten miles wide, and nearly all of it was cruel mountains with ice-green slopes and knife-edge crests, or dense huddled forests. A kingdom like that shouldn't be any trouble.

What he couldn't quite fathom was this feeling that it had *depth*. It seemed to contain far too much geography.

He rose and paced the floor to the balcony, with its unrivaled view of trees. It struck him that the trees were also looking back at him.

He could feel the resentment. But that was odd, because the people themselves hadn't objected. They didn't seem to object to anything very much. Verence had been popular enough, in his way. There'd been quite a turnout for the funeral; he recalled the lines of solemn faces. Not stupid faces. By no means stupid. Just preoccupied, as though what kings did wasn't really very important.

He found that almost as annoying as trees. A jolly good riot, now, that would have been more—more appropriate. One could have ridden out and hanged people, there would have been the creative tension so essential to the proper development of the state. Back down on the plains, if you kicked people they kicked back. Up here, when you kicked people they moved away and just waited patiently for your leg to fall off. How could a king go down in history ruling a people like that? You couldn't oppress them any more than you could oppress a mattress.

He had raised taxes and burned a few villages on general principles, just to show everyone who they were dealing with. It didn't seem to have any effect.

And then there were these witches. They haunted him.

"Fool!"

The Fool, who had been having a quiet doze behind the throne, awoke in terror.

"Yes!"

"Come hither, Fool."

The Fool jingled miserably across the floor.

"Tell me, Fool, does it always rain here?"

"Marry, nuncle—"

"Just answer the question," said Lord Felmet, with iron patience.

"Sometimes it stops, sir. To make room for the snow. And sometimes we get some right squand'ring orgulous fogs," said the Fool.

"Orgulous?" said the duke, absently.

The Fool couldn't stop himself. His horrified ears heard his mouth blurt out: "Thick, my lord. From the Latatian *orgulum*, a soup or broth."

But the duke wasn't listening. Listening to the prattle of underlings was not, in his experience, particularly worthwhile.

"I am bored, Fool."

"Let me entertain you, my lord, with many a merry quip and lightsome jest."

"Try me."

The Fool licked his dry lips. He hadn't actually expected this. King Verence had been happy enough just to give him a kick, or throw a bottle at his head. A *real* king.

"I'm waiting. Make me laugh."

The Fool took the plunge.

"Why, sirrah," he quavered, "why may a caudled fillhorse be deemed the brother to a hiren candle in the night?"

The duke frowned. The Fool felt it better not to wait.

"Withal, because a candle may be greased, yet a fillhorse be without a fat argier," he said and, because it was part of the joke, patted Lord Felmet lightly with his balloon on a stick and twanged his mandolin.

The duke's index finger tapped an abrupt tattoo on the arm of the throne.

"Yes?" he said. "And then what happened?"

"That, er, was by way of being the whole thing," said the Fool, and added, "My grandad thought it was one of his best."

"I daresay he told it differently," said the duke. He stood up. "Summon my huntsmen. I think I shall ride out on the chase. And you can come too."

"My lord, I cannot ride!"

For the first time that morning Lord Felmet smiled.

"Capital!" he said. "We will give you a horse that can't be ridden. Ha. Ha."

He looked down at his bandages. And afterward, he told himself, I'll get the armorer to send me up a file.

* * *

A year went past. The days followed one another patiently. Right back at the beginning of the multiverse they had tried all passing at the same time, and it hadn't worked.

Tomjon sat under Hwel's rickety table, watching his father as he walked up and down between the lattys, waving one arm and talking. Vitoller always waved his arms when he spoke; if you tied his hands behind his back he would be dumb.

"All right," he was saying, "how about *The King's Brides*?"

"Last year," said the voice of Hwel.

"All right, then. We'll give them *Mallo, the Tyrant of Klatch*," said Vitoller, and his larynx smoothly changed gear as his voice became a great rolling thing that could rattle the windows across the width of the average town square. "'In blood I came, And by blood rule, That none will dare assay these walls of blood—'"

"We did it the year before," said Hwel calmly. "Anyway, people are fed up with kings. They want a bit of a chuckle."

"They are not fed up with *my* kings," said Vitoller. "My dear boy, people do not come to the theater to laugh, they come to Experience, to Learn, to Wonder—"

"To laugh," said Hwel, flatly. "Have a look at this one."

Tomjon heard the rustle of paper and the creak of wickerwork as Vitoller lowered his weight onto a props basket.

"*A Wizard of Sorts*," Vitoller read. "*Or, Please Yourself.*"

Hwel stretched his legs under the table and dislodged Tomjon. He hauled the boy out by one ear.

"What's this?" said Vitoller. "Wizards? Demons? Imps? Merchants?"

"I'm rather pleased with Act II, Scene IV," said Hwel, propelling the toddler toward the props box. "Comic Washing Up with Two Servants."

"Any death-bed scenes?" said Vitoller hopefully.

"No-o," said Hwel. "But I can do you a humorous monologue in Act III."

"A humorous monologue!"

"All right, there's room for a soliloquy in the last act," said Hwel hurriedly. "I'll write one tonight, no problem."

"And a stabbing," said Vitoller, getting to his feet. "A foul murder. That always goes down well."

He strode away to organize the setting up of the stage.

Hwel sighed, and picked up his quill. Somewhere behind the sacking walls was the town of Hangdog, which had somehow allowed itself to be built in a hollow perched in the nearly sheer walls of a canyon. There was plenty of flat ground in the Ramtops. The problem was that nearly all of it was vertical.

Hwel didn't like the Ramtops, which was odd because it was traditional dwarf country and he was a dwarf. But he'd been banished from his tribe years ago, not only because of his claustrophobia but also because he had a tendency to daydream. It was felt by the local dwarf king that this is not a valuable talent for someone who is supposed to swing a pickaxe without forgetting what he is supposed to hit with it, and so Hwel had been given a very small bag of gold, the tribe's heartfelt best wishes, and a firm goodbye.

It had happened that Vitoller's strolling players had been passing through at the time, and the dwarf had ventured one small copper coin on a performance of *The Dragon of the Plains*. He had watched it without a muscle moving in his face, gone back to his lodgings, and in the morning had knocked on Vitoller's latty with the first draft of *King Under the Mountain*. It wasn't in fact very good, but Vitoller had been perceptive enough to see that inside the hairy bullet head was an imagination big enough to bestride the world and so, when the strolling players strolled off, one of them was running to keep up.

Particles of raw inspiration sleet through the universe all the time. Every once in a while one of them hits a receptive mind, which then invents DNA or the flute sonata form or a way of making light bulbs wear out in half the time. But most of them miss. Most people go through their lives without being hit by even one.

Some people are even more unfortunate. They get them *all*.

Such a one was Hwel. Enough inspirations to equip a complete history of the performing arts poured continuously into a small heavy skull designed by evolution to do nothing more spectacular than be remarkably resistant to axe blows.

He licked his quill and looked bashfully around the camp. No one was watching. He carefully lifted up the *Wizard* and revealed another stack of paper.

It was another potboiler. Every page was stained with sweat and the words themselves scrawled across the manuscript in a trellis of blots and crossings-out and tiny scribbled insertions. Hwel stared at it for a moment, alone in a world that consisted of him, the next blank page and the shouting, clamoring voices that haunted his dreams.

He began to write.

Free of Hwel's never-too-stringent attention, Tomjon pushed open the lid of the props hamper and, in the methodical way of the very young, began to unpack the crowns.

The dwarf stuck out his tongue as he piloted the errant quill across the ink-speckled page. He'd found room for the star-crossed lovers, the comic grave-diggers and the hunchback king. It was the cats and the roller skates that were currently giving him trouble . . .

A gurgle made him look up.

"For goodness sake, lad," he said. "It hardly fits. Put it back."

The Disc rolled into winter.

Winter in the Ramtops could not honestly be described as a magical frosty wonderland, each twig laced with confections of brittle ice. Winter in the

Ramtops didn't mess about; it was a gateway straight through to the primeval coldness that lived before the creation of the world. Winter in the Ramtops was several yards of snow, the forests a mere collection of shadowy green tunnels under the drifts. Winter meant the coming of the lazy wind, which couldn't be bothered to blow around people and blew right through them instead. The idea that Winter could actually be enjoyable would never have occurred to Ramtop people, who had eighteen different words for snow.*

The ghost of King Verence prowled the battlements, bereft and hungry, and stared out across his beloved forests and waited his chance.

It was a winter of portents. Comets sparkled against the chilled skies at night. Clouds shaped mightily like whales and dragons drifted over the land by day. In the village of Razorback a cat gave birth to a two-headed kitten, but since Greebo, by dint of considerable effort, was every male ancestor for the last thirty generations this probably wasn't all that portentous.

However, in Bad Ass a cockerel laid an egg and had to put up with some very embarrassing personal questions. In Lancre town a man swore he'd met a man who had actually seen with his own eyes a tree get up and walk. There was a short sharp shower of shrimps. There were odd lights in the sky. Geese

---

* All of them, unfortunately, unprintable.

walked backward. Above all of this flared the great curtains of cold fire that were the Aurora Coriolis, the Hublights, whose frosty tints illuminated and colored the midnight snows.

There was nothing the least unusual about any of this. The Ramtops, which as it were lay across the Disc's vast magical standing wave like an iron bar dropped innocently across a pair of subway rails, were so saturated with magic that it was constantly discharging itself into the environment. People would wake up in the middle of the night, mutter, "Oh, it's just another bloody portent," and go back to sleep.

Hogswatchnight came around, marking the start of another year. And, with alarming suddenness, nothing happened.

The skies were clear, the snow deep and crisped like icing sugar.

The freezing forests were silent and smelled of tin. The only things that fell from the sky were the occasional fresh showers of snow.

A man walked across the moors from Razorback to Lancre town without seeing a single marshlight, headless dog, strolling tree, ghostly coach or comet, and had to be taken in by a tavern and given a drink to unsteady his nerves.

The stoicism of the Ramtoppers, developed over the years as a sovereign resistance to the thaumaturgical chaos, found itself unable to cope with the sudden change. It was like a noise which isn't heard until it stops.

Granny Weatherwax heard it now as she lay snug

under a pile of quilts in her freezing bedroom. Hogswatchnight is, traditionally, the one night of the Disc's long year when witches are expected to stay at home, and she'd had an early night in the company of a bag of apples and a stone hotwater bottle. But something had awoken her from her doze.

An ordinary person would have crept downstairs, possibly armed with a poker. Granny simply hugged her knees and let her mind wander.

It hadn't been in the house. She could feel the small, fast minds of mice, and the fuzzy minds of her goats as they lay in their cozy flatulence in the outhouse. A hunting owl was a sudden dagger of alertness as it glided over the rooftops.

Granny concentrated harder, until her mind was full of the tiny chittering of the insects in the thatch and the woodworm in the beams. Nothing of interest there.

She snuggled down and let herself drift out into the forest, which was silent except for the occasional muffled thump as snow slid off a tree. Even in midwinter the forest was full of life, usually dozing in burrows or hibernating in the middle of trees.

All as usual. She spread herself further, to the high moors and secret passes where the wolves ran silently over the frozen crust; she touched their minds, sharp as knives. Higher still, and there was nothing in the snowfields but packs of vermine.*

---

* The vermine is a small black and white furry creature, much famed for its pelt. It is a more careful relative of the lemming; it only throws itself over small pebbles.

Everything was as it should be, with the exception that nothing was right. There was something—yes, there was something *alive* out there, something young and ancient and . . .

Granny turned over the feeling in her mind. Yes. That was it. Something forlorn. Something lost. And . . .

Feelings were never simple, Granny knew. Strip them away and there were others underneath . . .

Something that, if it didn't stop feeling lost and forlorn very soon, was going to get *angry*.

And still she couldn't find it. She could feel the tiny minds of chrysalises down under the frozen leaf mold. She could sense the earthworms, which had migrated below the frost line. She could even sense a few people, who were hardest of all—human minds were thinking so many thoughts all at the same time that they were nearly impossible to locate; it was like trying to nail fog to the wall.

Nothing there. Nothing there. The feeling was all around her, and there was nothing to cause it. She'd gone down about as far as she could, to the smallest creature in the kingdom, and there was nothing there.

Granny Weatherwax sat up in bed, lit a candle and reached for an apple. She glared at her bedroom wall.

She didn't like being beaten. There was something out there, something drinking in magic, something growing, something that seemed so alive it was all around the house, and she couldn't find it.

She reduced the apple to its core and placed it

carefully in the tray of the candlestick. Then she blew out the candle.

The cold velvet of the night slid back into the room.

Granny had one last try. Perhaps she was looking in the wrong way . . .

A moment later she was lying on the floor with the pillow clasped around her head.

And to think she had expected it to be *small* . . .

Lancre Castle shook. It wasn't a violent shaking, but it didn't need to be, the construction of the castle being such that it swayed slightly even in a gentle breeze. A small turret toppled slowly into the depths of the misty canyon.

The Fool lay on his flagstones and shivered in his sleep. He appreciated the honor, if it was an honor, but sleeping in the corridor always made him dream of the Fools' Guild, behind whose severe gray walls he had trembled his way through seven years of terrible tuition. The flagstones were slightly softer than the beds there, though.

A few feet away a suit of armor jingled gently. Its pike vibrated in its mailed glove until, swishing through the night air like a swooping bat, it slid down and shattered the flagstone by the Fool's ear.

The Fool sat up and realized he was still shivering. So was the floor.

In Lord Felmet's room the shaking sent cascades of dust down from the ancient four-poster. He awoke from a dream that a great beast was tramping around the castle, and decided with horror that it might be true.

A portrait of some long-dead king fell off the wall. The duke screamed.

The Fool stumbled in, trying to keep his balance on a floor that was now heaving like the sea, and the duke staggered out of bed and grabbed the little man by his jerkin.

"What's happening?" he hissed. "Is it an earthquake?"

"We don't have them in these parts, my lord," said the Fool, and was knocked aside as a chaise longue drifted slowly across the carpet.

The duke dashed to the window, and looked out at the forests in the moonlight. The white-capped trees shook in the still night air.

A slab of plaster crashed onto the floor. Lord Felmet spun around and this time his grip lifted the Fool a foot off the floor.

Among the very many luxuries the duke had dispensed with in his life was that of ignorance. He liked to feel he knew what was going on. The glorious uncertainties of existence held no attraction for him.

"It's the witches, isn't it?" he growled, his left cheek beginning to twitch like a landed fish. "They're out there, aren't they? They're putting an Influence on the castle, aren't they?"

"Marry, nuncle—" the Fool began.

"They run this country, don't they?"

"No, my lord, they've never—"

"*Who asked you?*"

The Fool was trembling with fear in perfect antiphase to the castle, so that he was the only thing that now appeared to be standing perfectly still.

"Er, you did, my lord," he quavered.

"Are you arguing with me?"

"No, my lord!"

"I thought so. You're in league with them, I suppose?"

"My lord!" said the Fool, really shocked.

"You're all in league, you people!" the duke snarled. "The whole bunch of you! You're nothing but a pack of ringleaders!"

He flung the Fool aside and thrust the tall windows open, striding out into the freezing night air. He glared out over the sleeping kingdom.

"Do you all hear me?" he screamed. "I am the king!"

The shaking stopped, catching the duke off-balance. He steadied himself quickly, and brushed the plaster dust off his nightshirt.

"Right, then," he said.

But this was worse. Now the forest was listening. The words he spoke vanished into a great vacuum of silence.

There was something out there. He could feel it. It was strong enough to shake the castle, and now it was watching him, listening to him.

The duke backed away, very carefully, fumbling behind him for the window catch. He stepped carefully into the room, shut the windows and hurriedly pulled the curtains across.

"I am the king," he repeated, quietly. He looked at the Fool, who felt that something was expected of him.

The man is my lord and master, he thought. I

have eaten his salt, or whatever all that business was. They told me at Guild school that a Fool should be faithful to his master until the very end, after all others have deserted him. Good or bad doesn't come into it. Every leader needs his Fool. There is only loyalty. That's the whole thing. Even if he is clearly three-parts bonkers, I'm his Fool until one of us dies.

To his horror he realized the duke was weeping.

The Fool fumbled in his sleeve and produced a rather soiled red and yellow handkerchief embroidered with bells. The duke took it with an expression of pathetic gratitude and blew his nose. Then he held it away from him and gazed at it with demented suspicion.

"Is this a dagger I see before me?" he mumbled.

"Um. No, my lord. It's my handkerchief, you see. You can sort of tell the difference if you look closely. It doesn't have as many sharp edges."

"*Good* fool," said the duke, vaguely.

Totally mad, the Fool thought. Several bricks short of a bundle. So far around the twist you could use him to open wine bottles.

"Kneel beside me, my Fool."

The Fool did so. The duke laid a soiled bandage on his shoulder.

"Are you loyal, Fool?" he said. "Are you trustworthy?"

"I swore to follow my lord until death," said the Fool hoarsely.

The duke pressed his mad face close to the Fool, who looked up into a pair of bloodshot eyes.

"I didn't want to," he hissed conspiratorially. "They made me do it. I didn't want—"

The door swung open. The duchess filled the doorway. In fact, she was nearly the same shape.

"Leonal!" she barked.

The Fool was fascinated by what happened to the duke's eyes. The mad red flame vanished, was sucked backward, and was replaced by the hard blue stare he had come to recognize. It didn't mean, he realized, that the duke was any less mad. Even the coldness of his sanity was madness in a way. The duke had a mind that ticked like a clock and, like a clock, it regularly went cuckoo.

Lord Felmet looked up calmly.

"Yes, my dear?"

"What is the meaning of all this?" she demanded.

"Witches, I suspect," said Lord Felmet.

"I really don't think—" the Fool began. Lady Felmet's glare didn't merely silence him, it almost nailed him to the wall.

"That is clearly apparent," she said. "You are an idiot."

"A Fool, my lady."

"As well," she added, and turned back to her husband.

"So," she said, smiling grimly. "Still they defy you?"

The duke shrugged. "How should I fight magic?" he said.

"With words," said the Fool, without thinking, and was instantly sorry. They were both staring at him.

"What?" said the duchess.

The Fool dropped his mandolin in his embarrassment.

"In—in the Guild," said the Fool, "we learned that words can be more powerful even than magic."

"Clown!" said the duke. "Words are just words. Brief syllables. Sticks and stones may break my bones—" he paused, savoring the thought—"but words can never hurt me."

"My lord, there are such words that can," said the Fool. "Liar! Usurper! Murderer!"

The duke jerked back and gripped the arms of the throne, wincing.

"Such words have no truth," said the Fool, hurriedly. "But they can spread like fire underground, breaking out to burn—"

"It's true! It's true!" screamed the duke. "I hear them, all the time!" He leaned forward. "It's the witches!" he hissed.

"Then, then, then they can be fought with other words," said the Fool. "Words can fight even witches."

"What words?" said the duchess, thoughtfully.

The Fool shrugged. "Crone. Evil eye. Stupid old woman."

The duchess raised one thick eyebrow.

"You are not entirely an idiot, are you," she said. "You refer to rumor."

"Just so, my lady." The Fool rolled his eyes. What had he got himself into?

"It's the witches," whispered the duke, to no one in particular. "We must tell the world about the witches.

They're evil. They make it come back, the blood. Even sandpaper doesn't work."

There was another tremor as Granny Weatherwax hurried along the narrow, frozen pathways in the forest. A lump of snow slipped off a tree branch and poured over her hat.

This wasn't right, she knew. Never mind about the—whatever it was—but it was unheard of for a witch to go out on Hogswatchnight. It was against all tradition. No one knew why, but that wasn't the point.

She came out onto the moorland and pounded across the brittle heather, which had been scoured of snow by the wind. There was a crescent moon near the horizon, and its pale glow lit up the mountains that towered over her. It was a different world up there, and one even a witch would rarely venture into; it was a landscape left over from the frosty birth of the world, all green ice and knife-edge ridges and deep, secret valleys. It was a landscape never intended for human beings—not hostile, anymore than a brick or cloud is hostile, but terribly, terribly uncaring.

Except that, this time, it was watching her. A mind quite unlike any other she had ever encountered was giving her a great deal of its attention. She glared up at the icy slopes, half expecting to see a mountainous shadow move against the stars.

"Who are you?" she shouted. "What do you want?"

Her voice bounced and echoed among the rocks.

There was a distant boom of an avalanche, high among the peaks.

On the crest of the moor, where in the summer partridges lurked among the bushes like small whirring idiots, was a standing stone. It stood roughly where the witches' territories met, although the boundaries were never formally marked out.

The stone was about the same height as a tall man, and made of bluish tinted rock. It was considered intensely magical because, although there was only one of it, *no one had ever been able to count it*; if it saw anyone looking at it speculatively, it shuffled behind them. It was the most self-effacing monolith ever discovered.

It was also one of the numerous discharge points for the magic that accumulated in the Ramtops. The ground around it for several yards was bare of snow, and steamed gently.

The stone began to edge away, and watched her suspiciously from behind a tree.

She waited for ten minutes until Magrat came hurrying up the path from Mad Stoat, a village whose good-natured inhabitants were getting used to ear massage and flower-based homeopathic remedies for everything short of actual decapitation.* She was out of breath, and wore only a shawl over a nightdress that, if Magrat had anything to reveal, would have been very revealing.

"You felt it too?" she said.

---

* They worked. Witches' remedies generally did, regardless of the actual form of delivery.

Granny nodded. "Where's Gytha?" she said.

They looked down the path that led to Lancre town, a huddle of lights in the snowy gloom.

There was a party going on. Light poured out into the street. A line of people were winding in and out of Nanny Ogg's house, from inside which came occasional shrieks of laughter and the sounds of breaking glass and children grizzling. It was clear that family life was being experienced to its limits in that house.

The two witches stood uncertainly in the street.

"Do you think we should go in?" said Magrat diffidently. "It's not as though we were invited. And we haven't brought a bottle."

"Sounds to me as if there's a deal too many bottles in there already," said Granny Weatherwax disapprovingly. A man staggered out of the doorway, burped, bumped into Granny, said, "Happy Hogswatchnight, missus," glanced up at her face and sobered up instantly.

"*Miss*," snapped Granny.

"I am most frightfully sorry—" he began.

Granny swept imperiously past him. "Come, Magrat," she commanded.

The din inside hovered around the pain threshold. Nanny Ogg got around the Hogswatchnight tradition by inviting the whole village in, and the air in the room was already beyond the reach of pollution controls. Granny navigated through the press of bodies by the sound of a cracked voice explaining to the world at large that, compared to an unbelievable variety of other animals, the hedgehog was quite fortunate.

Nanny Ogg was sitting in a chair by the fire with a quart mug in one hand, and was conducting the reprise with a cigar. She grinned when she saw Granny's face.

"What ho, my old boiler," she screeched above the din. "See you turned up, then. Have a drink. Have two. Wotcher, Magrat. Pull up a chair and call the cat a bastard."

Greebo, who was curled up in the inglenook and watching the festivities with one slit yellow eye, flicked his tail once or twice.

Granny sat down stiffly, a ramrod figure of decency.

"We're not staying," she said, glaring at Magrat, who was tentatively reaching out toward a bowl of peanuts. "I can see you're busy. We just wondered whether you might have noticed—anything. Tonight. A little while ago."

Nanny Ogg wrinkled her forehead.

"Our Darron's eldest was sick," she said. "Been at his dad's beer."

"Unless he was *extremely* ill," said Granny, "I doubt if it was what I was referring to." She made a complex occult sign in the air, which Nanny totally ignored.

"Someone tried to dance on the table," she said. "Fell into our Reet's pumpkin dip. We had a good laugh."

Granny waggled her eyebrows and placed a meaningful finger alongside her nose.

"I was alluding to things of a *different* nature," she hinted darkly.

Nanny Ogg peered at her.

"Something wrong with your eye, Esme?" she hazarded.

Granny Weatherwax sighed.

"Extremely worrying developments of a magical tendency are even now afoot," she said loudly.

The room went quiet. Everyone stared at the witches, except for Darron's eldest, who took advantage of the opportunity to continue his alcoholic experiments. Then, swiftly as they had fled, several dozen conversations hurriedly got back into gear.

"It might be a good idea if we can go and talk somewhere more private," said Granny, as the comforting hubbub streamed over them again.

They ended up in the washhouse, where Granny tried to give an account of the mind she had encountered.

"It's out there somewhere, in the mountains and the high forests," she said. "And it is very big."

"I thought it was looking for someone," said Magrat. "It put me in mind of a large dog. You know, lost. Puzzled."

Granny thought about this. Now she came to think of it . . .

"Yes," she said. "Something like that. A *big* dog."

"Worried," said Magrat.

"Searching," said Granny.

"And getting angry," said Magrat.

"Yes," said Granny, staring fixedly at Nanny.

"Could be a troll," said Nanny Ogg. "I left best part of a pint in there, you know," she added reproachfully.

"I know what a troll's mind feels like, Gytha," said Granny. She didn't snap the words out. In fact it was the quiet way she said them that made Nanny hesitate.

"They say there's really big trolls up toward the Hub," said Nanny slowly. "And ice giants, and big hairy wossnames that live above the snowline. But you don't mean anything like that, do you?"

"No."

"Oh."

Magrat shivered. She told herself that a witch had absolute control over her own body, and the goosepimples under her thin nightdress were just a figment of her own imagination. The trouble was, she had an excellent imagination.

Nanny Ogg sighed.

"We'd better have a look, then," she said, and took the lid off the copper.

Nanny Ogg never used her washhouse, since all her washing was done by the daughters-in-law, a tribe of gray-faced, subdued women whose names she never bothered to remember. It had become, therefore, a storage place for dried-up old bulbs, burnt-out cauldrons and fermenting jars of wasp jam. No fire had been lit under the copper for ten years. Its bricks were crumbling, and rare ferns grew around the firebox. The water under the lid was inky black and, according to rumor, bottomless; the Ogg grandchildren were encouraged to believe that monsters from the dawn of time dwelt in its depths, since Nanny believed that a bit of thrilling and pointless terror was an essential ingredient of the magic of childhood.

In summer she used it as a beer cooler.

"It'll have to do. I think perhaps we should join hands," she said. "And you, Magrat, make sure the door's shut."

"What are you going to try?" said Granny. Since they were on Nanny's territory, the choice was entirely up to her.

"I always say you can't go wrong with a good Invocation," said Nanny. "Haven't done one for years."

Granny Weatherwax frowned. Magrat said, "Oh, but you can't. Not here. You need a cauldron, and a magic sword. And an octogram. And spices, and all sorts of stuff."

Granny and Nanny exchanged glances.

"It's not her fault," said Granny. "It's all them grimmers she was bought." She turned to Magrat.

"You don't need none of that," she said. "You need headology." She looked around the ancient washroom.

"You just use whatever you've got," she said.

She picked up the bleached copper stick, and weighed it thoughtfully in her hand.

"We conjure and abjure thee by means of this—" Granny hardly paused—"sharp and terrible copper stick."

The waters in the boiler rippled gently.

"See how we scatter—" Magrat sighed—"rather old

washing soda and some extremely hard soap flakes in thy honor. Really, Nanny, I don't think—"

"Silence! Now you, Gytha."

"*And I invoke and bind thee* with the balding scrubbing brush of Art and the washboard of Protection," said Nanny, waving it. The wringer attachment fell off.

"Honesty is all very well," whispered Magrat, wretchedly, "but somehow it isn't the same."

"You listen to me, my girl," said Granny. "Demons don't care about the outward shape of things. It's what *you* think that matters. Get on with it."

Magrat tried to imagine that the bleached and ancient bar of lye soap was the rarest of scented whatever, ungulants or whatever they were, from distant Klatch. It was an effort. The gods alone knew what kind of demon would respond to a summoning like this.

Granny was also a little uneasy. She didn't much care for demons in any case, and all this business with incantations and implements whiffed of wizardry. It was pandering to the things, making them feel important. Demons ought to come when they were called.

But protocol dictated that the host witch had the choice, and Nanny quite liked demons, who were male, or apparently so.

At this point Granny was alternately cajoling and threatening the nether world with two feet of bleached wood. She was impressed at her own daring.

The waters seethed a little, became very still and

then, with a sudden movement and a little popping noise, mounded up into a head. Magrat dropped her soap.

It was a good-looking head, maybe a little cruel around the eyes and beaky about the nose, but nevertheless handsome in a hard kind of way. There was nothing surprising about this; since the demon was only extending an image of itself into this reality, it might as well make a good job of it. It turned slowly, a gleaming black statue in the fitful moonlight.

"*Well?*" it said.

"Who're you?" said Granny, bluntly.

The head revolved to face her.

"*My name is unpronounceable in your tongue, woman,*" it said.

"I'll be the judge of that," warned Granny, and added, "Don't you call me woman."

"*Very well. My name is WxrtHltl-jwlpklz,*" said the demon smugly.

"Where were you when the vowels were handed out? Behind the door?" said Nanny Ogg.

"Well, Mr.—" Granny hesitated only fractionally— "WxrtHltl-jwlpklz, I except you're wondering why we called you here tonight."

"*You're not supposed to say that,*" said the demon. "*You're supposed to say—*"

"Shut up. We have the sword of Art and the octogram of Protection, I warn you."

"*Please yourself. They look like a washboard and a copper stick to me,*" sneered the demon.

Granny glanced sideways. The corner of the washroom was stacked with kindling wood, with a big heavy sawhorse in front of it. She stared fixedly at the demon and, without looking, brought the stick down hard across the thick timber.

The dead silence that followed was broken only by the two perfectly-sliced halves of the sawhorse teetering backward and forward and folding slowly into the heap of kindling.

The demon's face remained impassive.

"*You are allowed three questions,*" it said.

"Is there something strange at large in the kingdom?" said Granny.

It appeared to think about it.

"And no lying," said Magrat earnestly. "Otherwise it'll be the scrubbing brush for you."

"*You mean stranger than usual?*"

"Get on with it," said Nanny. "My feet are freezing out here."

"*No. There is nothing strange.*"

"But we felt it—" Magrat began.

"Hold on, hold on," said Granny. Her lips moved soundlessly. Demons were like genies or philosophy professors—if you didn't word things *exactly* right, they delighted in giving you absolutely accurate and completely misleading answers.

"Is there something in the kingdom that wasn't there before?" she hazarded.

"*No.*"

Tradition said that there could be only three questions. Granny tried to formulate one that couldn't be deliberately misunderstood. Then she decided that this was playing the wrong kind of game.

"What the hell's going on?" she said carefully. "And no mucking about trying to wriggle out of it, otherwise I'll boil you."

The demon appeared to hesitate. This was obviously a new approach.

"Magrat, just kick that kindling over here, will you?" said Granny.

"*I protest at this treatment,*" said the demon, its voice tinged with uncertainty.

"Yes, well, we haven't got time to bandy legs with you all night," said Granny. "These word games might be all right for wizards, but we've got other fish to fry."

"Or boil," said Nanny.

"*Look,*" said the demon, and now there was a whine of terror in its voice. "*We're not supposed to volunteer information just like that. There are rules, you know.*"

"There's some old oil in the can on the shelf, Magrat," said Nanny.

"*If I simply tell you——*" the demon began.

"Yes?" said Granny, encouragingly.

"*You won't let on, will you?*" it implored.

"Not a word," promised Granny.

"Lips are sealed," said Magrat.

"*There is nothing new in the kingdom,*" said the demon, "*but the land has woken up.*"

"What do you mean?" said Granny.

"*It's unhappy. It wants a king that cares for it.*"

"How——" Magrat began, but Granny waved her into silence.

"You don't mean people, do you?" she said. The glistening head shook. "No, I didn't think so."

"What—" Nanny began. Granny put a finger to her lips.

She turned and walked to the washhouse's window, a dusty spiderweb graveyard of faded butterfly wings and last summer's bluebottles. A faint glow beyond the frosted panes suggested that, against all reason, a new day would soon dawn.

"Can you tell us why?" she said, without turning around. She'd felt the mind of a whole country . . .

She was rather impressed.

"I'm just a demon. What do I know? Only what is, not the why and how of it."

"I see."

"May I go now?"

"Um?"

"Please?"

Granny jerked upright again.

"Oh. Yes. Run along," she said distractedly. "Thank you."

The head didn't move. It hung around, like a hotel porter who has just carried fifteen suitcases up ten flights of stairs, shown everyone where the bathroom is, plumped up the pillows, and feels he has adjusted all the curtains he is going to adjust.

"You wouldn't mind banishing me, would you?" said the demon, when no one seemed to be taking the hint.

"What?" said Granny, who was thinking again.

"Only I'd feel better for being properly banished. 'Run along' lacks that certain something," said the head.

"Oh. Well, if it gives you any pleasure. Magrat!"

"Yes?" said Magrat, startled.

Granny tossed the copper stick to her.

"Do the honors, will you?" she said.

Magrat caught the stick by what she hoped Granny was imagining as the handle, and smiled.

"Certainly. Right. OK. Um. Begone, foul fiend, unto the blackest pit—"

The head smiled contentedly as the words rolled over it. This was more like it.

It melted back into the waters of the copper like candlewax under a flame. Its last contemptuous comment, almost lost in the swirl, was, *"Run aaaalonggg . . ."*

Granny went home alone as the cold pink light of dawn glided across the snow, and let herself into her cottage.

The goats were uneasy in their outhouse. The starlings muttered and rattled their false teeth under the roof. The mice were squeaking behind the kitchen dresser.

She made a pot of tea, conscious that every sound in the kitchen seemed slightly louder than it ought to be. When she dropped the spoon into the sink it sounded like a bell being hit with a hammer.

She always felt uncomfortable after getting involved in organized magic or, as she would put it, out of sorts with herself. She found herself wandering around the place looking for things to do and then forgetting them when they were half-complete. She paced back and forth across the cold flagstones.

It is at times like this that the mind finds the oddest jobs to do in order to avoid its primary purpose, i.e. thinking about things. If anyone had been watching they would have been amazed at the sheer dedication with which Granny tackled such tasks as cleaning the teapot stand, rooting ancient nuts out of the fruit bowl on the dresser, and levering fossilized bread crusts out of the cracks in the flagstones with the back of a teaspoon.

Animals had minds. People had minds, although human minds were vague foggy things. Even insects had minds, little pointy bits of light in the darkness of non-mind.

Granny considered herself something of an expert on minds. She was pretty certain things like countries didn't have minds.

They weren't even *alive*, for goodness sake. A country was, well, was—

Hold on. Hold on . . . A thought stole gently into Granny's mind and sheepishly tried to attract her attention.

There was a way in which those brooding forests could have a mind. Granny sat up, a piece of antique loaf in her hand, and gazed speculatively at the fireplace. Her mind's eye looked through it, out at the snow-filled aisles of trees. Yes. It had never occurred to her before. Of course, it'd be a mind made up of all the other little minds inside it; plant minds, bird minds, bear minds, even the great slow minds of the trees themselves . . .

She sat down in her rocking chair, which started to rock all by itself.

She'd often thought of the forest as a sprawling creature, but only metterforically, as a wizard would put it; drowsy and purring with bumblebees in the summer, roaring and raging in autumn gales, curled in on itself and sleeping in the winter. It occurred to her that in addition to being a collection of other things, the forest was a thing in itself. Alive, only not alive in the way that, say, a shrew was alive.

And *much slower*.

That would have to be important. How fast did a forest's heart beat? Once a year, maybe. Yes, that sounded about right. Out there the forest was waiting for the brighter sun and longer days that would pump a million gallons of sap several hundred feet into the sky in one great systolic thump too big and loud to be heard.

And it was at about this point that Granny bit her lip.

She'd just thought the word "systolic," and it certainly wasn't in her vocabulary.

Somebody was inside her head with her.

Some thing.

Had she just thought all those thoughts, or had they been thought *through* her?

She glared at the floor, trying to keep her ideas to herself. But her mind was being watched as easily as if her head was made of glass.

Granny Weatherwax got to her feet and opened the curtains.

And they were out there on what—in warmer months—was the lawn. And every single one of them was staring at her.

After a few minutes Granny's front door opened. This was an event in its own right; like most Ramtoppers Granny lived her life via the back door. There were only three times in your life when it was proper to come through the front door, and you were carried every time.

It opened with considerable difficulty, in a series of painful jerks and thumps. A few flakes of paint fell onto the snowdrift in front of the door, which sagged inward. Finally, when it was about halfway open, the door wedged.

Granny sidled awkwardly through the gap and out onto the hitherto undisturbed snow.

She had put her pointed hat on, and the long black cloak which she wore when she wanted anyone who saw her to be absolutely clear that she was a witch.

There was an elderly kitchen chair half buried in snow. In summer it was a handy place to sit and do whatever hand chores were necessary, while keeping one eye on the track. Granny hauled it out, brushed the snow off the seat, and sat down firmly with her knees apart and her arms folded defiantly. She stuck out her chin.

The sun was well up but the light on this Hogswatchday was still pink and slanting. It glowed on the great cloud of steam that hung over the assembled creatures. They hadn't moved, although every now and again one of them would stamp a hoof or scratch itself.

Granny looked up at a flicker of movement. She hadn't noticed before, but every tree around her garden was so heavy with birds that it looked as though a strange brown and black spring had come early.

Occupying the patch where the herbs grew in summer were the wolves, sitting or lolling with their tongues hanging out. A contingent of bears was crouched behind them, with a platoon of deer beside them. Occupying the metterforical stalls was a rabble of rabbits, weasels, vermine, badgers, foxes and miscellaneous creatures who, despite the fact that they live their entire lives in a bloody atmosphere of hunter and hunted, killing or being killed by claw, talon and tooth, are generally referred to as woodland folk.

They rested together on the snow, their normal culinary relationships entirely forgotten, trying to outstare her.

Two things were immediately apparent to Granny. One was that this seemed to represent a pretty accurate cross-section of the forest life.

The other she couldn't help saying aloud.

"I don't know what this spell is," she said. "But I'll tell you this for nothing—when it wears off, some of you little buggers had better get moving."

None of them stirred. There was no sound except for an elderly badger relieving itself with an embarrassed expression.

"Look," said Granny. "What can I do about it? It's no good you coming to me. He's the new lord. This is his kingdom. I can't go meddling. It's not *right* to go meddling, on account of I can't interfere with people ruling. It has to sort itself out, good or bad. Fundamental rule of magic, is that. You can't go around ruling people with spells, because you'd have to use more and more spells all the time." She sat back, grateful that long-standing tradition didn't allow the Crafty and the Wise to rule. She remembered what it had felt like to wear the crown, even for a few seconds.

No, things like crowns had a troublesome effect on clever folk; it was best to leave all the reigning to the kind of people whose eyebrows met in the middle when they tried to think. In a funny sort of way, they were much better at it.

She added, "People have to sort it out for themselves. Well-known fact."

She felt that one of the larger stags was giving her a particularly doubting look.

"Yes, well, so he killed the old king," she conceded. "That's nature's way, ain't it? Your lot know all about this. Survival of the wossname. You wouldn't know what an heir was, unless you thought it was a sort of rabbit."

She drummed her fingers on her knees.

"Anyway, the old king wasn't much of a friend to you, was he? All that hunting, and such."

Three hundred pairs of dark eyes bored in at her.

"It's no good you all looking at me," she tried. "I can't go around mucking about with kings just because you don't like them. Where would it all end? It's not as if he's done me any harm."

She tried to avoid the gaze of a particularly cross-eyed stoat.

"All right, so it's selfish," she said. "That's what bein' a witch is all about. Good day to you."

She stamped inside, and tried to slam the door. It stuck once or twice, which rather spoiled the effect.

Once inside she drew the curtains and sat down in the rocking chair and rocked fiercely.

"That's the whole point," she said. "I can't go around meddling. That's the whole point."

The lattys lurched slowly over the rutted roads, toward yet another little city whose name the company couldn't quite remember and would instantly forget. The winter sun hung low over the damp, misty cabbage fields of the Sto Plains, and the foggy silence magnified the creaking of the wheels.

Hwel sat with his stubby legs dangling over the backboard of the last latty.

He'd done his best. Vitoller had left the education of Tomjon in his hands; "You're better at all that business," he'd said, adding with his usual tact, "Besides, you're more his height."

But it wasn't working.

"Apple," he repeated, waving the fruit in the air.

Tomjon grinned at him. He was nearly three years old, and hadn't said a word anyone could understand. Hwel was harboring dark suspicions about the witches.

"But he seems bright enough," said Mrs. Vitoller, who was traveling inside the latty and darning the chain mail. "He knows what things are. He does what he's told. I just wish you'd speak," she said softly, patting the boy on the cheek.

Hwel gave the apple to Tomjon, who accepted it gravely.

"I reckon them witches did you a bad turn, missus," said the dwarf. "You know. Changelings and whatnot. There used to be a lot of that sort of thing. My great-great-grandmother said it was done to us, once. The fairies swapped a human and a dwarf. We never realized until he started banging his head on things, they say—"

> *"They say this fruit be like unto the world*
> *So sweet. Or like, say I, the heart of man*
> *So red without and yet within, unclue'd,*
> *We find the worm, the rot, the flaw.*
> *However glows his bloom the bite*
> *Proves many a man be rotten at the core."*

The two of them swiveled around to stare at Tomjon, who nodded to them and proceeded to eat the apple.

"That was the Worm speech from *The Tyrant*," whispered Hwel. His normal grasp of the language temporarily deserted him. "Bloody hell," he said.

"But he sounded just like—"

"I'm going to get Vitoller," said Hwel, and dropped off the tailboard and ran through the frozen puddles to the front of the convoy, where the actor-manager was whistling tunelessly and, yes, strolling.

"What ho, *b'zugda-hiara*,"* he said cheerfully.

"You've got to come at once! He's talking!"

"Talking?"

---

* A killing insult in Dwarfish, but here used as a term of endearment. It means "lawn ornament."

Hwel jumped up and down. "He's *quoting*!" he shouted. "You've got to come! He sounds just like—"

"Me?" said Vitoller, a few minutes later, after they had pulled the lattys into a grove of leafless trees by the roadside. "Do I sound like that?"

"Yes," chorused the company.

Young Willikins, who specialized in female roles, prodded Tomjon gently as he stood on an upturned barrel in the middle of the clearing.

"Here, boy, do you know my speech from *Please Yourself*?" he said.

Tomjon nodded. " 'He is not dead, I say, who lies beneath the stone. For if Death could but hear—' "

They listened in awed silence as the endless mists rolled across the dripping fields and the red ball of the sun floated down the sky. When the boy had finished hot tears were streaming down Hwel's face.

"By all the gods," he said, when Tomjon had finished, "I must have been on damn good form when I wrote that." He blew his nose noisily.

"Do I sound like that?" said Willikins, his face pale.

Vitoller patted him gently on the shoulder.

"If you sounded like that, my bonny," he said, "you wouldn't be standing arse-deep in slush in the middle of these forsaken fields, with nothing but liberated cabbage for thy tea."

He clapped his hands.

"No more, no more," he said, his breath making puffs of steam in the freezing air. "Backs to it, everybody. We must be outside the walls of Sto Lat by sunset."

As the grumbling actors awoke from the spell and wandered back to the shafts of the lattys Vitoller beckoned to the dwarf and put his arm around his shoulders, or rather around the top of his head.

"Well?" he said. "You people know all about magic, or so it is said. What do you make of it?"

"He spends all his time around the stage, master. It's only natural that he should pick things up," said Hwel vaguely.

Vitoller leaned down.

"Do you believe that?"

"I believe I heard a voice that took my doggerel and shaped it and fired it back through my ears and straight into my heart," said Hwel simply. "I believe I heard a voice that got behind the crude shape of the words and said the things I had meant them to say, but had not the skill to achieve. Who knows where such things come from?"

He stared impassively into Vitoller's red face. "He may have inherited it from his father," he said.

"But—"

"And who knows what witches may achieve?" said the dwarf.

Vitoller felt his wife's hand pushed into his. As he stood up, bewildered and angry, she kissed him on the back of the neck.

"Don't torture yourself," she said. "Isn't it all for the best? Your son has declaimed his first word."

Spring came, and ex-King Verence still wasn't taking being dead lying down. He prowled the castle relentlessly, seeking for a way in which its ancient stones would release their grip on him.

He was also trying to keep out of the way of the other ghosts.

Champot was all right, if a bit tiresome. But Verence had backed away at the first sight of the Twins, toddling hand in hand along the midnight corridors, their tiny ghosts a memorial to a deed darker even than the usual run of regicidal unpleasantness.

And then there was the Troglodyte Wanderer, a rather faded monkeyman in a furry loincloth who apparently happened to haunt the castle merely because it had been built on his burial mound. For no obvious reason a chariot with a screaming woman in it occasionally rumbled through the laundry room. As for the kitchen . . .

One day he'd given in, despite everything old Champot had said, and had followed the smells of cooking into the big, hot, high domed cavern that served the castle as kitchen and abattoir. Funny thing, that. He'd never been down there since his childhood. Somehow kings and kitchens didn't go well together.

It was *full* of ghosts.

But they weren't human. They weren't even proto-human.

They were stags. They were bullocks. They were rabbits, and pheasants, and partridges, and sheep, and pigs. There were even some round blobby things that looked unpleasantly like the ghosts of oysters. They were packed so tightly that in fact they merged and mingled, turning the kitchen into a silent, jostling nightmare of teeth and fur and horns, half-seen and misty. Several noticed him, and there was a weird blarting of noises that sounded far-off, tinny and unpleasantly out of register. Through them all the cook and his assistants wandered quite unconcernedly, making vegetarian sausages.

Verence had stared for half a minute and then fled, wishing that he still had a real stomach so that he could stick his fingers down his throat for forty years and bring up everything he'd eaten.

He'd sought solace in the stables, where his beloved hunting dogs had whined and scratched at the door and had generally been very ill-at-ease at his sensed but unseen presence.

Now he haunted—and how he hated the word—the Long Gallery, where paintings of long-dead kings looked down at him from the dusty shadows. He would have felt a lot more kindly toward them if he hadn't met a number of them gibbering in various parts of the premises.

Verence had decided that he had two aims in death. One was to get out of the castle and find his son, and the other was to get his revenge on the duke. But not by killing him, he'd decided, even if he could find a way, because an eternity in that giggling idiot's company would lend a new terror to death.

He sat under a painting of Queen Bemery (670–722), whose rather stern good looks he would have felt a whole lot happier about if he hadn't seen her earlier that morning walking through the wall.

Verence tried to avoid walking through walls. A man had his dignity.

He became aware that he was being watched.

He turned his head.

There was a cat sitting in the doorway, subjecting him to a slow blink. It was a mottled gray and extremely fat . . .

No. It was extremely *big*. It was covered with so much scar tissue that it looked like a fist with fur on it. Its ears were a couple of perforated stubs, its eyes two yellow slits of easy-going malevolence, its tail a twitching series of question marks as it stared at him.

Greebo had heard that Lady Felmet had a small white female cat and had strolled up to pay his respects.

Verence had never seen an animal with so much built-in villainy. He didn't resist as it waddled across the floor and tried to rub itself against his legs, purring like a waterfall.

"Well, well," said the king, vaguely. He reached down and made an effort to scratch it behind the two ragged bits on top of its head. It was a relief to find someone else besides another ghost who could see him, and Greebo, he couldn't help feeling, was a distinctly unusual cat. Most of the castle cats were either pampered pets or flat-eared kitchen and stable habitués who generally resembled the very rodents they lived on. This cat, on the other hand, was its own animal. All cats give that impression, of course, but instead of the mindless animal self-absorption that passes for secret wisdom in the creatures, Greebo radiated genuine intelligence. He also radiated a smell that would have knocked over a wall and caused sinus trouble in a dead fox.

Only one type of person kept a cat like this.

The king tried to hunker down, and found he was sinking slightly into the floor. He pulled himself together and drifted upward. Once a man allowed himself to go native in the ethereal world there would be no hope for him, he felt.

Only close relatives and the psychically inclined, Death had said. There weren't many of either in the castle. The duke qualified under the first heading, but his relentless self-interest made him about as psychically useful as a carrot. As for the rest, only the cook and the Fool seemed to qualify, but the cook spent a lot of his time weeping in the pantry because he wasn't being allowed to roast anything more bloody than a parsnip and the Fool was already such a bundle of nerves that Verence had given up his attempts to get through.

A witch, now. If a witch wasn't psychically inclined, then he, King Verence, was a puff of wind. He had to get a witch into the castle. And then . . .

He'd got a plan. In fact, it was more than that; it was a Plan. He spent months over it. He hadn't got anything else to do, except think. Death had been right about that. All that ghosts had were thoughts, and although thoughts in general had always been alien to the king the absence of any body to distract him with its assorted humors had actually given him the chance to savor the joys of cerebration. He'd never had a Plan before, or at least one that

went much further than "Let's find something
and kill it." And here, sitting in front of him washing itself, was the key.

"Here, pussy," he ventured. Greebo gave him a
penetrating yellow stare.

"Cat," the king amended hastily, and backed away,
beckoning. For a moment it seemed that the cat
wouldn't follow and then, to his relief, Greebo stood
up, yawned, and padded toward him. Greebo didn't
often see ghosts, and was vaguely interested in this
tall, bearded man with the see-through body.

The king led him along a dusty side corridor and
toward a lumber room crammed with crumbling
tapestries and portraits of long-dead kings.
Greebo examined it critically, and then sat down
in the middle of the dusty floor, looking at the king
expectantly.

"There's plenty of mice and things in here, d'you
see," said Verence. "And the rain blows in through
the broken window. Plus there's all these tapestries
to sleep on.

"Sorry," the king added, and turned to the door.

This was what he had been working on all these
months. When he was alive he had always taken a
lot of care of his body, and since being dead he had
taken care to preserve its shape. It was too easy to
let yourself go and become all fuzzy around the
edges; there were ghosts in the castle who were
mere pale blobs. But Verence had wielded iron self-
control and exercised—well, had thought hard
about exercise—and fairly bulged with spectral
muscles. Months of pumping ectoplasm had left

him in better shape than he had ever been, apart from being dead.

Then he'd started out small, with dust motes. The first one had nearly killed him,* but he'd persevered and progressed to sand grains, then whole dried peas; he still didn't dare venture into the kitchens, but he had amused himself by oversalting Felmet's food a pinch at a time until he pulled himself together and told himself that poisoning wasn't honorable, even against vermin.

Now he leaned all his weight on the door, and with every microgramme of his being forced himself to become as heavy as possible. The sweat of auto-suggestion dripped off his nose and vanished before it hit the floor. Greebo watched with interest as ghostly muscles moved on the king's arms like footballs mating.

The door began to move, creaked, then accelerated and hit the doorway with a thump. The latch clicked into place.

It bloody well had to work now, Verence told himself. He'd never be able to lift the latch by himself. But a witch would certainly come looking for her cat—wouldn't she?

In the hills beyond the castle the Fool lay on his stomach and stared into the depths of a little lake. A couple of trout stared back at him.

Somewhere on the Disc, reason told him, there

---

* In a manner of speaking.

must be someone more miserable than he was. He wondered who it was.

He hadn't asked to be a Fool, but it wouldn't have mattered if he had, because he couldn't recall anyone in his family ever listening to anything he said after Dad ran away.

Certainly not Grandad. His earliest memory was of Grandad standing over him making him repeat the jokes by rote, and hammering home every punchline with his belt; it was thick leather, and the fact that it had bells on didn't improve things much.

Grandad was credited with seven official new jokes. He'd won the honorary cap and bells of the Grand Prix des Idiots Blithering at Ankh-Morpork four years in a row, which no one else had ever done, and presumably they made him the funniest man who ever lived. He had worked hard at it, you had to give him that.

The Fool recalled with a shudder how, at the age of six, he'd timidly approached the old man after supper with a joke he'd made up. It was about a duck.

It had earned him the biggest thrashing of his life, which even then must have presented the old joker with a bit of a challenge.

"You will learn, my lad—" he recalled, with every sentence punctuated by jingling cracks—"that there is nothing more serious than jesting. From now on you will never—" the old man paused to change hands—"never, never, ever utter a joke that has not been approved by the Guild. Who are you to decide what is amusing? Marry, let the untutored giggle at unskilled banter; it is the laughter of the ignorant. Never. Never. Never let me catch you joculating again."

After that he'd gone back to learning the three hundred and eighty-three Guild-approved jokes, which was bad enough, and the glossary, which was a lot bigger and much worse.

And then he'd been sent to Ankh, and there, in the bare, severe rooms, he'd found there were books other than the great heavy brass-bound *Monster Fun Book*. There was a whole circular world out there, full of weird places and people doing interesting things, like . . .

Singing. He could hear singing.

He raised his head cautiously, and jumped at the tinkle of the bells on his cap. He gripped the hated things hurriedly.

The singing went on. The Fool peeped cautiously through the drift of meadowsweet that was providing him with perfect concealment.

The singing wasn't particularly good. The only word the singer appeared to know was "la," but she was making it work hard. The general tune gave the impression that the singer believed that people were supposed to sing "lalala" in certain circumstances, and was determined to do what the world expected of her.

The Fool risked raising his head a little further, and saw Magrat for the first time.

She had stopped dancing rather self-consciously through the narrow meadow and was trying to plait some daisies in her hair, without much success.

The Fool held his breath. On long nights on the hard flagstones he had dreamed of women like her. Although, if he really thought about it, not much like her; they were better endowed around the chest, their noses weren't so red and pointed, and their hair tended to flow more. But the Fool's libido was bright enough to tell the difference between the impossible and the conceivably attainable, and hurriedly cut in some filter circuits.

Magrat was picking flowers and talking to them. The Fool strained to hear.

"Here's Woolly Fellwort," she said. "And Treacle Wormseed, which is for inflammation of the ears . . ."

Even Nanny Ogg, who took a fairly cheerful view of the world, would have been hard put to say anything complimentary about Magrat's voice. But it fell on the Fool's ears like blossom.

". . . and Five-leaved False Mandrake, sovereign against fluxes of the bladder. Ah, and here's Old Man's Frogbit. That's for constipation."

The Fool stood up sheepishly, in a carillon of jingles. To Magrat it was as if the meadow, hitherto supporting nothing more hazardous than clouds of pale blue butterflies and a few self-employed bumblebees, had sprouted a large red-and-yellow demon.

It was opening and shutting its mouth. It had three menacing horns.

An urgent voice at the back of her mind said: You should run away now, like a timid gazelle; this is the accepted action in these circumstances.

Common sense intervened. In her most optimistic moments Magrat would not have compared herself to a gazelle, timid or otherwise. Besides, it added, the basic snag about running away like a timid gazelle was that in all probability she would easily outdistance him.

"Er," said the apparition.

Uncommon sense, which, despite Granny Weatherwax's general belief that Magrat was several sticks short of a bundle, she still had in sufficiency, pointed out that few demons tinkled pathetically and appeared to be quite so breathless.

"Hallo," she said.

The Fool's mind was also working hard. He was beginning to panic.

Magrat shunned the traditional pointed hat, as worn by the other witches, but she still held to one of the most fundamental rules of witchcraft. It's not much use being a witch unless you look like one. In her case this meant lots of silver jewelry with octograms, bats, spiders, dragons and other symbols of everyday mysticism; Magrat would have painted her fingernails black, except that she didn't think she would be able to face Granny's withering scorn.

It was dawning on the Fool that he had surprised a witch.

"Whoops," he said, and turned to run for it.

"Don't—" Magrat began, but the Fool was already pounding down the forest path that led back to the castle.

Magrat stood and stared at the wilting posy in her hands. She ran her fingers through her hair and a shower of wilted petals fell out.

She felt that an important moment had been allowed to slip out of her grasp as fast as a greased pig in a narrow passageway.

She felt an overpowering urge to curse. She knew a great many curses. Goodie Whemper had been really imaginative in that department; even the creatures of the forest used to go past her cottage at a dead run.

She couldn't find a single one that fully expressed her feelings.

"Oh, bugger," she said.

It was a full moon again that night, and most unusually all three witches arrived at the standing stone early; it was so embarrassed by this that it went and hid in some gorse bushes.

"Greebo hasn't been home for two days," said Nanny Ogg, as soon as she arrived. "It's not like him. I can't find him anywhere."

"Cats can look after themselves," said Granny Weatherwax. "Countries can't. I have intelligence to report. Light the fire, Magrat."

"Mmm?"

"I said, light the fire, Magrat."

"Mmm? Oh. Yes."

The two old women watched her drift vaguely across the moorland, tugging absently at dried-up whin clumps. Magrat seemed to have her mind on something.

"Doesn't seem to be her normal self," said Nanny Ogg.

"Yes. Could be an improvement," said Granny shortly, and sat down on a rock. "She should of got it lit before we arrived. It's her job."

"She means well," said Nanny Ogg, studying Magrat's back reflectively.

"I used to mean well when I was a girl, but that didn't stop the sharp end of Goodie Filter's tongue. Youngest witch serves her time, you know how it is. We had it tougher, too. Look at her. Doesn't even wear the pointy hat. How's anyone going to *know*?"

"You got something on *your* mind, Esme?" said Nanny.

Granny nodded gloomily.

"Had a visit yesterday," she said.

"Me too."

Despite her worries, Granny was slightly annoyed at this. "Who from?" she said.

"The mayor of Lancre and a bunch of burghers. They're not happy about the king. They want a king they can trust."

"I wouldn't trust any king a burgher could trust," said Granny.

"Yes, but it's not good for anyone, all this taxing and killing folk. The new sergeant they've got is a keen man when it comes to setting fire to cottages, too. Old Verence used to do it too, mind, but . . . well . . ."

"I know, I know. It was more personal," said Granny. "You felt he *meant* it. People like to feel they're valued."

"This Felmet hates the kingdom," Nanny went

on. "They all say it. They say when they go to talk to him he just stares at them and giggles and rubs his hand and twitches a bit."

Granny scratched her chin. "The old king used to shout at them and kick them out of the castle, mind. He used to say he didn't have time for shopkeepers and such," she added, with a note of personal approval.

"But he was always very gracious about it," said Nanny Ogg. "And he—"

"The kingdom is worried," said Granny.

"Yes, I already said."

"I didn't mean the people, I meant the kingdom."

Granny explained. Nanny interrupted a few times with brief questions. It didn't occur to her to doubt anything she heard. Granny Weatherwax never made things up.

At the end of it she said, "Well."

"My feelings exactly."

"Fancy that."

"Quite so."

"And what did the animals do then?"

"Went away. *It* had brought them there, it let them go."

"No one et anyone else?"

"Not where I saw."

"Funny thing."

"Right enough."

Nanny Ogg stared at the setting sun.

"I don't reckon a lot of kingdoms do that sort of thing," she said. "You saw the theater. Kings and such are killing one another the whole time. Their kingdoms just make the best of it. How come this one takes offense all of a sudden?"

"It's been here a long time," said Granny.

"So's everywhere," said Nanny, and added, with the air of a lifetime student, "Everywhere's been where it is ever since it was first put there. It's called geography."

"That's just about land," said Granny. "It's not the same as a kingdom. A kingdom is made up of all sorts of things. Ideas. Loyalties. Memories. It all sort of exists together. And then all these things create some kind of life. Not a body kind of life, more like a living idea. Made up of everything that's alive and what they're thinking. And what the people *before* them thought."

Magrat reappeared and began to lay the fire with the air of one in a trance.

"I can see you've been thinking about this a lot," said Nanny, speaking very slowly and carefully. "And this kingdom wants a better king, is that it?"

"No! That is, yes. Look—" she leaned forward— "it doesn't have the same kind of likes and dislikes as people, right?"

Nanny Ogg leaned back. "Well, it wouldn't, would it," she ventured.

"It doesn't care if people are good or bad. I don't think it could even *tell*, anymore than you could tell if an ant was a good ant. But it expects the king to care for it."

"Yes, but," said Nanny wretchedly. She was becoming a bit afraid of the gleam in Granny's eye. "Lots of people have killed each other to become king of Lancre. They've done all kinds of murder."

"Don't matter! Don't matter!" said Granny, waving her arms. She started counting on her fingers. "For why," she said. "One, kings go around killing each other because it's all part of destiny and such and doesn't count as murder, and two, they killed for the kingdom. That's the important bit. But this new man just wants the power. He hates the kingdom."

"It's a bit like a dog, really," said Magrat. Granny looked at her with her mouth open to frame some suitable retort, and then her face softened.

"Very much like," she said. "A dog doesn't care if its master's good or bad, just so long as it likes the dog."

"Well, then," said Nanny. "No one and nothing likes Felmet. What are we going to do about it?"

"Nothing. You know we can't meddle."

"You saved that baby," said Nanny.

"That's not meddling!"

"Have it your way," said Nanny. "But maybe one day he'll come back. Destiny again. And you said we should hide the crown. It'll all come back, mark my words. Hurry up with that tea, Magrat."

"What are you going to do about the burghers?" said Granny.

"I told them they'll have to sort it out themselves. Once we use magic, I said, it'd never stop. You know that."

"Right," said Granny, but there was a hint of wistfulness in her voice.

"I'll tell you this, though," said Nanny. "They

didn't like it much. They was muttering when they left."

Magrat blurted out, "You know the Fool, who lives up at the castle?"

"Little man with runny eyes?" said Nanny, relieved that the conversation had returned to more normal matters.

"Not that little," said Magrat. "What's his name, do you happen to know?"

"He's just called Fool," said Granny. "No job for a man, that. Running around with bells on."

"His mother was a Beldame, from over Blackglass way," said Nanny Ogg, whose knowledge of the genealogy of Lancre was legendary. "Bit of a beauty when she was younger. Broke many a heart, she did. Bit of a scandal there, I did hear. Granny's right, though. At the end of the day, a Fool's a Fool."

"Why d'you want to know, Magrat?" said Granny Weather-wax.

"Oh . . . one of the girls in the village was asking me," said Magrat, crimson to the ears.

Nanny cleared her throat, and grinned at Granny Weatherwax, who sniffed aloofly.

"It's a steady job," said Nanny. "I'll grant you that."

"Huh," said Granny. "A man who tinkles all day. No kind of husband for anyone, I'd say."

"You—she'd always know where he was," said Nanny, who was enjoying this. "You'd just have to listen."

"Never trust a man with horns on his hat," said Granny flatly.

Magrat stood up and pulled herself together, giving the impression that some bits had to come quite a long way.

"You're a pair of silly old women," she said quietly. "And I'm going home."

She marched off down the path to her village without another word.

The old witches stared at one another.

"Well!" said Nanny.

"It's all these books they read today," said Granny. "It overheats the brain. You haven't been putting ideas in her head, have you?"

"What do you mean?"

"You *know* what I mean."

Nanny stood up. "I certainly don't see why a girl should have to be single her whole life just because you think it's the right thing," she said. "Anyway, if people didn't have children, where would we be?"

"None of your girls is a witch," said Granny, also standing up.

"They *could* have been," said Nanny defensively.

"Yes, if you'd let them work it out for themselves, instead of encouragin' them to throw themselves at men."

"They're good-lookin'. You can't stand in the way of human nature. You'd know that if you'd ever—"

"If I'd ever what?" said Granny Weatherwax, quietly.

They stared at one another in shocked silence. They could both feel it, the tension creeping into their bodies from the ground itself, the hot, aching feeling that they'd started something they must finish, no matter what.

"I knew you when you were a gel," said Nanny sullenly. "Stuck-up, you were."

"At least I spent most of the time upright," said Granny. "Disgustin', that was. Everyone thought so."

"How would you know?" snapped Nanny.

"You were the talk of the whole village," said Granny.

"And you were, too! They called you the Ice Maiden. Never knew that, did you?" sneered Nanny.

"I wouldn't sully my lips by sayin' what they called you," shouted Granny.

"Oh yes?" shrieked Nanny. "Well, let me tell you, my good woman—"

"Don't you dare talk to me in that tone of voice! I'm not anyone's good woman—"

"*Right!*"

There was another silence while they stared at one another, nose to nose, but this silence was a whole quantum level of animosity higher than the last one; you could have roasted a turkey in the heat of this silence. There was no more shouting. Things had got far too bad for shouting. Now the voices came in low and full of menace.

"I should have known better than to listen to Magrat," growled Granny. "This coven business is ridiculous. It attracts entirely the wrong sort of people."

"I'm very glad we had this little talk," hissed Nanny Ogg. "Cleared the air."

She looked down.

"*And* you're in my territory, madam."

"*Madam!*"

Thunder rolled in the distance. The permanent Lancre storm, after a trip through the foothills, had drifted back toward the mountains for a one-night stand. The last rays of sunset shone livid through the clouds, and fat drops of water began to thud on the witches' pointed hats.

"I really don't have time for all this," snapped Granny, trembling. "I have far more important things to do."

"And me," said Nanny.

"Good night to you."

"And you."

They turned their backs on one another and strode away into the downpour.

The midnight rain drummed on Magrat's curtained windows as she thumbed her way purposefully through Goodie Whemper's books of what, for want of any better word, could be called natural magic.

The old woman had been a great collector of such things and, most unusually, had written them down; witches didn't normally have much use for literacy. But book after book was filled with tiny, meticulous handwriting detailing the results of patient experiments in applied magic. Goodie Whemper had, in fact, been a research witch.*

---

* Someone has to do it. It's all very well calling for eye of newt, but do you mean Common, Spotted or Great Crested? Which eye, anyway?

Magrat was looking up love spells. Every time she shut her eyes she saw a red-and-yellow figure on the darkness inside. Something had to be done about it.

She shut the book with a snap and looked at her notes. First, she had to find out his name. The old peel-the-apple trick should do that. You just peeled an apple, getting one length of peel, and threw the peel behind you; it'd land in the shape of his name. Millions of girls had tried it and had inevitably been disappointed, unless the loved one was called Scscs. That was because they hadn't used an unripe Sunset Wonder picked three minutes before noon on the first frosty day in the autumn and peeled left-handedly using a silver knife with a blade less than half an inch wide; Goodie had done a lot of experimenting and was quite explicit on the subject. Magrat always kept a few by for emergencies, and this probably was one.

She took a deep breath, and threw the peel over her shoulder.

She turned slowly.

I'm a witch, she told herself. This is just another spell. There's nothing to be frightened of. Get a grip of yourself, girl. *Woman*.

Will tapioca do just as well? If we substitute egg white will the spell a) work b) fail ar c) melt the bottom out of the cauldron? Goodie Whemper's curiosity about such things was huge and insatiable.**

** Nearly insatiable. It was probably satiated in her last flight to test whether a broomstick could survive having its bristles pulled out one by one in midair. According to the small black raven she had trained as a flight recorder, the answer was almost certainly no.

She looked down, and bit the back of her hand out of nervousness and embarrassment.

"Who'd have thought it?" she said aloud.

It had worked.

She turned back to her notes, her heart fluttering. What was next? Ah, yes—gathering fern seed in a silk handkerchief at dawn. Goodie Whemper's tiny handwriting went on for two pages of detailed botanical instructions which, if carefully followed, resulted in the kind of love potion that had to be kept in a tightly-stoppered jar at the bottom of a bucket of iced water.

Magrat pulled open her back door. The thunder had passed, but now the first gray light of the new day was drowned in a steady drizzle. But it still qualified as dawn, and Magrat was determined.

Brambles tugging at her dress, her hair plastered against her head by the rain, she set out into the dripping forest.

The trees shook, even without a breeze.

Nanny Ogg was also out early. She hadn't been able to get any sleep anyway, and besides, she was worried about Greebo. Greebo was one of her few blind spots. While intellectually she would concede that he was indeed a fat, cunning, evil-smelling multiple rapist, she nevertheless instinctively pictured him as the small fluffy kitten he had been decades before. The fact that he had once chased a female wolf up a tree and seriously surprised a she-bear who had been innocently digging for roots didn't stop her worrying that something bad might happen to him.

It was generally considered by everyone else in the kingdom that the only thing that might slow Greebo down was a direct meteorite strike.

Now she was using a bit of elementary magic to follow his trail, although anyone with a sense of smell could have managed it. It had led her through the damp streets and to the open gates of the castle.

She gave the guards a nod as she went through. It didn't occur to either of them to stop her because witches, like beekeepers and big gorillas, went where they liked. In any case, an elderly lady banging a bowl with a spoon was probably not the spearhead of an invasion force.

Life as a castle guard in Lancre was extremely boring. One of them, leaning on his spear as Nanny went past, wished there could be some excitement in his job. He will shortly learn the error of his ways. The other guard pulled himself together, and saluted.

"Mornin', Mum."

"Mornin', our Shawn," said Nanny, and set off across the inner courtyard.

Like all witches Nanny Ogg had an aversion to front doors. She went around the back and entered the keep via the kitchens. A couple of maids curtsied to her. So did the head housekeeper, whom Nanny Ogg vaguely recognized as a daughter-in-law, although she couldn't remember her name.

And so it was that when Lord Felmet came out of his bedroom he saw, coming along the passage toward him, a witch. There was no doubt about it. From the tip of her pointed hat to her boots, she was a witch. And she was coming for him.

* * *

Magrat slid helplessly down a bank. She was soaked to the skin and covered in mud. Somehow, she thought bitterly, when you read these spells you always think of it being a fine sunny morning in late spring. And she had forgotten to check what bloody kind of bloody fern it bloody was.

A tree tipped a load of raindrops onto her. Magrat pushed her sodden hair out of her eyes and sat down heavily on a fallen log, from which grew great clusters of pale and embarrassing fungus.

It had seemed such a lovely idea. She'd had great hopes of the coven. She was sure it wasn't right to be a witch alone, you could get funny ideas. She'd dreamed of wise discussions of natural energies while a huge moon hung in the sky, and then possibly they'd try a few of the old dances described in some of Goodie Whemper's books. Not actually *naked*, or skyclad as it was rather delightfully called, because Magrat had no illusions about the shape of her own body and the older witches seemed solid across the hems, and anyway that wasn't absolutely necessary. The books said that the old-time witches had sometimes danced in their shifts. Magrat had wondered about how you danced in shifts. Perhaps there wasn't room for them all to dance at once, she'd thought.

What she hadn't expected was a couple of crochety old women who were barely civil at the best of times and simply didn't enter into the spirit of things. Oh, they'd been kind to the baby, in their own way, but she couldn't help feeling that if a witch was kind to someone it was entirely for deeply self-ish reasons.

And when they did magic, they made it look as ordinary as housekeeping. They didn't wear any occult jewelry. Magrat was a great believer in occult jewelry.

It was all going wrong. And she was going home.

She stood up, wrapped her damp dress around her, and set off through the misty woods . . .

. . . and heard the running feet. Someone was coming through them at high speed, without caring who heard him, and over the top of the sound of breaking twigs was a curious dull jingling. Magrat sidled behind a dripping holly bush and peered cautiously through the leaves.

It was Shawn, the youngest of Nanny Ogg's sons, and the metal noise was caused by his suit of chain mail, which was several sizes too big for him. Lancre is a poor kingdom, and over the centuries the chain mail of the palace guards has had to be handed down from one generation to another, often on the end of a long stick. This one made him look like a bullet-proof bloodhound.

She stepped out in front of him.

"Is that you, Miss Magrat?" said Shawn, raising the flap of mail that covered his eyes. "It's mam!"

"What's happened to her?"

"*He's* locked her up! Said she was coming to poison him! And I can't get down to the dungeons to see because there's all new guards! They say she's been put in chains—" Shawn frowned—"and that means something horrible's going to happen. You know what she's like when she loses her temper. We'll never hear the last of it, miz."

"Where were you going?" demanded Magrat.

"To fetch our Jason and our Wane and our Darron and our—"

"Wait a moment."

"Oh, Miss Magrat, suppose they try to torture her? You know what a tongue she's got on her when she gets angry—"

"I'm thinking," said Magrat.

"He's put his own bodyguards on the gates and everything—"

"Look, just shut up a minute, will you, Shawn?"

"When our Jason finds out, he's going to give the duke a real seeing-to, miz. He says it's about time someone did."

Nanny Ogg's Jason was a young man with the build and, Magrat had always thought, the brains of a herd of oxen. Thick-skinned though he was, she doubted whether he could survive a hail of arrows.

"Don't tell him yet," she said thoughtfully. "There could be another way . . ."

"I'll go and find Granny Weatherwax, shall I, miz?" said Shawn, hopping from one leg to another. "*She'll* know what to do, she's a witch."

Magrat stood absolutely still. She had thought she was angry before, but now she was furious. She was wet and cold and hungry and this *person*—once upon a time, she heard herself thinking, she would have burst into tears at this point.

"Oops," said Shawn. "Um. I didn't mean. Whoops. Um . . ." He backed away.

"If you happen to see Granny Weatherwax," said Magrat slowly, in tones that should have etched her words into glass, "you can tell her that I will sort it all out. Now go away before I turn you into a frog. You look like one anyway."

She turned, hitched up her skirts, and ran like hell toward her cottage.

Lord Felmet was one of nature's gloaters. He was good at it.

"Quite comfortable, are we?" he said.

Nanny Ogg considered this. "Apart from these stocks, you mean?" she said.

"I am impervious to your foul blandishments," said the duke. "I scorn your devious wiles. You are to be tortured, I'll have you know."

This didn't appear to have the required effect. Nanny was staring around the dungeon with the vaguely interested gaze of a sightseer.

"And then you will be burned," said the duchess.

"OK," said Nanny.

"OK?"

"Well, it's bloody freezing down here. What's that big wardrobe thing with the spikes?"

The duke was trembling. "Aha," he said. "Now you realize, eh? That, my dear lady, is an Iron Maiden. It's the latest thing. Well may you—"

"Can I have a go in it?"

"Your pleas fall on deaf . . ." The duke's voice trailed off. His twitch started up.

The duchess leaned forward until her big red face was inches away from Nanny's nose.

"This insouciance gives you pleasure," she hissed, "but soon you will laugh on the other side of your face!"

"It's only got this side," said Nanny.

The duchess fingered a tray of implements lovingly. "We shall see," she said, picking up a pair of pliers.

"And you need not think any others of your people will come to your aid," said the duke, who was sweating despite the chill. "We alone hold the keys to this dungeon. Ha ha. You will be an example to all those who have been spreading malicious rumors about me. Do not protest your innocence! I hear the voices all the time, lying . . ."

The duchess gripped him ferociously by the arm. "Enough," she rasped. "Come, Leonal. We will let her reflect on her fate for a while."

". . . the faces . . . wicked lies . . . I wasn't there, and anyway he fell . . . my porridge, all salty . . ." murmured the duke, swaying.

The door slammed behind them. There was a click of locks and a thudding of bolts.

Nanny was left alone in the gloom. A flickering torch high on the wall only made the surrounding darkness more forbidding. Strange metal shapes, designed for no more exalted purpose than the destruct-testing of the human body, cast unpleasant shadows. Nanny Ogg stirred in her chains.

"All right," she said. "I can see you. Who are you?"

King Verence stepped forward.

"I saw you making faces behind him," said Nanny Ogg. "All I could do to keep a straight face myself."

"I wasn't making faces, woman, I was scowling."

Nanny squinted. "'Ere, I know you," she said. "You're dead."

"I prefer the term 'passed over,'" said the king.

"I'd bow,"* said Nanny. "Only there's all these chains and things. You haven't seen a cat around here, have you?"

"Yes. He's in the room upstairs, asleep."

Nanny appeared to relax. "That's all right, then," she said. "I was beginning to worry." She stared around the dungeon again. "What's that big bed thing over there?"

"The rack," said the king, and explained its use. Nanny Ogg nodded.

"What a busy little mind he's got," she said.

"I fear, madam, that I may be responsible for your present predicament," said Verence, sitting down on or at least just above a handy anvil. "I wished to attract a witch."

"I suppose you're no good at locks?"

"I fear they would be beyond my capabilities as yet . . . but surely—" the ghost of the king waved a hand in a vague gesture which encompassed the dungeon, Nanny and the manacles—"to a witch all this is just so much—"

---

* Witches never curtsy.

"Solid iron," said Nanny. "You might be able to walk through it, but I can't."

"I didn't realize," said Verence. "I thought witches could do magic."

"Young man," said Nanny, "you will oblige me by shutting up."

"Madam! I am a king!"

"You are also dead, so I wouldn't aspire to hold any opinions if I was you. Now just be quiet and wait, like a good boy."

Against all his instincts, the king found himself obeying. There was no gainsaying that tone of voice. It spoke to him across the years, from his days in the nursery. Its echoes told him that if he didn't eat it all up he would be sent straight to bed.

Nanny Ogg stirred in her chains. She hoped they would turn up soon.

"Er," said the king uneasily. "I feel I owe you an explanation . . ."

"Thank you," said Granny Weatherwax, and because Shawn seemed to be expecting it, added, "You've been a good boy."

"Yes'm," said Shawn. "M'm?"

"Was there something else?"

Shawn twisted the end of his chain-mail vest out of embarrassment. "It's not true what everyone's been saying about our mam, is it, m'm?" he said. "She doesn't go around putting evil curses on folk. Except for Daviss the butcher. And old Cakebread, after he kicked her cat. But they wasn't what you'd call real curses, was they, m'm?"

"You can stop calling me m'm."

"Yes, m'm."

"They've been saying that, have they?"

"Yes, m'm."

"Well, your mam does upset people sometimes."

Shawn hopped from one leg to another.

"Yes, m'm, but they says terrible things about you, m'm, savin' your presence, m'm."

Granny stiffened.

"What things?"

"Don't like to say, m'm."

"What things?"

Shawn considered his next move. There weren't many choices.

"A lot of things what aren't true, m'm," he said, establishing his credentials as early as possible. "All sorts of things. Like, old Verence was a bad king and you helped him on the throne, and you caused that bad winter the other year, and old Norbut's cow dint give no milk after you looked at it. Lot of lies, m'm," he added, loyally.

"Right," said Granny.

She shut the door in his panting face, stood in thought for a moment, and retired to her rocking chair.

Eventually she said, once more, "Right."

A little later she added, "She's a daft old besom, but we can't have people going around doing things to witches. Once you've lost your respect, you ain't got a thing. I don't remember looking at old Norbut's cow. Who's old Norbut?"

She stood up, took her pointed hat from its hook

behind the door and, glaring into the mirror, skewered it in place with a number of ferocious hatpins. They slid on one by one, as unstoppable as the wrath of God.

She vanished into the outhouse for a moment and came back with her witch's cloak, which served as a blanket for sick goats when not otherwise employed.

Once upon a time it had been black velvet; now it was just black. It was carefully and slowly fastened by a tarnished silver brooch.

No samurai, no questing knight, was ever dressed with as much ceremony.

Finally Granny drew herself up, surveyed her dark reflection in the glass, gave a thin little smile of approval, and left via the back door.

The air of menace was only slightly dispelled by the sound of her running up and down outside, trying to get her broomstick started.

Magrat was also regarding herself in the mirror.

She'd dug out a startlingly green dress that was designed to be both revealing and clinging, and would have been if Magrat had anything to display or cling to, so she'd shoved a couple of rolled-up stockings down the front in an effort to make good the more obvious deficiencies. She had also tried a spell on her hair, but it was naturally magic-resistant and already the natural shape was beginning to assert itself (a dandelion clock at about 2 p.m.).

Magrat had also tried makeup. This wasn't an unqualified success. She didn't have much practice.

She was beginning to wonder if she'd overdone the eyeshadow.

Her neck, fingers and arms between them carried enough silverware to make a full-sized dinner service, and over everything she had thrown a black cloak lined with red silk.

In a certain light and from a carefully chosen angle, Magrat was not unattractive. Whether any of these preparations did anything for her is debatable, but they did mean that a thin veneer of confidence overlaid her trembling heart.

She drew herself up and turned this way and that. The clusters of amulets, magical jewelry and occult bangles on various parts of her body jingled together; any enemy wouldn't only have to be blind to fail to notice that a witch was approaching, he'd have to be deaf as well.

She turned to her worktable and examined what she rather self-consciously, and never in Granny's hearing, called her Tools of the Craft. There was the white-handled knife, used in the preparation of magical ingredients. There was the black-handled knife, used in the magical workings themselves; Magrat had carved so many runes into its handle it was in constant danger of falling in half. They were undoubtedly powerful, but . . .

Magrat shook her head regretfully, went over to the kitchen dresser and took out the breadknife. Something told her that at times like these a good sharp breadknife was probably the best friend a girl could have.

* * *

"I spy, with my little eye," said Nanny Ogg, "something beginning with P."

The ghost of the king stared wearily around the dungeons.

"Pliers," he suggested.

"No."

"Pilliwinks?"

"That's a pretty name. What is it?"

"It's a kind of thumbscrew. Look," said the king.

"It's not that," said Nanny.

"Choke-pear?" he said desperately.

"That's a C, and anyway I don't know what it is," said Nanny Ogg. The king obligingly indicated it on the tray, and explained its use.

"Definitely not," said Nanny.

"Smouldering Boot of Punishment?" said the king.

"You're a bit too good at these names," said Nanny sharply. "You sure you didn't use them when you were alive?"

"Absolutely, Nanny," said the ghost.

"Boys that tell lies go to a bad place," warned Nanny.

"Lady Felmet had most of them installed herself, it's the truth," said the king desperately; he felt his position to be precarious enough without having any bad places to worry about.

Nanny sniffed. "Right, then," she said, slightly mollified. "It was 'pinchers.'"

"But pinchers is just another name for pl—" the king began, and stopped himself in time. During his adult life he'd been afraid of no man, beast or combination of the two, but Nanny's voice brought back old memories of schoolroom and nursery, of life under strict orders given by stern ladies in long skirts, and nursery food—mostly gray and brown—which seemed indigestible at the time but now appeared a distant ambrosia.

"That's five to me," said Nanny happily.

"They'll be back soon," said the king. "Are you sure you'll be all right?"

"If I'm not, precisely how much help can you be?" said Nanny.

There was the sound of bolts sliding back.

There was already a crowd outside the castle as Granny's broomstick wobbled uncertainly toward the ground. They went quiet as she strode forward, and parted to let her pass. She had a basket of apples under her arm.

"There's a witch in the dungeons," someone whispered to Granny. "And foul tortures, they say!"

"Nonsense," said Granny. "It couldn't be. I expect Nanny Ogg has just gone to advize the king, or something."

"They say Jason Ogg's gone to fetch his brothers," said a stallholder, in awe.

"I really advize you all to return home," said Granny Weatherwax. "There has probably been a misunderstanding. Everyone knows a witch cannot be held against her will."

"It's gone too far this time," said a peasant. "All this burning and taxing and now this. I blame you witches. It's got to stop. I know my rights."

"What rights are they?" said Granny.

"Dunnage, cowhage-in-ordinary, badinage, left-overs, scrommidge, clary and spunt," said the peasant promptly. "And acornage, every other year, and the right to keep two-thirds of a goat on the common. Until he set fire to it. It was a bloody good goat, too."

"A man could go far, knowing his rights like you do," said Granny. "But right now he should go home."

She turned and looked at the gates. There were two extremely apprehensive guards on duty. She walked up to them, and fixed one of them with a look.

"I am a harmless old seller of apples," she said, in a voice more appropriate for the opening of hostilities in a middle-range war. "Pray let me past, dearie." The last word had knives in it.

"No one must enter the castle," said one of the guards. "Orders of the duke."

Granny shrugged. The apple-seller gambit had never worked more than once in the entire history of witchcraft, as far as she knew, but it was traditional.

"I know you, Champett Poldy," she said. "I recall I laid out your grandad and I brought you into the world." She glanced at the crowds, which had regathered a little way off, and turned back to the guard, whose face was already a mask of terror. She leaned a little closer, and said, "I gave you your first good hiding in this valley of tears and by all the gods if you cross me now I will give you your last."

There was a soft metallic noise as the spear fell out of the man's fearful fingers. Granny reached and gave the trembling man a reassuring pat on the shoulder.

"But don't worry about it," she added. "Have an apple."

She made to step forward, and a second spear barred her way. She looked up with interest.

The other guard was not a Ramtopper, but a city-bred mercenary brought up to swell the ranks depleted in recent years. His face was a patchwork of scar tissue. Several of the scars rearranged themselves into what was possibly a sneer.

"So that's witches' magic, is it?" said the guard. "Pretty poor stuff. Maybe it frightens these country idiots, woman, but it doesn't frighten me."

"I imagine it takes a lot to frighten a big strong lad like you," said Granny, reaching up to her hat.

"And don't you try to put the wind up me, neither." The guard stared straight ahead, and rocked gently on the balls of his feet. "Old ladies like you, twisting people around. It shouldn't be stood for, like they say."

"Just as you like," said Granny, pushing the spear aside.

"Listen, I *said*—" the guard began, and grabbed Granny's shoulder. Her hand moved so quickly it hardly seemed to move at all, but suddenly he was clutching at his arm and moaning.

Granny replaced the hatpin in her hat and ran for it.

* * *

"We will begin," said the duchess, leering, "with the Showing of the Implements."

"Seen 'em," said Nanny. "Leastways, all the ones beginning with P, S, I, T and W."

"Then let us see how long you can keep that light conversational tone. Light the brazier, Felmet," snapped the duchess.

"Light the brazier, Fool," said the duke.

The Fool moved slowly. He hadn't expected any of this. Torturing people hadn't been on his mental agenda. Hurting old ladies in cold blood wasn't his cup of tea, and actually hurting witches in blood of any temperature whatsoever failed to be an entire twelve-course banquet. Words, he'd said. All this probably came under the heading of sticks and stones.

"I don't like doing this," he murmured under his breath.

"Fine," said Nanny Ogg, whose hearing was superb. "I'll remember that you didn't like it."

"What's that?" said the duke sharply.

"Nothing," said Nanny. "Is this going to take long? I haven't had breakfast."

The Fool lit a match. There was the faintest disturbance in the air beside him, and it went out. He swore, and tried another. This time his shaking hands managed to get it as far as the brazier before it, too, flared and darkened.

"Hurry up, man!" said the duchess, laying out a tray of tools.

"Doesn't seem to want to light—" muttered the

Fool, as another match became a fluttering streak of flame and then went out.

The duke snatched the box from his trembling fingers and caught him across the cheek with a handful of rings.

"Can no orders of mine be obeyed?" he screamed. "Infirm of purpose! Weak! Give me the box!"

The Fool backed away. Someone he couldn't see was whispering things he couldn't quite make out in his ear.

"Go outside," hissed the duke, "and see that we are not disturbed!"

The Fool tripped over the bottom step, turned and, with a last imploring look at Nanny, scampered through the door. He capered a little bit, out of force of habit.

"The fire isn't completely necessary," said the duchess. "It merely assists. Now, woman, will you confess?"

"What to?" said Nanny.

"It's common knowledge. Treason. Malicious witchcraft. Harboring the king's enemies. Theft of the crown—"

A tinkling noise made them look down. A blood-stained dagger had fallen off the bench, as though someone had tried to pick it up but just couldn't get the strength together. Nanny heard the king's ghost swear under its breath, or what would have been its breath.

"—and spreading false rumors," finished the duchess.

"—salt in my food—" said the duke, nervously, staring at the bandages on his hand. He kept getting the feeling that there was a fourth person in the dungeon.

"If you *do* confess," said the duchess, "you will merely be burned at the stake. And, please, no humorous remarks."

"What false rumors?"

The duke closed his eyes, but the visions were still there. "Concerning the accidental death of the late King Verence," he whispered hoarsely. The air swirled again.

Nanny sat with her head cocked to one side, as though listening to a voice only she could hear. Except that the duke was certain that he could hear something too, not exactly a voice, something like the distant sighing of the wind.

"Oh, I don't know nothing false," she said. "I know you stabbed him, and *you* gave him the dagger. It was at the top of the stairs." She paused, head cocked, nodded, and added, "Just by the suit of armor with the pike, and *you* said, 'If it's to be done, it's better if it's done quickly,' or something, and then you snatched the king's own dagger, the very same what is now lying on the floor, out of his belt and—"

"You lie! There were no witnesses. We made . . . there was nothing to witness! I heard someone in the dark, but there was no one there! There couldn't have been anyone seeing anything!" screamed the duke. His wife scowled at him.

"Do shut up, Leonal," she said. "I think within

these four walls we can dispense with that sort of thing."

"Who told her? Did you tell her?"

"And calm down. No one told her. She's a witch, for goodness sake, they find out about these things. Second glance, or something."

"Sight," said Nanny.

"Which you will not possess much longer, my good woman, unless you tell us who else knows and indeed, assist us on a number of other matters," said the duchess grimly. "And you will do so, believe me. I am skilled in these things."

Granny glanced around the dungeon. It was beginning to get crowded. King Verence was bursting with such angry vitality that he was very nearly apparent, and was furiously trying to get a grip on a knife. But there were others behind—wavering, broken shapes, not exactly ghosts but memories, implanted in the very substances of the walls themselves by sheer pain and terror.

"My own dagger! The bastards! They killed me with my own dagger," said the ghost of King Verence silently, raising his transparent arms and imploring the netherworld in general to witness this ultimate humiliation. "Give me strength . . ."

"Yes," said Nanny. "It's worth a try."

"And now we will commence," said the duchess.

"What?" said the guard.

"I SAID," said Magrat, "I've come to sell my lovely apples. Don't you listen?"

"There's not a sale on, is there?" The guard was

extremely nervous since his colleague had been taken off to the infirmary. He hadn't taken the job in order to deal with this sort of thing.

It dawned on him.

"You're not a witch, are you?" he said, fumbling awkwardly with his pike.

"Of course not. Do I look like one?"

The guard looked at her occult bangles, her lined cloak, her trembling hands and her face. The face was particularly worrying. Magrat had used a lot of powder to make her face pale and interesting. It combined with the lavishly applied mascara to give the guard the impression that he was looking at two flies that had crashed into a sugar bowl. He found his fingers wanted to make a sign to ward off the evil eyeshadow.

"Right," he said uncertainly. His mind was grinding through the problem. She was a witch. Just lately there'd been a lot of gossip about witches being bad for your health. He'd been told not to let witches pass, but no one had said anything about apple sellers. Apple sellers were not a problem. It was witches that were the problem. She'd said she was an apple seller and he wasn't about to doubt a witch's word.

Feeling happy with this application of logic, he stood to one side and gave an expansive wave.

"Pass, apple seller," he said.

"Thank you," said Magrat sweetly. "Would you like an apple?"

"No, thanks. I haven't finished the one the other witch gave me." His eyes rolled. "Not a witch. Not a witch, an apple seller. An apple seller. She ought to know."

"How long ago was this?"

"Just a few minutes . . ."

Granny Weatherwax was not lost. She wasn't the kind of person who ever became lost. It was just that, at the moment, while she knew exactly where SHE was, she didn't know the position of anywhere else. Currently she had arrived in the kitchens again, precipitating a breakdown in the cook, who was trying to roast some celery. The fact that several people had tried to buy apples from her wasn't improving her temper.

Magrat found her way to the Great Hall, empty and deserted at this time of day except for a couple of guards who were playing dice. They wore the tabards of Felmet's own personal bodyguard, and stopped their game as soon as she appeared.

"Well, well," said one, leering. "Come to keep us company, have you, my pretty."*

"I was looking for the dungeons," said Magrat, to whom the words "sexual harassment" were a mere collection of syllables.

"Just fancy," said one of the guards, winking at the other. "I reckon we can help you there." They got up and stood either side of her; she was aware of two chins you could strike matches on and an overpowering smell of stale beer. Frantic signals from outlying portions of her mind began to break down

---

* No one knows why men say things like this. Any minute now he is probably going to say he likes a girl with spirit.

her iron-hard conviction that bad things only happened to bad people.

They escorted her down several flights of steps into a maze of dank, arched passageways as she sought hurriedly for some polite way of disengaging herself.

"I should warn you," she said, "I am not, as I may appear, a simple apple seller."

"Fancy that."

"I am, in fact, a witch."

This did not make the impression she had hoped. The guards exchanged glances.

"Fair enough," said one. "I've always wondered what it was like to kiss a witch. Around here they do say you gets turned into a frog."

The other guard nudged him. "I reckon, then," he said, in the slow, ripe tones of one who thinks that what he is about to say next is going to be incredibly funny, "you kissed one years ago."

The brief guffaw was suddenly interrupted when Magrat was flung against the wall and treated to a close up view of the guard's nostrils.

"Now listen to me, sweetheart," he said. "You ain't the first witch we've had down here, if witch you be, but you could be lucky and walk out again. If you are nice to us, d'you see?"

There was a shrill, short scream from somewhere nearby.

"That, you see," said the guard, "was a witch having it the hard way. You could do us all a favor, see? Lucky you met us, really."

His questing hand stopped its wandering. "What's

this?" he said to Magrat's pale face. "A knife? A knife? I reckon we've got to take that very seriously, don't you, Hron?"

"You got to tie her hands and gag her," said Hron hurriedly. "They can't do no magic if they can't speak or wave their hands about . . ."

"You can take your hands off her!"

All three stared down the passage at the Fool. He was jingling with rage.

"Let her go this minute!" he shouted. "Or I'll report you!"

"Oh, you'll report us, will you?" said Hron. "And will anyone listen to you, you earwax-colored little twerp?"

"This is a witch we have here," said the other guard. "So you can go and tinkle somewhere else." He turned back to Magrat. "I like a girl with spirit," he said, incorrectly as it turned out.

The Fool advanced with the bravery of the terminally angry.

"I told you to let her go," he repeated.

Hron drew his sword and winked at his companion.

Magrat struck. It was an unplanned, instinctive blow, its stopping power considerably enhanced by the weight of rings and bangles; her arm whirred around in an arc that connected with her captor's jaw and spun him twice before he folded up in a heap with a quiet little sigh, and incidentally with several symbols of occult significance enbossed on his cheek.

Hron gaped at him, and then looked at Magrat.

He raised his sword at about the same moment that the Fool cannoned into him, and the two men went down in a struggling heap. Like most small men the Fool relied on the initial mad rush to secure an advantage and was at a loss for a follow-through, and it would probably have gone hard with him if Hron hadn't suddenly become aware that a bread-knife was pressed to his neck.

"Let go of him," said Magrat, pushing her hair out of her eyes.

He stiffened. "You're wondering whether I really would cut your throat," panted Magrat. "I don't know either. Think of the fun we could have together, finding out."

She reached down with her other hand and hauled the Fool to his feet by his collar.

"Where did that scream come from?" she said, without taking her eyes off the guard.

"It was down this way. They've got her in the torture dungeon and I don't like it, it's going too far, and I couldn't get in and I came to look for someone—"

"Well, you've found me," said Magrat.

"You," she said to Hron, "will stay here. Or run away, for all I care. But you won't follow us."

He nodded, and stared after them as they hurried down the passage. "The door's locked," said the Fool. "There's all sorts of noises, but the door's locked."

"Well, it's a dungeon, isn't it?"

"They're not supposed to lock from the inside!"

It was, indeed, unbudgeable. Silence came from the other side—a busy, thick silence that crawled through the cracks and spilled out into the passage, a kind of silence that is worse than screams.

The Fool hopped from one foot to the other as Magrat explored the door's rough surface.

"Are you really a witch?" he said. "They said you were a witch, are you really? You don't look like a witch, you look very, that is . . ." He blushed. "Not like a, you know, crone at all, but absolutely beautiful . . ." His voice trailed into silence . . .

I am totally in control of the situation, Magrat told herself. I never thought I would be, but I am thinking absolutely clearly.

And she realized, in an absolutely clear way, that her padding had slipped down to her waist, her head felt as though a family of unhygienic birds had been nesting in it, and her eyeshadow had not so much run as sprinted. Her dress was torn in several places, her legs were scratched, her arms were bruised, and for some reason she felt on top of the world.

"I think you'd better stand back, Verence," she said. "I'm not sure how this is going to work."

There was a sharp intake of breath.

"How did you know my name?"

Magrat sized up the door. The oak was old, centuries old, but she could sense just a little sap under a surface varnished by the years into something that was nearly as tough as stone. Normally what she had in mind would require a day's planning and a bagful of exotic ingredients. At least, so she'd always believed. Now she was prepared to doubt it. If you could conjure demons out of washtubs, you could do anything.

She became aware that the Fool had spoken.

"Oh, I expect I heard it somewhere," she said vaguely.

"I shouldn't think so, I never use it," said the Fool. "I mean, it's not a popular name with the duke. It was me mam, you see. They like to name you after kings, I suppose. My grandad said I had no business having a name like that and he said I shouldn't go around—"

Magrat nodded. She was looking around the dank tunnel with a professional's eye.

It wasn't a promising place. The old oak planks had been down here in the darkness all these years, away from the clock of the seasons . . .

On the other hand . . . Granny had said that somehow all trees were one tree, or something like that. Magrat thought she understood it, although she didn't know exactly what it meant. And it was springtime up there. The ghost of life that still lived in the wood must know that. Or if it had forgotten, it must be told.

She put her palms flat on the door again and shut her eyes, tried to think her way out through the stone, out of the castle, and into the thin, black soil of the mountains, into the air, into the sunlight . . .

The Fool was merely aware that Magrat was standing very still. Then her hair stood out from her head, gently, and there was a smell of leaf mold.

And then, without warning, the hammer that can drive a marshmallow-soft toadstool through six inches of solid pavement or an eel across a thousand miles of hostile ocean to a particular pond in an up-land field, struck up through her and into the door.

She stepped back carefully, her mind stunned, fighting against a desperate urge to bury her toes into the rock and put forth leaves. The Fool caught her, and the shock nearly knocked him over.

Magrat sagged against the faintly jingling body, and felt triumphant. She had done it! And with no artificial aids! If only the others could have seen this . . .

"Don't go near it," she mumbled. "I think I gave it rather . . . a lot." The Fool was still holding her toastrack body in his arms and was too overcome to utter a word, but she still got a reply.

"I reckon you did," said Granny Weatherwax, stepping out of the shadows. "I never would have thought of it myself."

Magrat peered at her.

"You've been here all the time?"

"Just a few minutes." Granny glanced at the door. "Good technique," she said, "but it's old wood. Been in a fire, too, I reckon. Lot of iron nails and stuff in there. Can't see it working, I'd have tried the stones if it was me, but—"

She was interrupted by a soft "pop."

There was another, and then a whole series of them together, like a shower of meringues.

Behind her, very gently, the door was breaking into leaf.

Granny stared at it for a few seconds, and then met Magrat's terrified gaze.

"Run!" she yelled.

They grabbed the Fool and scurried into the shelter of a convenient buttress.

The door gave a warning creak. Several of its planks twisted in vegetable agony and there was a shower of rock splinters when nails were expelled like thorns from a wound, ricocheting off the stonework. The Fool ducked as part of the lock whirred over his head and smashed into the opposite wall.

The lower parts of the planks extended questing white roots, which slithered across the damp stone to the nearest crack and began to auger in. Knotholes bulged, burst and thrust out branches which hit the stones of the doorway and tumbled them aside. And all the time there was a low groan, the sound of the cells of the wood trying to contain the surge of raw life pounding through them.

"If it had been *me*," said Granny Weatherwax, as part of the ceiling caved in further along the passage, "I wouldn't have done it like that. Not that I'm objecting, mind you," she said, as Magrat opened her mouth. "It's a reasonable job. I think you might have overdone it a bit, that's all."

"Excuse me," said the Fool.

"I can't do rocks," said Magrat.

"Well, no, rocks is an acquired taste—"

"Excuse me."

The two witches stared at him, and he backed away.

"Weren't you supposed to be rescuing someone?" he said.

"Oh," said Granny. "Yes. Come on, Magrat. We'd better see what she's been getting up to."

"There were screams," said the Fool, who couldn't help feeling they weren't taking things seriously enough.

"I daresay," said Granny, pushing him aside and stepping over a writhing taproot. "If anyone locked *me* in a dungeon, there'd be screams."

There was a lot of dust inside the dungeon, and by the nimbus of light around its one torch Magrat could dimly make out two figures cowering in the furthest corner. Most of the furniture had been overturned and scattered across the floor; it didn't look as though any of it had been designed to be the last word in comfort. Nanny Ogg was sitting quite calmly in what appeared to be a sort of stocks.

"Took your time," she observed. "Let me out of this, will you? I'm getting cramp."

And there was the dagger.

It spun gently in the middle of the room, glinting when the turning blade caught the light.

"My own dagger!" said the ghost of the king, in a voice only the witches could hear. "All this time and I never knew it! My own dagger! They bloody well did me in with my own bloody knife!"

He took another step toward the royal couple, waving the dagger. A faint gurgle escaped from the lips of the duke, glad to be out of there.

"He's doing well, isn't he," said Nanny, as Magrat helped her out of her prison.

"Isn't that the old king? Can they see him?"

"Shouldn't think so."

King Verence staggered slightly under the weight. He was too old for such poltergeist activity; you had to be an adolescent for this . . .

"Let me just get a grip on this thing," he said. "Oh, damn . . ."

The knife dropped from the ghost's tenuous grasp and clattered to the floor. Granny Weatherwax stepped forward smartly and put her foot on it.

"The dead shouldn't kill the living," she said. "It could be a dangerous wossname, precedent. We'd all be outnumbered, for one thing."

The duchess surfaced from her terror first. There had been knives swooping through the air and exploding doors, and now these women were defying her in her own dungeons. She couldn't be sure how she was supposed to react to the supernatural items, but she had very firm ideas about how she should tackle the last one.

Her mouth opened like the gateway to a red hell. "Guards!" she yelled, and spotted the Fool hovering near the door. "Fool! Fetch the guards!"

"They're busy. We were just leaving," said Granny. "Which one of you is the duke?"

Felmet stared pink-eyed up at her from his half-crouch in the corner. A thin dribble of saliva escaped from the corner of his mouth, and he giggled.

Granny looked closer. In the center of those streaming eyes something else looked back at her.

"I'm going to give you no cause," she said quietly. "But it would be better for you if you left this country. Abdicate, or whatever."

"In favor of whom?" said the duchess icily. "A witch?"

"I won't," said the duke.

"What did you say?"

The duke pulled himself upright, brushed some of the dust off his clothes, and looked Granny full in the face. The coldness in the center of his eyes was larger.

"I said I won't," he said. "Do you think a bit of simple conjuring would frighten me? I am the king by right of conquest, and you cannot change it. It is as simple as that, witch."

He moved closer.

Granny stared at him. She hadn't faced anything like this before. The man was clearly mad, but at the heart of his madness was a dreadful cold sanity, a core of pure interstellar ice in the center of the furnace. She'd thought him weak under a thin shell of strength, but it went a lot further than that. Somewhere deep inside his mind, somewhere beyond the event horizon of rationality, the sheer pressure of insanity had hammered his madness into something harder than diamond.

"If you defeat me by magic, magic will rule," said the duke. "And you can't do it. And any king raised with your help would be under your power. Hag-ridden, I might say. That which magic rules, magic destroys. It would destroy you, too. You know it. Ha. Ha."

Granny's knuckles whitened as he moved closer.

"You could strike me down," he said. "And per-haps you could find someone to replace me. But he would have to be a fool indeed, because he would know he was under your evil eye, and if he mispleased you, why, his life would be instantly forfeit. You could protest all you wished, but he'd know he ruled with your permission. And that would make him no king at all. Is this not true?"

Granny looked away. The other witches hung back, ready to duck.

"I *said*, is this not true?"

"Yes," said Granny. "It is true . . ."

"Yes."

". . . but there is one who could defeat you," said Granny slowly.

"The child? Let him come when he is grown. A young man with a sword, seeking his destiny." The duke sneered. "Very romantic. But I have many years to prepare. Let him try."

Beside him King Verence's fist smashed through the air and quite failed to connect.

The duke leaned closer until his nose was an inch from Granny's face.

"Get back to your cauldrons, wyrd sisters," he said softly.

Granny Weatherwax stalked through the passages of Lancre Castle like a large, angry bat, the duke's laughter echoing around her head.

"You could give him boils or something," said Nanny Ogg. "Hemorrhoids are good. That's allowed. It won't stop him ruling, it just means he'll have to rule standing up. Always good for a laugh, that. Or piles."

Granny Weatherwax said nothing. If fury were heat, her hat would have caught fire.

"Mind you, that'd probably make him worse," said Nanny, running to keep up. "Same with toothache." She gave a sideways glance at Granny's twitching features.

"You needn't fret," she said. "They didn't do anything much. But thanks, anyway."

"I ain't worried about you, Gytha Ogg," snapped Granny. "I only come along 'cos Magrat was fretting. What I say is, if a witch can't look after herself, she's got no business calling herself a witch."

"Magrat done well with the woodwork, I thought."

Even in the grip of her sullen fury, Granny Weatherwax spared a nod.

"She's coming along," she said. She looked up and down the corridor, and then leaned closer to Nanny Ogg's ear.

"I ain't going to give him the pleasure of saying it," she said, "but he's got us beaten."

"Well, I don't know," said Nanny. "Our Jason and a few sharp lads could soon—"

"You saw some of his guards. These aren't the old sort. These are a tough kind."

"We could give the boys just a bit of help—"

"It wouldn't work. People have to sort this sort of thing out for themselves."

"If you say so, Esme," said Nanny meekly.

"I do. Magic's there to be ruled, not for ruling."

Nanny nodded and then, remembering a promise, reached down and picked up a fragment of stone from the rubble on the tunnel floor.

"I thought you'd forgotten," said the ghost of the king, by her ear.

Further down the passage the Fool was capering after Magrat.

"Can I see you again?" he said.

"Well . . . I don't know," said Magrat, her heart singing a smug song.

"How about tonight?" said the Fool.

"Oh, no," said Magrat. "I'm very busy tonight." She had intended to curl up with a hot milk drink and Goodie Whemper's notebooks on experimental astrology, but instinct told her that any suitor should have an uphill struggle put in front of him, just to make him keener.

"Tomorrow night, then?" the Fool persisted.

"I think I should be washing my hair."

"I could get Friday night free."

"We do a lot of work at night, you see—"

"The afternoon, then."

Magrat hesitated. Perhaps instinct had got it wrong. "Well—" she said.

"About two o'clock. In the meadow by the pond, all right?"

"Well—"

"See you there, then. All right?" said the Fool desperately.

"Fool!" The duchess's voice echoed along the passage, and a look of terror crossed his face.

"I've got to go," he said. "The meadow, OK? I'll wear something so you recognize me. All right?"

"All right," echoed Magrat, hypnotized by the

sheer pressure of his persistence. She turned and ran after the other witches.

There was pandemonium outside the castle. The crowd that had been there at Granny's arrival had grown considerably, and had flowed in through the now unguarded gateway and lapped around the keep. Civil disobedience was new to Lancre, but its inhabitants had already mastered some of its more elementary manifestations, viz, the jerking of rakes and sickles in the air with simple up-and-down motions accompanied by grimaces and cries of "Gerrh!," although a few citizens, who hadn't quite grasped the idea, were waving flags and cheering. Advanced students were already eyeing the more combustible buildings inside the walls. Several sellers of hot meat pies and sausages in a bun had appeared from nowhere* and were doing a brisk trade. Pretty soon someone was going to throw something.

The three witches stood at the top of the steps that led to the keep's main door and surveyed the seas of faces.

"There's our Jason," said Nanny happily. "And Wane and Darron and Kev and Trev and Nev—"

"I will remember their faces," said Lord Felmet, emerging between them and putting a hand on their shoulders. "And do you see my archers, on the walls?"

---

* They always do, everywhere. No one sees them arrive. The logical explanation is that the franchise includes the stall, the paper hat and a small gas-powered time machine.

"I see 'em," said Granny grimly.

"Then smile and wave," said the duke. "So that the people may know that all is well. After all, have you not been to see me today on matters of state?"

He leaned closer to Granny.

"Yes, there are a hundred things you could do," he said. "But the ending would always be the same." He drew back. "I'm not an unreasonable man, I hope," he added, in cheerful tones. "Perhaps, if you persuade the people to be calm, I may be prevailed upon to moderate my rule somewhat. I make no promises, of course."

Granny said nothing.

"Smile and wave," commanded the duke.

Granny raised one hand in a vague motion and produced a brief rictus that had nothing whatsoever to do with humor. Then she scowled and nudged Nanny Ogg, who was waving and mugging like a maniac.

"No need to get carried away," she hissed.

"But there's our Reet and our Sharleen and their babbies," said Nanny. "Coo-eee!"

"Will you shut up, you daft old besom!" snapped Granny. "And pull yourself together!"

"Jolly good, well done," said the duke. He raised his hands, or at least his hand. The other still ached. He'd tried the grater again last night, but it hadn't worked.

"People of Lancre," he cried, "do not be afeared! I am your friend. I will protect you from the witches! They have agreed to leave you in peace!"

Granny stared at him as he spoke. He's one of

these here maniac depressives, she said. Up and down like a wossname. Kill you one minute and ask you how you're feeling the next.

She became aware that he was looking at her expectantly.

"What?"

"I said, I'll now call upon the respected Granny Weatherwax to say a few words, ha ha," he said.

"You said that, did you?"

"Yes!"

"You've gone a long way too far," said Granny.

"I have, haven't I!" The duke giggled.

Granny turned to the expectant crowds, which went silent.

"Go home," she said.

There was a further long silence.

"Is that all?" said the duke.

"Yes."

"What about pledges of eternal allegiance?"

"What about them? Gytha, will you stop waving at people!"

"Sorry."

"And now we are going to go, too," said Granny.

"But we were getting on so well," said the duke.

"Come, Gytha," said Granny icily. "And where's Magrat got to?"

Magrat looked up guiltily. She had been deep in conversation with the Fool, although it was the kind of conversation where both parties spend a lot of time looking at their feet and picking at their fingernails. Ninety percent of true love is acute, earburning embarrassment.

"We're leaving," said Granny.

"Friday afternoon, remember," hissed the Fool.

"Well, if I can," said Magrat.

Nanny Ogg leered.

And so Granny Weatherwax swept down the steps and through the crowds, with the other two running behind her. Several of the grinning guards caught her eye and wished they hadn't, but here and there, among the watching crowd, was a barely suppressed snigger. She hurtled through the gateway, across the drawbridge and through the town. Granny walking fast could beat most other people at a run.

Behind them the duke, who had crested the latest maniac peak on the switchback of his madness and was coasting speedily toward the watersplash of despair, laughed.

"Ha ha."

Granny didn't stop until she was outside the town and under the welcoming eaves of the forest. She turned off the road and flumped down on a log, her face in her hands.

The other two approached her carefully. Magrat patted her on the back.

"Don't despair," she said. "You handled it very well, we thought."

"I ain't despairing, I'm thinking," said Granny. "Go away."

Nanny Ogg raised her eyebrows at Magrat in a warning fashion. They backed off to a suitable distance although, with Granny in her present mood, the next universe might not be far enough, and sat down on a moss-grown stone.

"Are you all right?" said Magrat. "They didn't do anything, did they?"

"Never laid a finger on me," said Nanny. She sniffed. "They're not your real royalty," she added. "Old King Gruneweld, for one, he wouldn't have wasted time waving things around and menacing people. It'd been bang, needles right under the fingernails from the word go, and no messing. None of this evil laughter stuff. He was a *real* king. Very gracious."

"He was threatening to burn you."

"Oh, I wouldn't of stood for it. I see you've got a follower," said Nanny.

"Sorry?" said Magrat.

"The young fellow with the bells," said Nanny. "And the face like a spaniel what's just been kicked."

"Oh, him." Magrat blushed hotly under her pale makeup. "Really, he's just this man. He just follows me around."

"Can be difficult, can that," said Nanny sagely.

"Besides, he's so small. And he *capers* all over the place," said Magrat.

"Looked at him carefully, have you?" said the old witch.

"Pardon?"

"You haven't, have you? I thought not. He's a very clever man, that Fool. He ought to have been one of them actor men."

"What do you mean?"

"Next time you have a look at him like a witch, not like a woman," said Nanny, and gave Magrat a conspiratorial nudge. "Good bit of work with the door back there," she added. "Coming on well, you are. I hope you told him about Greebo."

"He said he'd let him out directly, Nanny."

There was a snort from Granny Weatherwax.

"Did you hear the sniggering in the crowd?" she said. "Someone sniggered!"

Nanny Ogg sat down beside her.

"And a couple of them pointed," she said. "I know."

"It's not to be borne!"

Magrat sat down on the other end of the log.

"There's other witches," she said. "There's lots of witches further up the Ramtops. Maybe they can help."

The other two looked at her in pained surprise.

"I don't think we need go *that* far," sniffed Granny. "*Asking* for *help*."

"Very bad practice," nodded Nanny Ogg.

"But you asked a demon to help you," said Magrat.

"No, we didn't," said Granny.

"Right. We didn't."

"We ordered it to assist."

"S'right."

Granny Weatherwax stretched out her legs and looked at her boots. They were good strong boots, with hobnails and crescent-shaped scads; you couldn't believe a cobbler had made them, someone had laid down a sole and *built* up from there.

"I mean, there's that witch over Skund way," she

said. "Sister Whosis, wossname, her son went off to be a sailor—you know, Gytha, her who sniffs and puts them antimassacres on the backs of chairs soon as you sits down—"

"Grodley," said Nanny Ogg. "Sticks her little finger out when she drinks her tea and drops her Haitches all the time."

"Yes. Hwell. I haven't hlowered myself to talk to her hever since that business with the gibbet, you recall. I daresay she'd just love to come snooping haround here, running her fingers over heverything and sniffling, telling us how to do things. Oh, yes. *Help*. We'd all be in a fine to-do if we went around helping all the time."

"Yes, and over Skund way the trees talk to you and walk around of night," said Nanny. "Without even asking permission. Very poor organization."

"Not really good organization, like we've got here?" said Magrat.

Granny stood up purposefully.

"I'm going home," she said.

There are thousands of good reasons why magic doesn't rule the world. They're called witches and wizards, Magrat reflected, as she followed the other two back to the road.

It was probably some wonderful organization on the part of Nature to protect itself. It saw to it that everyone with any magical talent was about as ready to cooperate as a she-bear with toothache, so all that dangerous power was safely dissipated as random bickering and rivalry. There were differences in style, of course. Wizards assassinated each other in drafty corridors, witches just cut one another dead in the street. And they were all as self-centered as a spinning top. Even when they help other people, she thought, they're secretly doing it for themselves. Honestly, they're just like big children.

Except for me, she thought smugly.

"She's very upset, isn't she," said Magrat to Nanny Ogg.

"Ah, well," said Nanny. "There's the problem, see. The more you get used to magic, the more you don't want to use it. The more it gets in your way. I expect, when you were just starting out, you learned a few spells from Goodie Whemper, maysherestinpeace, and you used them all the time, didn't you?"

"Well, yes. Everyone does."

"Well-known fact," agreed Nanny. "But when you get along in the Craft, you learn that the hardest magic is the sort you don't use at all."

Magrat considered the proposition cautiously. "This isn't some kind of Zen, is it?" she said.

"Dunno. Never seen one."

"When we were in the dungeons, Granny said something about trying the rocks. That sounded like pretty hard magic."

"Well, Goodie wasn't much into rocks," said Nanny. "It's not really hard. You just prod their memories. You know, of the old days. When they were hot and runny."

She hesitated, and her hand flew to her pocket. She gripped the lump of castle stone and relaxed.

"Thought I'd forgotten it, for a minute," she said, lifting it out. "You can come out now."

He was barely visible in the brightness of day, a mere shimmer in the air under the trees. King Verence blinked. He wasn't used to daylight.

"Esme," said Nanny. "There's someone to see you."

Granny turned slowly and squinted at the ghost.

"I saw you in the dungeon, didn't I?" she said. "Who're you?"

"Verence, King of Lancre," said the ghost, and bowed. "Do I have the honor of addressing Granny Weatherwax, doyenne of witches?"

It has already been pointed out that just because Verence came from a long line of kings didn't mean that he was basically stupid, and a year without the distractions of the flesh had done wonders as well. Granny Weatherwax considered herself totally unsusceptible to buttering up, but the king was expertly applying the equivalent of the dairy surplus of quite a large country. Bowing was a particularly good touch.

A muscle twitched at the corner of Granny's mouth. She gave a stiff little bow in return, because she wasn't quite sure what "doyenne" meant.

"I'm her," she conceded.

"You can get up now," she added, regally.

King Verence remained kneeling, about two inches above the actual ground.

"I crave a boon," he said urgently.

"Here, how did you get out of the castle?" said Granny.

"The esteemed Nanny Ogg assisted me," said the king. "I reasoned, if I am anchored to the stones of

Lancre, then I can also go where the stones go. I am afraid I indulged in a little trickery to arrange matters. Currently I am haunting her apron."

"Not the first, either," said Granny, automatically.

"Esme!"

"And I beg you, Granny Weatherwax, to restore my son to the throne."

"Restore?"

"You know what I mean. He is in good health?"

Granny nodded. "The last time we Looked at him, he was eating an apple," she said.

"It is his destiny to be King of Lancre!"

"Yes, well. Destiny is tricky, you know," said Granny.

"You will not help?"

Granny looked wretched. "It's meddling, you see," she said. "It always goes wrong if you meddle in politics. Like, once you start, you can't stop. Fundamental rule of magic, is that. You can't go around messing with fundamental rules."

"You're not going to help?"

"Well . . . naturally, one day, when your lad is a bit older . . ."

"Where is he now?" said the king, coldly.

The witches avoided one another's faces.

"We saw him safe out of the country, you see," said Granny awkwardly.

"Very good family," Nanny Ogg put in quickly.

"What kind of people?" said the king. "Not commoners, I trust?"

"Absolutely not," said Granny with considerable firmness as a vision of Vitoller floated across her imagination. "Not common at all. Very uncommon. Er."

Her eyes implored Magrat for help.

"They were Thespians," said Magrat firmly, her voice radiating such approval that the king found himself nodding automatically.

"Oh," he said. "Good."

"Were they?" whispered Nanny Ogg. "They didn't look it."

"Don't show your ignorance, Gytha Ogg," sniffed Granny. She turned back to the ghost of the king. "Sorry about that, your majesty. It's just her showing off. She don't even know where Thespia *is*."

"Wherever it is, I hope that they know how to school a man in the arts of war," said Verence. "I know Felmet. In ten years he'll be dug in here like a toad in a stone."

The king looked from witch to witch. "What kind of kingdom will he have to come back to? I hear what the kingdom is becoming, even now. Will you watch it change, over the years, become shoddy and mean?" The king's ghost faded.

His voice hung in the air, faint as a breeze.

"Remember, good sisters," he said, "the land and the king are one."

And he vanished.

The embarrassed silence was broken by Magrat blowing her nose.

"One what?" said Nanny Ogg.

"We've got to do something," said Magrat, her voice choked with emotion. "Rules or no rules!"

"It's very vexing," said Granny, quietly.

"Yes, but what are you going to do?" she said.

"Reflect on things," said Granny. "Think about it all."

"You've been thinking about it for a year," Magrat said.

"One what? Are one what?" said Nanny Ogg.

"It's no good just reacting," said Granny. "You've got to—"

A cart came bouncing and rumbling along the track from Lancre. Granny ignored it.

"—give these things careful consideration."

"You don't know what to do, do you?" said Magrat.

"Nonsense. I—"

"There's a cart coming, Granny."

Granny Weatherwax shrugged. "What you youngsters don't realize—" she began.

Witches never bothered with elementary road safety. Such traffic as there was on the roads of Lancre either went around them or, if this was not possible, waited until they moved out of the way. Granny Weatherwax had grown up knowing this for a fact; the only reason she didn't die knowing that it wasn't was that Magrat, with rather better reflexes, dragged her into the ditch.

It was an interesting ditch. There were jiggling corkscrew things in it which were direct descendants of things which had been in the primordial soup of creation. Anyone who thought that ditchwater was dull could have spent an instructive half-hour in that ditch with a powerful microscope. It also had nettles in it, and now it had Granny Weatherwax.

She struggled up through the weeds, incoherent with rage, and rose from the ditch like Venus Anadyomene, only older and with more duckweed.

"T-t-t," she said, pointing a shaking finger at the disappearing cart.

"It was young Nesheley from over Inkcap way," said Nanny Ogg, from a nearby bush. "His family were always a bit wild. Of course, his mother was a Whipple."

"He ran us down!" said Granny.

"You could have got out of the way," said Magrat.

"*Get out of the way?*" said Granny. "We're witches! People get out of *our* way!" She squelched onto the track, her finger still pointing at the distant cart. "By Hoki, I'll make him wish he'd never been born—"

"He was quite a big baby, I recall," said the bush. "His mother had a terrible time."

"It's never happened to me before, ever," said Granny, still twanging like a bowstring. "I'll teach him to run us down as though, as though, as though we was ordinary people!"

"He already knows," said Magrat. "Just help me get Nanny out of this bush, will you?"

"I'll turn his—"

"People haven't got any respect anymore, that's what it is," said Nanny, as Magrat helped her with the thorns. "It's all due to the king being one, I expect."

"We're witches!" screamed Granny, turning her face toward the sky and shaking her fists.

"Yes, yes," said Magrat. "The harmonious balance

of the universe and everything. I think Nanny's a bit tired."

"What've I been doing all this time?" said Granny, with a rhetorical flourish that would have made even Vitoller gasp.

"Not a lot," said Magrat.

"Laughed at! Laughed at! On my own roads! In my own country!" screamed Granny. "That just about does it! I'm not taking ten more years of this! I'm not taking another *day* of it!"

The trees around her began to sway and the dust from the road sprang up into writhing shapes that tried to swirl out of her way. Granny Weatherwax extended one long arm and at the end of it unfolded one long finger and from the tip of its curving nail there was a brief flare of octarine fire.

Half a mile down the track all four wheels fell off the cart at once.

"Lock up a witch, would he?" Granny shouted at the trees.

Nanny struggled to her feet.

"We'd better grab her," she whispered to Magrat. The two of them leapt at Granny and forced her arms down to her sides.

"I'll bloody well show him what a witch could do!" she yelled.

"Yes, yes, very good, very *good*," said Nanny. "Only perhaps not just now and not just like this, eh?"

"Wyrd sisters, indeed!" Granny yelled. "I'll make his—"

"Hold her a minute, Magrat," said Nanny Ogg, and rolled up her sleeve.

"It can be like this with the highly-trained ones," she said, and brought her plam around in a slap that lifted both witches off their feet. On such a flat, final note the universe might have ended.

At the conclusion of the breathless silence which followed Granny Weatherwax said, "Thank you."

She adjusted her dress with some show of dignity, and added, "But I meant it. We'll meet tonight at the stone and do what must be done. Ahem."

She reset the pins in her hat and set off unsteadily in the direction of her cottage.

"Whatever happened to the rule about not meddling in politics?" said Magrat, watching her retreating back.

Nanny Ogg massaged some life back into her fingers.

"By Hoki, that woman's got a jaw like an anvil," she said. "What was that?"

"I said, what about this rule about not meddling?" said Magrat.

"Ah," said Nanny. She took the girl's arm. "The thing is," she explained, "as you progress in the Craft, you'll learn there is another rule. Esme's obeyed it all her life."

"And what's that?"

"When you break rules, break 'em good and hard," said Nanny, and grinned a set of gums that were more menacing than teeth.

The duke smiled out over the forest.

"It works," he said. "The people mutter against the witches. How do you do it, Fool?"

"Jokes, nuncle. And gossip. People are halfway ready to believe it anyway. Everyone respects the witches. The point is that no one actually likes them very much."

Friday afternoon, he thought. I'll have to get some flowers. And my best suit, the one with the silver bells. Oh gosh.

"This is very pleasing. If it goes on like this, Fool, you shall have a knighthood."

This was no. 302, and the Fool knew better than to let a feed line go hungry. "Marry, nuncle," he said wearily, ignoring the spasm of pain that crawled across the duke's face, "if'n I had a Knighthood (Night Hood), why, it would keep my ears Warm in Bedde; i'faith, if many a Knight is a Fool, why, should a—"

"Yes, yes, all right," snapped Lord Felmet. In fact he was feeling much better already. His porridge hadn't been over-salted this evening, and there was a decently empty feel about the castle. There were no more voices on the cusp of hearing.

He sat down on the throne. It felt really comfortable for the first time.

The duchess sat beside him, her chin on her hand, watching the Fool intently. This bothered him. He thought he knew where he stood with the duke, it was just a matter of hanging on until his madness curved back to the cheerful stage, but the duchess genuinely frightened him.

"It seems that words are extremely powerful," she said.

"Indeed, lady."

"You must have made a lengthy study."

The Fool nodded. The power of words had sustained him through the hell of the Guild. Wizards and witches used words as if they were tools to get things done, but the Fool reckoned that words were things in their own right.

"Words can change the world," he said.

Her eyes narrowed.

"So you have said before. I remain unconvinced. Strong men change the world," she said. "Strong men and their deeds. Words are just like marzipan on a cake. Of course you think words are important. You are weak, you have nothing else."

"Your ladyship is wrong."

The duchess's fat hand drummed impatiently on the arm of her throne.

"You had better," she said, "be able to substantiate that comment."

"Lady, the duke wishes to chop down the forests, is this not so?"

"The trees talk about me," whispered Lord Felmet. "I hear them whisper when I go riding. They tell lies about me!"

The duchess and the Fool exchanged glances.

"But," the Fool continued, "this policy has met with fanatical opposition."

"What?"

"People don't like it."

The duchess exploded. "What does that matter?" she roared. "We rule! They will do what we say or they will be pitilessly executed!"

The Fool bobbed and capered and waved his hands in a conciliatory fashion.

"But, my love, we will run out of people," murmured the duke.

"No need, no need!" said the Fool desperately. "You don't have to do that at all! What you do is, you—" he paused for a moment, his lips moving quickly—"you embark upon a far-reaching and ambitious plan to expand the agricultural industry, provide long-term employment in the sawmills, open new land for development, and reduce the scope for banditry."

This time the duke looked baffled. "How will I do that?" he said.

"Chop down the forests."

"But you said—"

"Shut up, Felmet," said the duchess. She subjected the Fool to another long, thoughtful stare.

"Exactly how," she said, eventually, "does one go about knocking over the houses of people one does not like?"

"Urban clearance," said the Fool.

"I was thinking of burning them down."

"*Hygienic* urban clearance," the Fool added promptly.

"And sowing the ground with salt."

"Marry, I suspect that is hygienic urban clearance and a program of environmental improvements. It might be a good idea to plant a few trees as well."

"No more trees!" shouted Felmet.

"Oh, it's all right. They won't survive. The important thing is to have planted them."

"But I also want us to raise taxes," said the duchess.

"Why, nuncle—"

"And I am not your nuncle."

"N'aunt?" said the Fool.

"No."

"Why . . . prithee . . . you need to finance your ambitious program for the country."

"Sorry?" said the duke, who was getting lost again.

"He means that chopping down trees costs money," said the duchess. She smiled at the Fool. It was the first time he had ever seen her look at him as if he was other than a disgusting little cockroach. There was still a large element of cockroach in her glance, but it said: good little cockroach, you have learned a trick.

"Intriguing," she said. "But can your words change the past?"

The Fool considered this.

"More easily, I think," he said. "Because the past is what people remember, and memories are words. Who knows how a king behaved a thousand years ago? There is only recollection, and stories. And plays, of course."

"Ah, yes. I saw a play once," said Felmet. "Bunch of funny fellows in tights. A lot of shouting. The people liked it."

"You tell me history is what people are told?" said the duchess.

The Fool looked around the throne room and found King Gruneberry the Good (906–967).

"*Was* he?" he said, pointing. "Who knows, now? What was he good *at*? But he will be Gruneberry the Good until the end of the world."

The duke was leaning forward in his throne, his eyes gleaming.

"I want to be a *good* ruler," he said. "I want people to like me. I would like people to remember me fondly."

"Let us assume," said the duchess, "that there were other matters, subject to controversy. Matters of historical record that had . . . been clouded."

"I didn't do it, you know," said the duke, quickly. "He slipped and fell. That was it. Slipped and fell. I wasn't even there. He attacked me. It was self-defense." His voice fell to a mumble. "I have no recollection of it at this time," he murmured. He rubbed his dagger hand, although the word was becoming inappropriate.

"Be quiet, husband," snapped the duchess. "I know you didn't do it. I wasn't there with you, you may recall. It was I who didn't hand you the dagger." The duke shuddered again.

"And now, Fool," said Lady Felmet. "I was saying, I believe, that perhaps there are matters that should be *properly recorded*."

"Marry, that you were not there at the time?" said the Fool, brightly.

It is true that words have power, and one of the things they are able to do is get out of someone's mouth before the speaker has the chance to stop them. If words were sweet little lambs, then the Fool watched them bound cheerfully away into the flame-thrower of the duchess's glare.

"Not *where*?" she said.

"Anywhere," said the Fool hastily.

"Stupid man! Everyone is somewhere."

"I mean, you were everywhere but at the top of the stairs," said the Fool.

"Which stairs?"

"Any stairs," said the Fool, who was beginning to sweat. "I distinctly remember not seeing you!"

The duchess eyed him for a while.

"So long as you remember it," she said. The duchess rubbed her chin, which made an audible rasping noise.

"Reality is only weak words, you say. Therefore, words are reality. But how can words become history?"

"It was a very good play, the play that I saw," said Felmet dreamily. "There were fights, and no one really died. Some very good speeches, I thought."

There was another sandpapery sound from the duchess.

"Fool?" she said.

"Lady?"

"Can you write a play? A play that will go around the world, a play that will be remembered long after rumor has died?"

"No, lady. It is a special talent."

"But can you find someone who has it?"

"There are such people, lady."

"Find one," murmured the duke. "Find the best. Find the best. The truth will out. Find one."

The storm was resting. It didn't want to be, but it was. It had spent a fortnight understudying a famous anticyclone over the Circle Sea, turning up every day, hanging around in the cold front, grateful for a chance to uproot the occasional tree or whirl a farmhouse to any available emerald city of its choice. But the big break in the weather had never come.

It consoled itself with the thought that even the really great storms of the past—the Great Gale of 1789, for example, of Hurricane Zelda and Her Amazing Raining Frogs—had gone through this sort of thing at some stage in their career. It was just part of the great tradition of the weather.

Besides, it had had a good stretch in the equivalent of pantomime down on the plains, bringing seasonal snow and terminal frostbite to millions. It just had to be philosophical about being back up here now with nothing much to do except wave the heather about. If weather was people, this storm would be filling in time wearing a cardboard hat in a hamburger hell.

Currently it was observing three figures moving slowly over the moor, converging with some determination on a bare patch where the standing stone stood, or usually stood, though just at the moment it wasn't visible.

It recognized them as old friends and connoisseurs, and conjured up a brief unseasonal roll of thunder as a form of greeting. This was totally ignored.

"The bloody stone's gone," said Granny Weatherwax. "However many there is of it."

Her face was pale. It might also have been drawn; if so, then it was by a very neurotic artist. She looked as though she meant business. Bad business.

"Light the fire, Magrat," she added automatically.

"I daresay we'll all feel better for a cup of tea," said Nanny Ogg, mouthing the words like a mantra. She fumbled in the recesses of her shawl. "With something in it," she added, producing a small bottle of applejack.

"Alcohol is a deceiver and tarnishes the soul," said Magrat virtuously.

"I never touch the stuff," said Granny Weatherwax. "We should keep a clear head, Gytha."

"Just a drop in your tea isn't drinking," said Nanny. "It's medicine. It's a chilly old wind up here, sisters."

"Very well," said Granny. "But just a drop."

They drank in silence. Eventually Granny said, "Well, Magrat. You know all about the coven business. We might as well do it right. What do we do next?"

Magrat hesitated. She wasn't up to suggesting dancing naked.

"There's a song," she said. "In praise of the full moon."

"It ain't full," Granny pointed out. "It's wossname. Bulging."

"Gibbous," said Nanny obligingly.

"I think it's in praise of full moons in general," Magrat hazarded. "And then we have to raise our consciousness. It really ought to be full moon for that, I'm afraid. Moons are very important."

Granny gave her a long, calculating look.

"That's modern witchcraft for you, is it?" she said.

"It's part of it, Granny. There's a lot more."

Granny Weatherwax sighed. "Each to her own, I suppose. I'm blowed if I'll let a ball of shiny rock tell *me* what to do."

"Yes, bugger all that," said Nanny. "Let's curse somebody."

The Fool crept cautiously along the nighttime corridors. He wasn't taking any chances either. Magrat had given him a graphic account of Greebo's general disposition, and the Fool had borrowed a couple of gloves and a sort of metal wimple from the castle's store of hereditary chain mail.

He reached the lumber room, lifted the latch cautiously, pushed the door and then flung himself against the wall.

The corridor became slightly darker as the more intense darkness inside the room spilled out and mingled with the rather lighter darkness already there.

Apart from that, nothing. The number of spitting, enraged balls of murderous fur pouring through the door was zero. The Fool relaxed, and slipped inside.

Greebo dropped on his head.

It had been a long day. The room did not offer the kind of full life that Greebo had come to expect and demand. The only point of interest had been the discovery, around mid-morning, of a colony of mice who had spent generations eating their way through a priceless tapestry history of Lancre and had just got as far as King Murune (709–745), who met a terrible fate,* when they did, too. He had sharpened his claws on a bust of Lancre's only royal vampire, Queen Grimnir the Impaler (1514–1553, 1553–1557, 1557–1562, 1562–1567 and 1568–1573). He had performed his morning ablutions on a portrait of an unknown monarch, which was beginning to dissolve. Now he was bored, and also angry.

He raked his claws across the place where the Fool's ears should have been, and was rewarded with nothing more than a metallic scraping noise.

"Who's a good boy, den?" said the Fool. "Wowsa wowsa whoosh."

This intrigued Greebo. The only other person who had ever spoken to him like this was Nanny Ogg; everyone else addressed him as "Yarrgeroffou-tofityahbarstard." He leaned down very carefully, intrigued by the new experience.

From the Fool's point of view an upside-down cat face lowered itself slowly into his field of vision, wearing an expression of evil-eyed interest.

"Does oo want to go home, den?" said the Fool hopefully. "Look, Mr. Door is *open*."

Greebo increased his grip. He had found a friend.

The Fool shrugged, very carefully, turned, and walked back into the passage. He made his way down through the hall, out into the courtyard,

---

* Involving a red hot poker, a privy, ten pounds of live eels, a three mile stretch of frozen river, a butt of wine, a couple of tulip bulbs, a number of poisoned eardrops, an oyster and a large man with a mallet. King Murune didn't make friends easily.

around the side of the guardroom and out through the main gate, nodding—carefully—to the guards.

"Man just went past with a cat on his head," one of them remarked, after a minute or two's reflection.

"See who it was?"

"The Fool, I think."

There was a thoughtful pause. The second guard shifted his grip on his halberd.

"It's a rotten job," he said. "But I suppose someone's got to do it."

"We ain't going to curse anyone," said Granny firmly. "It hardly ever works if they don't know you've done it."

"What you do is, you send him a doll of himself with pins in."

"No, Gytha."

"All you have to do is get hold of some of his toenails," Nanny persisted, enthusiastically.

"No."

"Or some of his hair or anything. I've got some pins."

"*No.*"

"Cursing people is morally unsound and extremely bad for your karma," said Magrat.

"Well, I'm going to curse him anyway," said Nanny. "Under my breath, like. I could of caught my death in that dungeon for all he cared."

"We ain't going to curse him," said Granny. "We're going to replace him. What did you do with the old king?"

"I left the rock on the kitchen table," said Nanny. "I couldn't stand it anymore."

"I don't see why," said Magrat. "He seemed very pleasant. For a ghost."

"Oh, *he* was all right. It was the others," said Nanny.

"Others?"

"'Pray carry a stone out of the palace so's I can haunt it, good mother,' he says," said Nanny Ogg. "'It's bloody boring in here, Mistress Ogg, excuse my Klatchian,' he says, so of course I did. I reckon they was all listening. Ho yes, they all thinks, all aboard, time for a bit of a holiday. I've nothing against ghosts. Especially royal ghosts," she added loyally. "But my cottage isn't the place for them. I mean, there's some woman in a chariot yelling her head off in the washhouse. I ask you. And there's a couple of little kiddies in the pantry, and men without heads all over the place, and someone screaming under the sink, and there's this little hairy man wandering around looking lost and everything. It's not right."

"Just so long as he's not here," said Granny. "We don't want any men around."

"He's a ghost, not a man," said Magrat.

"We don't have to go into details," Granny said icily.

"But you can't put the old king back on the throne," said Magrat. "Ghosts can't rule. You'd never get the crown to stay on. It'd drop through."

"We're going to replace him with his son," said Granny. "Proper succession."

"Oh, we've been through all that," said Nanny, dismissively. "In about fifteen years' time, perhaps, but—"

"Tonight," said Granny.

"A child on the throne? He wouldn't last five minutes."

"Not a child," said Granny quietly. "A grown man. Remember Aliss Demurrage?"

There was silence. Then Nanny Ogg sat back.

"Bloody hell," she whispered. "You ain't going to try that, are you?"

"I mean to have a go."

"Bloody hell," said Nanny again, very quietly, and added, "you've been thinking about this, have you?"

"Yes."

"See here, Esme. I mean, Black Aliss was one of the best. I mean, you're very good at, well, headology and thinking and that. I mean, Black Aliss, well, she just upped and went at it."

"You saying I couldn't do it, are you?"

"Excuse me," said Magrat.

"No. No. Of course not," said Nanny, ignoring her. "Right."

"Only . . . well, she was a, you know, a hoyden of witches, like the king said."

"Doyenne," said Granny, who had looked it up. "Not hoyden."

"Excuse me," said Magrat, louder this time. "Who was Black Aliss? And," she added quickly, "none of this exchanging meaningful glances and talking over my head. There's three witches in this coven, remember?"

"She was before your time," said Nanny Ogg. "Before mine, really. She lived over Skund way. Very powerful witch."

"If you listen to rumor," said Granny.

"She turned a pumpkin into a royal coach once," said Nanny.

"Showy," said Granny Weatherwax. "That's no help to anyone, turning up at a ball smelling like a pie. And that business with the glass slipper. Dangerous, to my mind."

"But the biggest thing she ever did," said Nanny, ignoring the interruption, "was to send a whole palace to sleep for a hundred years until . . ." She hesitated. "Can't remember. Was there rose bushes involved, or was it spinning wheels in that one? I think some princess had to finger . . . no, there was a prince. That was it."

"Finger a prince?" said Magrat, uneasily.

"No . . . he had to kiss her. Very romantic, Black Aliss was. There was always a bit of romance in her spells. She liked nothing better than Girl meets Frog."

"Why did they call her Black Aliss?"

"Fingernails," said Granny.

"And teeth," said Nanny Ogg. "She had a sweet tooth. Lived in a real gingerbread cottage. Couple of kids shoved her in her own oven at the end. Shocking."

"And you're going to send the castle to sleep?" said Magrat.

"She never sent the castle to sleep," said Granny. "That's just an old wives' tale," she added, glaring at Nanny. "She just stirred up time a little. It's not as hard as people think. Everyone does it all the time. It's like rubber, is time. You can stretch it to suit yourself."

Magrat was about to say, that's not right, time is time, every second lasts a second, that's what it's for, that's its *job* . . .

And then she recalled weeks that had flown past and afternoons that had lasted forever. Some minutes had lasted hours, some hours had gone past so quickly she hadn't been aware they'd gone past at all . . .

"But that's just people's perception," she said. "Isn't it?"

"Oh, yes," said Granny, "of course it is. It all is. What difference does that make?"

"A hundred years'd be over-egging it, mind," said Nanny.

"I reckon fifteen'd be a nice around number," said Granny. "That means the lad will be eighteen at the finish. We just do the spell, go and fetch him, he can manifest his destiny, and everything will be nice and neat."

Magrat didn't comment on this, because it had occurred to her that destinies sounded easy enough when you talked about them but were never very bankable where real human beings were concerned. But Nanny Ogg sat back and tipped another generous measure of apple brandy in her tea.

"Could work out nice," she said. "A bit of peace and quiet for fifteen years. If I recall the spell, after you say it you have to fly around the castle before cock crow."

"I wasn't thinking about that," said Granny. "It wouldn't be right. Felmet would still be king all that time. The kingdom would still get sick. No, what I was thinking of doing was moving the whole kingdom."

She beamed at them.

"The whole of Lancre?" said Nanny.

"Yes."

"Fifteen years into the future?"

"Yes."

Nanny looked at Granny's broomstick. It was a well-made thing, built to last, apart from the occasional starting problem. But there were limits.

"You'll never do it," she said. "Not around the whole kingdom in that. That's all the way up to Powderknife and down to Drumlin's Fell. You just couldn't carry enough magic."

"I've thought of that," said Granny.

She beamed again. It was terrifying.

She explained the plan. It was dreadful.

A minute later the moor was deserted, as the witches hurried to their tasks. It was silent for a while, apart from the squeak of bats and the occasional rustle of the wind in the heather.

Then there was a bubbling from the nearby peat bog. Very slowly, crowned with a thicket of sphagnum moss, the standing stone surfaced and peered around the landscape with an air of deep distrust.

Greebo was really enjoying this. At first he thought his new friend was taking him to Magrat's cottage, but for some reason he'd wandered off the path in the dark and was taking a stroll in the forest. In one of the more interesting bits, Greebo had always felt. It was a hummocky area, rich in hidden potholes and small, intense swamps, full of mist even in fine weather. Greebo often came up here on the off-chance that a wolf was lying up for the day.

"I thought cats could find their own way home," the Fool muttered.

He cursed himself under his breath. It would have been easy to take this wretched creature back to Nanny Ogg's house, which was only a few streets away, almost in the shadow of the castle. But then he'd had the idea of delivering it to Magrat. It would impress her, he thought. Witches were very keen on cats. And then she'd be bound to ask him in, for a cup of tea or something . . .

He put his foot in another water-filled hole. Something wriggled underneath it. The Fool groaned, and stepped back onto a tumescent mushroom.

"Look, cat," he said. "You've got to come down, right? And then you can find your way home and I'll follow you. Cats are good at seeing in the dark and finding their own way home," he added hopefully.

He reached up. Greebo sank his claws into his arm as a friendly warning, and found to his surprise that this had no effect on chain mail.

"There's a good cat," said the Fool, and lowered him to the ground. "Go on, find your way home. Any home will do."

Greebo's grin gradually faded, until there was nothing left but the cat. This was nearly as spooky as the opposite way around.

He stretched and yawned to hide his embarrassment. Being called a good cat in the middle of one of his favorite stalking grounds wasn't going to do anything for his prowl-credibility. He disappeared into the undergrowth.

The Fool peered into the gloom. It dawned on him that while he liked forests, he liked them at one remove, as it were; it was nice to know that they were there, but the forests of the mind were not quite the same as real forests that, for example, you got lost in. They had more mighty oaks and fewer brambles. They also tended to be viewed in daylight, and the trees didn't have malevolent faces and long scratchy branches. The trees of the imagination were proud giants of the forest. Most of the trees here appeared to be vegetable gnomes, mere trellises for fungi and ivy.

The Fool was vaguely aware that you could tell which direction the Hub lay by seeing which side of the trees the moss grew on. A quick inspection of the nearby trunks indicated that, in defiance of all normal geography, the Hub lay everywhere.

Greebo had vanished.

The Fool sighed, removed his chain mail protection, and tinkled gently through the night in search of high ground. High ground seemed a good idea. The ground he was on at the moment appeared to be trembling. He was sure it shouldn't do that.

Magrat hovered on her broomstick several hundred feet above the Turnwise borders of Lancre, looking down on a sea of mist through which the occasional treetop poked like a seaweed-covered rock at high tide. A bulging moon floated above her, probably gibbous again. Even a decent thin crescent would have been better, she felt. More appropriate.

She shivered, and wondered where Granny Weatherwax was at this moment.

The old witch's broomstick was known and feared throughout the skies of Lancre. Granny had been introduced to flying quite late in life, and after some initial suspicion had taken to it like a bluebottle to an ancient fish head. A problem, however, was that Granny saw every flight simply as a straight line from A to B and was unable to get alongside the idea that other users of the air might have any rights whatsoever; the flight migration patterns of an entire continent had been changed because of that simple fact. High-speed evolution among local birds had developed a generation that flew on their backs, so that they could keep a watchful eye on the skies.

Granny's implicit belief that everything should get out of her way extended to other witches, very tall trees and, on occasion, mountains.

Granny had also browbeaten the dwarfs who lived under the mountains and in fear of their lives into speeding the thing up. Many an egg had been laid in midair by unsuspecting fowls who had suddenly glimpsed Granny bearing down on them, scowling over the top of the broomstick.

"Oh dear," thought Magrat. "I hope she hasn't happened to someone."

A midnight breeze turned her gently around in the air, like an unsupported weathercock. She shivered and squinted at the moonlit mountains, the high Ramtops, whose freezing crags and ice-green chasms acknowledged no king or cartographer. Only on the Rimward side was Lancre open to the world; the rest of its borders looked as jagged as a wolf's mouth and far more impassable. From up here it was possible to see the whole kingdom . . .

There was a ripping noise in the sky above her, a blast of wind that spun her around again, and a Doppler-distorted cry of, "Stop dreaming, girl!"

She gripped the bristles with her knees and urged the stick upward.

It took several minutes to catch up with Granny, who was lying almost full length along her broomstick to reduce wind resistance. Dark treetops roared far below them as Magrat came alongside. Granny turned to her, holding her hat on with one hand.

"Not before time," she snapped. "I don't reckon this one's got more'n a few minutes flight left. Come on, get a move on."

She reached out a hand. So did Magrat. Unsteadily, the broomsticks bucking and dipping in one another's slipstream, they touched fingertips.

Magrat's arm tingled as the power flowed up it.* Granny's broomstick jerked forward.

"Leave me a bit," shouted Magrat. "I've got to get down!"

"Shouldn't be difficult," screamed Granny, above the noise of the wind.

---

* Possibly the first attempt at the in-flight refuelling of a broomstick.

"I mean get down safely!"

"You're a witch, ain't you? By the way, did you bring the cocoa? I'm freezing up here!"

Magrat nodded desperately, and with her spare hand passed up a straw bag.

"Right," said Granny. "Well done. See you at Lancre Bridge."

She uncurled her fingers.

Magrat whirled away in the buffeting wind, clinging tightly to a broomstick which now, she feared, had about as much buoyancy as a bit of firewood. It certainly wasn't capable of sustaining a full-grown woman against the beckoning fingers of gravity.

As she plunged down toward the forest roof in a long shallow dive she reflected that there was possibly something complimentary in the way Granny Weatherwax resolutely refused to consider other people's problems. It implied that, in her considerable opinion, they were quite capable of sorting them out by themselves.

Some kind of Change spell was probably in order.

Magrat concentrated.

Well, that seemed to work.

Nothing in the sight of mortal man had in fact changed. What Magrat had achieved was a mere adjustment of the mental processes, from a bewildered and slightly frightened woman gliding inexorably toward the inhospitable ground to a clearheaded, optimistic and positive thinking woman who had really got it together, was taking full responsibility for her own life and in general knew where she was coming from although, unfortunately, where she was *heading* had not changed in any way. But she felt a lot better about it.

She dug her heels in and forced the broomstick to yield the last dregs of its power in a brief burst, sending it skimming erratically a few feet from the trees. As it sagged again and started to plow a furrow among the midnight leaves she tensed herself, prayed to whatever gods of the forest might be listening that she would land on something soft, and let go.

There are three thousand known major gods on the Disc, and research theologians discover more every week. Apart from the minor gods of rock, tree and water, there are two that haunt the Ramtops—Hoki, half a man, half a goat, and entirely a bad practical joker, who was banished from Dunmanifestin for pulling the old exploding mistletoe joke on Blind Io, chief of all the gods; and also Herne the Hunted, the terrified and apprehensive deity of all small furry creatures whose destiny it is to end their lives as a brief, crunchy squeak . . .

Either could have been candidates for the small miracle which then occurred, for—in a forest full of cold rocks, jagged stumps and thorn bushes—Magrat landed on something soft.

Granny, meanwhile, was accelerating toward the mountains on the second leg of the journey. She consumed the regrettably tepid cocoa and, with proper environmental consideration, dropped the bottle as she passed over an upland lake.

It turned out that Magrat's idea of sustaining food was two rounds of egg and cress sandwiches with the crusts cut off and, Granny noticed before the wind whipped it away, a small piece of parsley placed with consideration and care on top of each one. Granny regarded them for some time. Then she ate them.

A chasm loomed, still choked with winter snow. Like a tiny spark in the darkness, a dot of light against the hugeness of the Ramtops, Granny tackled the maze of the mountains.

Back in the forest, Magrat sat up and absentmindedly pulled a twig from her hair. A few yards away the broomstick dropped through the trees, showering leaves.

A groan and a small, half-hearted tinkle caused her to peer into the gloom. An indistinct figure was on its hands and knees, searching for something.

"Did I land on you?" said Magrat.

"Someone did," said the Fool.

They crawled nearer to one another.

"You?"

"You!"

"What are you doing here?"

"Marry, I was walking along the ground," said the Fool. "A lot of people do, you know. I mean, I know it's been done before. It's not original. It probably lacks imagination but, well, it's always been good enough for me."

"Did I hurt you?"

"I think I've got one or two bells that won't be the same again."

The Fool scrabbled through the leafmould, and finally located his hated hat. It clonked.

"Totally crushed, i'faith," he said, putting it on

anyway. He seemed to feel better for that, and went on, "Rain, yes, hail, yes, even lumps of rock. Fish and small frogs, OK. Women no, up till now. Is it going to happen again?"

"You've got a bloody hard head," said Magrat, pulling herself to her feet.

"Modesty forbids me to comment," said the Fool, and then remembered himself and added, quickly, "Prithee."

They stared at one another again, their minds racing.

Magrat thought: Nanny said look at him properly. I'm looking at him. He just looks the same. A sad thin little man in a ridiculous jester's outfit, he's practically a hunchback.

Then, in the same way that a few random bulges in a cloud can suddenly become a galleon or a whale in the eye of the beholder, Magrat realized that the Fool was not a little man. He was at least of average height, but he *made* himself small, by hunching his shoulders, bandying his legs and walking in a half-crouch that made him appear as though he was capering on the spot.

I wonder what else Gytha Ogg noticed? she thought, intrigued.

He rubbed his arm and gave her a lopsided grin.

"I suppose you haven't got any idea where we are?" he said.

"Witches never get lost," said Magrat firmly. "Although they can become temporarily mislaid. Lancre's over *that* way, I think. I've got to find a hill, if you'll excuse me."

"To see where you are?"

"To see when, I think. There's a lot of magic going on tonight."

"Is there? Then I think I'll accompany you," the Fool added chivalrously, after peering cautiously into the tree-haunted gloom that apparently lay between him and his flagstones. "I wouldn't want anything to happen to you."

Granny lay low over the broomstick as it plunged through the trackless chasms of the mountains, leaning from side to side in the hope that this might have some effect on the steering which seemed, strangely, to be getting worse. Falling snow behind her was whipped and spiraled into odd shapes by the wind of her passage. Rearing waves of crusted snow, poised all winter over the glacial valleys, trembled and then began the long, silent fall. Her flight was punctuated by the occasional boom of an avalanche.

She looked down at a landscape of sudden death and jagged beauty, and knew it was looking back at her, as a dozing man may watch a mosquito. She wondered if it realized what she was doing. She wondered if it'd make her fall any softer, and mentally scolded herself for such softness. No, the land wasn't like that. It didn't bargain. The land gave hard, and took hard. A dog always bit deepest on the veterinary hand.

And then she was through, vaulting so low over the last peak that one of her boots filled with snow, and barrelling down toward the lowlands.

The mist, never far away in the mountains, was

back again, but this time it was making a fight of it and had become a thick, silver sea in front of her. She groaned.

Somewhere in the middle of it Nanny Ogg floated, taking the occasional pull from a hip flask as a preventative against the chill.

And thus it was that Granny, her hat and iron-gray hair dripping with moisture, her boots shedding lumps of ice, heard the distant and muffled sound of a voice enthusiastically explaining to the invisible sky that the hedgehog had less to worry over than just about any other mammal. Like a hawk that has spotted something small and fluffy in the grass, like a wandering interstellar flu germ that has just seen a nice blue planet drifting by, Granny turned the stick and plunged down through the choking billows.

"Come on!" she screamed, drunk with speed and exhilaration, and the sound from five hundred feet overhead put a passing wolf severely off its supper. "This minute, Gytha Ogg!"

Nanny Ogg caught her hand with considerable reluctance and the pair of broomsticks swept up again and into the clear, starlit sky.

The Disc, as always, gave the impression that the Creator has designed it specifically to be looked at from above. Streamers of cloud in white and silver stretched away to the Rim, stirred into thousand-mile swirls by the turning of the world. Behind the speeding brooms the sullen roof of the fog was dragged up into a curling tunnel of white vapor, so that the watching gods—and they were certainly watching—could see the terrible flight as a furrow in the sky.

A thousand feet and rising fast into the frosty air, the two witches were bickering again.

"It was a bloody stupid idea," moaned Nanny. "I never liked heights."

"Did you bring something to drink?"

"Certainly. You said."

"Well?"

"I drank it, didn't I," said Nanny. "Sitting around up there at my age. Our Jason would have a fit."

Granny gritted her teeth. "Well, let's have the power," she said. "I'm running out of up. Amazing how—"

Granny's voice ended in a scream as, without any warning at all, her broomstick pinwheeled sharply across the clouds and dropped from sight.

The Fool and Magrat sat on a log on a small outcrop that looked out across the forest. The lights of Lancre town were in fact not very far away, but neither of them had suggested leaving.

The air between them crackled with unspoken thoughts and wild surmisings.

"You've been a Fool long?" said Magrat, politely. She blushed in the darkness. In that atmosphere it sounded the most impolite of questions.

"All my life," said the Fool bitterly. "I cut my teeth on a set of bells."

"I suppose it gets handed on, from father to son?" said Magrat.

"I never saw much of my father. He went off to

be Fool for the Lords of Quirm when I was small," said the Fool. "Had a row with my grandad. He comes back from time to time, to see my mam."

"That's terrible."

There was a sad jingle as the Fool shrugged. He vaguely recalled his father as a short, friendly little man, with eyes like a couple of oysters. Doing something as brave as standing up to the old boy must have been quite outside his nature. The sound of two suits of bells shaken in anger still haunted his memory, which was full enough of bad scenes as it was.

"Still," said Magrat, her voice higher than usual and with a vibrato of uncertainty, "it must be a happy life. Making people laugh, I mean."

When there was no reply she turned to look at the man. His face was like stone. In a low voice, talking as though she was not there, the Fool spoke.

He spoke of the Guild of Fools and Joculators in Ankh-Morpork.

Most visitors mistook it at first sight for the offices of the Guild of Assassins, which in fact was the rather pleasant, airy collection of buildings next door (the Assassins always had plenty of money); sometimes the young Fools, slaving at their rote in rooms that were always freezing, even in high summer, heard the young Assassins at play over the wall and envied them, even though, of course, the number of piping voices grew noticeably fewer toward the end of them (the Assassins also believed in competitive examination).

In fact all sorts of sounds managed to breach the

high grim windowless walls, and from keen questioning of servants the younger Fools picked up a vision of the city beyond. There were taverns out there, and parks. There was a whole bustling world, in which the students and apprentices of the various Guilds and Colleges took a full ripe part, either by playing tricks on it, running through it shouting, or throwing parts of it up. There was laughter which paid no attention to the Five Cadences or Twelve Inflections. And—although the students debated this news in the dormitories at night—there was apparently unauthorized humor, delivered freestyle, with no reference to the *Monster Fun Book* or the Council or anyone.

Out there, beyond the stained stonework, people were telling jokes without reference to the Lords of Misrule.

It was a sobering thought. Well, not a sobering thought in actual fact, because alcohol wasn't allowed in the Guild. But if it was, it would have been.

There was nowhere more sober than the Guild.

The Fool spoke bitterly of the huge, redfaced Brother Prankster, of evenings learning the Merry Jests, of long mornings in the freezing gymnasium learning the Eighteen Pratfalls and the accepted trajectory for a custard pie. And juggling. Juggling! Brother Jape, a man with a soul like cold boiled string, taught juggling. It wasn't that the Fool was bad at juggling that reduced him to incoherent fury. Fools were *expected* to be bad at juggling, especially if juggling inherently funny items like custard pies, flaming torches or extremely sharp cleavers. What had Brother Jape laying about him in red-hot, clanging rage was the fact that the Fool was bad at juggling *because he wasn't any good at it.*

"Didn't you want to be anything else?" said Magrat.

"What else is there?" said the Fool. "I haven't seen anything else I could be."

Student Fools were allowed out, in the last year of training, but under a fearsome set of restrictions. Capering miserably through the streets he'd seen wizards for the first time, moving like dignified carnival floats. He'd seen the surviving assassins, foppish, giggling young men in black silk, as sharp as knives underneath; he'd seen priests, their fantastic costumes only slightly marred by the long rubber sacrificial aprons they wore for major services. Every trade and profession had its costume, he saw, and he realized for the first time that the uniform he was wearing had been carefully and meticulously designed for no other purpose than making its wearer look like a complete and utter pillock.

Even so, he'd persevered. He'd spent his whole life persevering.

He persevered precisely because he had absolutely no talent, and because grandfather would have flayed him alive if he didn't. He memorized the authorized jokes until his head rang, and got up even earlier in the morning to juggle until his elbows creaked. He had perfected his grasp of the comic vocabulary until only the very senior Lords could understand him. He'd capered and clowned with an impenetrable grim determination and he'd graduated top of his year and had been awarded the Bladder of Honor. He'd dropped it down the privy when he came home.

Magrat was silent.

The Fool said, "How did you get to be a witch?"

"Um?"

"I mean, did you go to a school or something?"

"Oh. No. Goodie Whemper just walked down to the village one day, got all us girls lined up, and chose me. You don't choose the Craft, you see. It chooses you."

"Yes, but when do you actually become a witch?"

"When the other witches treat you as one, I suppose." Magrat sighed. "If they ever do," she added. "I thought they would after I did that spell in the corridor. It was pretty good, after all."

"Marry, 'twas a rite of passage," said the Fool, unable to stop himself. Magrat gave him a blank look. He coughed.

"The other witches being those two old ladies?" he said, relapsing into his usual gloom.

"Yes."

"Very strong characters, I imagine."

"Very," said Magrat, with feeling.

"I wonder if they ever met my grandad," said the Fool.

Magrat looked at her feet.

"They're quite nice really," she said. "It's just that, well, when you're a witch you don't think about other people. I mean, you *think* about them, but you don't actually think about their feelings, if you see what I mean. At least, not unless you think about it." She looked at her feet again.

"You're not like that," said the Fool.

"Look, I wish you'd stop working for the duke," said Magrat desperately. "You know what he's like. Torturing people and setting fire to their cottages and everything."

"But I'm his Fool," said the Fool. "A Fool has to be loyal to his master. Right up until he dies. I'm afraid it's tradition. Tradition is very important."

"But you don't even like being a Fool!"

"I hate it. But that's got nothing to do with it. If I've got to be a Fool, I'll do it properly."

"That's really stupid," said Magrat.

"Foolish, I'd prefer."

The Fool had been edging along the log. "If I kiss you," he added carefully, "do I turn into a frog?"

Magrat looked down at her feet again. They shuffled themselves under her dress, embarrassed at all this attention.

She could sense the shades of Gytha Ogg and Esme Weatherwax on either side of her. Granny's specter glared at her. *A witch is master of every situation*, it said.

Mistress, said the vision of Nanny Ogg, and made a brief gesture involving much grinning and waving of forearms.

"We shall have to see," she said.

It was destined to be the most impressive kiss in the history of foreplay.

Time, as Granny Weatherwax had pointed out, is

a subjective experience. The Fool's years in the Guild had been an eternity whereas the hours with Magrat on the hilltop passed like a couple of minutes. And, high above Lancre, a double handful of seconds extended like taffy into hours of screaming terror.

"Ice!" screamed Granny. "It's iced up!"

Nanny Ogg came alongside, trying vainly to match courses with the tumbling, bucking broomstick. Octarine fire crackled over the frozen bristles, shorting them out at random. She leaned over and snatched a handful of Granny's skirt.

"I tole you it was daft!" she shouted. "You went all through all that wet mist and then up into the cold air, you daft besom!"

"You let go of my skirt, Gytha Ogg!"

"Come on, grab hold o'mine. You're on fire at the back there!"

They shot through the bottom of the cloud bank and screamed in unison as the shrub-covered ground emerged from nowhere and aimed itself directly at them.

And *went past*.

Nanny looked down a black perspective at the bottom of which a boil of white water was dimly visible. They had flown over the edge of Lancre Gorge.

Blue smoke was pouring out of Granny's broomstick but she hung on, determined, and forced it around.

"What the hell you doing?" roared Nanny.

"I can follow the river," Granny Weatherwax screamed, above the crackle of flames. "Don't you worry!"

"You come aboard, d'you hear? It's all over, you can't do it . . ."

There was a small explosion behind Granny and several handfuls of burning bristles broke off and whirled away into the booming depths of the gorge. Her stick jerked sideways and Nanny grabbed her around the shoulders as a gout of fire snapped another binding.

The blazing broomstick shot from between her legs, twisted in the air, and went straight upward, trailing sparks and making a noise like a wet finger dragged around the top of a wineglass.

This left Nanny flying upside down, supporting Granny Weatherwax at arm's length. They stared into one another's face and screamed.

"I can't pull you up!"

"Well I can't climb up, can I? Act your age, Gytha!"

Nanny considered this. Then she let go.

Three marriages and an adventurous girlhood had left Nanny Ogg with thigh muscles that could crack coconuts, and the G-forces sucked at her as she forced the speeding stick down and around in a tight loop.

Ahead of her she made out Granny Weatherwax dropping like a stone, one hand clutching her hat, the other trying to prevent gravity from seeing up her skirts. She urged the stick forward until it creaked, snatched the falling witch around the waist, fought the plunging stick back up to level flight, and sagged.

The subsequent silence was broken by Granny

Weatherwax saying, "Don't you ever do that again, Gytha Ogg."

"I promise."

"Now turn us around. We're heading for Lancre Bridge, remember?"

Nanny obediently turned the broomstick, brushing the canyon walls as she did so.

"It's still miles to go," she said.

"I mean to do it," said Granny. "There's plenty of night left."

"Not enough, I'm thinking."

"A witch doesn't know the meaning of the word 'failure,' Gytha."

They shot up into the clear air again. The horizon was a line of golden light as the slow dawn of the Disc sped across the land, bulldozing the suburbs of the night.

"Esme?" said Nanny Ogg, after a while.

"What?"

"It means 'lack of success.'"

They flew in chilly silence for several seconds.

"I was speaking wossname. Figuratively," said Granny.

"Oh. Well. You should of said."

The line of light was bigger, brighter. For the first time a flicker of doubt invaded Granny Weatherwax's mind, puzzled to find itself in such unfamiliar surroundings.

"I wonder how many cockerels there are in Lancre?" she said quietly.

"Was that one of them wossname questions?"

"I was just wondering."

Nanny Ogg sat back. There were thirty-two of crowing age, she knew. She knew because she'd worked it out last night—*tonight*—and had given Jason his instructions. She had fifteen grown-up children and innumerable grandchildren and great-grandchildren, and they'd had most of the evening to get into position. It should be enough.

"Did you hear that?" said Granny. "Over Razorback way?"

Nanny looked innocently across the misty landscape. Sound traveled very clearly in these early hours.

"What?" she said.

"Sort of an 'urk' noise?"

"No."

Granny spun around.

"Over there," she said. "I definitely heard it this time. Something like 'cock-a-doo-arrgh.'"

"Can't say I did, Esme," said Nanny, smiling at the sky. "Lancre Bridge up ahead."

"And over there! Right down there! It was a definite squawk!"

"Dawn chorus, Esme, I expect. Look, only half a mile to go."

Granny glared at the back of her colleague's head.

"There's something going on here," she said.

"Search me, Esme."

"Your shoulders are shaking!"

"Lost my shawl back there. I'm a bit chilly. Look, we're nearly there."

Granny glared ahead, her mind a maze of suspicions. She was going to get to the bottom of this. When she had time.

The damp logs of Lancre's main link to the outside world drifted gently underneath them. From the chicken farm half a mile away came a chorus of strangled squawks and a thud.

"And that? What was that, then?" demanded Granny.

"Fowl pest. Careful, I'm bringing us down."

"Are you laughing at me?"

"Just pleased for you, Esme. You'll go down in history for this, you know."

They drifted between the timbers of the bridge. Granny Weatherwax alighted cautiously on the greasy planking and adjusted her dress.

"Yes. Well," she added, nonchalantly.

"Better than Black Aliss, everyone'll say," Nanny Ogg went on.

"Some people will say anything," said Granny. She peered over the parapet at the foaming torrent far below, and then up at the distant outcrop on which stood Lancre Castle.

"Do you think they will?" she added, nonchalantly.

"Mark my words."

"Hmm."

"But you've got to complete the spell, mind."

Granny Weatherwax nodded. She turned to face the dawn, raised her arms, and completed the spell.

It is almost impossible to convey the sudden passage of fifteen years and two months in words.

It's a lot easier in pictures, when you just use a calendar with lots of pages blowing off, or a clock with hands moving faster and faster until they blur, or trees bursting into blossom and fruiting in a matter of seconds . . .

Well, *you* know. Or the sun becomes a fiery streak across the sky, and days and nights flicker past jerkily like a bad zoetrope, and the fashions visible in the clothes shop across the road whip on and off faster than a lunchtime stripper with five pubs to do.

There are any amount of ways, but they won't be required because, in fact, none of this happened.

The sun *did* jerk sideways a bit, and it seemed that the trees on the rimward side of the gorge were rather taller, and Nanny couldn't shake off the sensation that someone had just sat down heavily on her, squashed her flat, and then opened her out again.

This was because the kingdom did not, in so many words, move through time in the normal flickering sky, high-speed photography sense of the word. It moved around it, which is much cleaner, considerably easier to achieve, and saves all that traveling around trying to find a laboratory opposite a dress shop that will keep the same dummy in the window for sixty years, which has traditionally been the most time-consuming and expensive bit of the whole business.

The kiss lasted more than fifteen years.

Not even frogs can manage that.

The Fool drew back, his eyes glazed, his expression one of puzzlement.

"Did you feel the world move?" he said.

Magrat peered over his shoulder at the forest.

"I think she's done it," she said.

"Done what?"

Magrat hesitated. "Oh. Nothing. Nothing much, really."

"Shall we have another try? I don't think we got it quite right that time."

Magrat nodded.

This time it lasted only fifteen seconds. It seemed longer.

A tremor ran through the castle, shaking the breakfast tray from which the Duke Felmet, much to his relief, was eating porridge that wasn't too salty.

It was felt by the ghosts that now filled Nanny Ogg's cottage like a rugby team in a telephone box.

It spread to every henhouse in the kingdom, and a number of hands relaxed their grip. And thirty-two purple-faced cockerels took a deep breath and crowed like maniacs, but they were too late, too late . . .

"I still reckon you were up to something," said Granny Weatherwax.

"Have another cup of tea," said Nanny pleasantly.

"You won't go and put any drink in it, will you," Granny said flatly. "It was the drink what did it last night. I would never have put myself forward like that. It's shameful."

"Black Aliss never done anything like it," said

Nanny, encouragingly. "I mean, it was a hundred years, all right, but it was only one castle she moved. I reckon anyone could do a castle."

Granny's frown puckered at the edge.

"And she let all weeds grow over it," she observed primly.

"Right enough."

"Very well done," said King Verence, eagerly. "We all thought it was superb. Being in the ethereal plane, of course, we were in a position to observe closely."

"Very good, your graciousness," said Nanny Ogg. She turned and observed the crowding ghosts behind him, who hadn't been granted the privilege of sitting at, or partly through, the kitchen table.

"But you lot can bugger off back to the outhouse," she said. "The cheek! Except the kiddies, they can stay," she added. "Poor little mites."

"I am afraid it feels so good to be out of the castle," said the king.

Granny Weatherwax yawned.

"Anyway," she said, "we've got to find the boy now. That's the next step."

"We shall look for him directly after lunch."

"Lunch?"

"It's chicken," said Nanny. "And you're tired. Besides, making a decent search will take a long time."

"He'll be in Ankh-Morpork," said Granny. "Mark my words. Everyone ends up there. We'll start with Ankh-Morpork. You don't have to search for people when destiny is involved, you just wait for them in Ankh-Morpork."

Nanny brightened up. "Our Karen got married to an innkeeper from there," she said. "I haven't seen the baby yet. We could get free board and everything."

"We needn't actually go. The whole point is that he should come *here*. There's something about that city," said Granny. "It's like a drain."

"It's five hundred miles away!" said Magrat. "You'll be away for ages!"

"I can't help it," said the Fool. "The duke's given me special instructions. He trusts me."

"Huh! To hire more soldiers, I expect?"

"No. Nothing like that. Not as bad as that." The Fool hesitated. He'd introduced Felmet to the world of words. Surely that was better than hitting people with swords? Wouldn't that buy time? Wouldn't it be best for everybody, in the circumstances?

"But you don't have to go! You don't *want* to go!"

"That doesn't have much to do with it. I promised to be loyal to him—"

"Yes, yes, until you're dead. But you don't even *believe* that! You were telling me how much you hated the whole Guild and everything!"

"Well, yes. But I still have to do it. I gave my word."

Magrat came close to stamping her foot, but didn't sink so low.

"Just when we were getting to know one another!" she shouted. "You're pathetic!"

The Fool's eyes narrowed. "I'd only be pathetic if I broke my word," he said. "But I may be incredibly ill-advized. I'm sorry. I'll be back in a few weeks, anyway."

"Don't you understand I'm asking you not to listen to him?"

"I said I'm sorry. I couldn't see you again before I go, could I?"

"I shall be washing my hair," said Magrat stiffly.

"When?"

"Whenever!"

Hwel pinched the bridge of his nose and squinted wearily at the wax-spattered paper.

The play wasn't going at all well.

He'd sorted out the falling chandelier, and found a place for a villain who wore a mask to conceal his disfigurement, and he'd rewritten one of the funny bits to allow for the fact that the hero had been born in a handbag. It was the clowns who were giving him trouble again. They kept changing every time he thought about them. He preferred them in twos, that was traditional, but now there seemed to be a third one, and he was blowed if he could think of any funny lines for him.

His quill moved scratchily over the latest sheet of paper, trying to catch the voices that had streamed through his dreaming mind and had seemed so funny at the time.

His tongue began to stick out of the corner of his mouth. He was sweating.

This iss My Little Study, he wrote. *Hey, with a Little Study youe could goe a Long Way. And I wishe youed start now. Iffe You can't leave yn a Cab then leave yn a Huff. Iff thates too soone, thenn leave yn a minute and a Huff. Say, have you Gott a Pensil? A crayon?*—

Hwel stared at this in horror. On the page it looked nonsensical, ridiculous. And yet, and yet, in the thronged auditorium of his mind . . .

He dipped the quill in the inkpot, and chased the echoes further.

Seconde Clown: Atsa right, Boss.

Third Clowne: [businesse with bladder on stick] *Honk. Honk.*

Hwel gave up. Yes, it was funny, he *knew* it was funny, he'd heard the laughter in his dreams. But it wasn't right. Not yet. Maybe never. It was like the other idea about the two clowns, one fat, one thin . . . *Thys ys amain Dainty Messe youe have got me into, Stanleigh* . . . He had laughed until his chest ached, and the rest of the company had looked at him in astonishment. But in his dreams it was hilarious.

He laid down the pen and rubbed his eyes. It must be nearly midnight, and the habit of a lifetime told him to spare the candles although, for a fact, they could afford all the candles they could eat now, whatever Vitoller might say.

Hour gongs were being struck all across the city and nightwatchmen were proclaiming that it was indeed midnight and also that, in the face of all the evidence, all was well. Many of them got as far as the end of the sentence before being mugged.

Hwel pushed open the shutters and looked out at Ankh-Morpork.

It would be tempting to say the twin city was at

its best this time of year, but that wouldn't be entirely correct. It was at its most *typical*.

The river Ankh, the cloaca of half a continent, was already pretty wide and silt laden when it reached the city's outskirts. By the time it left it didn't so much flow as exude. Owing to the accretion of the mud of centuries the bed of the river was in fact higher than some of the low lying areas and now, with the snow melt swelling the flow, many of the low-rent districts on the Morpork side were flooded, if you can use that word for a liquid you could pick up in a net. This sort of thing happened every year and would have caused havoc with the drains and sewage systems, so it is just as well that the city didn't have very many. Its inhabitants merely kept a punt handy in the back yard and, periodically, built another story on the house.

It was reckoned to be very healthy there. Very few germs were able to survive.

Hwel looked across a sort of misty sea in which buildings clustered like a sandcastle competition at high tide. Flares and lighted windows made pleasing patterns on the iridescent surface, but there was one glare of light, much closer to hand, which particularly occupied his attention.

On a patch of slightly higher ground by the river, bought by Vitoller for a ruinous sum, a new building was rising. It was growing even by night, like a mushroom—Hwel could see the cressets burning all along the scaffolding as the hired craftsmen and even some of the players themselves refused to let the mere shade of the sky interrupt their labors.

New buildings were rare in Morpork, but this was even a new *type* of building.

The *Dysk*.

Vitoller had been aghast at the idea at first, but young Tomjon had kept at him. And everyone knew that once the lad had got the feel of it he could persuade water to flow uphill.

"But we've *always* moved around, laddie," said Vitoller, in the desperate voice of one who knows that, at the end of it all, he's going to lose the argument. "I can't go around settling down at my time of life."

"It's not doing you any good," said Tomjon firmly. "All these cold nights and frosty mornings. You're not getting any younger. We should stay put somewhere, and let people come to us. And they will, too. You know the crowds we're getting now. Hwel's plays are famous."

"It's not my plays," Hwel had said. "It's the players."

"I can't see me sitting by a fire in a stuffy room and sleeping on feather beds and all that nonsense," said Vitoller, but he'd seen the look on his wife's face and had given in.

And then there had been the theater itself. Making water run uphill was a parlor trick compared to getting the cash out of Vitoller but, it was a fact, they had been doing well these days. Ever since Tomjon had been big enough to wear a ruff and say two words without his voice cracking.

Hwel and Vitoller had watched the first few beams of the wooden framework go up.

"It's against nature," Vitoller had complained, leaning on his stick. "Capturing the spirit of the theater, putting it in a cage. It'll kill it."

"Oh, I don't know," said Hwel diffidently. Tomjon had laid his plans well, he'd devoted an entire evening to Hwel before even broaching the subject to his father, and now the dwarf's mind was on fire with the possibilities of backdrops and scenery changes and wings and flies and magnificent engines that could lower gods from the heavens and trapdoors that could raise demons from hell. Hwel was no more capable of objecting to the new theater than a monkey was of resenting a banana plantation.

"Damn thing hasn't even got a name," Vitoller had said. "I should call it the *Golde Mine*, because that's what it's costing me. Where's the money going to come from, that's what I'd like to know."

In fact they'd tried a lot of names, none of which suited Tomjon.

"It's got to be a name that means everything," he said. "Because there's everything inside it. The whole world on the stage, do you see?"

And Hwel had said, knowing as he said it that what he was saying was exactly right, "The Disc."

And now the Dysk was nearly done, and still he hadn't written the new play.

He shut the window and wandered back to his desk, picked up the quill, and pulled another sheet of paper toward him. A thought struck him. The whole world *was* a stage, to the gods . . .

Presently he began to write.

All the Disc it is but an Theater, he wrote, *Ane alle men and wymmen are but Players.* He made the mistake of pausing, and another inspiration sleeted down, sending his train of thought off along an entirely new track.

He looked at what he had written and added: *Except Those who selle popcorn.*

After a while he crossed this out, and tried: *Like unto thee Staje of a Theater ys the World, whereon alle Persons strut as Players.*

This seemed a bit better.

He thought for a bit, and continued conscientiously: *Sometimes they walke on. Sometimes they walke off.*

He seemed to be losing it. Time, time, what he needed was an infinity . . .

There was a muffled cry and a thump from the next room. Hwel dropped the quill and pushed open the door cautiously.

The boy was sitting up in bed, white-faced. He relaxed when Hwel came in.

"Hwel?"

"What's up, lad? Nightmares?"

"Gods, it was terrible! I saw them again! I really thought for a minute that—"

Hwel, who was absent-mindedly picking up the clothes that Tomjon had strewn around the room, paused in his work. He was keen on dreams. That was when the ideas came.

"That what?" he said.

"It was like . . . I mean, I was sort of *inside* something, like a bowl, and there were these three terrible faces peering in at me."

"Aye?"

"Yes, and then they all said, 'All hail . . .' and then they started arguing about my name, and then they said, 'Anyway, who shall be king hereafter?' And then one of them said, 'Here after what?' and one of the other two said, 'Just hereafter, girl, it's what you're supposed to say in these circumstances, you might try and make an effort,' and then they all peered closer, and one of the others said, 'He looks a bit peaky, I reckon it's all that foreign food,' and then the youngest one said, 'Nanny, I've told you already, there's no such place as Thespia,' and then they bickered a bit, and one of the old ones said, 'He can't hear us, can he? He's tossing and turning a bit,' and the other one said, 'You know I've never been able to get sound on this thing, Esme,' and then they bickered some more, and it went cloudy, and then . . . I woke up . . ." he finished lamely. "It was horrible, because every time they came close to the bowl it sort of magnified everything, so all you could see was eyes and nostrils."

Hwel hoisted himself onto the edge of the narrow bed.

"Funny old things, dreams," he said.

"Not much funny about that one."

"No, but I mean, last night, I had this dream about a little bandy-legged man walking down a road," said Hwel. "He had a little black hat on, and he walked as though his boots were full of water."

Tomjon nodded politely.

"Yes?" he said. "And—?"

"Well, that was it. And nothing. He had this little

cane which he twirled and, you know, it was incredibly . . ."

The dwarf's voice trailed off. Tomjon's face had that familiar expression of polite and slightly condescending puzzlement that Hwel had come to know and dread.

"Anyway, it was very amusing," he said, half to himself. But he knew he'd never convince the rest of the company. If it didn't have a custard pie in it somewhere, they said, it wasn't funny.

Tomjon swung his legs out of bed and reached for his britches.

"I'm not going back to sleep," he said. "What's the time?"

"It's after midnight," said Hwel. "And you know what your father said about going to bed late."

"I'm not," said Tomjon, pulling on his boots. "I'm getting up early. Getting up early is very healthy. And now I'm going out for a very healthy drink. You can come too," he added, "to keep an eye on me."

Hwel gave him a doubting look.

"You also know what your father says about going out drinking," he said.

"Yes. He said he used to do it all the time when he was a lad. He said he'd think nothing of quaffing ale all night and coming home at 5 a.m., smashing windows. He said he was a bit of a roister-doister, not like these white-livered people today who can't hold their drink." Tomjon adjusted his doublet in front of the mirror, and added, "You know, Hwel, I reckon responsible behavior is something to get when you grow older. Like varicose veins."

Hwel sighed. Tomjon's memory for ill-judged remarks was legendary.

"All right," he said. "Just the one, though. Somewhere decent."

"I promise." Tomjon adjusted his hat. It had a feather in it.

"By the way," he said, "exactly how does one quaff?"

"I think it means you spill most of it," said Hwel.

If the water of the river Ankh was rather thicker and more full of personality than ordinary river water, so the air in the Mended Drum was more crowded than normal air. It was like dry fog.

Tomjon and Hwel watched it spilling out into the street. The door burst open and a man came through backward, not actually touching the ground until he hit the wall on the opposite side of the street.

An enormous troll, employed by the owners to keep a measure of order in the place, came out dragging two more limp bodies which he deposited on the cobbles, kicking them once or twice in soft places.

"I reckon they're roistering in there, don't you?" said Tomjon.

"It looks like it," said Hwel. He shivered. He hated taverns. People always put their drinks down on his head.

They scurried in quickly while the troll was holding one unconscious drinker up by one leg and banging his head on the cobbles in a search for concealed valuables.

Drinking in the Drum has been likened to diving in a swamp, except that in a swamp the alligators don't pick your pockets first. Two hundred eyes watched the pair as they pushed their way through the crowd to the bar, a hundred mouths paused in the act of drinking, cursing or pleading, and ninety-nine brows crinkled with the effort of working out whether the newcomers fell into category A, people to be frightened of or B, people to frighten.

Tomjon walked through the crowd as though it was his property and, with the impetuosity of youth, rapped on the bar. Impetuosity was not a survival trait in the Mended Drum.

"Two pints of your finest ale, landlord," he said, in tones so carefully judged that the barman was astonished to find himself obediently filling the first mug before the echoes had died away.

Hwel looked up. There was an extremely big man on his right, wearing the outside of several large bulls and more chains than necessary to moor a warship. A face that looked like a building site with hair on it glared down at him.

"Bloody hell," it said. "It's a bloody lawn ornament."

Hwel went cold. Cosmopolitan as they were, the people of Morpork had a breezy, no-nonsense approach to the nonhuman races, i.e. hit them over the head with a brick and throw them in the river. This did not apply to trolls, naturally, because it is very difficult to be racially prejudiced against creatures seven feet tall who can bite through walls, at least for very long. But people three feet high were absolutely *designed* to be discriminated against.

The giant prodded Hwel on the top of his head.

"Where's your fishing rod, lawn ornament?" he said.

The barman pushed the mugs across the puddled counter.

"Here you are," he said, leering. "One pint. And one half pint."

Tomjon opened his mouth to speak, but Hwel nudged him sharply in the knee. Put up with it, put up with it, slip out as soon as possible, it was the only way . . .

"Where's your little pointy hat, then?" said the bearded man.

The room had gone quiet. This looked like being cabaret time.

"I *said*, where's your pointy hat, dopey?"

The barman got a grip of the blackthorn stick with nails in which lived under the counter, just in case, and said, "Er—"

"I was talking to the lawn ornament here."

The man took the dregs of his own drink and poured them carefully over the silent dwarf's head.

"I ain't drinking here again," he muttered, when even this failed to have any effect. "It's bad enough they let monkeys drink here, but pygmies—"

Now the silence in the bar took on a whole new intensity in which the sound of a stool being slowly pushed back was like the creak of doom. All eyes swiveled to the other end of the room, where sat the one drinker in the Mended Drum who came into category C.

What Tomjon had thought was an old sack hunched over the bar was extending arms and—other arms, except that they were its legs. A sad, rubbery face turned toward the speaker, its expression as melancholy as the mists of evolution. Its funny lips curled back. There was absolutely nothing funny about its teeth.

"Er," said the barman again, his voice frightening even him in that terrible simian silence. "I don't think you meant that, did you? Not about monkeys, eh? You didn't really, did you?"

"What the hell's that?" hissed Tomjon.

"I think it's an orangutan," said Hwel. "An ape."

"A monkey's a monkey," said the bearded man, at which several of the Drum's more percipient customers started to edge for the door. "I mean, so what? But these bloody lawn ornaments—"

Hwel's fist struck out at groin height.

Dwarfs have a reputation as fearsome fighters. Any race of three-foot tall people who favor axes and go into battle as into a championship tree-felling competition soon get talked about. But years of wielding a pen instead of a hammer had relieved Hwel's punches of some of their stopping power, and it could have been the end of him when the big man yelled and drew his sword if a pair of delicate, leathery hands hadn't instantly jerked the thing from his grip and, with only a small amount of effort, bent it double.*

---

* An explanation may be needed at this point. The Librarian of the magic library at Unseen University, the Disc's premier college of wiz-

When the giant growled, and turned around, an arm like a couple of broom handles strung together with elastic and covered with red fur unfolded itself in a complicated motion and smacked him across the jaw so hard that he rose several inches in the air and landed on a table.

By the time that the table had slid into another table and overturned a couple of benches there was enough impetus to start the night's overdue brawl, especially since the big man had a few friends with him. Since no one felt like attacking the ape, who had dreamily pulled a bottle from the shelf and smashed the bottom off on the counter, they hit whoever happened to be nearest, on general principles. This is absolutely correct etiquette for a tavern brawl.

Hwel walked under a table and dragged Tomjon, who was watching all this with interest, after him.

"So this is roistering. I always wondered."

"I think perhaps it would be a good idea to leave," said the dwarf firmly. "Before there's, you know, any trouble."

There was a thump as someone landed on the table above them, and a tinkle of broken glass.

---

ardry, had been turned into an orangutan some years previously by a magical accident in that accident-prone academy, and since then had strenuously resisted all well-meaning efforts to turn him back. For one thing, longer arms and prehensile toes made getting around the higher shelves a whole lot easier, and being an ape meant you didn't have to bother with all this *angst* business. He had also been rather pleased to find that his new body, although looking deceptively like a rubber sack full of water, gave him three times the strength and twice the reach of his old one.

"Is it real roistering, do you suppose, or merely rollicking?" said Tomjon, grinning.

"It's going to be bloody murder in a minute, my lad!"

Tomjon nodded, and crawled back out into the fray. Hwel heard him thump on the bar counter with something and call for silence.

Hwel put his arms over his head in panic.

"I didn't mean—" he began.

In fact calling for silence was a sufficiently rare event in the middle of a tavern brawl that silence was what Tomjon got. And silence was what he filled.

Hwel started as he heard the boy's voice ring out, full of confidence and absolutely first-class projection.

"Brothers! And yet may I call all men brother, for on this night—"

The dwarf craned up to see Tomjon standing on a chair, one hand raised in the prescribed declamatory fashion. Around him men were frozen in the act of giving one another a right seeing-to, their faces turned to his.

Down at tabletop height Hwel's lips moved in perfect synchronization with the words as Tomjon went through the familiar speech. He risked another look.

The fighters straightened up, pulled themselves together, adjusted the hang of their tunics, glanced apologetically at one another. Many of them were in fact standing to attention.

Even Hwel felt a fizz in his blood, and he'd written

those words. He'd slaved half a night over them, years ago, when Vitoller had declared that they needed another five minutes in Act III of *The King of Ankh*.

"Scribble us something with a bit of spirit in it," he'd said. "A bit of zip and sizzle, y'know. Something to summon up the blood and put a bit of backbone in our friends in the ha'penny seats. And just long enough to give us time to change the set."

He'd been a bit ashamed of that play at the time. The famous Battle of Morpork, he strongly suspected, had consisted of about two thousand men lost in a swamp on a cold, wet day, hacking one another into oblivion with rusty swords. What would the last King of Ankh have said to a pack of ragged men who knew they were outnumbered, outflanked and outgeneralled? Something with bite, something with edge, something like a drink of brandy to a dying man; no logic, no explanation, just words that would reach right down through a tired man's brain and pull him to his feet by his testicles.

Now he was seeing its effect.

He began to think the walls had fallen away, and there was a cold mist blowing over the marshes, its choking silence broken only by the impatient cries of the carrion birds . . .

And this voice.

And he'd written the words, they were *his*, no half-crazed king had ever really spoken like this. And he'd written all this to fill in a gap so that a castle made of painted sacking stretched over a frame could be shoved behind a curtain, and this voice was taking the coal dust of his words and filling the room with diamonds.

I *made* these words, Hwel thought. But they don't belong to me. They belong to him.

Look at those people. Not a patriotic thought among them, but if Tomjon asked them, this bunch of drunkards would storm the Patrician's palace tonight. And they'd probably succeed.

I just hope his mouth never falls into the wrong hands . . .

As the last syllables died away, their white-hot echoes searing across every mind in the room, Hwel shook himself and crawled out of hiding and jabbed Tomjon on the knee.

"Come away now, you fool," he hissed. "Before it wears off."

He grasped the boy firmly by the arm, handed a couple of complimentary tickets to the stunned barman, and hurried up the steps. He didn't stop until they were a street away.

"I thought I was doing rather well there," said Tomjon.

"A good deal too well, I reckon."

The boy rubbed his hands together. "Right. Where shall we go next?"

"*Next?*"

"Tonight is young!"

"No, *tonight* is dead. It's *today* that's young," said the dwarf hurriedly.

"Well, I'm not going home yet. Isn't there somewhere a bit more friendly? We haven't actually drunk anything."

Hwel sighed.

"A troll tavern," said Tomjon. "I've heard about them. There's some down in the Shades.* I'd like to see a troll tavern."

"They're for trolls only, boy. Molten lava to drink and rock music and cheese 'n' chutney flavored pebbles."

"What about dwarf bars?"

"You'd hate it," said Hwel, fervently. "Besides, you'd run out of headroom."

"Low dives, are they?"

"Look at it like this—how long do you think you could sing about gold?"

" 'It's yellow and it goes chink and you can buy things with it,' " said Tomjon experimentally, as they strolled through the crowds on the Plaza of Broken Moons. "Four seconds, I think."

"Right. Five hours of it gets a bit repetitive." Hwel kicked a pebble gloomily. He'd investigated a few dwarf bars last time they were in town, and hadn't approved. For some reason his fellow expatriates, who at home did nothing more objectionable than mine a bit of iron ore and hunt small creatures, felt impelled, once in the big city, to wear chain mail underwear, go around with axes in their belts, and call themselves names like Timkin Rumbleguts. And no one could beat a city dwarf when it came to quaffing. Sometimes they missed their mouths altogether.

---

* The Shades is an ancient part of Ankh-Morpork considered considerably more unpleasant and disreputable than the rest of the city. This always amazes visitors.

"Anyway," he added, "you'd get thrown out for being too creative. The actual words are, 'Gold, gold, gold, gold, gold, gold.'"

"Is there a chorus?"

"'Gold, gold, gold, gold, gold,'" said Hwel.

"You left out a 'gold' there."

"I think it's because I wasn't cut out to be a dwarf."

"Cut *down*, lawn ornament," said Tomjon.

There was a little hiss of indrawn breath.

"Sorry," said Tomjon hurriedly. "It's just that father—"

"I've known your father for a long time," said Hwel. "Through thick and thin, and there was a damn sight more thin than thick. Since before you were bor—" He hesitated. "Times were hard in those days," he mumbled. "So what I'm saying is . . . well, some things you earn."

"Yes. I'm sorry."

"You see, just—" Hwel paused at the mouth of a dark alley. "Did you hear something?" he said.

They squinted into the alley, once again revealing themselves as newcomers to the city. Morporkians don't look down dark alleys when they hear strange noises. If they see four struggling figures their first instinct is not to rush to anyone's assistance, or at least not to rush to the assistance of the one who appears to be losing and on the wrong end of someone else's boot. Nor do they shout "Oi!" Above all, they don't look surprised when the assailants, instead of guiltily running off, flourish a small piece of cardboard in front of them.

"What's this?" said Tomjon.

"It's a clown!" said Hwel. "They've mugged a clown!"

" 'Theft Licence'?" said Tomjon, holding the card up to the light.

"That's right," said the leader of the three. "Only don't expect us to do you too,' cos we're on our way home."

"S'right," said one of his assistants. "It's the thingy, the quota."

"But you were kicking him!"

"Worl, not a lot. Not what you'd call actual kicking."

"More foot nudging, sort of thing," said the third thief.

"Fair's fair. He bloody well went and fetched Ron here a right thump, didn't he?"

"Yeah. Some people have no idea."

"Why, you heartless—" Hwel began, but Tomjon laid a cautioning hand on his head.

The boy turned the card over. The obverse read:

J. H. "Flannelfoot" Boggis and Nephews
Bespoke Thieves
"The Old Firm"
(Estblshd AM 1789)
All type Theft carryed out Professionly and
with Disgression
Houses cleared. 24-hr service.
No job too small.
LET US QUOTE YOU FOR OUR
FAMILY RATE

"It seems to be in order," he said reluctantly.

Hwel paused in the act of helping the dazed victim to his feet.

"In order?" he shouted. "To rob someone?"

"We'll give him a chitty, of course," said Boggis. "Lucky we found him first, really. Some of these newcomers in the business, they've got no idea."*

"Cowboys," agreed a nephew.

"How much did you steal?" said Tomjon.

Boggis opened the clown's purse, which was stuck in his belt. Then he went pale.

"Oh, bleeding hell," he said. The Nephews clustered around.

"We're for it, sort of thing."

"Second time this year, uncle."

---

* Ankh-Morpork's enviable system of licensed criminals owes much to the current Patrician, Lord Vetinari. He reasoned that the only way to police a city of a million inhabitants was to recognize the various gangs and robber guilds, give them professional status, invite the leaders to large dinners, allow an acceptable level of street crime *and then make the guild leaders responsible for enforcing it*, on pain of being stripped of their new civic honors along with large areas of their skins. It worked. Criminals, it turned out, made a very good police force; unauthorized robbers soon found, for example, that instead of a night in the cells they could now expect an eternity at the bottom of the river.

However, there was the problem of apportioning the crime statistics, and so there arose a complex system of annual budgeting, chits and allowances to see that a) the members could make a reasonable living and b) no citizen was robbed or assaulted more than an agreed number of times. Many foresighted citizens in fact arranged to get an acceptable minimum of theft, assault, etc, over at the beginning of the financial year, often in the privacy and comfort of their own homes, and thus be able to walk the streets quite safely for the rest of the year. It all ticked over extremely peacefully and efficiently, demonstrating once again that compared to the Patrician of Ankh, Machiavelli could not have run a whelk stall.

Boggis glared at the victim.

"Well, how was I to know? I wasn't to know, was I? I mean, look at him, how much would *you* expect him to have on him? Couple of coppers, right? I mean, we'd never have done for him, only it was on our way home. You try and do someone a favor, this is what happens."

"How much has he got, then?" said Tomjon.

"There must be a hundred silver dollars in here," moaned Boggis, waving a purse. "I mean, that's not my league. That's not my class. I can't handle that sort of money. You've got to be in the Guild of Lawyers or something to steal that much. It's way over my quota, is that."

"Give it back then," said Tomjon.

"But I done him a receipt!"

"They've all got, you know, numbers on," explained the younger of the nephews. "The Guild checks up, sort of . . ."

Hwel grabbed Tomjon's hand.

"Will you excuse us a moment?" he said to the frantic thief, and dragged Tomjon to the other side of the alley.

"OK," he said. "Who's gone mad? Them? Me? You?"

Tomjon explained.

"It's legal?"

"Up to a certain point. Fascinating, isn't it? Man in a pub told me about it, sort of thing."

"But he's stolen *too much*?"

"So it appears. I gather the Guild is very strict about it."

There was a groan from the victim hanging between them. He tinkled gently.

"Look after him," said Tomjon. "I'll sort this out."

He went back to the thieves, who were looking very worried.

"My client feels," he said, "that the situation could be resolved if you give the money back."

"Ye-es," said Boggis, approaching the idea as if it was a brand new theory of cosmic creation. "But it's the receipt, see, we have to fill it up, time and place, signed and everything . . ."

"My client feels that possibly you could rob him of, let us say, five copper pieces," said Tomjon, smoothly.

"—I bloody don't!—" shouted the Fool, who was coming around.

"That represents two copper pieces as the going rate, plus expenses of three copper pieces for time, call-out fees—"

"Wear and tear on cosh," said Boggis.

"Exactly."

"Very fair. Very fair." Boggis looked over Tomjon's head at the Fool, who was now completely conscious and very angry. "Very fair," he said loudly. "Statesmanlike. Much obliged, I'm sure." He looked down at Tomjon. "And anything for yourself, sir?" he added. "Just say the word. We've got a special on GBH this season. Practically painless, you'll barely feel a thing."

"Hardly breaks the skin," said the older nephew. "Plus you get choice of limb."

"I believe I am well served in that area," said Tomjon smoothly.

"Oh. Well. Right you are then. No problem."

"Which merely leaves," continued Tomjon, as the thieves started to walk away, "the question of legal fees."

The gentle grayness at the stump of the night flowed across Ankh-Morpork. Tomjon and Hwel sat on either side of the table in their lodgings, counting.

"Three silver dollars and eighteen copper pieces in profit, I make it," said Tomjon.

"That was amazing," said the Fool. "I mean, the way they volunteered to go home and get some more money as well, after you gave them that speech about the rights of man."

He dabbed some more ointment on his head.

"And the youngest one started to cry," he added. "Amazing."

"It wears off," said Hwel.

"You're a dwarf, aren't you?"

Hwel didn't feel he could deny this.

"I can tell you're a Fool," he said.

"Yes. It's the bells, isn't it?" said the Fool wearily, rubbing his ribs.

"Yes, and the bells." Tomjon grimaced and kicked Hwel under the table.

"Well, I'm very grateful," said the Fool. He stood up, and winced. "I'd really like to show my gratitude," he added. "Is there a tavern open around here?"

Tomjon joined him at the window, and pointed down the length of the street.

"See all those tavern signs?" he said.

"Yes. Gosh. There's hundreds."

"Right. See the one at the end, with the blue and white sign?"

"Yes. I think so."

"Well, as far as I know, that's the only one around here that's ever closed."

"Then pray allow me to treat you to a drink. It's the least I can do," said the Fool nervously. "And I'm sure the little fellow would like something to quaff."

Hwel gripped the edge of the table and opened his mouth to roar.

And stopped.

He stared at the two figures. His mouth stayed open.

It closed again with a snap.

"Something the matter?" said Tomjon.

Hwel looked away. It had been a long night. "Trick of the light," he muttered. "And I could do with a drink," he added. "A bloody good quaff."

In fact, he thought, why fight it? "I'll even put up with the singing," he said.

"Was' the nex' wor'?"

"S'gold. I think."

"Ah."

Hwel looked unsteadily into his mug. Drunkenness had this to be said for it, it stopped the flow of inspirations.

"And you left out the 'gold,'" he said.

"Where?" said Tomjon. He was wearing the Fool's hat.

Hwel considered this. "I reckon," he said, concentrating, "it was between the 'gold' and the 'gold.' An' I reckon," he peered again into the mug. It was empty, a horrifying sight. "I reckon," he tried again, and finally gave up, and substituted, "I reckon I could do with another drink."

"My shout this time," said the Fool. "Hahaha. My squeak. Hahaha." He tried to stand up, and banged his head.

In the gloom of the bar a dozen axes were gripped more firmly. The part of Hwel that was sober, and was horrified to see the rest of him being drunk, urged him to wave his hand at the beetling brows glaring at them through the gloom.

"S'all right," he said, to the bar at large. "He don't mean it, he ver' funny wossname, idiot. Fool. Ver' funny Fool, all way from wassisplace."

"Lancre," said the Fool, and sat down heavily on the bar.

"S'right. Long way away from wossname, sounds like foot disease. Don't know how to behave. Don't know many dwarfs."

"Hahaha," said the Fool, clutching his head. "Bit *short* of them where I come from."

Someone tapped Hwel on the shoulder. He turned and looked into a craggy, hairy face under an iron helmet. The dwarf in question was tossing a throwing axe up and down in a meaningful way.

"You ought to tell your friend to be a bit less funny,"

he suggested. "Otherwise he will be amusing the demons in Hell!"

Hwel squinted at him through the alcoholic haze.

"Who're you?" he said.

"Grabpot Thundergust," said the dwarf, striking his chain-mailed torso. "And I say—"

Hwel peered closer.

"Here, I know you," he said. "You got a cosmetics mill down Hobfast Street. I bought a lot of grease-paint off you last week—"

A look of panic crossed Thundergust's face. He leaned forward in panic. "Shutup, shutup," he whispered.

"That's right, it said the Halls of Elven Perfume and Rouge Co.," said Hwel happily.

"Ver' good stuff," said Tomjon, who was trying to stop himself from sliding off the tiny bench. "Especially your No. 19, Corpse Green, my father swears it's the best. First class."

The dwarf hefted his axe uneasily. "Well, er," he said. "Oh. But. Yes. Well, thank you. Only the finest ingredients, mark you."

"Chop them up with that, do you?" said Hwel innocently, pointing to the axe. "Or is it your night off?"

Thundergust's brows beetled again like a cockroach convention.

"Here, you're not with the theater?"

"Tha's us," said Tomjon. "Strolling players." He corrected himself. "Standing-still players now. Haha. Slidin'-down players now."

The dwarf dropped his axe and sat down on

the bench, his face suddenly softened with enthusiasm.

"I went last week," he said. "Bloody good, it was. There was this girl and this fellow, but she was married to this old man, and there was this other fellow, and they said he'd died, and she pined away and took poison, but then it turned out this man was the other man really, only he couldn't tell her on account of—" Thundergust stopped, and blew his nose. "Everyone died in the end," he said. "Very tragic. I cried all the way home, I don't mind telling you. She was so pale."

"No. 19 and a layer of powder," said Tomjon cheerfully. "Plus a bit of brown eyeshadow."

"Eh?"

"And a couple of hankies in the vest," he added.

"What's he saying?" said the dwarf to the company at, for want of a better word, large.

Hwel smiled into his tankard.

"Give 'em a bit of Gretalina's soliloquy, boy," he said.

"Right."

Tomjon stood up, hit his head, sat down and then knelt on the floor as a compromise. He clasped his hands to what would have been, but for a few chance chromosomes, his bosom.

"*You lie who call it Summer . . .*" he began.

The assembled dwarfs listened in silence for several minutes. One of them dropped his axe, and was noisily hushed by the rest of them.

"*. . . and melting snow. Farewell,*" Tomjon finished. "Drinks phial, collapses behind battlements, down

ladder, out of dress and into tabard for Comic Guard
No. 2, wait one, entrance left. *What ho, good—*"

"That's about enough," said Hwel quietly.

Several of the dwarfs were crying into their hel-
mets. There was a chorus of blown noses.

Thundergust dabbed at his eyes with a chain-
mail handkerchief.

"That was the most saddest thing I've ever heard,"
he said. He glared at Tomjon. "Hang on," he said, as
realization dawned. "He's a man. I bloody fell in
love with that girl on stage." He nudged Hwel.
"He's not a bit of an elf, is he?"

"Absolutely human," said Hwel. "I know his father."

Once again he stared hard at the Fool, who was
watching them with his mouth open, and looked
back at Tomjon.

Nah, he thought. Coincidence.

"S'acting," he said. "A good actor can be anything,
right?"

He could feel the Fool's eye boring into the back
of his short neck.

"Yes, but dressing up as women, it's a bit—" said
Thundergust doubtfully.

Tomjon slipped off his shoes and knelt down on
them, bringing his face level with the dwarf's. He
gave him a calculating stare for a few seconds, and
then adjusted his features.

And there were two Thundergusts. True, one of
them was kneeling and had apparently been shaved.

"What ho, what ho," said Tomjon in the dwarf's
voice.

This was by way of being a hilarious gag to the rest of the dwarfs, who had an uncomplicated sense of humor. As they gathered around the pair Hwel felt a gentle touch on the shoulder.

"You two are with a theater?" said the Fool, now almost sober.

"S'right."

"Then I've come five hundred miles to find you."

It was, as Hwel would have noted in his stage directions, Later the Same Day. The sounds of hammering as the Dysk theater rose from its cradle of scaffolding thumped through Hwel's head and out the other side.

He could remember the drinking, he was certain. And the dwarfs bought lots more rounds when Tomjon did his impersonations. Then they had all gone to another bar Thundergust knew, and then they'd gone to a Klatchian take-away, and after that it was just a blur . . .

He wasn't very good at quaffing. Too much of the drink actually landed in his mouth.

Judging by the taste in it, some incontinent creature of the night had also scored a direct hit.

"Can you do it?" said Vitoller.

Hwel smacked his lips to get rid of the taste.

"I expect," said Tomjon. "It sounded interesting, the way he told it. Wicked king ruling with the help of evil witches. Storms. Ghastly forests. True Heir to Throne in Life-and-Death Struggle. Flash of Dagger. Screams, alarums. Evil king dies. Good triumphs. Bells ring out."

"Showers of rose petals could be arranged," said Vitoller. "I know a man who can get them at practically cost."

They both looked at Hwel, who was drumming his fingers on his stool. All three found their attention drawn to the bag of silver the Fool had given Hwel. Even by itself it represented enough money to complete the Dysk. And there had been talk of more to follow. Patronage, that was the thing.

"You'll do it then, will you?" said Vitoller.

"It's got a certain something," Hwel conceded. "But . . . I don't know . . ."

"I'm not trying to pressure you," said Vitoller. All three pairs of eyes swiveled back to the money bag.

"It seems a bit fishy," Tomjon conceded. "I mean, the Fool is decent enough. But the way he tells it . . . it's very odd. His mouth says the words, and his eyes say something else. And I got the impression he'd much rather we believed his eyes."

"On the other hand," said Vitoller hurriedly, "what harm could it do? The pay's the thing."

Hwel raised his head.

"What?" he said muzzily.

"I said, the play's the thing," said Vitoller.

There was silence again, except for the drumming of Hwel's fingertips. The bag of silver seemed to have grown larger. In fact, it seemed to fill the room.

"The thing is—" Vitoller began, unnecessarily loudly.

"The way I see it—" Hwel began.

They both stopped.

"After you. Sorry."

"It wasn't important. Go ahead."

"I was going to say, we could afford to build the Dysk anyway," said Hwel.

"Just the shell and the stage," said Vitoller. "But not all the other things. Not the trapdoor mechanism, or the machine for lowering gods out of heaven. Or the big turntable, or the wind fans."

"We used to manage without all that stuff," said Hwel. "Remember the old days? All we had was a few planks and a bit of painted sacking. But we had a lot of spirit. If we wanted wind we had to make it ourselves." He drummed his fingers for a while. "Of course," he added quietly, "we should be able to afford a wave machine. A small one. I've got this idea about this ship wrecked on an island, where there's this—"

"Sorry." Vitoller shook his head.

"But we've had some huge audiences!" said Tomjon.

"Sure, lad. Sure. But they pay in ha'pennies. The artificers want silver. If we wanted to be rich men—people," he corrected hurriedly, "we should have been born carpenters." Vitoller shifted uneasily. "I already owe Chrystophrase the Troll more than I should."

The other two stared.

"He's the one that has people's limbs torn off!" said Tomjon.

"How much do you owe him?" said Hwel.

"It's all right," said Vitoller hurriedly, "I'm keeping up the interest payments. More or less."

"Yes, but how much does he want?"

"An arm and a leg."

The dwarf and boy stared at him in horror. "How could you have been so—"

"I did it for you two! Tomjon deserves a better stage, he doesn't want to go ruining his health sleeping in lattys and never knowing a home, and you, my man, you need somewhere settled, with all the proper things you ought to have, like trapdoors and . . . wave machines and so forth. You talked me into it, and I thought, they're right. It's no life out on the road, giving two performances a day to a bunch of farmers and going around with a hat afterward, what sort of future is that? I thought, we've got to get a place somewhere, with comfortable seats for the gentry, people who don't throw potatoes at the stage. I said, blow the cost. I just wanted you to—"

"All right, all right!" shouted Hwel. "I'll write it!"

"I'll act it," said Tomjon.

"I'm not forcing you, mind," said Vitoller. "It's your own choice."

Hwel frowned at the table. There were, he had to admit, some nice touches. Three witches was good. Two wouldn't be enough, four would be too many. They could be meddling with the destinies of mankind, and everything. Lots of smoke and green light. You could do a lot with three witches. It was surprising no one had thought of it before.

"So we can tell this Fool that we'll do it, can we?" said Vitoller, his hand on the bag of silver.

And of course you couldn't go wrong with a good

storm. And there was the ghost routine that Vitoller had cut out of *Please Yourself*, saying they couldn't afford the muslin. And perhaps he could put Death in, too. Young Dafe would make a damn good Death, with white make-up and platform soles . . .

"How far away did he say he'd come from?" he said.

"The Ramtops," and the playmaster. "Some little kingdom no one has ever heard of. Sounds like a chest infection."

"It'd take months to get there."

"I'd like to go, anyway," said Tomjon. "That's where I was born."

Vitoller looked at the ceiling. Hwel looked at the floor. Anything was better, just at that moment, than looking at each other's face.

"That's what you said," said the boy. "When you did a tour of the mountains, you said."

"Yes, but I can't remember where," said Vitoller. "All those little mountain towns looked the same to me. We spent more time pushing the lattys across rivers and dragging them up hills than we ever did on the stage."

"I could take some of the younger lads and we could make a summer of it," said Tomjon. "Put on all the old favorites. And we could still be back by Soulcake Day. You could stay here and see to the theater, and we could be back for a Grand Opening." He grinned at his father. "It'd be good for them," he said slyly. "You always said some of the young lads don't know what a real acting life is like."

"Hwel's still got to write the play," Vitoller pointed out.

Hwel was silent. He was staring at nothing at all. After a while one hand fumbled in his doublet and brought out a sheaf of paper, and then disappeared in the direction of his belt and produced a small corked ink pot and a bundle of quills.

They watched as, without once looking at them, the dwarf smoothed out the paper, opened the ink pot, dipped a quill, held it poised like a hawk waiting for its prey, and then began to write.

Vitoller nodded at Tomjon.

Walking as quietly as they could, they left the room.

Around mid-afternoon they took up a tray of food and a bundle of paper.

The tray was still there at teatime. The paper had gone.

A few hours later a passing member of the company reported hearing a yell of "It can't work! It's back to front!" and the sound of something being thrown across the room.

Around supper Vitoller heard a shouted request for more candles and fresh quills.

Tomjon tried to get an early night, but sleep was murdered by the sound of creativity from the next room. There were mutterings about balconies, and whether the world really needed wave machines. The rest was silence, except for the insistent scratching of quills.

Eventually, Tomjon dreamed.

"*Now. Have we got everything this time?*"

"*Yes, Granny.*"

"*Light the fire, Magrat.*"

"*Yes, Granny.*"

"*Right. Let's see now—*"

"*I wrote it all down, Granny.*"

"*I can read, my girl, thank you very much. Now, what's this. 'Round about the cauldron go, In the poisoned entrails throw . . .' What are these supposed to be?*"

"*Our Jason slaughtered a pig yesterday, Esme.*"

"*These look like perfectly good chitterlin's to me, Gytha. There's a couple of decent meals in them, if I'm any judge.*"

"*Please, Granny.*"

"*There's plenty of starvin' people in Klatch who wouldn't turn up their nose at 'em, that's all I'm saying . . . All right, all right. 'Whole grain wheat and lentils too, In the cauldron seethe and stew'? What happened to the toad?*"

"*Please, Granny. You're slowing it down. You know Goodie was against all unnecessary cruelty. Vegetable protein is a perfectly acceptable substitute.*"

"*That means no newt or fenny snake either, I suppose?*"

"*No, Granny.*"

"*Or tiger's chaudron?*"

"*Here.*"

"*What the hell's this, excuse my Klatchian?*"

"*It's a tiger's chaudron. Our Wane bought it off a merchant from forn parts.*"

"*You sure?*"

"*Our Wane asked special, Esme.*"

"*Looks like any other chaudron to me. Oh, well. 'Double hubble, stubble trouble, Fire burn and cauldron bub—' WHY isn't the cauldron bubbling, Magrat?*"

Tomjon awoke, shivering. The room was dark. Outside a few stars pierced the mists of the city, and there was the occasional whistle of burglars and footpads as they went about their strictly lawful occasions.

There was silence from the next room, but he could see the light of a candle under the door.

He went back to bed.

Across the turgid river the Fool had also awakened. He was staying in the Fool's Guild, not out of choice but because the duke hadn't given him any money for anything else, and getting to sleep had been difficult in any case. The chilly walls had brought back too many memories. Besides, if he listened hard he could hear the muted sobs and occasional whimpers from the students' dormitories, as they contemplated with horror the life that lay ahead of them.

He punched the rock-hard pillow, and sank into a fitful sleep. Perchance to dream.

"*Slab and grue, yes. But it doesn't say* how *slab and grue.*"

"*Goodie Whemper recommended testing a bit in a cup of cold water, like toffee.*"

"*How inconvenient that we didn't think to bring one, Magrat.*"

"*I think we should be getting on, Esme. The night's nearly gone.*"

"*Just don't blame me if it doesn't work properly, that's all. Lessee . . . 'Baboon hair and . . .' Who's got the ba-*

boon hair? Oh, thank you, Gytha, though it looks more like cat hair to me, but never mind. 'Baboon hair and mandrake root,' and if that's real mandrake I'm very surprised, 'carrot juice and tongue of boot,' I see, a little humor, I suppose . . ."

"Please hurry!"

"All right, all right. 'Owl hoot and glow-worm glimmer. Boil—and then allow to simmer.'"

"You know, Esme, this doesn't taste half bad."

"You're not supposed to drink it, you daft doyenne!"

Tomjon sat bolt upright in bed. That was them again, the same faces, the bickering voices, distorted by time and space.

Even after he looked out of the window, where fresh daylight was streaming through the city, he could still hear the voices grumbling into the distance, like old thunder, fading away . . .

"I for one didn't believe it about the tongue of boot."

"It's still very runny. Do you think we should put some corn-flour into it?"

"It won't matter. Either he's on his way, or he isn't . . ."

He got up and doused his face in the washbasin.

Silence rolled in swathes from Hwel's room. Tomjon slipped on his clothes and pushed open the door.

It looked as though it had snowed indoors, great heavy flakes that had drifted into odd corners of the room. Hwel sat at his low table in the middle of the floor, his head pillowed on a pile of paper, snoring.

Tomjon tiptoed across the room and picked up a discarded ball of paper at random. He smoothed it out and read:

KING: Now, I'm just going to put the crown on this
   bush here, and you will tell me if anyone tries to
   take it, won't you?
GROUNDLINGS: Yes!
KING: Now if I could just find my horsey . . .
          (*1st assassin pops up behind rock.*)
AUDIENCE: Behind you!
                (*1st assassin disappears.*)
KING: You're trying to play tricks on old Kingy, you
   naughty . . .

There was a lot of crossing out, and a large blot.
Tomjon threw it aside and selected another ball at
random.

KING: Is this a ~~duck knife~~ dagger I see ~~behind beside
   in front of~~ before me, its ~~beak~~ handle pointing at
   ~~me~~ my hand?
1ST MURDERER: I'faith, it is not so. ~~Oh on it isn't!~~
2ND MURDERER: Thou speakest truth, sire. ~~Oh yes
   it is!~~

Judging by the creases in the paper, this one had
been thrown at the wall particularly hard. Hwel
had once explained to Tomjon his theory about inspirations, and by the look of it a whole shower had
fallen last night.
   Fascinated by this insight into the creative processes,
however, Tomjon tried a third discarded attempt:

QUEEN: Faith, there is a sound without! Mayhap
   it is my husband returning! Quick, into the gar-

derobe, and wait not upon the order of your going!

MURDERER: Marry, but your maid still has my pantoufles!

MAID (*opening door*): The Archbishop, your majesty.

PRIEST (*under bed*): Bless my soul!

(*Divers alarums*)

Tomjon wondered vaguely what divers alarums, which Hwel always included somewhere in the stage directions, actually were. Hwel always refused to say. Perhaps they referred to dangerous depths, or lack of air pressure.

He sidled toward the table and, with great care, pulled the sheaf of paper from under the sleeping dwarf's head, lowering it gently onto a cushion.

The top sheet read:

~~Verence Felmet Small God's Eve~~ A Night Of ~~Knives Daggers~~ Kings, by, Hwel of Vitoller's Men. A ~~Comedy~~ Tragedy in ~~Eight Five Six Three~~ Nine Acts.

Characters: Felmet, A Good King.

Verence, A Bad King.

Wethewacs, Ane Evil Witch

Hogg, Ane Likewise Evil Witch

Magerat, Ane Sirene . . .

Tomjon flicked over the page.

Scene: ~~A Drawing Room Ship at Sea Street in Pseudopolis~~ Blasted Moor. Enter Three Witches . . .

The boy read for a while and then turned to the last page.

Gentles, leave us dance and sing, and wish good health unto the king. (Exeunt all, singing falala, etc. Shower of rose petals. Ringing of bells. Gods descend from heaven, demons rise from hell, much ado with turntable, etc.) The End.

Hwel snored.

In his dreams gods rose and fell, ships moved with cunning and art across canvas oceans, pictures jumped and ran together and became flickering images; men flew on wires, flew without wires, great ships of illusion fought against one another in imaginary skies, seas opened, ladies were sawn in half, a thousand special effects men giggled and gibbered. Through it all he ran with his arms open in desperation, knowing that none of this really existed or ever would exist and all he *really* had was a few square yards of planking, some canvas and some paint on which to trap the beckoning images that invaded his head.

Only in our dreams are we free. The rest of the time we need wages.

"It's a good play," said Vitoller, "apart from the ghost."

"The ghost stays," said Hwel sullenly.

"But people always jeer and throw things. Anyway, you know how hard it is to get all the chalk dust out of the clothes."

"The ghost stays. It's a dramatic necessity."

"You *said* it was a dramatic necessity in the last play."

"Well, it was."

"And in *Please Yourself*, and in *A Wizard of Ankh*, and all the rest of them."

"I like ghosts."

They stood to one side and watched the dwarf artificers assembling the wave machine. It consisted of half a dozen long spindles, covered in complex canvas spirals painted in shades of blue and green and white, and stretching the complete width of the stage. An arrangement of cogs and endless belts led to a treadmill in the wings. When the spirals were all turning at once people with weak stomachs had to look away.

"Sea battles," breathed Hwel. "Shipwrecks. Tritons. Pirates!"

"Squeaky bearings, laddie," groaned Vitoller, shifting his weight on his stick. "Maintenance expenses. Overtime."

"It does look extremely . . . intricate," Hwel admitted. "Who designed it?"

"A daft old chap in the Street of Cunning Artificers," said Vitoller. "Leonard of Quirm. He's a painter really. He just does this sort of thing for a hobby. I happened to hear that he's been working on this for months. I just snapped it up quick when he couldn't get it to fly."

They watched the mock waves turn.

"You're bent on going?" said Vitoller, at last.

"Yes. Tomjon's still a bit wild. He needs an older head around the place."

"I'll miss you, laddie. I don't mind telling you. You've been like a son to me. How old are you, exactly? I never did know."

"A hundred and two."

Vitoller nodded gloomily. He was sixty, and his arthritis was playing him up.

"You've been like a father to me, then," he said.

"It evens out in the end," said Hwel diffidently. "Half the height, twice the age. You could say that on the overall average we live about the same length of time as humans."

The playmaster sighed. "Well, I don't know what I will do without you and Tomjon around, and that's a fact."

"It's only for the summer, and a lot of the lads are staying. In fact it's mainly the apprentices that are going. You said yourself it'd be good experience."

Vitoller looked wretched and, in the chilly air of the half-finished theater, a good deal smaller than usual, like a balloon two weeks after the party. He prodded some wood shavings distractedly with his stick.

"We grow old, Master Hwel. At least," he corrected himself, "I grow old and you grow older. We have heard the gongs at midnight."

"Aye. You don't want him to go, do you?"

"I was all for it at first. You know. Then I thought, there's destiny afoot. Just when things are going well, there's always bloody destiny. I mean, that's where he came from. Somewhere up in the mountains. Now fate is calling him back. I shan't see him again."

"It's only for the summer—"

Vitoller held up a hand. "Don't interrupt. I'd got the right dramatic flow there."

"Sorry."

Flick, flick, went the stick on the wood shavings, knocking them into the air.

"I mean, you know he's not my flesh and blood."

"He's your son, though," said Hwel. "This hereditary business isn't all it's cracked up to be."

"It's fine of you to say that."

"I mean it. Look at me. I wasn't supposed to be writing plays. Dwarfs aren't even supposed to be able to *read*. I shouldn't worry too much about destiny, if I was you. I was destined to be a miner. Destiny gets it wrong half the time."

"But you said he looks like the Fool person. I can't see it myself, mark you."

"The light's got to be right."

"Could be some destiny at work there."

Hwel shrugged. Destiny was funny stuff, he knew. You couldn't trust it. Often you couldn't even see it. Just when you knew you had it cornered, it turned out to be something else—coincidence, maybe, or providence. You barred the door against it, and it was standing behind you. Then just when you thought you had it nailed down it walked away with the hammer.

He used destiny a lot. As a tool for his plays it

was even better than a ghost. There was nothing like a bit of destiny to get the old plot rolling. But it was a mistake to think you could spot the shape of it. And as for thinking it could be controlled . . .

Granny Weatherwax squinted irritably into Nanny Ogg's crystal ball. It wasn't a particularly good one, being a greenish glass fishing float brought back from forn seaside parts by one of her sons. It distorted everything including, she suspected, the truth.

"He's definitely on his way," she said, at last. "In a cart."

"A fiery white charger would have been favorite," said Nanny Ogg. "You know. Caparisoned, and that."

"Has he got a magic sword?" said Magrat, craning to see.

Granny Weatherwax sat back.

"You're a disgrace, the pair of you," she said. "I don't know—magic chargers, fiery swords. Ogling away like a couple of milkmaids."

"A magic sword *is* important," said Magrat. "You've got to have one. We could make him one," she added wistfully. "Out of thunderbolt iron. I've got a spell for that. You take some thunderbolt iron," she said uncertainly, "and then you make a sword out of it."

"I can't be having with that old stuff," said Granny. "You can wait days for the damn things to hit and then they nearly take your arm off."

"And a strawberry birthmark," said Nanny Ogg, ignoring the interruption.

The other two looked at her expectantly.

"A strawberry birthmark," she repeated. "It's one of those things you've got to have if you're a prince coming to claim your kingdom. That's so's everyone will know. O'course, I don't know how they know it's *strawberry*."

"Can't abide strawberries," said Granny vaguely, quizzing the crystal again.

In its cracked green depths, smelling of bygone lobsters, a minute Tomjon kissed his parents, shook hands or hugged the rest of the company, and climbed aboard the leading latty.

It must of worked, she told herself. Else he wouldn't be coming here, would he? All those others must be his trusty band of good companions. After all, common sense, he's got to come five hundred miles across difficult country, anything could happen.

I daresay the armor and swords is in the carts.

She detected a twinge of doubt, and set out to quell it instantly. There isn't any other reason for him to come, stands to reason. We got the spell exactly right. Except for the ingredients. And most of the poetry. And it probably wasn't the right time. And Gytha took most of it home for the cat, which couldn't of been proper.

But he's on his way. What can't speak, can't lie.

"Best put the cloth over it when you've done, Esme," said Nanny. "I always get worried someone'll peer in at me when I'm having my bath."

"He's on his way," said Granny, the satisfaction in her voice so strong you could have ground corn with it. She dropped the black velvet bag over the ball.

"It's a long road," said Nanny. "There's many a slip twixt dress and drawers. There could be bandits."

"We shall watch over him," said Granny.

"That's not right. If he's going to be king he ought to be able to fight his own battles," said Magrat.

"We don't want him to go wasting his strength," said Nanny primly. "We want him good and fresh for when he gets here."

"And then, I hope, we shall leave him to fight his battles in his own way," said Magrat.

Granny clapped her hands together in a business-like fashion.

"Quite right," she said. "Provided he looks like winning."

They had been meeting at Nanny Ogg's cottage. Magrat made an excuse to tarry after Granny left, around dawn, allegedly to help Nanny with tidying up.

"Whatever happened to not meddling?" she said.

"What do you mean?"

"You know, Nanny."

"It's not proper meddling," said Nanny awkwardly. "Just helping matters along."

"Surely you can't really think that!"

Nanny sat down and fidgeted with a cushion.

"Well, see, all this not meddling business is fine in the normal course of things," she said. "Not meddling is easy when you don't have to. And then I've got the family to think about. Our Jason's been in a couple of fights because of what people have been saying. Our Shawn was thrown out of the army. The way I see it, when we get the new king in, he should owe us a few favors. It's only fair."

"But only last week you were saying—" Magrat stopped, shocked at this display of pragmatism.

"A week is a long time in magic," said Nanny. "Fifteen years, for one thing. Anyway, Esme is determined and I'm in no mood to stop her."

"So what you're saying," said Magrat, icily, "is that this 'not meddling' thing is like taking a vow not to swim. You'll absolutely never break it unless of course you happen to find yourself in the water?"

"Better than drowning," Nanny said.

She reached up to the mantelpiece and took down a clay pipe that was like a small tar pit. She lit it with a spill from the remains of the fire, while Greebo watched her carefully from his cushion.

Magrat idly lifted the hood from the ball and glared at it.

"I think," she said, "that I will never really understand about witchcraft. Just when I think I've got a grip on it, it changes."

"We're all just people." Nanny blew a cloud of blue smoke at the chimney. "Everyone's just people."

"Can I borrow the crystal?" said Magrat suddenly.

"Feel free," said Nanny. She grinned at Magrat's back. "Had a row with your young man?" she said.

"I really don't know what you're talking about."

"Haven't seen him around for weeks."

"Oh, the duke sent him to—" Magrat stopped, and went on—"sent him away for something or other. Not that it bothers me at all, either way."

"So I see. Take the ball, by all means."

Magrat was glad to get back home. No one was about on the moors at night anyway, but over the last couple of months things had definitely been getting worse. On top of the general suspicion of witches, it was dawning on the few people in Lancre who had any dealings with the outside world that a) either more things had been happening than they had heard about before or b) time was out of joint. It wasn't easy to prove,* but the few traders who came along the mountain tracks after the winter seemed to be rather older than they should have been. Unexplained happenings were always more or less expected in the Ramtops because of the high magical potential, but several years disappearing overnight was a bit of a first.

---

* Because of the way time was recorded among the various states, kingdoms and cities. After all, when over an area of a hundred square miles the same year is variously the Year of the Small Bat, and Anticipated Monkey, the Hunting Cloud, Fat Cows, Three Bright Stallions and at least nine numbers recording the time since** assorted kings, prophets, and strange events were either crowned, born or happened, and each year has a different number of months, and some of them don't have weeks, and one of them refuses to accept the day as a measure of time, the only thing it is possible to be sure of is that good sex doesn't last long enough.***

**The calendar of the Theocracy of Muntab counts *down*, not up. No one knows why, but it might not be a good idea to hang around and find out.

***Except for the Zabingo tribe of the Great Nef, of course.

She locked the door, fastened the shutters, and carefully laid the green glass globe on the kitchen table.

She concentrated . . .

The Fool dozed under the tarpaulins of the river barge, heading up the Ankh at a steady two miles an hour. It wasn't an exciting method of transport but it got you there eventually.

He looked safe enough, but he was tossing and turning in his sleep.

Magrat wondered what it was like, spending your whole life doing something you didn't want to do. Like being dead, she considered, only worse, the reason being, you were alive to suffer it.

She considered the Fool to be weak, badly led and sorely in need of some backbone. And she was longing for him to get back, so she could look forward to never seeing him again.

It was a long, hot summer.

They didn't rush things. There was a lot of country between Ankh-Morpork and the Ramtops. It was, Hwel had to admit, fun. It wasn't a word dwarfs were generally at home with.

Please Yourself went over well. It always did. The apprentices excelled themselves. They forgot lines, and played jokes; in Sto Lat the whole third act of *Gretalina and Mellias* was performed against the backdrop for the second act of *The Mage Wars*, but no one seemed to notice that the greatest love scene in history was played on a set depicting a tidal wave sweeping across a continent. That was possibly because Tomjon was playing Gretalina. The effect was so disconcertingly riveting that Hwel made him swap roles for the next house, if you could apply the term to a barn hired for the day, and the effect still had more rivets than a suit of plate armor, including the helmet, and even though Gretalina in this case was now young Wimsloe, who was a bit simple and tended to stutter and whose spots might eventually clear up.

The following day, in some nameless village in the middle of an endless sea of cabbages, he let Tomjon play Old Miskin in *Please Yourself*, a role that Vitoller always excelled in. You couldn't let anyone play it who was under the age of forty, not unless you wanted an Old Miskin with a cushion up his jerkin and greasepaint wrinkles.

Hwel didn't consider himself old. His father had still been digging three tons of ore a day at the age of two hundred.

Now, he felt old. He watched Tomjon hobble off the stage, and for a fleeting instant knew what it was to be a fat old man, pickled in wine, fighting old wars that no one cared about anymore, hanging grimly onto the precipice of late middle-age for fear of dropping off into antiquity, but only with one hand, because with the other he was giving the finger to Death. Of course, he'd known that when he wrote the part. But he hadn't *known* it.

The same magic didn't seem to infuse the new play. They tried it a few times, just to see how it went. The audience watched attentively, and went home. They didn't even bother to throw anything.

It wasn't that they thought it was bad. They didn't think it was anything.

But all the right ingredients were there, weren't they? Tradition was full of people giving evil rulers a well-justified seeing to. Witches were always a draw. The apparition of Death was particularly good, with some lovely lines. Mix them all together . . . and they seemed to cancel out, become a mere humdrum way of filling the stage for a couple of hours.

Late at night, when the cast was asleep, Hwel would sit up in one of the carts and feverishly re-write. He rearranged scenes, cut lines, *added* lines, introduced a clown, included another fight, and tuned up the special effects. It didn't seem to have any effect. The play was like some marvelous intricate painting, a feast of impressions close to, a mere blur from the distance.

When the inspirations were sleeting fast he even tried changing the style. In the morning the early risers grew accustomed to finding discarded experiments decorating the grass around the carts, like extremely literate mushrooms.

Tomjon kept one of the strangest:

1ST WITCHE: He's late.

(*Pause*)

2ND WITCHE: He said he would come.

(*Pause*)

3RD WITCHE: He said he would come but he hasn't. This is my last newt. I saved it for him. And he hasn't come.

(*Pause*)

"I think," said Tomjon, later, "you ought to slow down a bit. You've done what was ordered. No one said it had to *sparkle*."

"It could, you know. If I could just get it right."

"You're absolutely sure about the ghost, are you?" said Tomjon. The way he threw the line away made it clear that he wasn't.

"There's nothing wrong with the ghost," snapped Hwel. "The scene with the ghost is the best I've done."

"I was just wondering if this is the right play for it, that's all."

"The ghost stays. Now let's get on, boy."

Two days later, with the Ramtops a blue and white wall that was beginning to dominate the Hubward horizon, the company was attacked. There wasn't much drama; they had just manhandled the lattys across a ford and were resting in the shade of a grove of trees, which suddenly fruited robbers.

Hwel looked along the line of half a dozen stained and rusty blades. Their owners seemed slightly uncertain about what to do next.

"We've got a receipt somewhere—" he began.

Tomjon nudged him. "These don't look like Guild thieves," he hissed. "They definitely look freelance to me."

It would be nice to say that the leader of the robbers was a black-bearded, swaggering brute, with a red headscarf and one gold earring and a chin you could clean pots with. Actually it would be practically compulsory. And, in fact, this was so. Hwel thought the wooden leg was overdoing it, but the man had obviously studied the role.

"Well now," said the bandit chief. "What have we here, and do they have any money?"

"We're actors," said Tomjon.

"That ought to answer both questions," said Hwel.

"And none of your repartee," said the bandit. "I've been to the city, I have. I know repartee when I see it and—" he half turned to his followers, raising an eyebrow to indicate that the next remark was going to be witty—"if you're not careful I can make a few *cutting* remarks of my own."

There was dead silence behind him until he made an impatient gesture with his cutlass.

"All right," he said, against a chorus of uncertain laughter. "We'll just take any loose change, valuables, food and clothing you might be having."

"Could I say something?" said Tomjon.

The company backed away from him. Hwel smiled at his own feet.

"You're going to beg for mercy, are you?" said the bandit.

"That's right."

Hwel thrust his hands deep into his pockets and looked up at the sky, whistling under his breath and trying not to break into a maniac grin. He was aware that the other actors were also looking expectantly at Tomjon.

He's going to give them the mercy speech from *The Troll's Tale*, he thought . . .

"The point I'd just like to make is that—" said Tomjon, and his stance changed subtly, his voice became deeper, his right hand flung out dramatically—"'The worth of man lies not in feats of arms, Or the fiery hunger o' the ravening—'"

It's going to be like when that man tried to rob us back in Sto Lat, Hwel thought. If they end up giving us their swords, what the hell can we do with them? And it's so embarrassing when they start crying.

It was at this moment that the world around him took a green tint and he thought he could make out, right on the cusp of hearing, other voices.

"There's men with swords, Granny!"

"—rend with glowing blades the marvel of the world—" Tomjon said, and the voices at the edge of imagination said, *"No king of mine is going to beg anything off anyone. Give me that milk jug, Magrat."*

"—the heart of compassion, the kiss—"

"That was a present from my aunt."

"—this jewel of jewels, this crown of crowns."

There was silence. One or two of the bandits were weeping silently into their hands.

Their chief said, "Is that it?"

For the first time in his life Tomjon looked nonplussed.

"Well, yes," he said. "Er. Would you like me to repeat it?"

"It was a good speech," the bandit conceded. "But I don't see what it's got to do with me. I'm a practical man. Hand over your valuables."

His sword came up until it was level with Tomjon's throat.

"And all the rest of you shouldn't be standing there like idiots," he added. "Come on. Or the boy gets it."

Wimsloe the apprentice raised a cautious hand.

"What?" said the bandit.

"A-are you s-sure you listened carefully, sir?"

"I won't tell you again! Either I hear the clink of coins, or you hear a gurgle!"

In fact what they all heard was a whistling noise, high in the air, and the crash as a milk jug, its sides frosted with the ice of altitude, dropped out of the sky onto the spike atop the chief's helmet.

The remaining bandits took one look at the results, and fled.

The actors stared down at the recumbent bandit. Hwel prodded a lump of frozen milk with his boot.

"Well, well," he said weakly.

"He didn't take any notice!" whispered Tomjon.

"A born critic," said the dwarf. It was a blue and white jug. Funny how little details stood out at a time like this. It had been smashed several times in the past, he could see, because the pieces had been carefully glued together again. Someone had really loved that jug.

"What we're dealing with here," he said, rallying some shreds of logic, "is a freak whirlwind. Obviously."

"But milk jugs don't just drop out of the sky," said Tomjon, demonstrating the astonishing human art of denying the obvious.

"I don't know about that. I've heard of fish and frogs and rocks," said Hwel. "There's nothing against crockery." He began to rally. "It's just one of these uncommon phenomenons. They happen all the time in this part of the world, there's nothing unusual about it."

They got back onto the carts and rode on in unaccustomed silence. Young Wimsloe collected every bit of jug he could find and stored them carefully in the props box, and spent the rest of the day watching the sky, hoping for a sugar basin.

The lattys toiled up the dusty slopes of the Ramtops, mere motes in the foggy glass of the crystal.

"Are they all right?" said Magrat.

"They're wandering all over the place," said Granny. "They may be good at the acting, but they've got something to learn about the traveling."

"It was a nice jug," said Magrat. "You can't get them like that anymore. I mean, if you'd have said what was on your mind, there was a flatiron, on the shelf."

"There's more to life than milk jugs."

"It had a daisy pattern around the top."

Granny ignored her.

"I think," she said, "it's time we had a look at this new king. Close up." She cackled.

"You cackled, Granny," said Magrat darkly.

"I did not! It was," Granny fumbled for a word, "a chuckle."

"I bet Black Aliss used to cackle."

"You want to watch out you don't end up the same way as she did," said Nanny, from her seat by the fire. "She went a bit funny at the finish, you know. Poisoned apples and suchlike."

"Just because I might have chuckled a . . . a bit roughly," sniffed Granny. She felt that she was being unduly defensive. "Anyway, there's nothing wrong with cackling. In moderation."

"I think," said Tomjon, "that we're lost."

Hwel looked at the baking purple moorland around them, which stretched up to the towering spires of the Ramtops themselves. Even in the height of summer there were pennants of snow flying from the highest peaks. It was a landscape of describable beauty.

Bees were busy, or at least endeavoring to look and sound busy, in the thyme by the trackside. Cloud shadows flickered over the alpine meadows. There was the kind of big, empty silence made by an environment that not only doesn't have any people in it, but doesn't need them either.

Or signposts.

"We were lost ten miles ago," said Hwel. "There's got to be a new word for what we are now."

"You said the mountains were honeycombed with dwarf mines," said Tomjon. "You said a dwarf could tell wherever he was in the mountains."

"*Underground*, I said. It's all a matter of strata and rock formations. Not on the surface. All the landscape gets in the way."

"We could dig you a hole," said Tomjon.

But it was a nice day and, as the road meandered through clumps of hemlock and pine, outposts of the forest, it was pleasant enough to let the mules go at their own pace. The road, Hwel felt, had to go somewhere.

This geographical fiction has been the death of many people. Roads don't necessarily have to go anywhere, they just have to have somewhere to start.

"We *are* lost, aren't we?" said Tomjon, after a while.

"Certainly not."

"Where are we, then?"

"The mountains. Perfectly clear on any atlas."

"We ought to stop and ask someone."

Tomjon gazed around at the rolling countryside. Somewhere a lonely curlew howled, or possibly it was a badgar—Hwel was a little hazy about rural matters, at least those that took place higher than about the limestone layer. There wasn't another human being within miles.

"Who did you have in mind?" he said sarcastically.

"That old woman in the funny hat," said Tomjon, pointing. "I've been watching her. She keeps ducking down behind a bush when she thinks I've seen her."

Hwel turned and looked down at a bramble bush, which wobbled.

"Ho there, good mother," he said.

The bush sprouted an indignant head.

"Whose mother?" it said.

Hwel hesitated. "Just a figure of speech, Mrs . . . Miss . . ."

"Mistress," snapped Granny Weatherwax. "And I'm a poor old woman gathering wood," she added defiantly.

She cleared her throat. "Lawks," she went on.

mules into a plod again, grum-

r later, the track ran out among a
se-sized boulders, Hwel laid down
ully and folded his arms. Tomjon

u think you're doing?" he said.
aid the dwarf grimly.
ing dark soon."
be here long," said Hwel.
Nanny Ogg gave up and came out
her rock.
pork, understand?" said Hwel sharply.
or leave it, OK? Now—which way's

n, left at the ravine, then you pick up the
t leads to a bridge, you can't miss it," said
romptly.
grabbed the reins. "You forgot about the

ger. Sorry. Lawks."
you're a humble old wood gatherer, I expect,"
went on.
ot on, lad," said Nanny cheerfully. "Just about
ake a start, as a matter of fact."
omjon nudged the dwarf.
You forgot about the river," he said. Hwel glared
im.
"Oh yes," he muttered, "and can you wait here
hile we go and find a river."
"To help you across," said Tomjon carefully.
Nanny Ogg gave him a bright smile. "There's a

"You did give me a fright, young master. My poor old heart."

There was silence from the carts. Then Tomjon said, "I'm sorry?"

"What?" said Granny.

"Your poor old heart what?"

"What about my poor old heart?" said Granny, who wasn't used to acting like an old woman and had a very limited repertoire in this area. But it's traditional that young heirs seeking their destiny get help from mysterious old women gathering wood, and she wasn't about to buck tradition.

"It's just that you mentioned it," said Hwel.

"Well, it isn't important. Lawks. I expect you're looking for Lancre," said Granny testily, in a hurry to get to the point.

"Well, yes," said Tomjon. "All day."

"You've come too far," said Granny. "Go back about two miles, and take the track on the right, past the stand of pines."

Wimsloe tugged at Tomjon's shirt.

"When you m-meet a m-mysterious old lady in the road," he said, "you've got to offer to s-share your lunch. Or help her across the r-river."

"You have?"

"It's t-terribly b-bad luck not to."

Tomjon gave Granny a polite smile.

"Would you care to share our lunch, good mo— old wo—ma'am?"

Granny looked doubtful.

"What is it?"

"Salt pork."

She shook her head. "Thanks all the same," she said graciously. "But it gives me wind."

She turned on her heel and set off through the bushes.

"We could help you across the river if you like," shouted Tomjon after her.

"What river?" said Hwel. "We're on the moor, there can't be a river in miles."

"Y-you've got to get them on y-your side," said Wimsloe. "Then t-they help you."

"Perhaps we should have asked her to wait while we went and looked for one," said Hwel sourly.

They found the turning. It led into a forest criss-crossed with as many tracks as a marshalling yard, the sort of forest where the back of your head tells you the trees are turning around to watch you as you go past and the sky seems to be very high up and a long way off. Despite the heat of the day a dank, impenetrable gloom hovered among the tree trunks, which crowded up to the track as if intending to obliterate it completely.

They were soon lost again, and decided that being lost somewhere where you didn't know where you were was even worse than being lost in the open.

"She could have given more explicit instructions," said Hwel.

"Like ask at the next crone," said Tomjon. "Look over there."

He stood up in the seat.

"Ho there, old . . . good . . ." he hazarded.

Magra[...]

"Just a[...]
held up a[...]
with nothi[...]
her temper.[...]

Wimsloe n[...]
his face in an i[...]

"Would you c[...]
wo . . . miss?" he [...]

"Meat is extrem[...]
said Magrat. "If y[...]
you'd be horrified."

"I think I would," [...]

"Did you know that[...]
five pounds of undigest[...]
at all times?" said Magra[...]
tures on nutrition had be[...]
families to hide in the cel[...]

"Whereas pine kernels and s[...]

"There aren't any rivers a[...]
helping over, are there?" said [...]

"Don't be silly," said Magrat.[...]
wood gatherer, lawks, collecting a [...]
hap directing lost travelers on the r[...]

"Ah," said Hwel, "I thought we'd [...]

"You fork left up ahead and turn [...]
stone with the crack in it, you can't [...]
Magrat.

"Fine," growled Hwel. "Well, we won'[...]
I'm sure you've got a lot of wood to colle[...]
forth."

He whistled th[...]
bling to himself.[...]
When, an hou[...]
landscape of ho[...]
the reins caref[...]
stared at him.

"What do yo[...]
"Waiting," [...]
"It'll be get[...]
"We won't [...]
Eventually[...]
from behin[...]
"It's salt [...]
"Take it [...]
Lancre?" [...]
"Keep [...]
track tha[...]
Nanny [...]
Hwel [...]
lawks."
"Bug[...]
"An[...]
Hwel[...]
"S[...]
to m[...]
T[...]
at [...]
w[...]

perfectly good bridge," she said. "But I wouldn't say no to a lift. Move over."

To Hwel's irritation Nanny Ogg hitched up her skirts and scrambled onto the board, inserting herself between Tomjon and the dwarf and then twisting like an oyster knife until she occupied half the seat.

"You mentioned salt pork," she said. "There wouldn't be any mustard, would there?"

"No," said Hwel sullenly.

"Can't abide salt pork without condiments," said Nanny conversationally. "But pass it over, anyway." Wimsloe wordlessly handed over the basket holding the troupe's supper. Nanny lifted the lid and gave it a critical assessment.

"That cheese in there is a bit off," she said. "It needs eating up quick. What's in the leather bottle?"

"Beer," said Tomjon, a fraction of a second before Hwel had the presence of mind to say, "Water."

"Pretty weak stuff," said Nanny, eventually. She fumbled in her apron pocket for her tobacco pouch.

"Has anyone got a light?" she inquired.

A couple of actors produced bundles of matches. Nanny nodded, and put the pouch away.

"Good," she said. "Now, has anyone got any tobacco?"

Half an hour later the lattys rattled over the Lancre Bridge, across some of the outlying farmlands, and through the forests that made up most of the kingdom.

"This is it?" said Tomjon.

"Well, not all of it," said Nanny, who had been expecting rather more enthusiasm. "There's lots more of it behind the mountains over there. But this is the flat bit."

"You call this flat?"

"Flattish," Nanny conceded. "But the air's good. That's the palace up there, offering outstanding views of the surrounding countryside."

"You mean forests."

"You'll like it here," said Nanny encouragingly.

"It's a bit small."

Nanny thought about this. She'd spent nearly all her life inside the boundaries of Lancre. It had always seemed about the right size to her.

"Bijou," she said. "Handy foreverywhere."

"Everywhere *where*?"

Nanny gave up. "Everywhere close," she said.

Hwel said nothing. The air *was* good, rolling down the unclimbable slopes of the Ramtops like a sinus wash, tinted with turpentine from the high forests. They passed through a gateway into what was, up here, probably called a town; the cosmopolitan he had become decided that, down on the plains, it would just about have qualified as an open space.

"There's an inn," said Tomjon doubtfully.

Hwel followed his gaze. "Yes," he said, eventually. "Yes, it probably is."

"When are we going to do the play?"

"I don't know. I think we just send up to the castle and say we're here." Hwel scratched his chin. "Fool said the king or whoever would want to see the script."

Tomjon looked around Lancre town. It seemed peaceful enough. It didn't look like the kind of place likely to turn actors out at nightfall. It needed the population.

"This is the capital city of the kingdom," said Nanny Ogg. "Well-designed streets, you'll notice."

"Streets?" said Tomjon.

"Street," corrected Granny. "Also houses in quite good repair, stone's throw from river—"

"Throw?"

"Drop," Nanny conceded. "Neat middens, look, and extensive—"

"Madam, we've come to entertain the town, not buy it," said Hwel.

Nanny Ogg looked sidelong at Tomjon.

"Just wanted you to see how attractive it is," she said.

"Your civic pride does you credit," said Hwel. "And now, please, leave the cart. I'm sure you've got some wood to gather. Lawks."

"Much obliged for the snack," said Nanny, climbing down.

"Meals," corrected Hwel.

Tomjon nudged him. "You ought to be more polite," he said. "You never know." He turned to Nanny. "Thank you, good—oh, she's gone."

"They've come to do a theater," said Nanny.

Granny Weatherwax carried on shelling beans in the sun, much to Nanny's annoyance.

"Well? Aren't you going to say something? I've been finding out things," she said. "Picking up information. Not sitting around making soup—"

"Stew."

"I reckon it's very important," sniffed Nanny.

"What kind of a theater?"

"They didn't say. Something for the duke, I think."

"What's he want a theater for?"

"They didn't say that, either."

"It's probably all a trick to get in the castle," Granny said knowingly. "Very clever idea. Did you see anything in the carts?"

"Boxes and bundles and such."

"They'll be full of armor and weapons, depend upon it."

Nanny Ogg looked doubtful.

"They didn't look very much like soldiers to me. They were awfully young and spotty."

"Clever. I expect in the middle of the play the king will manifest his destiny, right where everyone can see him. Good plan."

"That's another thing," said Nanny, picking up a bean pod and chewing it. "He doesn't seem to like the place much."

"Of course he does. It's in his blood."

"I brought him the pretty way. He didn't seem very impressed."

Granny hesitated.

"He was probably suspicious of you," she concluded. "He was probably too overcome to speak, really."

She put down the bowl of beans and looked thoughtfully at the trees.

"Have you got any family still working up at the castle?" she said.

"Shirt and Daff help out in the kitchens since the cook went off his head."

"Good. I'll have a word with Magrat. I think we should see this theater."

"Perfect," said the duke.

"Thank you," said Hwel.

"You've got it exactly spot on about that dreadful accident," said the duke. "You might almost have been there. Ha. Ha."

"You weren't, were you?" said Lady Felmet, leaning forward and glaring at the dwarf.

"I just used my imagination," said Hwel hurriedly. The duchess glared at him, suggesting that his imagination could consider itself lucky it wasn't being dragged off to the courtyard to explain itself to four angry wild horses and a length of chain.

"Exactly right," said the duke, leafing one-handedly through the pages. "This is exactly, exactly, exactly how it was."

"*Will have been*," snapped the duchess.

The duke turned another page.

"You're in this too," he said. "Amazing. It's a word for word how I'm going to remember it. I see you've got Death in it, too."

"Always popular," said Hwel. "People expect it."

"How soon can you act it?"

"Stage it," corrected Hwel, and added, "We've

tried it out. As soon as you like." And then we can get away from here, he said to himself, away from your eyes like two raw eggs and this female mountain in the red dress and this castle which seems to act like a magnet for the wind. This is not going to go down as one of my best plays, I know that much.

"How much did we say we were going to pay you?" said the duchess.

"I think you mentioned another hundred silver pieces," said Hwel.

"Worth every penny," said the duke.

Hwel left hurriedly, before the duchess could start to bargain. But he felt he'd gladly pay something to be out of this place. Bijou, he thought. Gods, how could anyone like a kingdom like this?

The Fool waited in the meadow with the lake. He stared wistfully at the sky and wondered where the hell Magrat was. This was, she said, *their* place; the fact that a few dozen cows also shared it at the moment didn't appear to make any difference.

She turned up in a green dress and a filthy temper.

"What's all this about a play?" she said.

The Fool sagged onto a willow log.

"Aren't you glad to see me?" he said.

"Well, yes. Of course. Now, this play . . ."

"My lord wants something to convince people that he is the rightful King of Lancre. Himself mostly, I think."

"Is that why you went to the city?"

"Yes."

"It's disgusting!"

The Fool sat calmly. "You would prefer the duchess's approach?" he said. "She just thinks they ought to kill everyone. She's good at that sort of thing. And then there'd be fighting, and everything. Lots of people would die anyway. This way might be easier."

"Oh, where's your spunk, man?"

"Pardon?"

"Don't you want to die nobly for a just cause?"

"I'd much rather live quietly for one. It's all right for you witches, you can do what you like, but I'm circumscribed," said the Fool.

Magrat sat down beside him. *Find out all about this play*, Granny had ordered. *Go and talk to that jingling friend of yours.* She'd replied, *He's very loyal. He might not tell me anything.* And Granny had said, *This is no time for half measures. If you have to, seduct him.*

"When's this play going to be, then?" she said, moving closer.

"Marry, I'm sure I'm not allowed to tell you," said the Fool. "The duke said to me, he said, don't tell the witches that it's tomorrow night."

"I shouldn't, then," agreed Magrat.

"At eight o'clock."

"I see."

"But meet for sherry beforehand at seven-thirty, i'faith."

"I expect you shouldn't tell me who *is* invited, either," said Magrat.

"That's right. Most of the dignitaries of Lancre. You understand I'm not telling you this."

"That's right," said Magrat.

"But I think you have a right to know what it is you're not being told."

"Good point. Is there still that little gate around the back, that leads to the kitchens?"

"The one that is often left unguarded?"

"Yes."

"Oh, we hardly ever guard it these days."

"Do you think there might be someone guarding it at around eight o'clock tomorrow?"

"Well, *I* might be there."

"Good."

The Fool pushed away the wet nose of an inquisitive cow.

"The duke will be expecting you," he added.

"You said he said we weren't to know."

"He said I mustn't tell you. But he also said, 'They'll come anyway, I hope they do.' Strange, really. He seemed in a very good mood when he said it. Um. Can I see you after the show?"

"Is that all he said?"

"Oh, there was something about showing witches their future. I didn't understand it. I really would like to see you after the show, you know. I brought—"

"I think I might be washing my hair," said Magrat vaguely. "Excuse me, I really ought to be going."

"Yes, but I brought you this pres—" said the Fool vaguely, watching her departing figure.

He sagged as she disappeared between the trees, and looked down at the necklace wound tightly between his nervous fingers. It was, he had to admit, terribly tasteless, but it was the sort of thing she liked, all silver and skulls. It had cost him too much.

A cow, misled by his horns, stuck its tongue in his ear.

It was true, the Fool thought. Witches *did* do unpleasant things to people, sometimes.

Tomorrow night came, and the witches went by a roundabout route to the castle, with considerable reluctance.

"If he wants us to be here, I don't want to go," said Granny. "He's got some plan. He's using headology on us."

"There's something up," said Magrat. "He had his men set fire to three cottages in our village last night. He always does that when he's in a good mood. That new sergeant is a quick man with the matches, too."

"Our Daff said she saw them actors practicin' this morning," said Nanny Ogg, who was carrying a bag of walnuts and a leather bottle from which rose a rich, sharp smell. "She said it was all shouting and stabbing and then wondering who done it and long bits with people muttering to themselves in loud voices."

"Actors," said Granny, witheringly. "As if the world weren't full of enough history without inventing more."

"They shout so loud, too," said Nanny. "You can hardly hear yourself talk." She was also carrying, deep in her apron pocket, a lump of haunted castle rock. The king was getting in free.

Granny nodded. But, she thought, it was going to be worth it. She hadn't got the faintest idea what Tomjon had in mind, but her inbuilt sense of drama assured her that the boy would be bound to do something important. She wondered if he would leap off the stage and stab the duke to death, and realized that she was hoping like hell that he would.

"All hail wossname," she said under her breath, "who shall be king here, after."

"Let's get a move on," said Nanny. "All the sherry'll be gone."

The Fool was waiting despondently inside the little wicket gate. His face brightened when he saw Magrat, and then froze in an expression of polite surprise when he saw the other two.

"There's not going to be any trouble, is there?" he said. "I don't want there to be any trouble. Please."

"I'm sure I don't know what you mean," said Granny regally, sweeping past.

"Wotcha, jinglebells," said Nanny, elbowing the man in the ribs. "I hope you haven't been keeping our girl here up late o'nights!"

"Nanny!" said Magrat, shocked. The Fool gave the terrified, ingratiating rictus of young men everywhere when confronted by importunate elderly women commenting on their intimately personal lives.

The older witches brushed past. The Fool grabbed Magrat's hand.

"I know where we can get a good view," he said.

She hesitated.

"It's all right," said the Fool urgently. "You'll be perfectly safe with me."

"Yes, I will, won't I," said Magrat, trying to look around him to see where the others had gone.

"They're staging the play outside, in the big court-yard. We'll get a lovely view from one of the gate towers, and no one else will be there. I put some wine up there for us, and everything."

When she still looked half-reluctant he added, "And there's a cistern of water and a fireplace that the guards use sometimes. In case you want to wash your hair."

The castle was full of people standing around in that polite, sheepish way affected by people who see each other all day and are now seeing each other again in unusual social circumstances, like an office party. The witches passed quite unremarked among them and found seats in the rows of benches in the main courtyard, set up before a hastily assembled stage.

Nanny Ogg waved her bag of walnuts at Granny.

"Want one?" she said.

An alderman of Lancre shuffled past her and pointed politely to the seat on her left.

"Is anyone sitting here?" he said.

"Yes," said Nanny.

The alderman looked distractedly at the rest of the benches, which were filling up fast, and then down at the clearly empty space in front of him. He hitched up his robes with a determined expression.

"I think that since the play is commencing to

start, your friends must find a seat elsewhere, when they arrive," he said, and sat down.

Within seconds his face went white. His teeth began to chatter. He clutched at his stomach and groaned.*

"I *told* you," said Nanny, as he lurched away. "What's the good of asking if you're not going to listen?" She leaned toward the empty seat. "Walnut?"

"No, thank you," said King Verence, waving a spectral hand. "They go right through me, you know."

"*Pray, gentles all, list to our tale . . .*"

"What's this?" hissed Granny. "Who's the fellow in the tights?"

"He's the Prologue," said Nanny. "You have to have him at the beginning so everyone knows what the play's about."

"Can't understand a word of it," muttered Granny. "What's a gentle, anyway?"

"Type of maggot," said Nanny.

"That's nice, isn't it? 'Hallo maggots, welcome to the show.' Puts people in a nice frame of mind, doesn't it?"

There was a chorus of "sshs."

"These walnuts are damn tough," said Nanny, spitting one out into her hand. "I'm going to have to take my shoe off to this one."

---

* The observant will realize that this was because the king was already seated there. It was not because the man had used the phrase "commence to start" in cold blood. But it ought to have been.

Granny subsided into unaccustomed, troubled silence, and tried to listen to the prologue. The theater worried her. It had a magic of its own, one that didn't belong to her, one that wasn't in her control. It changed the world, and said things were otherwise than they were. And it was worse than that. It was magic that didn't belong to magical people. It was commanded by ordinary people, who didn't know the rules. They altered the world because it sounded better.

The duke and duchess were sitting on their thrones right in front of the stage. As Granny glared at them the duke half turned, and she saw his smile.

I want the world the way it is, she thought. I want the past the way it was. The past used to be a lot better than it is now.

And the band struck up.

Hwel peered around a pillar and signaled to Wimsloe and Brattsley, who hobbled out into the glare of the torches.

OLD MAN (an Elder): *"What hath befell the land?"*

OLD WOMAN (a Crone): *"'Tis a terror—"*

The dwarf watched them for a few seconds from the wings, his lips moving soundlessly. Then he scuttled back to the guardroom where the rest of the cast were still in the last hasty stages of dressing. He uttered the stage manager's traditional scream of rage.

"C'mon," he ordered. "Soldiers of the king, at the double! And the witches—*where are the blasted witches?*"

Three junior apprentices presented themselves.

"I've lost my wart!"

"The cauldon's all full of yuk!"

"There's something living in this wig!"

"Calm down, calm down," screamed Hwel. "It'll all be all right on the night!"

"This is the night, Hwel!"

Hwel snatched a handful of putty from the makeup table and slammed on a wart like an orange. The offending straw wig was rammed on its owner's head, livestock and all, and the cauldron was very briefly inspected and pronounced full of just the right sort of yuk, nothing wrong with yuk like that.

On stage a guard dropped his shield, bent down to pick it up, and dropped his spear. Hwel rolled his eyes and offered up a silent prayer to any gods that might be watching.

It was already going wrong. The earlier rehearsals had their little teething troubles, it was true, but Hwel had known one or two monumental horrors in his time and this one was shaping up to be the worst. The company was more jittery than a potful of lobsters. Out of the corner of his ear he heard the on-stage dialogue falter, and scurried to the wings.

"—avenge the terror of thy father's death—" he hissed, and hurried back to the trembling witches. He groaned. Divers alarums. This lot were supposed to be terrorizing a kingdom. He had about a minute before the cue.

"Right!" he said, pulling himself together. "Now, what are you? You're evil hags, right?"

"Yes, Hwel," they said meekly.

"Tell me what you are," he commanded.

"We're evil hags, Hwel."

"Louder!"

"We've Evil Hags!"

Hwel stalked the length of the quaking line, then turned abruptly on his heel, "And what are you going to do?"

The 2nd Witche scratched his crawling wig.

"We're going to curse people?" he ventured. "It says in the script—"

"I-can't-HEAR-you!"

"We're going to curse people!" they chorused, springing to attention and staring straight ahead to avoid his gaze.

Hwel stumped back along the line.

"What are you?"

"We're hags, Hwel!"

"What kind of hags?"

"We're black and midnight hags!" they yelled, getting into the spirit.

"What kind of black and midnight hags?"

"*Evil* black and midnight hags!"

"Are you scheming?"

"Yeah!"

"Are you secret?"

"*Yeah!*"

Hwel drew himself to his full height, such as it was.

"What-are-you?" he screamed.

"We're scheming evil secret black and midnight hags!"

"Right!" He pointed a vibrating finger toward the

stage and lowered his voice and, at that moment, a dramatic inspiration dived through the atmosphere and slammed into his creative node, causing him to say, "Now I want you to get out there and give 'em hell. Not for me. Not for the goddam captain." He shifted the butt of an imaginary cigar from one side of his mouth to the other, and pushed back a nonexistent tin helmet, and rasped, "But for Corporal Walkowski and his little dawg."

They stared at him in disbelief.

On cue, someone shook a sheet of tin and broke the spell.

Hwel rolled his eyes. He'd grown up in the mountains, where thunderstorms stalked from peak to peak on legs of lightning. He remembered thunderstorms that left mountains a different shape and flattened whole forests. Somehow, a sheet of tin wasn't the same, no matter how enthusiastically it was shaken.

Just once, he thought, just once. Let me get it right just once.

He opened his eyes and glared at the witches.

"What are you hanging around here for?" he yelled. "Get out there and *curse* them!"

He watched them scamper onto the stage, and then Tomjon tapped him on the head.

"Hwel, there's no crown."

"Hmm?" said the dwarf, his mind wrestling with ways of building thunder-and-lightning machines.

"There's no crown, Hwel. I've got to wear a crown."

"Of course there's a crown. The big one with the

red glass, very impressive, we used it in that place with the big square—"

"I think we left it there."

There was another tinny roll of thunder but, even so, the part of Hwel that was living the play heard a faltering voice on stage. He darted to the wings.

"—I have smother'd many a babe—" he hissed, and sprinted back.

"Well, just find another one, then," he said vaguely. "In the props box. You're the Evil King, you've got to have a crown. Get on with it, lad, you're on in a few minutes. Improvise."

Tomjon wandered back to the box. He'd grown up among crowns, big golden crowns made of wood and plaster, studded with finest glass. He'd cut his teeth on the hat-brims of Authority. But most of them had been left in the Dysk now. He pulled out collapsible daggers and skulls and vases, the strata of the years and, right at the bottom, his fingers closed on something thin and crown shaped, which no one had ever wanted to wear because it looked so uncrownly.

It would be nice to say it tingled under his hand. Perhaps it did.

Granny was sitting as still as a statue, and almost as cold. The horror of realization was stealing over her.

"That's us," she said. "Round that silly cauldron. That's meant to be us, Gytha."

Nanny Ogg paused with a walnut halfway to her gums. She listened to the words.

"I never shipwrecked anybody!" she said. "They just said they shipwreck people! I never did!"

Up in the tower Magrat elbowed the Fool in the ribs.

"Green blusher," she said, staring at the 3rd Witche. "I don't look like that. I don't, do I?"

"Absolutely not," said the Fool.

"And that hair!"

The Fool peered through the crenellations like an over-eager gargoyle.

"It looks like straw," he said. "Not very clean, either."

He hesitated, picking at the lichened stonework with his fingers. Before he'd left the city he'd asked Hwel for a few suitable words to say to a young lady, and he had been memorizing them on the way home. It was now or never.

"I'd like to know if I could compare you to a summer's day. Because—well, June 12th was quite nice, and . . . Oh. You've gone . . ."

King Verence gripped the edge of his seat; his fingers went through it. Tomjon had strutted onto the stage.

"That's him, isn't it? That's my son?"

The uncracked walnut fell from Nanny Ogg's fingers and rolled onto the floor. She nodded.

Verence turned a haggard, transparent face toward her.

"But what is he doing? What is he saying?"

Nanny shook her head. The king listened with his

mouth open as Tomjon, lurching crabwise across the stage, launched into his major speech.

"I think he's meant to be you," said Nanny, distantly.

"But I never walked like that! Why's he got a hump on his back? What's happened to his leg?" He listened some more, and added, in horrified tones, "And I certainly never did *that*! Or that. Why is he saying I did that?"

The look he gave Nanny was full of pleading. She shrugged.

The king reached up, lifted off his spectral crown, and examined it.

"And it's my crown he's wearing! Look, this is it! And he's saying I did all those—" He paused for a minute, to listen to the latest couplet, and added, "All right. Maybe I did *that*. So I set fire to a few cottages. But everyone does that. It's good for the building industry, anyway."

He put the ghostly crown back on his head.

"Why's he saying all this about me?" he pleaded.

"It's art," said Nanny. "It wossname, holds a mirror up to life."

Granny turned slowly in her seat to look at the audience. They were staring at the performance, their faces rapt. The words washed over them in the breathless air. This was real. This was more real even than reality. This was history. It might not be true, but that had nothing to do with it.

Granny had never had much time for words. They were so insubstantial. Now she wished that she had found the time. Words were indeed insubstantial. They were as soft as water, but they were also as powerful as water and now they were rushing over the audience, eroding the levees of veracity, and carrying away the past.

That's us down there, she thought. Everyone knows who we really are, but the things down there are what they'll remember—three gibbering old baggages in pointy hats. All we've ever done, all we've ever been, won't exist anymore.

She looked at the ghost of the king. Well, he'd been no worse than any other king. Oh, he might burn down the odd cottage every now and again, in a sort of absent-minded way, but only when he was really angry about something, and he could give it up any time he liked. Where he wounded the world, he left the kind of wounds that healed.

Whoever wrote this Theater knew about the uses of magic. Even I believe what's happening, and I know there's no truth in it.

This is Art holding a Mirror up to Life. That's why everything is exactly the wrong way around.

We've lost. There is nothing we can do against this without becoming exactly what we aren't.

Nanny Ogg gave her a violent nudge in the ribs.

"Did you hear that?" she said. "One of 'em said we put babbies in the cauldron! They've done a slander on me! I'm not sitting here and have 'em say we put babbies in a cauldron!"

Granny grabbed her shawl as she tried to stand up.

"Don't do anything!" she hissed. "It'll make things worse."

"'Ditch-delivered by a drab,' they said. That'll be young Millie Hipwood, who didn't dare tell her mum and then went out gathering firewood. I was up all night with that one," Nanny muttered. "Fine girl she produced. It's a slander! What's a drab?" she added.

"Words," said Granny, half to herself. "That's all that's left. Words."

"And now there's a man with a trumpet come on. What's he going to do? Oh. End of Act One," said Nanny.

The words won't be forgotten, thought Granny. They've got a power to them. They're damn good words, as words go.

There was yet another rattle of thunder, which ended with the kind of crash made, for example, by a sheet of tin escaping from someone's hands and hitting the wall.

In the world outside the stage the heat pressed down like a pillow, squeezing the very life out of the air. Granny saw a footman bend down to the duke's ear. No, he won't stop the play. Of course he won't. He wants it to run its course.

The duke must have felt the heat of her gaze on the back of his neck. He turned, focused on her, and gave her a strange little smile. Then he nudged his wife. They both laughed.

Granny Weatherwax was often angry. She considered it one of her strong points. Genuine anger was one of the world's great creative forces. But you had to learn how to control it. That didn't mean you let it trickle away. It meant you dammed it, carefully, let it develop a working head, let it drown whole valleys of the mind and then, just when the whole structure was about to collapse, opened a tiny pipeline at the base and let the iron-hard stream of wrath power the turbines of revenge.

She felt the land below her, even through several feet of foundations, flagstones, one thickness of leather and two thicknesses of sock. She felt it waiting.

She heard the king say, "My own flesh and blood? Why has he done this to me? I'm going to confront him!"

She gently took Nanny Ogg's hand.

"Come, Gytha," she said.

Lord Felmet sat back in his throne and beamed madly at the world, which was looking good right at the moment. Things were working out better than he had dared to hope. He could feel the past melting behind him, like ice in the spring thaw.

On an impulse he called the footman back.

"Call the captain of the guard," he said, "and tell him to find the witches and arrest them."

The duchess snorted.

"Remember what happened last time, foolish man?"

"We left two of them loose," said the duke. "This time . . . all three. The tide of public feeling is on our side. That sort of thing affects witches, depend upon it."

The duchess cracked her knuckles to indicate her view of public opinion.

"You must admit, my treasure, that the experiment seems to be working."

"It would appear so."

"Very well. Don't just stand there, man. Before the play ends, tell him. Those witches are to be under lock and key."

Death adjusted his cardboard skull in front of the mirror, twitched his cowl into a suitable shape, stood back and considered the general effect. It was going to be his first speaking part. He wanted to get it right.

"Cower now, Brief Mortals," he said. "For I am Death, 'Gainst Whom No . . . no . . . no . . . Hwel, 'gainst whom no?"

"Oh, good grief, Dafe. ' 'Gainst whom no lock will hold nor fasten'd portal bar,' I really don't see why you have difficulty with . . . not that way up, you idiots!" Hwel strode off through the backstage mêlée in pursuit of a pair of importunate scene shifters.

"Right," said Death, to no one in particular. He turned back to the mirror.

" 'Gainst Whom No . . . Tumpty-Tum . . . nor Tumpty-Tumpty bar," he said, uncertainly, and flourished his scythe. The end fell off.

"Do you think I'm fearsome enough?" he said, as he tried to fix it on again.

Tomjon, who was sitting on his hump and trying to drink some tea, gave him an encouraging nod.

"No problem, my friend," he said. "Compared to a visit from you, even Death himself would hold no fears. But you could try a bit more hollowness."

"How d'you mean?"

Tomjon put down his cup. Shadows seemed to move across his face; his eyes sank, his lips drew back from his teeth, his skin stretched and paled.

"I HAVE COME TO GET YOU, YOU TERRIBLE ACTOR," he intoned, each syllable falling into place like a coffin lid. His features sprang back into shape.

"Like that," he said.

Dafe, who had flattened himself against the wall, relaxed a bit and gave a nervous giggle.

"Gods, I don't know how you do it," he said. "Honestly, I'll never be as good as you."

"There really isn't anything to it. Now run along, Hwel's fit to be tied as it is."

Dafe gave him a look of gratitude and ran off to help with the scene shifting.

Tomjon sipped his tea uneasily, the backstage noises whirring around him like so much fog. He was worried.

Hwel had said that everything about the play was fine, except for the play itself. And Tomjon kept thinking that the play itself was trying to force itself into a different shape. His mind had been hearing other words, just too faint for hearing. It was almost like eavesdropping on a conversation. He'd had to shout more to drown out the buzzing in his head.

This wasn't right. Once a play was written it was, well, written. It shouldn't come alive and start twisting itself around.

No wonder everyone needed prompting all the time. The play was writhing under their hands, trying to change itself.

Ye gods, he'd be glad to get out of this spooky castle, and away from this mad duke. He glanced around, decided that it would be some time before the next act was called, and wandered aimlessly in search of fresher air.

A door yielded to his touch and he stepped out onto the battlements. He pushed it shut behind him, cutting off the sounds of the stage and replacing them by a velvet hush. There was a livid sunset imprisoned behind bars of cloud, but the air was as still as a mill pond and as hot as a furnace. In the forest below some night bird screamed.

He walked to the other end of the battlements and peered down into the sheer depths of the gorge. Far beneath, the Lancre boiled in its eternal mists.

He turned, and walked into a draft of such icy coldness that he gasped.

Unusual breezes plucked at his clothing. There was a strange muttering in his ear, as though someone was trying to talk to him but couldn't get the speed right. He stood rigid for a moment, getting his breath, and then fled for the door.

"But we're *not* witches!"

"Why do you look like them, then? Tie their hands, lads."

"Yes, excuse me, but we're not *really* witches!"

The captain of the guard looked from face to face. His gaze took in the pointy hats, the disordered hair smelling of damp haystacks, the sickly green complexions and the herd of warts. Guard captain for the duke wasn't a job that offered long-term prospects for those who used initiative. Three witches had been called for, and these seemed to fit the bill.

The captain never went to the theater. When he was on the rack of adolescence he'd been badly frightened by a Punch and Judy show, and since then had taken pains to avoid any organized entertainment and had kept away from anywhere where crocodiles could conceivably be expected. He'd spent the last hour enjoying a quiet drink in the guardroom.

"I said tie their hands, didn't I?" he snapped.

"Shall we gag them as well, cap'n?"

"But if you'd just *listen*, we're with the theater—"

"Yes," said the captain, shuddering. "Gag them."

"Please . . ."

The captain leaned down and stared at three pairs of frightened eyes. He was trembling.

"That," he said, "is the last time *you*'ll eat anyone's sausage."

He was aware that now the soldiers were giving him odd looks as well. He coughed and pulled himself together.

"Very well then, my theatrical witches," he said. "You've done your show, and now it's time for your applause." He nodded to his men.

"Clap them in chains," he said.

Three other witches sat in the gloom behind the stage, staring vacantly into the darkness. Granny Weatherwax had picked up a copy of the script, which she peered at from time to time, as if seeking ideas.

"'Divers alarums and excursions'," she read, uncertainly.

"That means lots of terrible happenings," said Magrat. "You always put that in plays."

"Alarums and what?" said Nanny Ogg, who hadn't been listening.

"Excursions," said Magrat patiently.

"Oh." Nanny Ogg brightened a bit. "The seaside would be nice," she said.

"Do shut up, Gytha," said Granny Weatherwax. "They're not for you. They're only for divers, like it says. Probably so they can recover from all them alarums."

"We can't let this happen," said Magrat, quickly and loudly. "If this gets about, witches'll always be old hags with green blusher."

"And meddlin' in the affairs of kings," said Nanny. "Which we never do, as is well known."

"It's not the meddlin' I object to," said Granny Weatherwax, her chin on her hand. "It's the *evil* meddling."

"And the unkindness to animals," muttered Magrat. "All that stuff about eye of dog and ear of toad. *No one* uses that kind of stuff."

Granny Weatherwax and Nanny Ogg carefully avoided one another's faces.

"Drabe!" said Nanny Ogg bitterly.

"Witches just aren't like that," said Magrat. "We live in harmony with the great cycles of Nature, and do no harm to anyone, and it's wicked of them to say we don't. We ought to fill their bones with hot lead."

The other two looked at her with a certain amount of surprised admiration. She blushed, although not greenly, and looked at her knees.

"Goodie Whemper did a recipe," she confessed. "It's quite easy. What you do is, you get some lead, and you—"

"I don't think that would be appropriate," said Granny carefully, after a certain amount of internal struggle. "It could give people the wrong idea."

"But not for long," said Nanny wistfully.

"No, we can't be having with that sort of thing," said Granny, a little more firmly this time. "We'd never hear the last of it."

"Why don't we just change the words?" said Magrat. "When they come back on stage we could just put the 'fluence on them so they forget what they're saying, and give them some new words."

"I suppose you're an expert at theater words?" said Granny sarcastically. "They'd have to be the proper sort, otherwise people would suspect."

"Shouldn't be too difficult," said Nanny Ogg dismissively. "I've been studyin' it. You go tumpty-tumpty-tumpty."

Granny gave this some consideration.

"There's more to it than that, I believe," she said. "Some of those speeches were very good. I couldn't understand hardly any of it."

"There's no trick to it at all," Nanny Ogg insisted. "Anyway, half of them are forgetting their lines as it is. It'll be easy."

"We could put words in their mouths?" said Magrat.

Nanny Ogg nodded. "I don't know about *new* words," she said. "But we can make them forget these words."

They both looked at Granny Weatherwax. She shrugged.

"I suppose it's worth a try," she conceded.

"Witches as yet unborn will thank us for it," said Magrat ardently.

"Oh, good," said Granny.

"At last! What are you three playing at? We've been looking for you everywhere!"

The witches turned to see an irate dwarf trying to loom over them.

"Us?" said Magrat. "But we're not in—"

"Oh yes you are, remember, we put it in last week. Act Two, Downstage, around the cauldron. You haven't got to say anything. You're symbolizing occult forces at work. Just be as wicked as you can. Come on, there's good lads. You've done well so far."

Hwel slapped Magrat on the bottom. "Good complexion you've got there, Wilph," he said encouragingly. "But for goodness' sake use a bit more padding, you're still the wrong shape. Fine warts there, Billem. I must say," he added, standing back, "you look as nasty a bunch of hags as a body might hope to clap eyes on. Well done. Shame about the wigs. Now run along. Curtain up in one minute. Break a leg."

He gave Magrat another ringing slap on her rump, slightly hurting his hand, and hurried off to shout at someone else.

None of the witches dared to speak. Magrat and Nanny Ogg found themselves instinctively turning toward Granny.

She sniffed. She looked up. She looked around. She looked at the brightly lit stage behind her. She brought her hands together with a clap that echoed around the castle, and then rubbed them together.

"Useful," she said grimly. "Let's do the show right here."

Nanny squinted sullenly after Hwel. "Break your own leg," she muttered.

Hwel stood in the wings and gave the signal for the curtains. And for the thunder.

It didn't come.

"Thunder!" he hissed, in a voice heard by half the audience. "Get on with it!"

A voice from behind the nearest pillar wailed, "I went and bent the thunder, Hwel! It just goes clonk-clonk!"

Hwel stood silent for a moment, counting. The company watched him, awestruck but not, unfortunately, thunderstruck.

At last he raised his fists to the open sky and said, "I wanted a storm! Just a storm. Not even a big storm. Any storm. Now I want to make myself absolutely CLEAR! I have had ENOUGH! I want thunder right NOW!"

The stab of lightning that answered him turned the multihued shadows of the castle into blinding white and searing black. It was followed by a roll of thunder, on cue.

It was the loudest noise Hwel had ever heard. It seemed to start inside his head and work its way outward.

It went on and on, shaking every stone in the castle. Dust rained down. A distant turret broke away with balletic slowness and, tumbling end over end, dropped gently into the hungry depths of the gorge.

When it finished it left a silence that rang like a bell.

Hwel looked up at the sky. Great black clouds were blowing across the castle, blotting out the stars.

The storm was back.

It had spent ages learning its craft. It had spent years lurking in distant valleys. It had practiced for hours in front of a glacier. It had studied the great storms of the past. It had honed its art to perfection. And now, tonight, with what it could see was clearly an appreciative audience waiting for it, it was going to take them by, well . . . tempest.

Hwel smiled. Perhaps the gods *did* listen, after all. He wished he'd asked for a really good wind machine as well.

He gestured frantically at Tomjon.

"Get on with it!"

The boy nodded, and launched into his main speech.

"And now our domination is complete—"

Behind him on the stage the witches bent over the cauldron.

"It's just tin, this one," hissed Nanny. "And it's full of all yuk."

"And the fire is just red paper," whispered Magrat. "It looked so real from up there, it's just red paper! Look, you can poke it—"

"Never mind," said Granny. "Just look busy, and wait until I say."

As the Evil King and the Good Duke began the exchange that was going to lead to the exciting Duel Scene they became uncomfortably aware of activity behind them, and occasional chuckles from the audience. After a totally inappropriate burst of laughter Tomjon risked a sideways glance.

One of the witches was taking their fire to bits. Another one was trying to clean the cauldron. The third one was sitting with her arms folded, glaring at him.

"*The very soil cries out at tyranny*—" said Wimsloe, and then caught the expression on Tomjon's face and followed his gaze. His voice trailed into silence.

"'And calls me forth for vengeance,'" prompted Tomjon helpfully.

"B-but—" whispered Wimsloe, trying to point surreptitiously with his dagger.

"I wouldn't be seen dead with a cauldron like this," said Nanny Ogg, in a whisper loud enough to carry to the back of the courtyard. "Two days' work with a scourer and a bucket of sand, is this."

"'And calls me forth for vengeance,'" hissed Tomjon. Out of the tail of his eye he saw Hwel in the wings, frozen in an attitude of incoherent rage.

"How do they make it flicker?" said Magrat.

"Be quiet, you two," said Granny. "You're upsetting people." She raised her hat to Wimsloe. "Go ahead, young man. Don't mind us."

"Wha?" said Wimsloe.

"Aha, it calls you forth for vengeance, does it?" said Tomjon, in desperation. "And the heavens cry revenge, too, I expect."

On cue, the storm produced a thunderbolt that blew the top off another tower . . .

The duke crouched in his seat, his face a panorama of fear. He extended what had once been a finger.

"There they are," he breathed. "That's them. What are they doing in my play? Who said they could be in my play?"

The duchess, who was less inclined to deal in rhetorical questions, beckoned to the nearest guard.

On stage Tomjon was sweating under the load of the script. Wimsloe was incoherent. Now Gumridge, who was playing the part of the Good Duchess in a wig of flax, had lost the thread as well.

"Aha, thou callst me an evil king, though thou wisperest it so none save I may hear it," Tomjon croaked. "And thou hast *summoned the guard*, possibly by some most secret signal, owing nought to artifice of lips or tongue."

A guard came on crabwise, still stumbling from Hwel's shove. He stared at Granny Weatherwax.

"Hwel says what the hell's going on?" he hissed.

"What was that?" said Tomjon. "Did I hear you say *I come, my lady*?"

"Get these people off, he says!"

Tomjon advanced to the front of the stage.

"Thou babblest, man. See how I dodge thy tortoise spear. I *said*, see how I dodge thy tortoise spear. Thy spear, man. You're holding it in thy bloody hand, for goodness' sake."

The guard gave him a desperate, frozen grin.

Tomjon hesitated. Three other actors around him were staring fixedly at the witches. Looming up in front of him with all the inevitability of a tax demand was a sword fight during which, it was beginning to appear, he would have to parry his own wild thrusts and stab himself to death.

He turned to the three witches. His mouth opened.

For the first time in his life his awesome memory let him down. He could think of nothing to say.

Granny Weatherwax stood up. She advanced to the edge of the stage. The audience held its breath. She held up a hand.

"Ghosts of the mind and all device away, I bid the Truth to have—" she hesitated—"its tumpty-tumpty day."

Tomjon felt the chill engulf him. The others, too, jolted into life.

Up from out of the depths of their blank minds new words rushed, words red with blood and revenge, words that had echoed among the castle's stones, words stored in silicon, words that would have themselves heard, words that gripped their mouths so tightly that an attempt not to say them would result in a broken jaw.

"Do you fear him now?" said Gumridge. "And he so amazed with drink? Take his dagger, husband— you are a blade's width from the kingdom."

"I dare not," Wimsloe said, trying to look in astonishment at his own lips.

"Who will know?" Gumridge waved a hand toward the audience. He'd never act so well again. "See, there is only eyeless night. Take the dagger now, take the kingdom tomorrow. Have a stab at it, man."

Wimsloe's hand shook.

"I have it, wife," he said. "Is this a dagger I see before me?"

"Of course it's a bloody dagger. Come on, do it now. The weak deserve no mercy. We'll say he fell down the stairs."

"But people will suspect!"

"Are there no dungeons? Are there no pilliwinks? Possession is nine parts of the law, husband, when what you possess is a knife."

Wimsloe drew his arm back.

"I cannot! He has been kindness itself to me!"

"And you can be Death itself to him . . ."

Dafe could hear the voices a long way off. He adjusted his mask, checked the deathliness of his appearance in the mirror, and peered at the script in the empty backstage gloom.

"Cower Now, Brief Mortals," he said. "I Am Death, 'Gainst Who—'Gainst Who—"

WHOM.

"Oh, thanks," said the boy distractedly. "'Gainst Whom No Lock May Hold—"

WILL HOLD.

"*Will* Hold Nor Fasten'd Portal Bar, Here To—to—to—"

HERE TO TAKE MY TALLY ON THIS NIGHT OF KINGS.

Dafe sagged.

"You're so much better at it," he moaned. "You've got the right voice and you can remember the words." He turned around. "It's only three lines and Hwel will . . . have . . . my . . . guts . . . for."

He froze. His eyes widened and became two saucers of fear as Death snapped his fingers in front of the boy's rigid face.

FORGET, he commanded, and turned and stalked silently toward the wings.

His eyeless skull took in the line of costumes, the waxy debris of the makeup table. His empty nostrils snuffed up the mixed smells of mothballs, grease and sweat.

There was something here, he thought, that nearly belonged to the gods. Humans had built a world inside the world, which reflected it in pretty much the same way as a drop of water reflects the landscape. And yet . . . and yet . . .

Inside this little world they had taken pains to put all the things you might think they would want to escape from—hatred, fear, tyranny, and so forth. Death was intrigued. They thought they wanted to be taken out of themselves, and every art humans dreamt up took them further *in*. He was fascinated.

He was here for a very particular and precise purpose. There was a soul to be claimed. There was no time for inconsequentialities. But what was time, after all?

His feet did an involuntary little clicking dance

across the stones. Alone, in the gray shadows, Death tapdanced.

—THE NEXT NIGHT IN YOUR DRESSING ROOM THEY HANG A STAR—

He pulled himself together, adjusted his scythe, and waited silently for his cue.

He'd never missed one yet.

He was going to get out there and slay them.

"And you can be Death itself to him. Now!"

Death entered, his feet clicking across the stage.

COWER NOW, BRIEF MORTALS, he said, FOR I AM DEATH, 'GAINST WHOM NO . . . NO . . .'GAINST WHOM . . .

He hesitated. He hesitated, for the very first time in the eternity of his existence.

For although the Death of the Discworld was used to dealing with people by the million, at the same time every death was intimate and personal.

Death was seldom seen except by those of an occult persuasion and his clients themselves. The reason that no one else saw him was that the human brain is clever enough to edit sights too horrible for it to cope with, but the problem here was that several hundred people were in fact *expecting* to see Death at this point, and were therefore seeing him.

Death turned slowly and stared back at hundreds of watching eyes.

Even in the grip of the truth Tomjon recognized a fellow actor in distress, and fought for mastery of his lips.

"'. . . lock will hold . . .'" he whispered, through teeth fixed in a grimace.

Death gave him a manic grin of stagefright.

WHAT? he whispered, in a voice like an anvil being hit with a small lead hammer.

"'. . . lock will hold, nor fasten'd portal . . . ,'" said Tomjon encouragingly.

. . . LOCK WILL HOLD NOR FASTEN'D PORTAL . . . UH . . . repeated Death desperately, watching his lips.

"'. . . bar! . . .'"

BAR.

"No, I cannot do it!" said Wimsloe. "I will be seen! Down there in the hall, someone watches!"

"There is no one!"

"I feel the stare!"

"Dithering idiot! Must I put it in for you? See, his foot is upon the top stair!"

Wimsloe's face contorted with fear and uncertainty. He drew back his hand.

"No!"

The scream came from the audience. The duke was half-risen from his seat, his tortured knuckles at his mouth. As they watched he lurched forward between the shocked people.

"No! I did not do it! It was not like that! You cannot say it was like that! You were not there!" He stared at the upturned faces around him, and sagged.

"Nor was I," he giggled. "I was asleep at the time, you know. I remember it quite well. There was blood on the counterpane, there was blood on the floor, I could not wash off the blood, but these are not proper subjects for the inquiry. I cannot allow the discussion of national security. It was just a dream, and when I awoke, he'd be alive tomorrow. And tomorrow it wouldn't have happened because it was not done. And tomorrow you can say I did not know. And tomorrow you can say I had no recollection. What a noise he made in falling! Enough to wake the dead . . . who would have thought he had so much blood in him? . . ." By now he had climbed onto the stage, and grinned brightly at the assembled company.

"I hope that sorts it all out," he said. "Ha. Ha."

In the silence that followed Tomjon opened his mouth to utter something suitable, something soothing, and found that there was nothing he could say.

But another personality stepped into him, took over his lips, and spoke thusly:

"With my own bloody dagger, you bastard! I know it was you! I saw you at the top of the stairs, sucking your thumb! I'd kill you now, except for the thought of having to spend eternity listening to your whining. I, Verence, formerly King of—"

"What testimony is this?" said the duchess. She stood in front of the stage, with half a dozen soldiers beside her.

"These are just slanders," she added. "And treason to boot. The rantings of mad players."

"I was bloody King of Lancre!" shouted Tomjon.

"In which case you are the alleged victim," said the duchess calmly. "And unable to speak for the prosecution. It is against all precedent."

Tomjon's body turned toward Death.

"You were there! You saw it all!"

I SUSPECT I WOULD NOT BE CONSIDERED AN APPRO-
PRIATE WITNESS.

"Therefore there is no proof, and where there is
no proof there is no crime," said the duchess. She
motioned the soldiers forward.

"So much for your experiment," she said to her
husband. "I think my way is better."

She looked around the stage, and found the
witches.

"Arrest them," she said.

"No," said the Fool, stepping out of the wings.

"*What* did you say?"

"I saw it all," said the Fool, simply. "I was in the
Great Hall that night. You killed the king, my lord."

"I did not!" screamed the duke. "You were not
there! I did not see you there! I *order* you not to be
there!"

"You did not dare say this before," said Lady
Felmet.

"Yes, lady. But I must say it now."

The duke focused unsteadily on him.

"You swore loyalty unto death, my Fool," he
hissed.

"Yes, my lord. I'm sorry."

"You're *dead*."

The duke snatched a dagger from Wimsloe's unresisting hand, darted forward, and plunged it to
the hilt into the Fool's heart. Magrat screamed.

The Fool rocked back and forth unsteadily.

"Thank goodness that's over," he said, as Magrat

pushed her way through the actors and clasped him to what could charitably be called her bosom. It struck the Fool that he had never looked a bosom squarely in the face, at least since he was a baby, and it was particularly cruel of the world to save the experience until after he was dead.

He gently moved one of Magrat's arms and pulled the despicable horned cowl from his head, and tossed it as far as possible. He didn't have to be a Fool anymore or, he realized, bother about vows or anything. What with bosoms as well, death seemed to be an improvement.

"I didn't do it," said the duke.

No pain, thought the Fool. Funny, that. On the other hand, you obviously can't feel pain when you are dead. It would be wasted.

"You all saw that I didn't do it," said the duke.

Death gave the Fool a puzzled look. Then he reached into the recesses of his robes and pulled out an hourglass. It had bells on it. He gave it a gentle shake, which made them tinkle.

"I gave no orders that any such thing should be done," said the duke calmly. His voice came from a long way off, from wherever his mind was now. The company stared at him wordlessly. It wasn't possible to hate someone like this, only to feel acutely embarrassed about being anywhere near him. Even the Fool felt embarrassed, and he was dead.

Death tapped the hourglass, and then peered at it to see if it had gone wrong.

"You are all lying," said the duke, in tranquil tones. "Telling lies is naughty."

He stabbed several of the nearest actors in a dreamy, gentle way, and then held up the blade.

"You see?" he said. "No blood! It wasn't me." He looked up at the duchess, towering over him now like a red tsunami over a small fishing village.

"It was her," he said. "She did it."

He stabbed her once or twice, on general principles, and then stabbed himself and let the dagger drop from his fingers.

After a few seconds reflection he said, in a voice far nearer the worlds of sanity, "You can't get me now."

He turned to Death. "Will there be a comet?" he said. "There must be a comet when a prince dies. I'll go and see, shall I?"

He wandered away. The audience broke into applause.

"You've got to admit he was real royalty," said Nanny Ogg, eventually. "It only goes to show, royalty goes eccentric far better than the likes of you and me."

Death held the hourglass to his skull, his face radiating puzzlement.

Granny Weatherwax picked up the fallen dagger and tested the blade with her finger. It slid into the handle quite easily, with a faint squeaking noise.

She passed it to Nanny.

"There's your magic sword," she said.

Magrat looked at it, and then back at the Fool.

"Are you dead or not?" she said.

"I must be," said the Fool, his voice slightly muffled. "I think I'm in paradise."

"No, look, I'm serious."

"I don't know. But I'd like to breathe."

"Then you must be alive."

"Everyone's alive," said Granny. "It's a trick dagger. Actors probably can't be trusted with real ones."

"After all, they can't even keep a cauldron clean," said Nanny.

"Whether everyone is alive or not is a matter for me," said the duchess. "As ruler it is my pleasure to decide. Clearly my husband has lost his wits." She turned to her soldiers. "And I decree—"

"Now!" hissed King Verence in Granny's ear. "Now!"

Granny Weatherwax drew herself up.

"Be silent, woman!" she said. "The true King of Lancre stands before you!"

She clapped Tomjon on the shoulder.

"What, him?"

"Who, me?"

"Ridiculous," said the duchess. "He's a mummer, of sorts."

"She's right, miss," said Tomjon, on the edge of panic. "My father runs a theater, not a kingdom."

"He is the true king. We can prove it," said Granny.

"Oh, no," said the duchess. "We're not having that. There's no mysterious returned heirs in this kingdom. Guards—take him."

Granny Weatherwax held up a hand. The soldiers lurched from foot to foot, uncertainly.

"She's a witch, isn't she?" said one of them, tentatively.

"Certainly," said the duchess.

The guards shifted uneasily.

"We seen where they turn people into newts," said one.

"And then shipwreck them."

"Yeah, and alarum the divers."

"Yeah."

"We ought to talk about this. We ought to get extra for witches."

"She could do anything to us, look. She could be a drabe, even."

"Don't be foolish," said the duchess. "Witches don't do that sort of thing. They're just stories to frighten people."

The guard shook his head.

"It looked pretty convincing to me."

"Of course it did, it was *meant*—" the duchess began. She sighed, and snatched a spear out of the guard's hand.

"I'll show you the power of these witches," she said, and hurled it at Granny's face.

Granny moved her hand across at snakebite speed and caught the spear just behind the head.

"So," she said, "and it comes to this, does it?"

"You don't frighten me, wyrd sisters," said the duchess.

Granny stared her in the eye for a few seconds. She gave a grunt of surprise.

"You're right," she said. "We really don't, do we . . ."

"Do you think I haven't studied you? Your witch-craft is all artifice and illusion, to amaze weak minds. It holds no fears for me. Do your worst."

Granny studied her for a while.

"My worst?" she said, eventually. Magrat and Nanny Ogg shuffled gently out of her way.

The duchess laughed.

"You're clever," she said. "I'll grant you that much. And quick. Come on, hag. Bring on your toads and demons, I'll . . ."

She stopped, her mouth opening and shutting a bit without any words emerging. Her lips drew back in a rictus of terror, her eyes looked beyond Granny, beyond the world, toward something else. One knuckled hand flew to her mouth and she made a little whimpering noise. She froze, like a rabbit that has just seen a stoat and knows, without any doubt, that it is the last stoat that it will ever see.

"What have you done to her?" said Magrat, the first to dare to speak. Granny smirked.

"Headology," said Granny, and smirked. "You don't need any Black Aliss magic for it."

"Yes, but what have you *done*?"

"No one becomes like she is without building walls inside their head," she said. "I've just knocked them down. Every scream. Every plea. Every pang of guilt. Every twinge of conscience. All at once. There's a little trick to it."

She gave Magrat a condescending smile. "I'll show you one day, if you like."

Magrat thought about it. "It's horrible," she said.

"Nonsense," Granny smiled terribly. "Everyone wants to know their true self. Now, she does."

"Sometimes, you have to be kind to be cruel," said Nanny Ogg approvingly.

"I think it's probably the worst thing that could happen to anyone," said Magrat, as the duchess swayed backward and forward.

"For goodness' sake use your imagination, girl," said Granny. "There are far worse things. Needles under the fingernails, for one. Stuff with pliers."

"Red-hot knives up the jacksie," said Nanny Ogg. "Handle first, too, so you cut your fingers trying to pull them out—"

"This is simply the worst that I can do," said Granny Weatherwax primly. "It's all right and proper, too. A witch should act like that, you know. There's no need for any dramatic stuff. Most magic goes on in the head. It's headology. Now, if you'd—"

A noise like a gas leak escaped from the duchess's lips. Her head jerked back suddenly. She opened her eyes, blinked, and focused on Granny. Sheer hatred suffused her features.

"Guards!" she said. "I told you to take them!"

Granny's jaw sagged. "What?" she said. "But—but I showed you your true self . . ."

"I'm supposed to be upset by that, am I?" As the soldiers sheepishly grabbed Granny's arms the duchess pressed her face close to Granny's, her tremendous eyebrows a V of triumphant hatred. "I'm supposed to grovel on the floor, is that it? Well, old woman, I've seen exactly what I am, do you understand, and I'm proud of it! I'd do it all again, only hotter and longer! I enjoyed it, and I did it because I wanted to!"

She thumped the vast expanse of her chest.

"You gawping idiots!" she said. "You're so *weak*.

You really think that people are basically decent underneath, don't you?"

The crowd on the stage backed away from the sheer force of her exultation.

"Well, I've looked underneath," said the duchess. "I know what drives people. It's fear. Sheer, deep-down fear. There's not one of you who doesn't fear me, I can make you widdle your drawers out of terror, and now I'm going to take—"

At this point Nanny Ogg hit her on the back of the head with the cauldron.

"She does go on, doesn't she?" she said conversationally, as the duchess collapsed. "She was a bit eccentric, if you ask me."

There was a long, embarrassed silence.

Granny Weatherwax coughed. Then she treated the soldiers holding her to a bright, friendly smile, and pointed to the mound that was now the duchess.

"Take her away and put her in a cell somewhere," she commanded. The men snapped to attention, grabbed the duchess by her arms, and pulled her upright with considerable difficulty.

"Gently, mind," said Granny.

She rubbed her hands together and turned to Tomjon, who was watching her with his mouth open.

"Depend on it," she hissed. "Here and now, my lad, you don't have a choice. You're the King of Lancre."

"But I don't know how to be a king!"

"We all seed you! You had it down just right, including the shouting."

"That's just acting!"

"Act, then. Being a king is, is—" Granny hesitated, and snapped her fingers at Magrat. "What do you call them things, there's always a hundred of them in anything?"

Magrat looked bewildered. "Do you mean percents?" she said.

"Them," agreed Granny. "Most of the percents in being a king is acting, if you ask me. You ought to be good at it."

Tomjon looked for help into the wings, where Hwel should have been. The dwarf was in fact there, but he wasn't paying much attention. He had the script in front of him, and was rewriting furiously.

BUT I ASSURE YOU, YOU ARE NOT DEAD. TAKE IT FROM ME.

The duke giggled. He had found a sheet from somewhere and had draped it over himself, and was sidling along some of the castle's more deserted corridors. Sometimes he would go "whoo-oo" in a low voice.

This worried Death. He was used to people claiming that they were *not* dead, because death always came as a shock, and a lot of people had some trouble getting over it. But people claiming that they were dead with every breath in their body was a new and unsettling experience.

"I shall jump out on people," said the duke dreamily. "I shall rattle my bones all night, I shall perch on the roof and foretell a death in the house—"

THAT'S BANSHEES.

"I shall if I want," said the duke, with a trace of

earlier determination. "And I shall float through walls, and knock on tables, and drip ectoplasm on anyone I don't like. Ha. Ha."

IT WON'T WORK. LIVING PEOPLE AREN'T ALLOWED TO BE GHOSTS. I'M SORRY.

The duke made an unsuccessful attempt to float through a wall, gave up, and opened a door out onto a crumbling section of the battlements. The storm had died away a bit, and a thin rind of moon lurked behind the clouds like a ticket tout for eternity.

Death stalked through the wall behind him.

"Well then," said the duke, "if I'm *not* dead, why are you here?"

He jumped up onto the wall and flapped his sheet.

WAITING.

"Wait forever, bone face!" said the duke triumphantly. "I shall hover in the twilight world, I shall find some chains to shake, I shall—"

He stepped backward, lost his balance, landed heavily on the wall and slid. For a moment the remnant of his right hand scrabbled ineffectually at the stonework, and then it vanished.

Death is obviously potentially everywhere at the same time, and in one sense it is no more true to say that he was on the battlements, picking vaguely at non-existent particles of glowing metal on the edge of his scythe blade, than that he was waist-deep in the foaming, rock-toothed waters in the depths of Lancre gorge, his calcareous gaze sweeping downward and stopping abruptly at a point where the torrent ran a few treacherous inches over a bed of angular pebbles.

After a while the duke sat up, transparent in the phosphorescent waves.

"I shall haunt their corridors," he said, "and whisper under the doors on still nights." His voice grew fainter, almost lost in the ceaseless roar of the river. "I shall make basket chairs creak most alarmingly, just you wait and see."

Death grinned at him.

Now YOU'RE TALKING.

It started to rain.

Ramtop rain has a curiously penetrative quality which makes ordinary rain seem almost arid. It poured in torrents over the castle roofs, and somehow seemed to go right through the tiles and fill the Great Hall with a warm, uncomfortable moistness.*

The hall was crowded with half the population of Lancre. Outside, the rushing of the rain even drowned out the distant roar of the river. It soaked the stage. The colors ran and mingled in the painted backdrop, and one of the curtains sagged away from its rail and flapped sadly into a puddle.

Inside, Granny Weatherwax finished speaking.

"You forgot about the crown," whispered Nanny Ogg.

"Ah," said Granny. "Yes, the crown. It's on his head, d'you see? We hid it among the crowns when the actors left, the reason being, no one would look for it there. See how it fits him so perfectly."

---

* Like Bognor.

It was a tribute to Granny's extraordinary powers of persuasion that everyone did see how perfectly it fitted Tomjon. In fact the only one who didn't was Tomjon himself, who was aware that it was only his ears that were stopping it becoming a necklace.

"Imagine the sensation when he put it on for the first time," she went on. "I expect there was an eldritch tingling sensation."

"Actually, it felt rather—" Tomjon began, but no one was listening to him. He shrugged and leaned over to Hwel, who was still scribbling busily.

"Does eldritch mean uncomfortable?" he hissed.

The dwarf looked at him with unfocused eyes.

"What?"

"I said, does eldritch mean uncomfortable?"

"Eh? Oh. No. No, I shouldn't think so."

"What *does* it mean then?"

"Dunno. Oblong, I think." Hwel's glance returned to his scrawls as though magnetized. "Can you remember what he said after all those tomorrows? I didn't catch the bit after that . . ."

"And there wasn't any need for you to tell everyone I was—adopted," said Tomjon.

"That's how it was, you see," said the dwarf vaguely. "Best to be honest about these things. Now then, did he actually stab her, or just accuse her?"

"I don't want to be a king!" Tomjon whispered hoarsely. "Everyone says I take after dad!"

"Funny thing, all this taking after people," said the dwarf vaguely. "I mean, if I took after *my* dad, I'd be a hundred feet underground digging rocks, whereas—" His voice died away. He stared at the nib of his pen as though it held an incredible fascination.

"Whereas what?"

"Eh?"

"Aren't you even *listening*?"

"I knew it was wrong when I wrote it, I knew it was the wrong way round . . . What? Oh, yes. Be a king. It's a good job. It seems there's a lot of competition, at any rate. I'm very happy for you. Once you're a king, you can do anything you want."

Tomjon looked at the faces of the Lancre worthies around the table. They had a keen, calculating look, like the audience at a fatstock show. They were weighing him up. It crept upon him in a cold and clammy way that once he was king, he could do anything he wanted. Provided that what he wanted to do was be king.

"You could build your own theater," said Hwel, his eyes lighting up for a moment. "With as many trapdoors as you wanted, and magnificent costumes. You could act in a new play every night. I mean, it would make the Dysk look like a shed."

"Who would come to see me?" said Tomjon, sagging in his seat.

"Everyone."

"What, every night?"

"You could order them to," said Hwel, without looking up.

I knew he was going to say that, Tomjon thought. He can't really mean it, he added charitably. He's got his play. He doesn't really exist in this world, not right now at the moment.

He took off the crown and turned it over and over in his hands. There wasn't much metal in it, but it felt heavy. He wondered how heavy it would get if you wore it all the time.

At the head of the table was an empty chair containing, he had been assured, the ghost of his real father. It would have been nice to report that he had experienced anything more, when being introduced to it, than an icy sensation and a buzzing in the ears.

"I suppose I could help father pay off on the Dysk," he said.

"That would be nice, yes," said Hwel.

He spun the crown in his fingers and listened glumly to the talk flowing back and forth over his head.

"Fifteen years?" said the Mayor of Lancre.

"We had to," said Granny Weatherwax.

"I thought the baker was a bit early last week."

"No, no," said the witch impatiently. "It doesn't work like that. No one's lost anything."

"According to my figuring," said the man who doubled as Lancre's beadle, town clerk and grave-digger, "we've all lost fifteen years."

"No, we've all gained them," said the mayor. "It stands to reason. Time's like this sort of wiggly road, see, but we took a short cut across the fields."

"Not at all," said the clerk, sliding a sheet of paper across the table. "Look here . . ."

Tomjon let the waters of debate close over him again.

Everyone wanted him to be king. No one thought twice about what he wanted. His views didn't count.

Yes, that was it. No one wanted *him* to be king, not precisely *him*. He just happened to be convenient.

Gold does not tarnish, at least physically, but Tomjon felt that the thin band of metal in his hands had an unpleasant depth to its luster. It had sat on too many troubled heads. If you held it to your ear, you could hear the screams.

He became aware of someone else looking at him, their gaze playing across his face like a blowlamp on a lolly. He looked up.

It was the third witch, the young . . . the youngest one, with the intense expression and the hedgerow hairstyle. Sitting next to old Fool as though she owned a controlling interest.

It wasn't his face she was examining. It was his features. Her eyeballs were tracking him from nape to nose like a pair of calipers. He gave her a little brave smile, which she ignored. Just like everyone else, he thought.

Only the Fool noticed him, and returned the smile with an apologetic grin and a tiny conspiratorial wave of the fingers that said: "What are we doing here, two sensible people like us?" The woman was looking at him again, turning her head this way and that and narrowing her eyes. She kept glancing at Fool and back to Tomjon. Then she turned to the oldest witch, the only person in the entire hot, damp room who seemed to have acquired a mug of beer, and whispered in her ear.

The two started a spirited, whispered conversation. It was, thought Tomjon, a particularly feminine way of talking. It normally took place on doorsteps, with all the participants standing with their arms folded and, if anyone was so ungracious as to walk past, they'd stop abruptly and watch them in silence until they were safely out of earshot.

He became aware that Granny Weatherwax had stopped talking, and that the entire hall was staring at him expectantly.

"Hallo?" he said.

"It might be a good idea to hold the coronation tomorrow," said Granny. "It's not good for a kingdom to be without a ruler. It doesn't like it."

She stood up, pushed back her chair, and came and took Tomjon's hand. He followed her unprotestingly across the flagstones and up the steps to the throne, where she put her hands on his shoulders and pressed him gently down onto the threadbare red plush cushions.

There was a scraping of benches and chairs. He looked around in panic.

"What's happening now?" he said.

"Don't worry," said Granny firmly. "Everyone wants to come and swear loyalty to you. You just nod graciously and ask everyone what they do and if they enjoy it. Oh, and you'd better give them the crown back."

Tomjon removed it quickly.

"Why?" he said.

"They want to present it to you."

"But I've already got it!" said Tomjon desperately.

Granny gave a patient sigh.

"Only in the wossname, real sense," she said. "This is more ceremonial."

"You mean unreal?"

"Yes," said Granny. "But much more important."

Tomjon gripped the arms of the throne.

"Fetch me Hwel," he said.

"No, you must do it like that. It's precedent, you see, first you meet the—"

"I *said*, fetch me the dwarf. Didn't you hear me, woman?" This time Tomjon got the spin and pitch of his voice just right, but Granny rallied magnificently.

"I don't think you quite realize who you are talking to, young man," she said.

Tomjon half rose in his seat. He had played a great many kings, and most of them weren't the kind of kings who shook hands graciously and asked people whether they enjoyed their work. They were far more the type of kings who got people to charge into battle at five o'clock on a freezing morning *and still managed to persuade them that this was better than being in bed*. He summoned them all, and treated Granny Weatherwax to a blast of royal hauteur, pride and arrogance.

"We thought we were talking to a *subject*," he said. "Now do as we say!"

Granny's face was immobile for several seconds as she worked out what to do next. Then she smiled to herself, said lightly, "As you wish," and went and dislodged Hwel, who was still writing.

The dwarf gave a stiff bow.

"None of that," snapped Tomjon. "What do I do next?"

"I don't know. Do you want me to write an acceptance speech?"

"I told you. I don't want to be king!"

"Could be a problem with an acceptance speech, then," the dwarf agreed. "Have you really thought about this? Being king is a great role."

"But it's the only one you get to play!"

"Hmm. Well, just tell them 'no,' then."

"Just like that? Will it work?"

"It's got to be worth a try."

A group of Lancre dignitaries were approaching with the crown on a cushion. They wore expressions of constipated respect coupled with just a hint of self-satisfaction. They carried the crown as if it was a Present for a Good Boy.

The Mayor of Lancre coughed behind his hand.

"A proper coronation will take some time to arrange," he began, "but we would like—"

"No," said Tomjon.

The mayor hesitated. "Pardon?" he said.

"I won't accept it."

The mayor hesitated again. His lips moved and his eyes glazed slightly. He felt that he had got lost somewhere, and decided it would be best to start again.

"A proper coronation will take—" he ventured.

"It won't," said Tomjon. "I will not be king."

The mayor was mouthing like a carp.

"Hwel?" said Tomjon desperately. "You're good with words."

"The problem we've got here," said the dwarf, "is that 'no' is apparently not among the options when you are offered a crown. I think he could cope with 'maybe.'"

Tomjon stood up, and grabbed the crown. He held it above his head like a tambourine.

"Listen to me, all of you," he said. "I thank you for your offer, it's a great honor. But I can't accept it. I've worn more crowns than you can count, and the only kingdom I know how to rule has got curtains in front of it. I'm sorry."

Dead silence greeted this. They did not appear to have been the right words.

"Another problem," said Hwel conversationally, "is that you don't actually have a choice. You *are* the king, you see. It's a job you are lined up for when you're born."

"I'd be no good at it!"

"That doesn't matter. A king isn't something you're good at, it's something you are."

"You can't leave me here! There's nothing but forests!"

Tomjon felt the suffocating cold sensation again, and the slow buzzing in his ears. For a moment he thought he saw, faint as a mist, a tall sad man in front of him, stretching out a hand in supplication.

"I'm sorry," he whispered. "I really am."

Through the fading shape he saw the witches, watching him intently.

Beside him Hwel said, "The only chance you'd have is if there was another heir. You don't remember any brothers and sisters, do you?"

"I don't remember anyone! Hwel, I—"

There was another ferocious argument among the witches. And then Magrat was striding, striding across the hall, moving like a tidal wave, moving like a rush of blood to the head, shaking off Granny Weatherwax's restraining hand, bearing down on the throne like a piston, and dragging the Fool behind her.

"I say?"

"Er. Hallo*ee*!"

"Er, I say, excuse me, can anyone hear us?"

The castle up above was full of hubbub and general rejoicing, and there was no one to hear the polite and frantic voices that echoed along the dungeon passages, getting politer and more frantic with each passing hour.

"Um, I say? Excuse me? Billem's got this terrible *thing* about rats, if you don't mind. Cooeee!"

Let the camera of the mind's eye pan slowly back along the dim, ancient corridors, taking in the dripping fungi, the rusting chains, the damp, the shadows . . .

"Can anyone hear us? Look, it's really too much. There's been some laughable mistake, look, the wigs come right off . . ."

Let the plaintive echoes dwindle among the

cobwebbed corners and rodent-haunted tunnels, until they're no more than a reedy whisper on the cusp of hearing.

"I say? I say, excuse me, help?"

Someone is bound to come down here again one of these days.

Some time afterward Magrat asked Hwel if he believed in long engagements. The dwarf paused in the task of loading up the latty.*

"About a week, maximum," he said at last. "With matinees, of course."

A month went past. The early damp-earth odors of autumn drifted over the velvety-dark moors, where the watery starlight was echoed by one spark of a fire.

The standing stone was back in its normal place, but still poised to run if any auditors came into view.

The witches sat in careful silence. This was not going to rate among the hundred most exciting coven meetings of all time. If Mussorgsky had seen them, the night on the bare mountain would have been over by teatime.

Then Granny Weatherwax said, "It was a good banquet, I thought."

"I was nearly sick," said Nanny Ogg proudly. "And

---

* At least, of supervising the loading. Actual physical assistance was a little difficult because he had, the day before, slipped on something and broken his leg.

my Shirl helped out in the kitchen and brought me home some scraps."

"I heard," said Granny coldly. "Half a pig and three bottles of fizzy wine went missing, they say."

"It's nice that some people think of the old folk," said Nanny Ogg, completely unabashed. "I got a coronation mug, too." She produced it. "It says 'Viva Verence II Rex.' Fancy him being called Rex. I can't say it's a good likeness, mind you. I don't recall him having a handle sticking out of his ear."

There was another long, terribly polite pause. Then Granny said, "We were a bit surprised you weren't there, Magrat."

"We thought you'd be up at the top of the table, kind of thing," said Nanny. "We thought you'd have moved in up there."

Magrat stared fixedly at her feet.

"I wasn't invited," she said meekly.

"Well, I don't know about *invited*," said Granny. "We weren't *invited*. People don't have to invite witches, they just know we'll turn up if we want to. They soon find room for us," she added, with some satisfaction.

"You see, he's been very busy," said Magrat to her feet. "Sorting everything out, you know. He's very clever, you know. Underneath."

"Very sober lad," said Nanny.

"Anyway, it's full moon," said Magrat quickly. "You've got to go to coven meetings at full moon, no matter what other pressing engagements there may be."

"Have y—?" Nanny Ogg began, but Granny nudged her sharply in the ribs.

"It's a very good thing he's paying so much attention to getting the kingdom working again," said Granny, soothingly. "It shows proper consideration. I daresay he'll get around to everything, sooner or later. It's very demanding, being a king."

"Yes," said Magrat, her voice barely audible.

The silence that followed was almost solid. It was broken by Nanny, in a voice as bright and brittle as ice.

"Well, I brought a bottle of that fizzy wine with me," she said. "In case he'd . . . in case . . . in case we felt like a drink," she rallied, and waved it at the other two.

"I don't want any," said Magrat sullenly.

"You drink up, girl," said Granny Weatherwax. "It's a chilly night. It'd be good for your chest."

She squinted at Magrat as the moon drifted out from behind its cloud.

"Here," she said. "Your hair looks a bit grubby. It looks as though you haven't washed it for a month."

Magrat burst into tears.

The same moon shone down on the otherwise unremarkable town of Rham Nitz, some ninety miles from Lancre.

Tomjon left the stage to thunderous applause at the concluding act of *The Troll of Ankh*. A hundred people would go home tonight wondering whether trolls were really as bad as they had hitherto thought although, of course, this wouldn't actually stop them disliking them in any way whatsoever.

Hwel patted him on the back as he sat down at the makeup table and started scraping off the thick gray sludge that was intended to make him look like a walking rock.

"Well done," he said. "The love scene—just right. And when you turned around and roared at the wizard I shouldn't think there was a dry seat in the house."

"I know."

Hwel rubbed his hands together.

"We can afford a tavern tonight," he said. "So if we just—"

"We'll sleep in the carts," said Tomjon firmly, squinting at himself in the shard of mirror.

"But you know how much the Fo—the king gave us! It could be feather beds all the way home!"

"It's straw mattresses and a good profit for us," said Tomjon. "And that'll buy you gods from heaven and demons from hell and the wind and the waves and more trapdoors than you can count, my lawn ornament."

Hwel's hand rested on Tomjon's shoulder for a moment. Then he said, "You're right, boss."

"Certainly I am. How's the play going?"

"Hmm? What play?" said Hwel, innocently.

Tomjon carefully removed a plaster brow ridge.

"You know," he said. "That one. The Lancre King."

"Oh. Coming along. Coming along, you know. I'll get it right one of these days." Hwel changed the subject with speed. "You know, we could work our way down to the river and take a boat home. That would be nice, wouldn't it?"

"But we could work our way home over land and pick up some more cash. That would be better, wouldn't it?" Tomjon grinned. "We took one hundred and three pence tonight; I counted heads during the Judgment speech. That's nearly one silver piece after expenses."

"You're your father's son, and no mistake," said Hwel.

Tomjon sat back and looked at himself in the mirror.

"Yes," he said, "I thought I had better be."

Magrat didn't like cats and hated the idea of mousetraps. She'd always felt that it should be possible to come to some sort of arrangement with creatures like mice so that all available food was rationed in the best interest of all parties. This was a very humanitarian outlook, which is to say that it was not a view shared by mice, and therefore her moonlit kitchen was alive.

When there was a knocking at the door the entire floor appeared to rush toward the walls.

After a few seconds the knocking came again.

There was another pause. Then the knocking rattled the door on its hinges, and a voice cried, "Open in the name of the king!"

A second voice said, in hurt tones, "You don't have to shout like that. Why did you shout like that? I didn't order you to shout like that. It's enough to frighten anybody, shouting like that."

"Sorry, sire! It goes with the job, sire!"

"Just knock again. A bit more gently, please."

The knocking might have been a bit softer. Magrat's apron dropped off its hook on the back of the door.

"Are you sure I can't do it myself?"

"It's not done, sire, kings knocking at humble cottage doors. Best leave it to me. OPEN IN THE—"

"Sergeant!"

"Sorry, sire. Forgot myself."

"Try the latch."

There was the sound of someone being extremely hesitant.

"Don't like the sound of that, sire," said the invisible sergeant. "Could be dangerous. If you want my advice, sire, I'd set fire to the thatch."

"Set fire?"

"Yessire. We always do that if they don't answer the door. Brings them out a treat."

"I don't think that would be appropriate, sergeant. I think I'll try the latch, if it's all the same to you."

"Breaks my heart to see you do it, sire."

"Well, I'm sorry."

"You could at least let me buff it up for you."

"No!"

"Well, couldn't I just set fire to the privy—?"

"Absolutely not!"

"That chicken house over there looks as if it would go up like—"

"*Sergeant!*"

"Sire!"

"Go back to the castle!"

"What, and leave you all alone, sire?"

"This is a matter of extreme delicacy, sergeant. I am sure you are a man of sterling qualities, but there are times when even a king needs to be alone. It concerns a young woman, you understand."

"Ah. Point taken, sire."

"Thank you. Help me dismount, please."

"Sorry about all that, sire. Tactless of me."

"Don't mention it."

"If you need any help getting her alight—"

"*Please* go back to the castle, sergeant."

"Yes, sire. If you're sure, sire. Thank you, sire."

"Sergeant?"

"Yes, sire?"

"I shall need someone to take my cap and bells back to the Fools' Guild in Ankh-Morpork now I'm leaving. It seems to me you're the ideal man."

"Thank you, sire. Much obliged."

"It's your, ah, burning desire to be of service."

"Yes, sire?"

"Make sure they put you up in one of the guest rooms."

"Yes, sire. Thank you, sire."

There was the sound of a horse trotting away. A few seconds later the latch clonked and the Fool crept in.

It takes considerable courage to enter a witch's kitchen in the dark, but probably no more than it takes to wear a purple shirt with velvet sleeves and scalloped edges. It had this in its favor, though. There were no bells on it.

He had brought a bottle of sparkling wine and a bouquet of flowers, both of which had gone flat during the journey. He laid them on the table, and sat down by the embers of the fire.

He rubbed his eyes. It had been a long day. He wasn't, he felt, a good king, but he'd had a lifetime of working hard at being something he wasn't cut out to be, and he was persevering. As far as he could see, none of his predecessors had tried at all. So much to do, so much to repair, so much to organize . . .

On top of it all there was the problem with the duchess. Somehow he'd felt moved to put her in a decent cell in an airy tower. She was a widow, after all. He felt he ought to be kind to widows. But being kind to the duchess didn't seem to achieve much, she didn't understand it, she thought it was just weakness. He was dreadfully afraid that he might have to have her head cut off.

No, being a king was no laughing matter. He brightened up at the thought. There was that to be said about it.

And, after a while, he fell asleep.

The duchess was not asleep. She was currently half-way down the castle wall on a rope of knotted sheets, having spent the previous day gradually chipping away the mortar around the bars of her window although, in truth, you could hack your way out of the average Lancre Castle wall with a piece of cheese.

The fool! He'd given her cutlery, and plenty of bed-clothes! That was how these people reacted. They let their fear do their thinking for them. They were scared of her, even when they thought they had her in their power (and the weak never had the strong in their power, never truly in their power). If she'd thrown herself in prison, she would have found considerable satisfaction in making herself regret she'd ever been born. But they'd just given her blankets, and worried about her.

Well, she'd be back. There was a big world out there, and she knew how to pull the levers that made people do what she wanted. She wouldn't burden herself with a husband this time, either. Weak! He was the worst of them, no courage in him to be as bad as he knew he was, inside.

She landed heavily on the moss, paused to catch her breath and then, with the knife ready in her hand, slipped away along the castle walls and into the forest.

She'd go all the way down to the far border and swim the river there, or maybe build a raft. By morning she'd be too far away for them ever to find her, and she doubted very much that they'd ever come looking.

Weak!

She moved through the forest with surprising speed. There were tracks, after all, wide enough for carts, and she had a pretty good sense of direction. Besides, all she needed to do was go downhill. If she found the gorge then she just had to follow the flow.

And then there seemed to be too many trees.

There was still a track, and it went more or less in the right direction, but the trees on either side of it were planted rather more thickly than one might expect and, when she tried to turn back, there was no track at all behind her. She took to turning suddenly, half expecting to see the trees moving, but they were always standing stoically and firmly rooted in the moss.

She couldn't feel a wind, but there was a sighing in the treetops.

"All right," she said, under her breath. "All right. I'm going anyway. I *want* to go. But I will be back."

It was at this point that the track opened out into a clearing that hadn't been there the day before and wouldn't be there tomorrow, a clearing in which the moonlight glittered off assembled antlers and fangs and serried ranks of glowing eyes.

The weak banded together can be pretty despicable, but it dawned on the duchess that an alliance of the strong can be more of an immediate problem.

There was total silence for a few seconds, broken only by a faint panting, and then the duchess grinned, raised her knife, and charged the lot of them.

The front ranks of the massed creatures opened to let her pass, and then closed in again. Even the rabbits.

The kingdom exhaled.

On the moors under the very shadow of the peaks the mighty nocturnal chorus of nature had fallen silent. The crickets had ceased their chirping, the owls had hooted themselves into silence, and the wolves had other matters to attend to.

There was a song that echoed and boomed from cliff to cliff, and resounded up the high hidden valleys, causing miniature avalanches. It funnelled along the secret tunnels under glaciers, losing all meaning as it rang between the walls of ice.

To find out what was actually being sung you would have to go all the way back down to the dying fire by the standing stone, where the cross-resonances and waves of conflicting echoes focused on a small, elderly woman who was waving an empty bottle.

"—with a snail if you slow to a crawl, but the hedgehog—"

"It tastes better at the bottom of the bottle, doesn't it," Magrat said, trying to drown out the chorus.

"That's right," said Granny, draining her cup.

"Is there any more?"

"I think Gytha finished it, by the sound of it."

They sat on the fragrant heather and stared up at the moon.

"Well, we've got a king," said Granny. "And there's an end of it."

"It's thanks to you and Nanny, really," said Magrat, and hiccupped.

"Why?"

"None of them would have believed me if you hadn't spoken up."

"Only because we was asked," said Granny.

"Yes, but everyone knows witches don't lie, that's the important thing. I mean, everyone could see they *looked* so alike, but that could have been coincidence. You see," Magrat blushed, "I looked up *droit de seigneur*. Goodie Whemper had a dictionary."

Nanny Ogg stopped singing.

"Yes," said Granny Weatherwax. "Well."

Magrat became aware of an uncomfortable atmosphere.

"You did tell the truth, didn't you?" she said. "They really are brothers, aren't they?"

"Oh yes," said Gytha Ogg. "Definitely. I saw to his mother when your—when the new king was born. And to the queen when young Tomjon was born, and she told me who his father was."

"Gytha!"

"Sorry."

The wine was going to her head, but the wheels in Magrat's mind still managed to turn.

"Just a minute," she said.

"I remember the Fool's father," said Nanny Ogg, speaking slowly and deliberately. "Very personable young man, he was. He didn't get on with his dad, you know, but he used to visit sometimes. To see old friends."

"He made friends easily," said Granny.

"Among the ladies," agreed Nanny. "Very athletic, wasn't he? Could climb walls like nobody's business, I remember hearing."

"He was very popular at court," said Granny. "I know that much."

"Oh, yes. With the queen, at any rate."

"The king used to go out hunting such a lot," said Granny.

"It was that droit of his," said Nanny. "Always out and about with it, he was. Hardly ever home o'nights."

"Just a minute," Magrat repeated.

They looked at her.

"Yes?" said Granny.

"*You* told everyone they were brothers and that Verence was the older!"

"That's right."

"And you let everyone believe that—"

Granny Weatherwax pulled her shawl around her.

"We're bound to be truthful," she said. "But there's no call to be honest."

"No, no, what you're saying is that the King of Lancre isn't really—"

"What I'm saying *is*," said Granny firmly, "that we've got a king who is no worse than most and better than many and who's got his head screwed on right—"

"Even if it is against the thread," said Nanny.

"—and the old king's ghost has been laid to rest happy, there's been an enjoyable coronation and *some* of us got mugs we weren't entitled to, them being only for the kiddies and, all in all, things are a lot more satisfactory than they might be. That's what I'm saying. Never mind what should be or what might be or what ought to be. It's what things are that's important."

"But he's not really a king!"

"He might be," said Nanny.

"But you just said—"

"Who knows? The late queen wasn't very good at counting. Anyway, he doesn't know he isn't royalty."

"And you're not going to tell him, are you?" said Granny Weatherwax.

Magrat stared at the moon, which had a few clouds across it.

"No," she said.

"Right, then," said Granny. "Anyway, look at it like this. Royalty has to start somewhere. It might as well start with him. It looks as though he means to take it seriously, which is a lot further than most of them take it. He'll do."

Magrat knew she had lost. You always lost against Granny Weatherwax, the only interest was in seeing exactly how. "But I'm surprised at the two of you, I really am," she said. "You're witches. That means you have to care about things like truth and tradition and destiny, don't you?"

"That's where you've been getting it all wrong," said Granny. "Destiny *is* important, see, but people go wrong when they think it controls them. It's the other way around."

"Bugger destiny," agreed Nanny.

Granny glared at her.

"After all, you never thought being a witch was going to be easy, did you?"

"I'm learning," said Magrat. She looked across the moor, where a thin rind of dawn glowed on the horizon.

"I think I'd better be off," she said. "It's getting early."

"Me too," said Nanny Ogg. "Our Shirl frets if I'm not home when she comes to get my breakfast."

Granny carefully scuffed over the remains of the fire.

"When shall we three meet again?" she said. "Hmm?"

The witches looked at one another sheepishly.

"I'm a bit busy next month," said Nanny. "Birthdays and such. Er. And the work has really been piling up with all this hurly-burly. You know. And there's all the ghosts to think about."

"I thought you sent them back to the castle," said Granny.

"Well, they didn't want to go," said Nanny vaguely. "To be honest, I've got used to them around the place. They're company of an evening. They hardly scream at all, now."

"That's nice," said Granny. "What about you, Magrat?"

"There always seems to be such a lot to do at this time of year, don't you find?" said Magrat.

"Quite," said Granny Weatherwax, pleasantly. "It's no good getting yourself tied down to appointments all the time, is it? Let's just leave the whole question open, shall we?"

They nodded. And, as the new day wound across the landscape, each one busy with her own thoughts, each one a witch alone, they went home.*

---

* There is a school of thought that says that witches and wizards can never go home. They went, though, just the same.

THE END

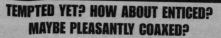